HERO'S
TORCH

Published in the United States of America by
Blue Murder Projekt Publishing
thebluemurderprojekt19@outlook.com

Cover design: 19

Cover model: Complete Destruction.
Used with permission.

HERO'S TORCH

BY

19

For SM Johnson

for helping me reach the place
where the sky goes black

The secret to happiness is freedom, and the secret to freedom is courage.

—Thucydides

DYS·TO·PI·A

(dîs-to¹pê-e) noun

1. An imaginary place or state in which the condition of life is extremely bad, as from deprivation, oppression, or terror.

2. A work describing such a place or state: "dystopias such as Brave New World"

children

It was almost silent in the basement of the Church.

Faded chains of colored paper hung in loops from the low ceiling. Pages from Christian coloring books were taped to the peeling walls, all sharing a similar lack of creativity. No doodles in the margins, no Jesus with blue hair, no Moses with a green face. Nothing to distinguish them from one another except the crooked, sprawling names.

It was almost silent, except for the hum of air purifiers and the crying of thirty-one children.

The crying happened the same way every single tithe. They would sit on parent's laps, clinging to hands, some of them worrying at bottles or toys, just waiting—but without fail, one would start to cry.

Then two, then ten.

Here on Earth the tears were never dramatic, never the hysterical siren pitch that meant a tantrum or a bloody knee. Here the weeping was restrained, almost identical from child to child, like those rows of Biblical faces.

Sometimes mothers and fathers cried too, pale and shaking, shushing their children, eyes moving frantically from door to child to door again.

Oberon stood outside, listening to the muffled terror. He turned so his guards couldn't see his eyes drifting closed, kept his lips pressed closed to keep the corners from turning upward. His entourage fidgeted behind him, shifting boots, a slight cough.

Their impatience was irrelevant.

He waited, until he was calm and still, hands loose and easy in the pockets of his long black coat.

The Septarch never touched anything.

Not here.

He stepped inside, flanked by his guards. They were largely there for the sake of appearance. No one had physically attacked him since the Lazarus outpost incident sixteen years earlier. That had been a surprise, and those were increasingly rare. And it had been over so quickly.

1

The memory flickered through him, quick and red, dissolved his urge to smile. Nostalgia? Was that the word for this feeling?

The crying stopped, as if someone had thrown a switch. All the eyes in the room dropped to the floor. No one moved. They didn't dare.

It was the same, every time.

"All of them passed?"

He directed this pointless question at no one in particular, enjoying the silent struggle among his servants. Nobody wanted to be the one to speak. He could feel them hoping, or perhaps praying he wouldn't turn and ask again. An offense like that always meant blood.

"Yes, Lord Septarch. These are the ones that have been found suitable in the preliminary tests."

Oberon didn't look at at the one who'd dared to answer him. He made a small cruel motion as if he might speak again, certain they weren't even breathing. When he nodded there was no sigh of relief. They knew better.

Little trinities of mother-father-child were sitting in folding chairs in one long row. The trembling set in and passed around the room like a quick contagion. This world, all worlds, just machines, turning in perfect sync at his slightest decision.

Exactly as it should be.

Sometimes that exhausted him.

He'd seen these children or their twins hundreds of times, on dozens of planets. Repetition had bleached this of any amusement it had once held. This thought filled him with exasperation and exhaustion. He chose almost at random, bothering to gesture, trusting his guards to follow his gaze. "This one. That one. These two."

Two forgettable girls, a boy with platinum hair, none of them interesting enough to look at twice.

He turned to leave.

Behind him, the screams began. A woman collapsed, making a sound like shorn metal, her face buried in her husband's lap, her hands hanging limp, brushing the tile floor. Her little girl was the first one he had chosen.

Outside, a black electric car was waiting for him, crouched like a predator beast. He got in, relief warring with disappointment as the door slid closed between himself and Earth. He didn't spare a look at the utility transport being loaded with his new property. He wasn't interested in background details.

Cayle sat beside him, pressing pills into his hand. His tanned face was made of creases under a careless white shock of hair. The startlingly blue eyes behind his glasses were both kind and worried.

Oberon took the pills, waved away the offer of water. Beyond the one-way window was the empty street, empty sidewalk, buildings caked with pollution. A holographic billboard in the sky, a cross that dissolved into a Bible verse that melted in turn into a list of route changes and Zone restrictions. Back to the cross again.

"I hate this planet." Oberon tossed the pills into his mouth and chewed them.

Cayle was accustomed to the Septarch's mercurial moods. He'd been Oberon's personal physician for much longer than a human lifetime, and was overall free of the crippling fear that paralyzed most of his guards. Still, he always had the pills ready and waiting. There was a difference between bravery and stupidity. "One more, but not for a few days."

"I know my schedule," Oberon snapped. He leaned his forehead against the cool glass. Maybe he'd arrange a contest, a game of wits, persistence or creativity for the little ones to struggle through. Something more amusing than waiting and crying. Something that might fascinate him for a while.

"Did you want to stay here?" Cayle's voice had that papery tension that meant he was pretending not to be worried.

The sigh escaped before he could stop it. "No. Just get me to the spaceport."

ısolation

Two hundred miles away, an act of sabotage was in progress.

Or maybe it was better described as *event art*.

"Radio...live transmission," Leander sang to himself, around a mouthful of wires. This was much easier on clear nights, when the poison count was green and he didn't need a mask to keep from dying. This line of work often required more hands than he possessed, and peripheral vision was a tremendous perk when avoiding cops and security bots.

He was a narrow sculpture of bone and thin young muscle, with wide inquisitive eyes of an improbable green. His disaster area of coffee-colored hair was stuffed under a black knit cap. He was pressed against the wall where the shadows were thickest, nearly invisible in clothing that was illegally black and illegally torn, sloppy asymmetrical swipes of ebony makeup hiding the blades of his cheekbones, the sharp angles of his nose and chin.

He had two minutes and twelve seconds until the robot passed by again. The song was two minutes long, and when he reached the end of it he would have twelve seconds to escape.

"Listen to the silence...let it ring on..."

His bag was cutting a bruise into his shoulder. He spent two precious seconds adjusting it, pulled the wire slowly and firmly until it surrendered a half-inch of slack.

"Bang," he muttered, grinning, and touched copper to copper. A spark stung his wrist above his glove. There was an anguished mechanical screech from around the corner of the building as the metal security shield over the windows rolled itself up.

One, smash a window with his bag, or more precisely, the brick he'd stowed in the bottom.

Two, grab as many boards and passcards as possible.

Three, leave a gift in exchange: a small gadget from his pocket. He flipped it on with his thumbnail, and a tiny light on one side blinked into cheerful life. He pitched it into the broken window.

Four, run into the alley on the other side of the building.

He groped past the stolen merchandise in his bag for a smooth cylinder. He knocked off the plastic cap, sprayed three dripping neon-red sixes on the brick wall, dropped the paint can and scaled the fence at the end of the alley. The barbed wire along the top had rusted into a pathetic joke. It smeared his shadowsuit with orange, and tore the knee of his pants. That was fine. Better than when he'd torn open his forearm, and staggered home with his sock tied around the wound.

He ran two blocks, counting under his breath.

Hopefully the robot would be in the blast radius. The State Police could have that little favor for free, not that they'd care. Factories churned the damn copbots out by the hundreds, designed and built by the lowest bidder. It was not uncommon for them to fall out of the air and lie sparking and twitching on the sidewalk, shrieking garbled codes and sending all kinds of film to any computers within sensor range.

Radio. Live transmission.

It wasn't much of a bang. There was a whoosh, and a pressure change that ruffled his hair and made him swallow. No alarm. The falling debris was what made the noise, a pattering rain of clumps, clinks, and more ominous thumps.

Zone Seven Technological Supply was over.

They deserved it for having a goddamned system that was twenty years out of date. He almost felt sorry for the idiots.

Almost.

He'd been rummaging through the school computer system, sifting through payout records when he'd learned that since he'd eliminated the competition, these bastards now distributed all wristunits in the quadrant.

The wristunits were as simple as they were grotesque–stylish, useful, convenient watch-sized tracking devices the State required everyone to wear at all times.

For safety, of course, though they never said *whose*.

You could call other people on them, like a comm, check the weather, the time, your mail, the scores for a dozen sports. You could summon a doctor or a fireman, a policeman or a priest anytime you liked.

Or, you know, They could summon *you*. Or summon a few dozen copbots to surround you.

He loathed them as the cattle-tags they were, and had mysterious and continual bad luck with his own. He just couldn't seem to stop losing it or breaking it. Actually, his own replacement unit had probably been one of tonight's casualties.

The State would not have been amused to learn that the Tri-Six Terrorist was a fourteen-year-old boy.

Leander let himself edge into a fast walk. He took a side trip into another alley, pulled the brick out of his bag and tossed it in a recycle bin. He had a long walk ahead of him, and his bag was heavy enough already. He'd built a bastardized motor scooter with silent engines for this kind of mission. On his test run the police had spotted him and seized it. Unauthorized vehicle. He hadn't even *known* about that law. He supposed he should have, because anything he wanted to do was, invariably, against the law.

He unzipped the outer pocket of his bag, pulled out four pills, and chewed them. They left his mouth gritty and tasting of sulfur.

He crept into the house, convinced the security console he had done no such thing, and tiptoed upstairs. The floor creaked in a new place, and he froze, waiting to hear the chime of his parents' door opening. He counted to one hundred, the drugs a mean voodoo drum in his skull. Nothing.

Once he was locked in his room he dropped his bag into his battered chair and fell across his bed. Safe.

He peeled off the gloves, buried them under a pile of dirty school uniforms, wriggled out of his shadowsuit of clothes, scrubbed his face with them before shoving them down there to keep the gloves company. He'd told his mother the rust stains—and occasional bloodstains—were souvenirs of scavenger hunts in junkyards. Whether she believed him or not, she didn't question him about it. He was always building things. Machines if they worked, sculptures if they didn't.

His room reeked of sandalwood. The bed was a snarl of mismatched sheets, a Republic of Earth flag crumpled at the footboard, the blue cross on a white background twisted into a crooked glyph. He'd painted every inch of the walls, the ceiling, a solid mural of earth browns, red and gray, flashes of magenta and green. Most of it was abstract, with occasional eyes, teeth, snakes, and flames. A mutant angel covered most of the ceiling.

Nowhere else on Earth was easy on his eyes.

He groped under his bed, came up with a gizmo that was supposed to be a perpetual motion machine, managed to break off one of the counterweights, and dropped it again with a sigh. On his second try, he came up with his earphones. The music was a violent counterpoint to the headache unfolding in his temples. He kicked at the flag until it was crammed between the bedframe and the mattress, keeping company with a compass, two computer disks, and the gas mask he'd outgrown when he was eight.

He sank into a barrage of disconnected images, his least favorite people, a fuzzy plan to get into the comm net and link it into his stereo. His Humanities teacher lying in a hallway, hands crammed against her ears, while the school's public address system blasted ancient rock bands at merciless volume.

So many explosions. So much fire.

ıconoclasm

Two hours later, his alarm beeped in his ears.

He dragged himself out of bed, pulled on his last clean uniform, emptied the stolen equipment out of his bag. He ate an amphetamine, wandered into the bathroom and brushed his teeth, and snuck down the stairs with his eyes half-closed.

He escaped the house without either parent seeing him.

Sunlight splattered down on him. A small saccharine panic unfurled in his chest when the door closed behind him. So much space. So many eyes. He had his backpack, made beautiful with electrical tape, wire, obscure stickers and painted graffiti. It was juju.

He was safe.

He buckled his mask over his head. He breathed in deep and quickly, getting his earphones situated around the bulk straps, listening to the hiss of the filter. The air through it was warm and bland. He missed the illegal smell of gasoline. He found the ghost of that scent in junkyards, but that wasn't the same. Ten years ago they'd had a neighbor with an antique car. Rubber wheels and a gasoline engine, a ferocious noise that kept him toddling across the yard desperate to indulge his fascination, with his mother in aggravated pursuit.

The man and his car were gone, now, the man sent to reconditioning camp, the car dismembered for scrap metal.

All this, and the planet is still toxic.

We might as well have kept the gasoline.

Now the streets were empty, most of the time, even the electrocars too expensive to use when it was a short walk to the public station, where the bastard tran would take him to the exasperating misery of school.

When Leander was twelve, he'd been allowed to choose an elective class. He'd picked Creative Arts, expecting the counselor to recite some script about the class being full, or a scheduling conflict with his required credits. Instead, she'd keyed in his code, and sent his schedule to his handscreen.

8

He stood in the doorway of the classroom, amazed. No desk terminals. There were angled tables, each with a massive sheet of white paper and a box of colored pencils, the kind with soft lead that made thick rich lines.

Each seat had an index card with a name. He found his, tucked his bag under his feet, and chewed his lip, impatiently. The kids came in, one by one. A skinny kid with hair the color of dirt glanced at Leander disdainfully. Leander gave him such a vicious look in return that he looked away.

The teacher was a heavy woman in standard issue gray, hair twisted into a repellent lumpy bun. "For your first day, let's have a little fun. We're going to draw something from the Bible."

Of course they were.

"Daniel and the lions, Adam and Eve, whatever you'd like."

There was plenty in the Bible he could stand to draw. Revelation alone would keep him busy for an entire semester.

Leander picked up a bright blue pencil.

The classroom vanished.

He was in a universe that consisted of the paper, and the evolving lines. He drew without stopping or erasing. It felt more like translating than creating.

The class was almost over. The teacher was making rounds, pausing at each table, offering suggestions, praise. Leander didn't look up. He drew faster, knowing that he would lose a lot of it once the bell rang.

She stopped behind Leander's desk.

He didn't stop drawing until she snatched the pencil out of his hand.

"What is this?" she demanded, her voice indignant, appalled.

The class fell silent.

It was Jesus.

The messiah was in a strange costume of dark shiny blue. He had black lipstick, and was bolted to a steel cross, with rivets through his wrists and ankles. His face and chest were studded with circuit boards. There were hundreds of meticulously drawn wires invading his flesh, a tiny blue wound at each point of penetration.

The teacher grabbed Leander's chin and forced his head back. "Is that supposed to be funny? How *dare* you draw something like

9

that?"

Leander was shaking.

He had never had a teacher yell at him like that in all his life. He had no idea what he'd even done wrong. Was she jealous? Had the class already ended, with him just sitting here?

He opened his mouth, and what came out was, "I'm not finished. Could I have my pencil back?"

She slapped him so hard he nearly fell out of his chair. It erased any coherent thought left in his brain. No one had ever hit him before, not outside of scuffles with other kids. His immediate and *intense* instinct was to hit her back. His face was hot, his mouth dry.

Her hand came down over his shoulder. *Wrinkled* his drawing. Snatched it, the motion punctuated by the soft hiss of tearing paper.

Leander went still.

Everyone was staring at him. None of them dared to say anything.

Bang.

He put his hands under the table, and slammed it upward, as hard as he could. It flipped over completely, crushing the kid across from him to the floor in a tangle of chairs. Colored pencils clattered against the tile. "That's *mine*—"

The teacher grabbed him, yanked his arm so hard that pain flared in the socket of his shoulder, into his ribs. She dragged him through the debris field and out the door, holding his sketch in her free hand away from her body, as though it might get her dirty.

Knocking over the table had earned him a beating with a wooden paddle an inch thick. It was delivered in front of the entire school, after his sketch had been displayed and loudly condemned as Satanic. The bruises ran from his waist to the backs of his knees, and they had taken more than a month to fade.

He had shown his father the bruises. Paul Schaiden had said

(you should've been)

several useless, lame things, and told him not to show his mother.

For once, Leander had obeyed.

He'd dreaded going back to school the next day, facing all those eyes, all those whispers. It never occurred to him he might have something far worse to fear.

10

When he badged in at the front gate two guards flanked him and told him he'd been transferred.

This was a pleasant state euphemism for kidnapping, as he'd discovered when they'd copgrabbed him by his upper arm on either side and escorted him to a humming black transport.

Six months of live-in priority counseling at the nearest recon.

This was a pleasant State euphemism for psychological torture.

For one hundred and eighty days, twelve hours a day, he was locked in a room with four of Them. They were great massive slabs of men with low foreheads, beady eyes. Their porky hands were made of fingers strangling on gold rings like tied-off sausages, heavy and dense enough to crush him like a drink can. They screamed at him like he was deaf or retarded, inches from his face, breath that belonged in a zoo, spit spraying in his eyes, on his mouth. He couldn't even wipe it off. Covering his ears had made them tape his hands to the chair.

They drugged him until he couldn't raise his head, let alone piece together Their insane ranting. They made no sense even when he was sober. Circular reasoning that always led back to Jesus, and he would see his sketch again, burning in the air in front of his eyes. Jesus, the entire fucking reason he was there in the first place.

When they weren't trying to deafen him they kept him in a cold cell that contained only a bed and a Bible. They woke him at random. He soon lost all sense of time.

Always exhausted, always hungry, always terrified, always taken back to that blindingly white room.

He'd never seen other...inmates? Patients?

Heretics?

Sometimes he'd thrown up. They'd poured buckets of water over him and started in again. At first he'd held his mouth open to drink some, desperate and dry from lips to stomach. After that they'd begun putting salt or vinegar in it. Long after that, he could no longer throw up, could no longer care about their breath, could no longer care about anything. It was as if he really had gone deaf, really had become retarded.

In the end he was sure he'd always been there. Escape was

impossible because everywhere else was a delusion. This empty white horror was the only real world.

After awhile he said, *sure, okay, fine,* over and over. He lied his way through a written evaluation. They pronounced him cured of his independent thought disorder.

For weeks after they'd let him go, he'd stayed in bed under all the blankets he could find, all his clothing piled on top. He didn't care if he was hot; he *had* to feel covered, hidden, needed to smell himself and his room, needed to be crowded close on all sides so that no other people would fit there anymore. When he'd been able to venture out, he kept gouging at his arms with his nails until he bled because he was afraid it was a dream and he was still there.

Paul could not go near him. It sent him into violent hysterics. It had been months before the voice and the bulk of any grown man was tolerable.

Soren knocked sometimes, and that sent him scrambling back into his

(hole)

bed, sobbing. She'd learned to call his name from the hallway, to almost sing to him that she was leaving water or food. He would wait until he was positive she was gone, crack the door, snatch whatever he'd been given and drag it inside, devour it before anyone could take it away from him.

In time he'd become more certain that he need only fear that place in sleep. Then he'd gone to his computer, finding it exactly as he remembered and yet so foreign it was almost untouchable.

He used the simple Overnet, no tricks, no treats, just the public boring channels any citizen might use.

He looked up *recon*.

He thought it was short for *reconnaissance,* or perhaps *reconditioning*. The first word made no sense, and the second was too easy. He could turn it around and around in his head like a puzzle piece, and it still didn't fit. Too easy. Too *gentle*.

Weeks of food and sleep and silence–and once he could stand it, music—made something, perhaps his soul, perhaps his sanity, that he'd thought withered and dead, begin to stir.

He went back to his computer, this time to the Undernet.

There, he learned from other survivors what that word meant

when They said it.

It wasn't short for *reconnaissance*, or *recondition*.

It was short for *reconquer*.

He thought of the Spanish swarming the Aztecs, of how he'd always secretly cheered for the rebel colonies that were discussed with such indignant disdain in history class. He thought of those thick ignorant men spraying spittle into his face with every bellowed insanity, trying to drive the demons out of a body that held only what was left of himself.

That weak and wounded thing in his chest began to warm, began to move, began to spin inside him, a gyroscope, a gear, a star, until it was hot enough to hurt. The longer he looked at that arrogant word–*reconquer*–the faster that internal rotation, the hotter that long lost fire. He could almost see it, red, and then yellow, and then white, then finally bluewhite so bright it would blind the galaxy, spinning so fast he was afraid to open his mouth because an inhuman shriek might come out, independent of his breath, endless.

He realized he was shaping the word with his lips, over and over, *reconquer*, but that was not the word echoing inside his skull.

Rage.

He'd been afraid he would never feel it again, had mourned its loss with what little emotion he had left, alone in the dark, alone in the light with those wide, stupid men. But here it was, a rage that should have set him ablaze, a rage too large for a skinny short kid to hold, but happy to be so housed, hissing and burning and still his own.

He found better words behind that one, and he was chanting a greeting, a declaration, an incantation.

A warning.

He remembered how to engage his voice, and first it was a hoarse whisper, and then a clumsy out-of-tune croak, and then shouting, and then shrieking.

Soren came running, the timid murmurs from the hallway forgotten in her fear for her son. She found him shouting in fury at that word on the screen, his voice failing on one word in three, but clear enough for her to grasp the mantra.

"YOU MOTHERFUCKERS NEVER CONQUERED ME. YOU MOTHERFUCKERS NEVER CONQUERED ME..."

This time, when she caught hold of Leander, he let her.

Even then, it had taken him a long, long time to heal.

School had begun insisting he return a *week* after he'd been released. Soren had cordially invited them to go and fuck themselves. She had filled out the paperwork to homeschool him until his health was restored. The school began a petty campaign of annoyance, demanding she fill out this form and that form, insisting they had not received this record or that signed waiver.

Finally, his mother printed copies of every single form and every piece of correspondence she had exchanged with them, a *fortune* in paper, brought them to the school. Leander was never told what kind of conversation *that* was. They figured out how to keep track of his files after that, but they also began sending schoolwork he was completely incapable of doing.

Soren did it herself, daring Paul with eyes as green as hemlock leaves to say one word to her.

Paul did not.

"I even drew monsters in the margins," she told him, curled up in his bed with him like he was a child, his clothes put away, his bedding clean and sweet around them. "Just for you, and just for *Them.*"

His head on her shoulder. Her heartbeat, her scent, so that he knew this was the real world.

"We're the monsters," he said to her, in the dim cheerful light of his desk lamp.

Green eyes looking into green eyes. Two smiles. A secret that his father could not see, could not share, would not have understood.

He lived on the Undernet after that. He wanted none of the Overnet's sanitized, perfumed Citizen bullshit. He wanted the black market to end all black markets, where you could get anything you wanted if you had enough credit.

He wanted information.

Credits were easy. He kept half a dozen accounts under names that would pass Overnet security checks but would lead the State

Police in circles if they ever got nosy. None of them had been found, and he had accrued a surprising amount of interest in his absence. Had it really been that long?

It made his head ache to think of how long. He had been twelve, now he was thirteen, and they'd stolen the birthday that was supposed to divide those two states in his head.

He hadn't even gotten a cake, and he always did *so* love anything that had to do with fire.

That thought made him smile, gave him a place to begin.

You read everything you can find, and you learn everything you ever want to know.

That was exactly what Leander did. And soon he had real wealth, a library of forbidden knowledge he kept in a place he swore They would ever enter again.

Inside his head.

Three months later, he had his birthday cake.

It was night in the wrong Zone, long after curfew. He was dressed in the first incarnation of his shadowsuit, dappled black and gray, his mother's eyeliner breaking the lines of his face. His body was bent in a strange pose, meant to alter the familiar shape of his body into something eyes would pass right over in the darkness, a heap of trash, a discarded skin.

At home he'd felt silly, tiptoeing into his bathroom in this costume, like a little kid playing at being a superhero.

Until he'd shown the mirror his teeth.

He had learned, and he had no intention of ever stopping.

A tiny controller was nestled deep in his pocket. His thumb was on it, ready, and that bluewhite familiar cyclone was whirling and shrieking inside him.

Click. Boom.

And a fire that reddened the sky above a plant that made processors for the fucking wristunits that tracked them all like cattle, a fire that exceeded his wildest expectations, a fire that all the screaming spitting preachers in all the Republic could not blow out.

Leander made a wish.

dysgenic

The vengeance fix of blowing up the Tech supply was already wearing thin. Maybe after school. If he ate a little more speed...

There were a few kids at the transport station, a few adults in workman's blues. The kids ignored him, but he got more than one disapproving look from the adults at his lack of a wristunit.

Cattle-tags.

The tran collected him, carried him towards eight hours of faded women hammering at him with incomprehensible lies, morals and ethics and never-ending ravings about Christ. Recon light. He sat alone in the back, wound up small and tight around the backpack on his knees, worrying his mask in his hands.

I want more than this.

Is there more than this?

The school was a crouching tumor, caged by ten-foot rusted fences topped with vicious spirals of razorwire. Only the front gate was ever used, and that one was manned by a little clump of pseudocops. The rest were kept locked, the badge panels dark and silent. Leander wondered who it was they thought actually *wanted* to get inside. Out, sure, but *in?*

School started with homeroom, with prayers and roll call and usually the meting out of punishments. On his way to these festivities he passed a group of girls exchanging horrified whispers. "Tri-Six...again, last night...they say he's from a cult in Zone Eight..."

Leander bit back a grin. One of the girls must have seen his expression, because they all shut up at once. He ignored them. If he hadn't known cloning was illegal, he would have sworn that they were all copies of the same shallow, empty-headed bitch.

He had no friends. Contacts, yes, but no friends. Some were physical people who would take a passcard out of his hand and leave a tiny package of drugs in return in one practiced motion. Others were user names who would trade with him in the virtual equivalents of very bad neighborhoods.

He could not imagine any other kind of interactions. The entire concept sounded like an excellent way to wind up back in recon. Holding a sustained conversation was a terrifying idea, letting someone into his room an utter impossibility. His interests and hobbies consisted of all the wrong things. Though he was a skilled and fluid liar, he couldn't imagine sustaining that for long enough to stand around and *talk* to people.

He listened to their chatter sometimes, not quite wistful, more curious and a little contemptuous. It all sounded the same. Church. Who had been arrested and why. Hours of detailed discussion about whichever safe and nauseating telecasts—badly veiled propaganda, to Leander's eyes—they were watching this week. Sports teams, and if there was anything Leander hated more than the sappy, preachy telecasts about fine, upstanding Christian families, it was organized sports.

Sometimes they would talk quietly of which boy or girl was cute. This was rare, and immediately ceased in the presence of adults. You weren't supposed to think about that until your parents suggested you start dating. Or presented you with someone to marry.

Leander had no idea how they could *tell* who was cute and who was not, though he gathered that he himself was not. His hair was too straight and long, his eyes too large and aware, not as empty and accepting as those of his classmates. He was half the size of most boys his age, all of whom looked ready to walk out of the classroom and onto a screen to join their heroes in chasing a fucking ball.

Too short, too many bones showing.

Too different.

Most of the other kids were genetically engineered into the bland sterile symmetry that was considered attractive. They all had the same Biblical names, all carried the same bags and wore the same uniforms. None of them added rips or pins or drawings in marker to make these things their own, and their snickers and stares made it clear what they thought of Leander's habit of doing so.

He didn't understand them, and he didn't understand why he was supposed to want to.

Once he reached his desk he didn't even get to turn his computer on before the teacher started reading off a handscreen. "The following students will report immediately to the Admin of Health."

Leander felt something collapse in the general vicinity of his throat. He just *knew*.

"Isaiah Lamkin...Daniel Foreman...Leander Schaiden..."

17

He sighed. The rest of the little bastards were too busy snickering at him to hear it. He was That Skinny Kid, the one who was, oh horrors, *natural* born, the one who looked at Weird Stuff on the computer terminals, the one who sometimes read *paper* books, the one who drew monsters in the margins of his homework. He was Probably A Devil Worshiper, telecast at eleven.

At first a few of them had mistaken him for an easy target. He had corrected this error without hesitation and without mercy, and now they left him alone, except for the snickers and the stares. That was fine. He cared more about the opinions of cockroaches. The other kids were fauna that had the aggravating habit of standing in clusters between him and wherever he wanted to go, but even that wasn't exactly deliberate. They were completely self-centered and not at all smart.

Their parents *bred* them that way, stupidity and all.

Leander imagined darling Mom and Dad, bringing a picture of whatever celebrity they wanted their designer kid to resemble, perhaps clicking through options on a terminal screen the way you could order food in restaurants. For the main course let's have the current taste in physical beauty, strength and glowing health, a side order of perfect teeth and perfect eyesight. For dessert, a perfectly average mind topped with a lack of curiosity.

One of Leander's earliest memories was of a telecast commercial. Of course when they came from the Republic you were supposed to call them Public Service Announcements. He'd been three, young enough to still be delighted by the tiresome little fanfare that signified an official proclamation. Sometimes it meant a bad person was in trouble, and his mother would carry him out of the room before he could watch. Sometimes it meant there would be airplanes or tanks.

The best things that followed that song were about spaceships. He could not contain his joy when this was the case, and would usually spend the rest of the day zooming around with one of Mommy's bowls on his head, pretending to be in space. Mommy and Daddy both didn't mind if he watched those, and sometimes Daddy would even play with him, though he had to be coaxed into putting his helmet on.

This time the screen filled with the face of a lovely African woman, her gorgeous mink-brown eyes gleaming with love and concern.

"Hello, friend. I'm Atarah Kent. I'm speaking to you today on behalf of the Council for Reproductive Services, and on behalf of your unborn children."

Her voice was smooth, rich and sweet, a voice like the maple candy a neighbor had once brought them. You wanted more and more.

At least, until it made you sick.

"This may be the most important message you ever hear. If you are planning to have children, please, stop what you're doing right now, and listen. Your child's future depends on it."

She paused, like a kindergarten teacher waiting for an unruly class to grow quiet. Once she decided she had everyone's attention, the real horror began.

"As you approach parenthood, I'm sure you're thinking of many ways to provide the best chance in life for your child. What parent wouldn't want that? Everyone wants a beautiful, healthy, well-adjusted family. And while you ponder the many possibilities God has blessed us with today, intelligence may seem like a wonderful gift to give your future child."

She was smiling a little. Then the smile dimmed like the light in a lamp Leander wasn't allowed to touch.

"But we all know that sometimes appearances can be deceptive. We have learned from the long dark years before the Revolution that the Tree of Knowledge does, indeed, bring death."

"Intelligence above and beyond what is needed to lead a productive life is not a gift, but a terrible curse, like many of the genetic diseases we have, by the grace of God, wiped from the face of the Earth. The CRS, after decades of research, has concluded that children with high to exceptional intelligence are often depressed, mistrustful, and find it hard to fit in with their peers."

He had been excited at the prospect of spaceships, and a little disappointed when it was only this nice lady, but willing to wait for the cartoon to return anyway. Now he was frozen in place, listening. Leander knew *depressed* because of a different commercial, one of a girl whose face was stuck on sadness. She cried a lot and stayed in bed all the time. That one had scary music, until the end, when the screen had a picture of Jesus, smiling with his arms out like he wanted a hug, over the words *Get Help* and a really long number.

Jesus himself never appeared in any telecasts. Apparently, he was offworld and would return soon, though Leander often wondered what other planet he was on, and why he didn't simply send a telecast back to Earth as many of the colonies did.

The nice lady was saying, "Almost one hundred percent have severe disciplinary problems. Serious and dangerous behavioral issues begin to occur as early as middle school, and are resistant to both medication and therapy. As adults, these children are fifty times more likely to turn to substance abuse, deviant sexual behavior, even violent and antisocial criminal activity."

Leander felt cold, the way he did when Mommy yelled at him for breaking something or not using his inside voice.

He knew *violent*.

That was a very bad word.

That was what happened to the bad people he wasn't allowed to watch.

"Some have even rejected the Church and our Lord and Savior, and at the end of their unhappy lives suffer the one true death, lost to you and to themselves forever."

Atarah Kent blinked those astounding eyes, almost a flutter, and touched one elegant finger tipped with a sculpted ivory nail under her lashes, as if finding it difficult to hold back tears.

Then she leaned forward, confiding, imploring.

"There is more to a full life and a loving Christian soul than academic brilliance. So much more."

A pause, to let this resonate, with her presumably now mesmerized viewers.

"When you select the traits for your new child, ask yourself— do I want a happy child, one that loves and trusts the Lord and the Church as His presence on Earth? Do I want a child loved by his friends, admired by his teachers, successful in his workplace, successful in raising her own children?"

"Do I want what's REALLY best for my child?"

"Please, don't make your family spend a lifetime paying the

price for your vanity. Ask your doctor how you can best achieve a well-balanced son or daughter."

"The State loves you, the Church loves you, and God loves us all, may He bless us and keep us and help us to choose wisely."

A sunny smile. Atarah Kent was proud of you, pleased you'd had this little talk, certain she'd succeeded. You agreed with her, of course you did. Why would the State or the Church lie to you?

"Amen."

Leander normally would've smiled back, though he understood the telecast people couldn't see him. He wasn't smiling now, because he knew the most important big word of all those the friendly brown lady had used.

Intelligence.

A few weeks earlier Mommy had taken him to a big white building, where he'd played funny, simple games with a doctor. He was very good at the games, but the doctor hadn't been pleased about that at all. He'd told Mommy in a voice almost like yelling that Leander's scores were so high they wanted to medicate him *immediately*. And he was angry that Mommy hadn't brought Leander in sooner, even though he didn't feel sick and had better games at home.

Mommy had answered the doctor right back. She used several words that earned Leander the mad face when he tried to say them. She did *not* use her inside voice. She slammed the door behind them, without wishing for God to bless the doctor, and left with her distressed and sniffling son in her arms.

As bright as Leander was, he was too new to the world to grasp what the telecasts really were. The telescreen was a friendly thing that brought him cartoons, chatted at him while his mother was busy. The word *propaganda* was still years in his future, but that sparkling word, *intelligence,* was not. It sounded like what happened when sunlight hit the water in the swimming pool they visited on Saturdays. He understood the meaning well enough, like many other words he couldn't say. He knew it was something he had a lot of, that the other children at the park lacked.

Until that gentle woman on the screen, he hadn't seen his intelligence as good or bad, just a part of himself like the dimples on his knees or his own fascinating toes. Now he was struggling with the idea that it was something that required guilt. No wonder the doctor got so mad when he was good at those games. Whatever *intelligence* was, he had quite a lot of it.

He understood enough to be frightened and hurt and ashamed, a wail forming down in his stomach that would soon escape out into the world.

Mommy had come in time to see the end of the commercial, alarmed by his sudden quiet stillness. She scooped him off the floor fast enough to startle him, swung him in a swoosh way up to the ceiling. This made him laugh, even when he was cutting teeth, even when he had the flu. He laughed now because he was supposed to. It was hollow, and it didn't last long. Then Mommy caught him close and held him so tight he squirmed a little until she let him breathe.

"Don't you ever listen to that nonsense, Leander," she said, her face so close to his that all he knew was her softness and her beauty, her wonderful warm summer smell, those bright green eyes so like his own. She was angry, he could tell, but not at him. Was she angry at the brown woman on the screen?

"Don't you ever listen to Them. They sound like nice people, but they're pretending so you'll believe their lies. Everything that comes out of that screen that starts with that stupid song and ends with that nonsense about the State and the Church is a lie. That's a secret, and you can't tell anyone EVER, not even Daddy, or we'll both get in trouble, but I promise you it's true."

He nodded, half afraid of the venom in her voice, half delighted that now they had a secret. "I don't have a bad thing?"

Mommy laughed, though he thought maybe hers was hollow too. "No, kitten. I have the most perfect baby in all the Republic, and I want you to get as smart as you can. Read everything you can find. Learn everything you ever want to know. Don't you listen to anyone who tells you otherwise. They're jealous, that's all. Do you understand?"

He nodded again, though he wasn't sure he did. He understood enough to make the lump of confused hurt in his chest dissolve like snow in spring. He reached for her chocolate-colored hair with both hands, demanding, "Kiss lots!"

She did. She was all the world, the sun, the moon, the stars he'd seen once when they went far away to something called a beach.

His universe. His father was a dim and distant satellite, a wobbly dead planet that sometimes drifted close enough to bask in Soren's light, her laughter, her rage, all the *no* she refused to set aside, all the *no* his father was afraid to say to anyone.

His father could not have any of their secret.

She carried Leander to his room and read the next chapter of *The Hobbit* to him, out of a real paper book, even though it wasn't bedtime. He loved her so much it made invisible parts of him ache.

Eleven years later, Leander had seen Atarah Kent make this earnest, nauseating speech into the camera hundreds of times, and he didn't even *like* to watch the telecasts. It was inescapable, broadcast during school at least once a week, that excruciating *Hello, friend* drawing his eyes whether he wanted to look or not.

He knew every blink, knew exactly the place where there was an almost-invisible pick on shoulder of her butterscotch sweater, a thread caught by a kitten or a ring or one of those ivory nails. He knew exactly when to watch her bottom lip for a single miniscule twitch he could never decipher. Amusement? Horror? A dying spasm of conscience?

He could recite every loathsome word.

He believed his mother, but he thought she had one detail wrong. They weren't jealous. They weren't intelligent enough to even begin to grasp why they should be.

They were ignorant, and it was apparently bliss.

He shouldered his bag, and slouched his way out into the corridor, walking into whatever doom They had planned for him, thinking something his mother liked to say.

I'd rather be weird than stupid.

thanateros

Sixteen kids sat in a room. No computer terminals, no keypad, just little tables, almost like his disastrous art class. Leander was told to put his bag under his seat. He was given a pencil, a narrow slip of paper with lettered and numbered boxes on it, and a thick booklet. His name was printed on the cover in narrow uptight handwriting above a rubber stamp: PERSONAL AND CONFIDENTIAL PER SECTION 579-14-27G ARCTURUS.

He had no idea what it meant.

He started to open it, but years of looking at a BEGIN TEST WHEN INSTRUCTED screen made him change his mind. He did flip it over to check out the back, and found it blank. He examined the green-printed slip while trying not to laugh. Were they going to feed this thing into a computer that still used vacuum tubes?

He'd never seen the teacher before. The man had the look of a natural-born, not quite symmetrical, not quite perfect, grayhaired and grayfaced, balding and paunchy with small thick glasses.

Will I look like that one day?

Leander tried to imagine this, wrinkled his nose. Then he caught a glimpse of the slack jaw and low forehead of the great hulking kid sitting the closest to his right, hands like hams, eyes small and dull and disinterested. There were worse things than gray hair and a pot belly.

The teacher put one hand on a disk copy of the Earth Standard Bible, raised the other, and turned so that the nearest camera could see him fully. He raised his voice, addressing eyes and ears in some distant unknown place.

"I, Mark Tobiah Polling, do solemnly swear that these tests will be absolutely without punitive consequences, regardless of the answers given. Neither parents, nor any employee of the school, the State, or the Church, or any lawful power of the Republic of Earth will be permitted to view your answers or the final results of this test, now or at any future time. This I do swear, so help me God."

Leander had heard speeches like that before, in telecasts of criminal trials. If you were found to have lied after such an oath, it was blasphemy. Executions for cardinal sins were neither quick nor painless.

This was now somewhere way beyond weird. And almost certainly real. This man did not look like he could bravely face a paper cut, let alone death by slow fire.

So he could write *fuck off* and these bastards couldn't do anything about it?

It *had* to be true. There were four cameras, one in each corner of the room. All four, along with sixteen witnesses had just seen the teacher swear.

Leander had heard of one camera being down, and was willing to accept that two might be down out of four, but cameras were monitored by living people and by the Overnet, and a malfunction resulted in the appearance of technicians from the State and a chaplain from the Church in mere minutes, with portable temporary cameras to record the repairs as well as the premises.

His attempts to shut them down himself had never been successful. Employee-level access had not gotten him around this, and to his surprise Council of Education access was just as unsuccessful. Whoever handled the surveillance was beyond his territory, and he'd wisely decided against poking around at any higher clearance. Instead he'd given the janitor and the cafeteria staff gigantic raises and everyone else an impressive pay cut. They were still sorting out his handiwork.

Mr. Polling lowered his hand. "These tests are for the purpose of research to improve public service in our schools. We ask—" He paused, and did an awkward swallow, as though something in his throat hurt. "We ask that you please be completely honest and answer every question fully. There is no time limit."

Leander hadn't heard a teacher say *please* since he was in preschool.

The gray man searched in the air for words. "This is very important." He looked at his hands when he said this, skipping the teacher trick of making eye contact with a few kids or speaking over their heads. Then he took four unsteady steps around to the back of his desk, sat down as though he were carrying a great weight. He put his hands on the desk, noticed how they were shaking, and put them in his lap instead.

Leander had never seen a teacher do *any* of that.

I don't like this.

He didn't look to see how the other kids were reacting. He could guess, from the stricken silence that followed instead of a rustling murmur. Even *they* were smart enough to have grasped that something was the opposite of right about their situation.

He flipped open the little packet, found it printed with precise tiny letters. He skimmed through the questions.

Do you ever take illegal drugs?

Do you masturbate?

Do you hate your mother or father?

Do you hate your teachers?

Do you believe in God?

All the questions were like that, *yes* or *no* answers, until the last four pages. There was only one question at the top of each page, with blank space underneath. Essay questions. Great.

How do you feel about the Church?

What do you think will happen when you die?

If you could kill someone and get away with it, would you? How would you do it?

Leander bit his lip.

I don't like this at all.

To lie, or not to lie. That was the first question.

He was too big to be dragged away from the telecasts, now. He'd seen hundreds of executions, maybe thousands. They were almost as popular as whatever sport was in season. He knew how long it could take someone to die. He looked at Mr. Polling again, at that face made of fear and flaws, and then down at this anachronism of a test.

He thought of the Very First Bomb. of how it had felt to stand in his favorite junkyard with his little controller ready to trigger it, of how afraid he'd been of the sound, of how afraid he'd been that there would *be* no sound.

He wasn't new to telling Them what he thought of Them. He did it with explosives and computer viruses and spraypaint all the time.

He picked up his pencil, thought for a long time, and colored in his first *yes.*

He didn't lie, except when the question felt like nosing around for a certain terrorist who liked to blow things up. No, never set anything on fire, never stolen anything, never broken anything on purpose. He hung on *Do you think enemies of the Republic should be jailed?* and went with *No.* He could always lie and say he thought they should be shot in the face, if anyone wanted clarification.

He kept coloring in the little rectangles on that long skinny slip of paper. They asked for it, and just this once, this fucking *once,* he was going to talk to someone. Not a friend, not a contact, but an enemy. Probably *the* enemy.

And that was it for multiple choice.

He glared at the essay questions. It was easy to pick out the answer They wanted when it was multiple choice, not that he'd bothered to do so, but this felt more dangerous than anything yet in this creepy computer-free room. It wasn't so bad when the answer only required a word or a sentence. These motherfuckers had a whole empty PAGE beneath each question.

That was a whole lot of rope to hang yourself with.

He gnawed his pencil, a pleasure that terminals and keypads lacked. Pondered that white, tempting space.

Then he grinned.

Nowhere did it specify *how* he had to answer.

How do you feel about the Church?

He considered a study of his own left hand making a particular ancient gesture. Too easy. And then the right idea came to him, emblazoned in his head like he had a telescreen in there the size of an execution arena.

He sketched what could've been any church in the Republic and probably in any of the colonies, too. Steeple, bell, cross, columns, wide sweep of steps, simple lines so that it had depth and perspective instead of looking like a cardboard cutout. Quick suggestion of trees beside it, some electrocars parked in front to give context and a sense of size.

Now came the fun part.

The flames were satisfying to draw, though he longed for color. He glanced at Mr. Polling. The man had wrapped his arms around himself, now, as if he was cold, and appeared to be

(rocking)

shivering.

No, he wouldn't ask. That was a great way to get told he couldn't answer this way, and he was enjoying it immensely.

He added some meteors hurtling towards the Church, and some tiny people running in apparent panic in the parking lot and on the steps, little stick arms waving over little oval heads. He set a few of the miniature people on fire, along with one of the trees. He added more victims in the foreground, these larger and more detailed than stick figures. A few were huddled around some fallen comrades, some of whom were in several pieces.

This was a waste of so many idiots running amok. He chewed his pencil, pondering an idea that was both awesome and silly, until he decided *fuck it*. There was nothing that a few dinosaurs couldn't make even cooler.

He put in a few pterodactyls high above the carnage, a tiny man screaming a tiny but unmistakable *O* of horror as one of them snatched him up and away from the world. Next he added a ravening pack of carnivores he was probably inventing. They were too large to be raptors and too graceful to be tyrannosaurs. They rampaged through the foreground, ripping one unlucky figure to shreds.

Plenty of beckoning space for additional mayhem. Lithe fluid shapes with unspeakable talons and dripping merciless teeth chased a woman that he decided was his cunt of an art teacher. He decorated her with a blanket-wrapped baby so minute it was hard to draw it with his dulling pencil. He had no idea if she *had* a baby, but he felt deliciously evil finishing the teardrop-shaped bundle, the head so little it was more a dot than a circle.

Still missing something. It needed a signature.

He drew himself, facing the Church so that the audience couldn't see his face, though anyone who knew his build and his too-long hair and the plethora of monsters on his backpack would recognize him. He was closer to the viewer than anyone else, sitting on the ground with his knees bent, an unidentifiable something that probably wasn't a cigarette in one hand, drifting a graceful wisp of smoke up into the air where it joined the thicker, darker swarm from the burning church.

When he was finished he was afraid of what he'd done, thinking of Jesus with wires in his head, thinking of a blurry crowd of faces while he was

(hurt)

No. Never fucking mind that.

Here they were, that blurry crowd of faces, and he bet getting fucking eaten alive hurt a lot more than some pervert hitting you with a piece of wood.

He was enjoying himself immensely. He looked around, to see if anyone had noticed and was running towards him to put a stop to it.

No, not yet, anyway. Next.

What do you think will happen when you die?

Well, that was some philosophy class bullshit right there. He was pretty sure God and Jesus and Hell were about as real as Big Brother in that long-banned book *1984*, but much like Big Brother, God didn't need to be real for his infuriating will to be enforced.

He'd never really considered what might be real if the fairy tales were lies.

He wrinkled his nose, and wrote the first thing came to mind: NOT A CLUE, in massive letters that filled the smugly blank paper below that aggravating question. It still looked sparse, so he drew a sea serpent across the bottom, with quick lazy ocean waves around it, and elaborate calligraphy that read: HERE THERE BE DRAGONS.

If you could kill someone and get away with it, would you? How would you do it?

This was more like it.

His pencil went immediately to the paper.

He drew himself in the glass dome head of a gargantuan robot, with improbable levers in each hand and a grin splitting his face from ear to ear. He was making the same slightly unhinged smile in real life without knowing it. In one massive pincer-hand he drew a man in a suit and tie, this time with eyes as round and horrified as his Edvard Munch mouth. He helpfully wrote PRIME MINISTER OF EARTH and drew a little arrow pointing to the screaming meat in question.

Continuity was hardly important, so he went ahead and drew his art teacher again in the other claw, brandished overhead like a trophy. She was limp and dollbroken as though the robot had already squished her, or perhaps shaken her. He labeled her simply BITCH.

Underneath this he wrote DESTROY ALL HUMANS. REDECORATE EARTH.

If that wasn't enough of an explanation as to how he intended to render the concept of *getting away with it* obsolete, they'd have to take off points.

There was still plenty of tempting space on the robot itself. He took advantage of this for quite some time, drawing cables and bolts and access panels and weapons arrays, and then random spines and spikes because he felt like it.

Almost. Needed a little shading, some depth. There.

Finished.

They'd said he could answer however he wanted, and he had.

He didn't put his pencil down. He was staring at REDECORATE EARTH but seeing himself surrounded by shrieking faces, voices hammering at him with nonsense that would've been amusing if he were not so small and so outnumbered and so very tired...

Was it too late to change his answers now? He could throw up, he supposed, a skill he'd perfected offloading drugs that didn't turn out to be friendly. He could bite the inside of his cheek, work up a mouthful of spit and blood, smear a little around his nose while pretending to wipe it, and voila, nosebleed. Cough up the mouthful all over his paper.

Apologize repeatedly and ask for another one.

Write something They would never look at twice.

The thought of it made him feel like he'd been using speed instead of sleep for too long. Stretched too thin, and empty. He flipped back to his burning church, and grinned again at how pleased he was with it. He looked at himself blissfully smoking pot while dinosaurs ate everyone he'd ever hated.

He did not throw up or bite the inside of his cheek.

There were only two other kids still working. Some had finished so quickly he was sure they'd simply immediately scrawled down whatever inane bullshit had wandered through their tiny minds. *Idiots.* Whatever else this was, it was better than algebra or biblical history.

He flipped the test back to the cover page, collected his answer sheet, and his bag. He got his dry mouth and his treacherous legs to cooperate, walked up to Mr. Polling's desk, and handed him this stack of heresies.

praelectus

The high point of the day was in physical training. They were learning archery. The coach made them wait for his signal to fire and to run out into the field to retrieve their arrows, but made no attempt to help them with technique. Leander figured out the important parts himself—the wind, and correcting for his own tendency to shoot low and to the left. When he aimed high and right he could drop the arrow into the yellow center of the target almost every time.

He wondered what it would be like to fire at something that was

(alive)

moving, and guessed that you'd fire where they were about to be, not where they actually were. You'd have to be able to predict what your prey would do, easy enough if prey was half as dumb as his classmates. One perfect genetically-enhanced princess decided to let go of the *bow* instead of the arrow and the string, and earned a prompt lesson in physics and a concussion for her trouble, along with an all-expenses paid trip to the infirmary. Atarah Kent had neglected to mention that stupidity sometimes came with painful side effects.

The wooden, declarative sound of his arrows hitting the target was soothing. He expected no praise and received none. The dirty looks he was collecting from the clone army were more satisfying than any praise. His arrows were embedded so deeply he had to plant his foot on the target to remove them. His grumbling classmates had a much longer hike to retrieve their own, scattered in the field of dust behind the gym. Sometimes the coach yelled until they broke into a grudging run instead of a sulky walk. They'd come trudging back at long last, glaring at Leander, patiently waiting at the firing line.

Why couldn't they do *this* all the time instead of fighting over a stupid ball?

When he got home his mother opened the door before he could even touch the keypad. Her leafgreen eyes were red and swollen. "Leander, get in here."

He followed her into the kitchen, wary. "What happened?"

31

She turned away from him and covered her face. "Sit down."

They know, he thought. Visions of prison, or worse, recon. Again. He ran through a mental list of his crimes. Vandalism. Arson. Theft. Heresy. Hacking. Drugs.

His mother leaned over the table.

He leaned back. Strategic retreat.

"Leander, did you take some test in school today?"

She didn't sound mad. She sounded terrified.

"Yeah. Some ethics thing. It was stupid," he said carefully. "Why? Did they telecomm you? Did I fail it, or something?"

"No," she said. Her face was white and sharp, like her bones were showing through it. "No, Leander, you didn't fail."

When Dad got home they shut themselves in the living room and locked him out.

Leander paced, creeping as close to the door as he could. He caught snatches of conversation, his mother mostly.

"...just a child...you know how he is...there has to be a way to get Them to let him..."

Them. Fuck.

He went into his room and hacked the intercom into the living room.

"Paul, he probably did that as a joke. He's just like I was at his age. Mad at everything with something to prove. This can't happen. If we tell them he was in recon—"

"They already know that, Soren. That's probably why he got picked in the first place."

"But this is *crazy!*"

She was crying.

Leander felt like he might sneeze or choke or maybe start crying himself. Would *she* go to recon too, for what he had done?

Those fucking LIARS. They had sworn on camera on a Bible.

They're pretending so you'll believe their lies.

"This can't be happening!" Soren was shouting at Paul. "Why the fuck do they let him *do* this? We have ships, airplanes, surface-to-space missiles, all those goddamned satellites...and they're still letting him do this? Why don't they just kill the bastard?"

Soren dissolved into sobbing.

Leander swallowed around a burning ache. He had never, ever heard her use the word *fuck* in front of Dad before. Never. Not even when he was six and he'd gashed open his forehead, and the car had run out of charge on the way to the hospital. And the Soren Schaiden that was still named *Mommy* in his heart didn't cry about things. She pulled her sword and started swinging.

Missiles? Had she actually used the word *missiles*?

Leander was an expert at assembling facts from fragments, at making a working whole from scattered junkyard parts. He had to be, because when the Church got through redacting almost everything he wanted to know, fragments were all that remained.

But he could not arrange this into anything that made any sense.

Maybe they had worked out from the test who he was. He tried to analyze this, and the whirling confusion in his head made him cover his face with his hands.

He'd been nailed for something. He was headed either for recon or prison. Did it really matter why?

Think. If you lose it, you're done. Now think.

Inhale. Exhale.

He stood in the middle of his room, his hands knotted in his hair like someone in a bad play.

It couldn't be about the Tri-Six business. The State's reaction to terrorism was swift and absolute. They wouldn't have bothered to arrest him. They'd have shot him on sight if they were feeling generous. If not, they'd have blown his house to smithereens and never mind his parents who were probably guilty too.

His shoulders pulled themselves in. His stomach muscles locked so hard it hurt him inside. He'd never considered that. Both of them, both of his parents dead because of his amusing little revenge game. *Both of them*, he insisted to himself, but it was Soren's face he saw, the bright summer scent of her in his throat.

This test will be absolutely without punitive consequences.

"Loophole," he muttered to himself.

That list, at the end of the oath. It reminded him of books he'd read about heathen, sinful, ancient Egypt. A negative confession. All the people who would *not* be told the contents of his answers. Parents, employees of the school, employees of the State, employees of the Church, and that last weird catch-all.

Or any other lawful power of the Republic of Earth.

So, nobody on Earth, nobody in any of the colonies.

Who or what did that leave?

Fairy tales, about as believable as an angry Hebrew deity with a white beard and sandals obsessed with what he did with his penis. Ghost stories about aliens, rogue colonists, disappearing colonies. Nonsense. That was wedged into the vow to cover anything they'd forgotten to mention. Legal notices were sneaky like that. *Covering their asses,* Soren would've said, ignoring Paul's frown.

Recon. That was their loophole.

They'd given the tests to some civilian doctor, like that bastard in the white coat with his games, someone with a face made of disgust and disapproval. Still neatly within the boundaries of the vow, maybe just handing them a list of names so they'd know who to take. They wouldn't consider that punishment. They'd consider it…health care.

Medication and therapy.

He made a little scared sound, involuntary, humiliating, but when he sucked in his breath the noise happened again when he exhaled. He wouldn't go back. He wouldn't survive it again. Not as himself.

There it was, the fear laid bare at last like so many bones.

He had no intention of letting that happen. If he changed again, *when* he changed again, it would be by choice.

He stood stricken by this for a moment. Here was information that he had not stolen from anywhere, not learned from anyone. *My mind is my own,* and that thought was a red apple that fit perfectly in his hand, smelling sweetly of growing things and the first warning of autumn in the air. There was both relief and panic in that simple revelation.

He sorted things on his bed. Two categories: keep, and destroy. A small mountain of illegal disks, books, and tiny cellophane packets of various drugs began to form.

He kept a few disks of things too dangerous to keep on the house computer. To this he added a few of his favorite killswitches, a sketchbook, his journal, and a miniature tin lunchbox of drugs he was unwilling to part with. He stuffed this miniscule pile into his backpack, looked longingly and regretfully at the row of paper books on his desk.

Too many, too heavy, too bad.

He piled up everything that had gotten the death sentence on his Earth flag, tied up the corners to make a lumpy sack he intended to burn. Those things could land

(Mom)

people in large, deep trouble.

He reset the intercom, hoping there wasn't a telltale click on his parents' end, and called down to the living room. It beeped twice, and Paul finally answered it. "What is it, son?"

"Um...am I still going to school tomorrow?"

Paul sighed. To Leander's horror it sounded as though he had been crying, too. "Yes. Same time as always."

Leander clicked the comm off. He was most certainly *not* going to school tomorrow.

He wasn't going to recon tomorrow, either.

The plan, if you could even call it that, was simple. He would run until they had him cornered, and force them to shoot him down. Maybe, if he got lucky, he could rig an explosion or something, take a few of the cops out with him. Even though there would be plenty more to take their places.

He pushed his bag of evidence over, lay on his back and fumbled his headphones on, dryswallowed two Valium.

Part of him deeper than dread could still feel that bluewhite shrieking place inside him, undimmed and undeterred. Most people would've agreed that he survived once and would do so again. Leander knew that was not exactly true. Last time he had come out of that place with most of the child in him burned away, a page torn out of a sketchbook and given to the fire. He had drawn three sixes on the next page in chemicals and ash.

He did *not* want to see what he might draw on the page after that. Trying to imagine it made his face twist, his eyes ache.

The drug slithered blue tendrils around his fear, unfolded his rage, and dragged him into a heavy, suffocating sleep.

precursor

Leander woke up in recon.

He flailed in panic and succeeded in knocking a jar of colored pens and a broken handscreen down onto his chest from the shelf over his bed.

He lay in this debris field, in his own room, gasping.

This must be how people feel living in a war zone.

This thought made him bark a ragged unhinged laugh that he stifled. Had he ever lived in anything *but* a war zone?

He got up, disconnected and numb.

The police were not waiting in the shower or on the stairs, or in the kitchen. His mother's houseplants were the same old cheerful green confusion. His father was the same old bulk as gray and solid as granite.

Reality should've had the decency to be *different* today.

He'd hoped his mother would be awake, in honor of his last day on Earth, but Soren was as nocturnal as her only son. When she was present in the morning it was usually because she was still up from the night before.

Leander slunk into his chair, folded his arms, examined his fingernails. He waited for his breakfast lecture, usually about his redecoration of his clothes, his backpack, or himself.

Son, it's not wise to draw attention to yourself. Can't you draw on paper? And what are these squiggles? Have you told your mother you need a haircut? What happened to your face?

You know They're only putting up with that for two reasons. One is that you're young, and two is that you're making it easy for Them to tell which wheel needs the grease.

Leander always ignored this useful and hateful advice. He drew on anything that tempted him with boring blank space. He did *not* want a haircut, and failed to see how anyone could *need* one. Maybe if it got so long he was tripping over it, but it barely covered his ears. What was the big deal? He *hated* it when they finally did force him to cut it. He felt robbed of something, hot and indignant that the Leander in the mirror looked more like They wanted him to look.

Silence. Coffee being slurped.

No lecture.

Paul was an engineer, who helped design the tunnels for the underground transit. Sometimes instead of several paragraphs detailing things he disliked about his son, he would talk about work, or pulled up news reports, read to Leander from the screen, and added his own editorial on The Way The World Is These Days.

Leander almost hoped his father would do that, even considered saying something like *How did that refit in Zone Three turn out?* or *What's going on with the news, Dad?* to coax Paul into being

(ordinary)

uh, better company. But Leander hadn't instigated a conversation with his father

(since art class)

in almost three years.

He no longer had the trick of it, if he ever had.

Paul sat with his large frame oddly hunched over the newspaper on his handscreen. His eyes didn't move, and he didn't scroll the page. He took nervous, noisy sips of coffee. No editorial appeared to be forthcoming.

He knows something. And whatever it is, he's so ashamed he won't even look at me.

This made him angry, abruptly and intensely.

(you should have been more careful)

He wished he could unravel his father to see if there were new colors underneath, some bright fascination, hidden, wasted under his blank skin. Some clue. If he knew that geography maybe he could read Paul's mind, like witches seeking the future in a gutted bird. Virgin reams of color, hidden by skin from all eyes for a lifetime, suddenly in his sight.

Did he really want to know what was going to happen? Would that stop the awful sensation clawing around inside him? Would that make it easier to breathe?

"Leander," Paul said.

Yes! Bitch about my hair! I drew a goat with three eyes on my shirt pocket just for you, bitch about that! Tell me how these ignorant kids who got arrested for smoking weed are lucky the kind fucking benevolent Church caught them before they died of a marijuana overdose!

That was such a frenzy he bit his lip, hard, afraid he'd said some of it out loud. Instead he sighed because he was supposed to, and mumbled something that rhymed with *sir,* also because he was supposed to. He resented the warm fall of relief in his stomach.

His brain was already writing the script.

Be a man.

Face up to what you've done.

You weren't raised that way.

You should have been more...

Yes, fine, he would nod, apologize, tell lies about why he intended to do better. Things would be normal again.

Boring, but normal.

His father fumbled for words. Leander thought of Mr. Polling, looking around in the air. He chewed one of his fingernails and wished he was still in bed.

"Is there still school today?"

Half the time even the school didn't know when the warning broadcasts had gone out. The levels of poison in the air rose and fell by the hour, and he never turned to the newscasts on the computer anymore. He got enough propaganda already.

"The count's not even in the yellow today." This was complete bullshit. He pulled an artificial face of adolescent annoyance, and his father made a halfhearted grin.

"When they give your workforce card, you'll miss being in school," Paul said for possibly the billionth time.

"Yeah," Leander agreed, on autopilot. His usual argument was that you got paid for work, and his father's argument was that when you were in school, your parents paid for everything, and you didn't need money. Apparently Paul had never tried to get narcotics without credits. When Leander did get his own, legal workforce card, he intended to hack that one, too, spend his days reading banned books and building illegal machines.

He got up, waiting for Paul to stop him. "See ya."

Paul waved, a lazy gesture that made Leander want to scream. "Have a good day."

Leander tried to imagine that. Eight hours of archery, or

possibly the sun going supernova.

"I will," he lied.

Paul nodded, as though this had affirmed some belief he carried in his worn useless brain. "Learn something," he added.

He smiled at that. It threatened to crack his face. "I always learn something." *Most of it would fucking horrify you.*

"Leander," his father called.

He stopped, gritting back a sigh, and ignoring a little pang of hope somewhere around his belt buckle. "Yes?"

"You come home right after school today." Paul took off his eyeglasses, rubbed at the bridge of his nose. "There's somewhere we have to go, tonight."

"All right," he said.

So *that* was when they would take him.

They didn't like to do it at your house, in case you had traps or bombs or mutant guard dogs or something, and sobbing parents didn't make for uplifting telecasts. They'd be waiting to swarm him like a Biblical plague.

No more Tri-Six. No more feeling like an underground comic-book hero.

He turned that idea over in his mind, and found he could not fathom it, could not believe in it, could not stand any more wondering and dread.

Run.

It almost made him laugh. There was nowhere to run. Earth was made of walls and guards and the ever-smaller spaces between them. He'd never even get out of the quadrant, let alone off the planet and past the Reach of the Republic.

"I love you, son," Paul said.

That one stopped Leander's heart and sent it hurtling upward, still and cold, dropped it to fall back into his chest with an impact that made him catch his breath. He was not sure if anything could've scared him more.

Leander paused, his hand on the door's keypad. He looked at his father a long time before he decided it wasn't worth the questions. His liar's skill had deserted him. He mumbled something that could not decide whether to be *thanks* or *you too*. The resulting garble sounded a bit like he'd said *gloves*.

He slammed the door behind him. The keypad beeped in protest, and he mashed at the buttons irritably until it shut up. His heart was still not right. It had become untethered, bouncing around like one of the fucking balls in phys ed, and he was still terrible at catching it.

He supposed he was lucky to have the parents he did. Kids who'd been in recon were often promptly shipped by their own parents to somewhere equally hideous, until they were grown. One prison in particular had been sending paper mail to his parents ever since his Jesus sketch. *St. Catherine's School and Hospital for Troubled Youth. We care about you!!! Healing minds and saving souls for the LORD!!!*

He doubted that their care was kind or loving. The truth behind the pretty Jesus facade was that you would be locked up until the rebellion was beaten out of you, no matter which saint, no matter how musical the slogan.

Leander had caught Soren ripping such mail into tiny, tiny fragments, and she'd given him the crooked grin that mirrored his own and said, "There's nothing about you I want Them to fix."

He sometimes wondered if his father didn't look at that junk mail in a completely different way than his mother did.

He could feel something in him, something...growing.

He wouldn't surrender it. Even if it hurt, and it often did.

It was his.

We're the monsters, he thought. And some of him wished he was three again, eleven again, as young as he had been yesterday, young enough to find Soren and cling to her. Old enough to go to a spaceport, leave the region, leave the planet.

Trapped.

He did a quick scan of the street, holding his breath, eyes already stinging. He was trying to make it look as though he was appreciating the foul air and the graygreen sky. No one in the neat rows of driveways was paying him any attention. No cops, human or mechanical.

He got his mask seated against his face, tightened the straps. When he removed it there would be an oblong line where the rubber seal pressed against his skin, starting at his hairline, snaking along in front of either ear to close under his chin, as though a surgeon had removed his real face and installed a replacement.

Leander took the little bundle of evidence out of his bookbag, and threw it into their neighbor's incinerator bin as he walked by, with what he hoped would look like casual ease to any invisible eyes.

Run, he thought again. There was pressure inside him, pushing too hard, heart already running doublespeed, feet light as air and eager to move faster, faster.

He rummaged through his bag and pulled out a handscreen. It confirmed what his stinging eyes had already explained. The poison levels were way up. School was closed for the day, if not the entire week.

The mask was filled with ghostsmell of rubber, nauseating under the flat blank taste of filtered air. Here was the familiar temptation to rip it off, breathe deep, suck in deadly air like a deprived addict. He wondered if he would convulse, screaming, vomiting up pale pink clots of lung tissue, tearing his hands to shreds on the cement.

They'd never find him in time, not without a wristunit. Patrols would stumble across him after dark. They'd take him for a junkie, kick him before they turned their flashlights on and saw him, blue as a drowned baby, the acid in the night dew already peeling his skin. The Tri-Six, a suicide on a street corner, and all of them deprived of their scapegoat.

He just wanted to live in a world that changed sometimes. He wished he had been born before the Revolution, seen it before the fences went up.

Staying home wasn't an option. Hours filled with long silences between himself and his father. His mother hurrying around, her voice transparent and cheerful, asking millions of casual questions. He'd improvise the correct responses until the rage under his skin threatened to rend him into pieces, and then escape to his room, burn incense, draw guillotines and sea monsters and alien horrors.

He knew this story much too well.

In his miniature tin box was a better way to spend his last day of freedom. Two alluring scary, tiny snips of paper that were supposedly LSD. He'd read all the censored, judgmental information his computer would give him on lysergic acid diethylamide, years ago, under the guise of a report for his ethics class. Then on to the

Undernet for actual data.

Tension inside him, rupturing soft delicate things.

Revelations.

He wanted one so badly he could feel it in his bones.

The little box was in his hand, and then the slip of cellophane, and then the two innocent-looking snips of paper.

He pulled his mask up for an instant, holding his breath, and tucked the papers between his cheek and gum.

"It isn't fair," he whispered.

The feeble sun succeeded in piercing a rainbow in the eyepiece of his mask, and he covered the lenses with his hands.

The whole world was a jigsaw puzzle, with all the little tabs trimmed off until it was all squares. It fit, but the picture didn't make any sense anymore. He was deviant beyond all chance of redemption, and he would not let them trim him smooth.

He uncovered his eyes and found he was looking up into the into the swampcolored sky, the sun hidden in dirty yellow haze.

He imagined the drifting satellites, cameras rendered mostly useless by the pollution below them. He raised both hands, and both middle fingers, just in case they could see him, grinning behind his mask.

"Bang. Smash," he whispered to himself.

Radio.

Live transmission.

kinetic energy

Thirty-six thousand miles over Leander's head, Oberon was sitting in his office on *Goya*. She was one of a fleet of three flagships he used on these missions of acquisition, a masterpiece of leather and chrome and recessed lighting and various amusements.

He was sick of every inch of this beloved ship.

Today had almost been productive. He'd rearranged the furniture, sent random obscene films to a lucky handful of victims, and sharpened his nails.

Now, he was sitting in his elaborate leather chair, staring out of the wide floor-to-ceiling window at Earth, spread out below him like a virtual map. He was in one of his brief and intense depressions, and he had rejected all offers of drugs, food, and entertainment. He wanted to sit and stare out the window, and wait for something to happen.

The problem with immortality was that you might wait a very long time.

He was toying with a glass of expensive wine. He tossed it over his shoulder to hear it shatter. He was angry, the subtle creeping fury that filled him with indiscriminate hatred.

It drove a muffled, terrified cry out of the new girl in his office.

He spun lazily in his chair to watch her frantically picking up glass. She wasn't pretty. She was made of overcorrected DNA, nerves, and apologies.

She'd been trying to get blood out of his carpet. So far she was spreading the stain around, making an even bigger mess, and she hadn't even started on the walls.

He didn't mind.

He knew the carpet would need to be replaced. He had sent for her to enjoy her reaction to seeing this elegant, civilized room splattered like an abattoir.

He was not enjoying it at all.

Sometimes the search was an adventure. He would tingle in the back of his throat, the palms of his hands, being led like royalty through an endless parade of church basements and hastily emptied town halls. The air was always thick with the scent of terror, and children would be arranged for him, lined up in rows like jewelry in a shop window.

Sometimes he would choose one, lead it far enough away to send the brat's parents into paroxysms of hysteria before pretending to change his mind, letting the squalling little abomination go.

Sometimes it was a draining waste of time and energy, a stunningly tiresome galactic joyride that accomplished nothing.

He sighed, in something like despair.

The only thing he liked about Earth was that a planetary theocracy produced children with fascinating psychological hang-ups. That, and the entertainment of the horrified looks he got on the rare occasions when he ventured out in public on this world. Hadn't it been Earth, last tithe or the one before, when a woman had brandished a crucifix in his face? He'd taken it from her, held it three feet over her head, his face expressionless, until her struggles to reach bored him. He'd dropped it in the dust and walked past her.

His eyes drifted to the paper on his desk. He had no problem with computers, a convenient thing since he himself contained several, but in the interest of complicating the lives of his servants he often insisted that everything had to be hand-written.

On the finest paper, in crimson ink. Without mistakes.

He picked up his schedule.

One more. One more selection before he could return to the Sphere, away from all this noise, dirt, religion.

He considered calling it off. Ordering them to drop out of orbit, set sail for home.

It was tempting.

But he only had four.

Four.

Three of which were so dull he had decided they were expendable. Not one of them intrigued him. It was the first time in years he'd had to travel this far before he'd found nine or ten or so, and he'd spent two weeks finding this miserable four.

There were only seventeen to choose from in this last group.

It was possible there were children being hidden from him. Or someone was paying his examiners to fail their children in the tests.

He would have to look into it.

The idea pleased him. Sometimes it was too easy to command

44

perfect obedience. He would have to make some changes, invent new rules. He missed having trials, interrogations, executions. He missed planning the perfect tortures, dressing in the perfect regalia. Watching their faces. Listening to their silly rationalizations, before they dissolved into frenzied incoherency.

Of course, he still did most of that, but it was nowhere near as amusing when it was arbitrary.

The girl made another small cry, and he glanced up to see her cradling a gashed and bleeding thumb.

His expression did not change.

He pretended to go back to his paperwork, gestured for her to fill and bring him a new glass. She did, crying quietly. There was a scarlet thumbprint on it.

He held it out to her, wordlessly, one eyebrow raised a fraction of an inch. She wiped the smear off with the hem of her skirt, and handed the glass back to him, careful not to let her fingers touch his.

He laughed, deliberately, to see if she would cringe. She did. Priceless. "What is your name?"

"Alyris," she said, her voice pale, thin.

Not a Biblical name. Not an Earth-engineered face, either—the result of engineered parents having natural children. Colony refugee. He could investigate her file to see if he was correct, but why? They were disposable. He had a thousand like her, and ten thousand more waiting for an open position on his staff. He often wondered why anyone would want to work here, though he supposed it sounded glamorous, compared to mucking around in a dying garden on a dying world.

"Alyris." Slowly, as if he were tasting the name to make sure he didn't like it. And there was an idea. "I want you to go over there and lick the floor."

She looked up at him, eyes stunned wide in disbelief. "What?"

"Lick. The floor. As in put your tongue against it. Go on," he said, amused.

She stared at him in abject horror.

Not you. No, it was never supposed to be you. Not even when you landed a job in the Imperial Palace.

He brought his new glass of wine to his mouth. He was trying not to laugh again. "Did you understand me?"

One puppet-jerk nod, and an overflow of tears.

"You won't die. Assuming you do it, that is."

That reminded her how to move, and it was back to the crimson splatter, rabbitfast, eyes dancing from him, to the blood, back to him.

No reprieve.

She knelt awkwardly, pushed back her hair, and leaned over, crying harder. He watched the muscles in her neck convulse. Gagging. Almost beautiful. She put out her tongue, tears bright on her eyelashes. He inhaled appreciatively. Blood and bleach and terror.

Yes, almost beautiful.

The door chimed.

He stabbed irritably at the camera controls in the chair's arm. A viewscreen on his desk slid up, turned itself so that he could see it.

It was Victoria, with an antigrav crate.

He considered, and keyed the door open.

She walked in, moving in her usual aimless style. The crate drifted in front of her, bobbing gently on its magnetic cushion, guided by the pressure of her fingertips. "A present," she said, smiling behind the wires lacing her lips together. Her voice was muffled, but understandable. It had taken her years to adapt that well.

He didn't get up, and he was careful not to look curious. "I don't need anything. I said you could come only if you left me alone," he told her, his voice cold.

"It's something you don't have."

If his pupils had been visible she'd have seen them dilate. "That, I would really like to see. Open it."

She touched the controls, and the top of the box unfolded like a Chinese puzzle. Oberon pretended not to watch. He opened an ivory candy dish on his desk and took a handful of the dried mushrooms inside. They tasted awful, but they were expensive, hallucinogenic, and difficult to obtain.

She cleared a space on his desk, without asking. He rescued his mushrooms and leaned back in his chair to give her room.

Victoria lifted a panel out of the crate that he recognized. A life support card.

He felt himself beginning to smile. "Will I like this?"

In answer she lifted out a small, limp package that looked suspiciously human. She laid the bundle down and unwrapped it.

When he saw what she had brought him he stood up, stepped away from his desk, horrified. "What is it?"

"A child," she said.

He came closer, fascinated, set his mushrooms down. It was a naked boy, colorless, like a deep-sea fish, with white skin, white hair, strangely elongated limbs.

When he spoke again it was to the maid trying her best to be invisible on the floor. "Get out."

Alyris did, to her credit in utter silence, though she walked as though he'd nearly killed her. Melodrama.

Victoria reached out and stroked the boy's bonecolored hair. Her fingernails were long, painted deep green. "Do you like him?"

"What is wrong with him?" Oberon asked her, revolted and fascinated.

"Albinism. Engineered out of the gene pool almost entirely. He's one of seven left in the system. Look," she said, and turned the boy's head, pried open one snowy eyelid. The iris of his eye was the deep strange rose of a tourmaline. "I know how you like eyes," she added, her mouth turned tight and mischievous.

"Incredible." Oberon lifted one limp hand, examined the fingers, stroked the inner wrist. The boy's skin was soft, slightly damp, seeming almost transparent. He dropped the child's hand back onto his chest, already reaching for the top drawer of his desk. searching for a smooth leather case. "I wonder."

"What do you wonder, Lord Septarch?"

Oberon snapped open the case, and pulled out a straight-razor.

"I wonder what color he is on the inside."

lysergia

Leander wanted to be alone.

His junkyard, he decided. More private than the library, and sometimes the source of some discarded wonder that gave him a whole new perspective on machinery. He hadn't been there in months and he missed scavenging, improvising, discovering. He'd gotten skilled enough at his career to steal precisely what he needed, but there was an artistry you only learned when you were covered in rust. And there would be peace and quiet, or at least a space free of small talk and questions and adult eyes.

The walk to the tran station took about a century. He kept looking back to make sure he hadn't gone right past it, distracted by internal attention. The tran he needed, routed to the southern border of Zone Seven, was the third to arrive.

It was packed, of course, due to the poison count. He had to sit with people on either side. The little tab of LSD in his mouth felt like the remnant of a spitball. He chewed it for a moment, then tucked it back inside his cheek with his tongue. He thought it had a faint electric, metallic flavor, like the taste of a key, but he might've been imagining that.

He felt nothing.

Maybe it took more time, more patience.

Or maybe he'd been cheated.

He didn't wait long. His muscles tightened, aching, as if he expected a fight or a beating. Tremors of tension made him shiver, the movements so obvious the man sitting next to him eyed him with wary mistrust. Or did he? Leander wasn't sure.

It was only nerves, he told himself.

He knew it wasn't true.

Vicious energy settled in his teeth. He could feel them growing, long and lean and lethally sharp. He reached up furtively and felt them, hesitant, half-expecting them to snap closed and take off most of his finger. His teeth didn't feel different when he touched them, but his mouth told another story. They were strong enough to bite through concrete, hunger streaming down from his lips to throat to stomach.

More. He wanted more.

He could see the blood flowing through his hands. He realized he had his arm about an inch away from his eyes. The man next to him really was watching him now, curious and revolted. Leander could see right through his skin, to the flesh below, red and gaping.

Saliva gushed into his mouth, nearly choking him.

He'd taken off his mask. He wanted to put it on again, but he wasn't sure he remembered how to open his backpack.

Last day...go ahead and bite them...last day...

He sat on his hands.

He was in a world composed of meat.

He could smell them.

And his teeth, merciless, were still growing.

It was long instinct that made him hit the switch for the tran to stop. It did so, with one last disagreeable sigh. The landscape beyond the marred windows was unfamiliar, though the coordinates on the display by the driver told him he was close enough for anti-government work.

It was all wrong. It was too clean. There were more street signs than he remembered, more benches. A hideous suspicion made him tug his headphones out of his ears, and he found he was correct.

It was much too quiet.

It's the acid, he told himself.

He didn't believe in what he was seeing, not even when the tran was a tiny noise in the distance, not even when he was standing on the street alone holding his breath out of reflex, his mask forgotten in his hand.

This is one serious drug. Really convincing.

He put the mask on when his eyes began to sting.

He walked, swooping staggering steps that made him glad the street was deserted. He was reasonably sure this, too, was not the drug. Something much worse.

Here was a street he had once known, the same gentle slope of hill, the same little bridge over what was left of a canal that was probably filled with instant death.

He would cross the bridge, and spread out to the left would be an artificial valley in a sea of pressed-metal buildings. It was a cemetery for machines, some a hundred years old, hulking like dinosaur bones, some gleaming derelict copbots, still warm, sometimes still sparking. A maze, tangled and intricate, filled with answers and questions and fabulous smells, filled with astounding noise that became a new kind of silence. Shredders and grinders and shouting and lifts, making a din that could drown out Earth.

He crossed the bridge. Spread out to the left was...nothing.

Nothing at all.

"No," he said, to no one.

The sound of it made him stop talking. Months. Maybe as long as a year, since he'd been here.

Too long.

Well, he'd wanted a world that changed sometimes, hadn't he?

The ratty haphazard buildings were gone. The dirty men who never asked him why he wanted so much wire and shrapnel were gone. The bones were gone.

His junkyard was gone.

Now there was raw red cemetery dirt.

Were they still under there, the machines, *his* machines? Or had They hauled them off to drop into some unimaginable furnace? Had They gotten the place shut down with any number of laws—*inciting curiosity*—or simply bought the land to make room for more tiny, identical houses?

He knew better than to stop. To mourn. He kept walking, and he made himself do it until that empty place was behind him.

Acid didn't feel like a sentient presence as some entheogens did. It was more like a swarm of nanotechs inside him, installing temporary perception upgrades.

Earth, or at least every part of it he had ever seen and certainly the part of it he was in now, was a terrible place to have one's senses enhanced.

He found more empty holes, like growing teeth had been knocked *out*. A cheerfully blank storefront with barren windows where he had once bought beads and bones and feathers and paint, an abandoned square of pavement where a man in a gargantuan straw hat gave out badly drawn comics with every purchase of a weird and wonderful sandwich.

They were planting those massive, spiny plants everywhere there was room. Nothing else would grow outdoors within miles of a city. *The eyesores,* his mother called them in disdain, turning back to her spoiled windowsill violets.

He wondered how long it took for one such delightful little mushroom of rebellion to grow in the dark, how much rage and courage it had taken to nurture each one. How little time it took Them to come in with their fucking earthmovers once They noticed. Or maybe they'd been hanging on for years, decades, only to find the same

(furnace)

end as all the other fallen.

The LSD upgrade was helpfully showing him a nation, a planet made of these empty places, of wounds that had once held teeth. And worse, it was showing him exactly what would grow in that raw red dirt. More news displays, more copbots whizzing around overhead, more of those grim and cheerless eyesore plants. Benches nobody used on streets where nobody walked, all the identical people neatly filed away in identical houses, all of this built over the graves of much better ideas.

Nowhere was safe.

Not on this planet, maybe not even beyond it, once they'd run out of originality to clean up.

It was his room he wanted now, the solace of bed and darkness, where he'd hidden from recon.

The LSD upgraded that understanding, too. Recon wasn't really a place, or an event, or anything you could leave behind. It was a process, and it was still going on, all around him.

Only two things here moved besides himself: bots darting around a few yards overhead, and the occasional passing trans. He considered catching one of the latter, but the idea of being boxed into a tiny space with

(grief)

other people sounded highly unwise.

He kept moving, through spaces that felt increasingly unreal.

At night his walks felt like adventures, the dark drawing a merciful veil over all Earth's embarrassing, slightly desperate normalcy. This walk felt like work, and the waste of what might've been an astounding drug if there had been anything about this fucking place worth magnifying.

So much horrifying light, and so many invisible eyes.

Bed, he thought, raw red dirt in his head.

Darkness, he thought, and that was a little better.

Music, he thought, and that was the best idea he'd had in all this terrible last day, one he didn't have to reach his room to indulge.

He put his headphones back on.

Later, he could not have said whether it made the long walk home more nightmarish or more bearable.

The keypad on the door of his house was a riddle he struggled to solve until his father opened it for him. "Leander. You're home early," he said, already turning back to his chair.

Leander fought to decipher this. "The count went up and they made us go home."

He stumbled towards the stairs, marveling at the genius of this. How clever of his brain, to construct such plausible lies, without his conscious input! He felt a rush of love for it, so intense he longed to unhinge it from the unfair cage of his skull, lavish it with kisses and admiration and praise.

That was so bizarre he stopped in the middle of the staircase, running it through his mind again. He had the urge to return to the bottom of the stairs and walk up again, as though his location was connected with his thoughts.

He imagined his brain in his hands, wet salty tissue open to his lips, his tongue, his teeth. Would it be soft, like the best meat, or rough and textured, like celery, cartilage?

If he ate his brain, would he draw in through his blood all that he already knew? With no brain, where would the data go?

"Leander," his father was saying.

"I know, we have to go out," his miraculous brain said. "I want to take a nap first. It's the count...I'm really tired."

"I'll call you when we need to leave," his father said.

Leander closed his bedroom door, locked out the world. He collapsed on his bed. The texture of the bedclothes ripped through his nerves, and he moaned, almost undone.

New. That was all he wanted, new. Something completely unlike Earth.

He could reach out with new invisible limbs and feel the solar system spinning around him. He was sure that if he tried he could make it spin faster, or slower, or even stop entirely.

The angel he'd painted on his ceiling folded and unfolded its wings, opened a mouth studded with sharp green teeth, sprouted new eyes in myriad colors, gestured him closer with languid fingers.

He closed his eyes to escape this painful complexity, and found yet more elaborations, wave after wave of them rattling his new teeth. Penetration. Chemical rape. The galaxy expanded around him, spinning lazily. He spread his arms wide, feeling the breeze ruffling his hair.

He thought, *Oh, if only I could draw all this.*

He let the revelations come.

"Leander?"

The knock came again. Leander groaned and wrapped his arms around his head, the sound still bouncing around in his skull. This time his brain appeared to be fresh out of brilliant lies. "I'm sick," he said. "Go away."

His mother's voice came again, worried and infuriating. "Leander, you have to get up. We can't be late."

"I can't go. I'm sick."

She overrode his privacy lock and opened the door a crack. The wedge of light from the hallway slammed into his cranium.

"Leander, we have to go. Even if you're sick."

She flicked on his overhead light, adding to his anguish, and leaned over him, her worried hands on him, cool and invasive. "Are you all right?"

He was not.

She tugged his arms away from his face, got a look at his eyes. "What did you take?"

He hated her then, ruining his visions, and he snapped, "Acid,"

53

to spite her, to see if her face would crumple.

His father's voice came up the stairs, tense and irritated. "Soren, what is it?"

His mother looked at him for a long time before she answered Paul. "Leander's not feeling well. I'll help him get ready. Go downstairs and get the damn car running, will you?"

She said to Leander, "I was known to frequent the opium dens when I was a little older than you. Who could blame us, the world being what it is?"

He was caught between delighted and appalled. "Does Dad know that?"

"Paul?" She laughed. "No. At least, he pretends he doesn't, and I'd like for it to stay that way."

She laid her hand on his forehead, still cool, but comforting now, no longer invasive. He loved her as suddenly as he'd hated her, and he turned his face and pressed a secret grateful kiss to her palm. She smelled like warm cookies and fresh milk, like unknown flowers. She was like him. Sometimes he forgot that.

Soren stroked his hair. "Can you stand?"

He did it for her, though it sent pain through his back, his thighs. His mother was small, scarcely bigger than he was, but she kept him upright all the way to the bathroom.

Once there, she undressed him, pushing away his protesting hands.

"I'm too old for this," he said.

She put her hands on her hips, her eyes exasperated, her mouth sad. "You're right. So am I."

She persuaded him into the tub. When he saw that she actually meant to wash him, he protested, feebly. He was too fucked-up to be genuinely embarrassed but well aware that he should be. She flicked a handful of water at his face, and when he recovered from this amusing indignity he lay limp and moveless, neither helping nor hindering her. The smell of the soap sent his mind wandering through soothing pictures of roses and rain.

She dried him, dressed him in his favorite civilian suit, the one that was a frowned-upon unusual shade of deep bluegreen. She brushed his hair for much too long. He was lost in texture, in circles of descending thought. "Thank you," he said, almost an afterthought.

She smoothed his hair one more time, though it didn't need it, cupped his head in her hands. "I've always been proud of you," she said, for no ears but his own.

She made him look at her with her Mom-magic, and when he saw what she meant his own eyes went wide. "Of everything you've done," she added, leaving no room for doubt.

He opened his mouth, closed it again. He had no idea what to say to that, and then it came to him.

"Kiss lots."

She did.

Soren half-carried Leander down the stairs and arranged him in the electrocar. He slumped, eyes closed. She pushed his bag into his hands, and got into the back seat beside him. Weird, for her to do that instead of sitting up front with his father, but Leander didn't mind.

"We could run. I've got enough charge to take us far away from the city," Soren said to Paul.

"They'll find us. There's no explaining that away. It's not worth the risk."

"He's my boy. Our only child. We'll never have another."

"He's too old, anyway. He'll never be chosen at his age."

Soren's response was to chew her thumbnail exactly the way Leander did when something unsettled him.

"Too old for what?" he asked, curious now. He was too *young* for everything he wanted to do. What could he possibly be too *old* for?

"Nothing, Leander. Don't worry about it," his mother told him, her voice uneven.

The motion of the engine soothed him. Soren had her arm around him. He snuggled closer, buried his face in her long hair, embraced the familiar weight of his bag.

auxilio ab alto

When he heard the engines power down, Leander sat up. "Where are we?"

"Ignatius Elementary Training Center," Soren told him, in the tone of voice that would've gotten Leander frowned at by his father for sarcasm.

"A school for little kids? Why?"

"It's a state-required exam," his father said before Soren could answer.

"They did that at our school last year," Leander said, annoyed. "And I just took a test. Yesterday."

"There've been two cases of Plague 14. They're being careful," his mother said. No sarcasm this time. Something else, though, hurried, too brittle.

Leander had to watch the news telecasts every day in school, and he lived on the Undernet. He hadn't heard about any Plague 14 cases in over a century. "I guess so," he said, into the silence.

Busy pictures were swarming in from every side. He wanted to lie down and never move again, but at the same time, he wanted to scream as loud as he could, run as fast as he could, get into a fight.

Two policemen were coming up to the car.

One of them gestured for his father to key down the window.

Leander sucked in his breath, tried to brace himself for the imagined torture of laser fire.

"We'll take the child. You can park over to the left, and someone will show you where you can wait."

I'm not a fucking child.

Fascist voices. No mercy. Just following orders. Leander's hands closed hard on his backpack. One of them opened the door on his side. "This way, son," he said, not looking Leander in the face. He wore a helmet with a dark blue UV shield, even though it was early evening, with formal blues, pins and braid and the elaborate cross on the right breast pocket. Leander watched the threads crawling in and out of the cloth like worms.

Under the tunic was the unmistakable stiff bulge of shield vest.

Riot gear? For a state-required exam in an *elementary* school?

Leander stood up, holding tight to his bag. "My mask..."

"The count went to green about two hours ago. You'll be all right," the policeman said, in a fake-friendly voice, familiar from a thousand social-consciousness telecasts.

Leander slung his bag over his shoulder, stuck his hands in his pockets. He gritted his teeth and tried to will the ground to stop billowing.

The policeman put his hand on Leander's neck, steering him towards the school building, the way they'd pushed him around in Priority. He thought about grabbing the man's ring finger and twisting it as hard as he could

(squishsnap)

and then he tried to walk without thinking at all.

At the double doors two policemen patted him down. He held his breath, waiting for them to search his bag, but they put it on a little scanning table and gave it back to him without a word. His escort pushed him inside, walking so fast Leander had to nearly run.

There was a long hallway, lined by heavy doors. Panic made his steps feel infinite. He sang to himself: *radio, live transmission.*

The song moved forward, and he knew this was no nightmare.

He wished he hadn't been smart enough to sing.

A boy sat on a folding chair, staring off into space, his hand tight around a bandage in the crook of his elbow. Behind one of the doors someone was crying, the sound snotty and muffled, a little kid failing to be quiet.

Three more policemen were huddled together, UV shields flipped up, drinking coffee and talking in serious tones. They fell silent as Leander was guided past them, three masks with staring expressionless eyes.

His own personal cop opened one of those heavy doors, nudged him into a room with two chairs and a portable exam table. "Strip down. The doctor will be here in a minute," the policeman told him.

There should have been no humanity in that voice. It should have been the blatting monotone of a security bot.

But there wasn't.

The voice was casual, calm, and definitely organic.

A real live human had told him to do that.

That was the scary part.

The door slammed.

It clicked.

He was locked in.

Leander stood shocked and furious.

After a moment he set his bag on a chair and fumbled out of his clothes. Naked, he sat on the edge of the examining table and tried not to look scared. His mind found the anonymous record of an unknown movie. *Name, rank, and serial number.* He tried to look brave, tried to *feel* brave.

After about twenty minutes the door opened.

A man with gray hair and thick glasses in a white lab coat came in, tailed by yet another policeman. He had an electronic notepad, and started firing questions even before the door closed.

"Name?"

He swallowed. "Leander Schaiden."

"Parents?"

Yes, I have two of them, thanks. "Paul and Soren Schaiden."

"Are you natural or engineered?"

"I'm...I'm normal. Natural." Leander was scrubbing his hands on his bare thighs. He didn't like this guy.

"Age?"

"Fourteen."

"Have you engaged in sexual relations with anyone of either sex?"

"What does that have to do with anything?"

"Have you engaged in—"

"No, all right? No." His voice shook. He could feel himself blushing. He wasn't sure if it was humiliation or anger.

He pried open Leander's mouth and ran his finger along his teeth. Leander gagged, and pulled away, glaring. The policeman stepped closer, his hand drifting towards the stun gun at his belt.

The doctor toggled the voice recorder on his notepad. "Male subject, circumcised. Five-four, approximately one-fifteen pounds. Perfect skin. Perfect teeth. Hair dark brown, eyes green. Delicate bone structure. Features more or less attractive, somewhat feminine. No visible signs of disease, although he appears to be underweight."

Two motherfuckers, one with a stunner, to control of one underweight kid. Either you fucks know I'm the Tri-Six or you're scared of your own shadows.

The doctor scanned him for heart rate and breathing, peered into his eyes. He put on rubber gloves, examined Leander's penis with rough heartless fingers. "Stand up and lean over the table."

Leander was so mad he was shaking. "Fuck off," he snarled, making a grab for his bag, preparing to shove his way out the door, naked or not.

The jolt was so fast Leander didn't realize the cop had stunned him. His tailbone hit the corner of the table, sending a blinding dull pain up into his spine. He tried to stand, hands curling into fists. The room went heavy, blurry, gray.

Then he was bent over, the edge of the table digging into his ribs. His arms were pinned behind him, cruel hard fingers grating the bones in his wrists together, and hands were spreading his buttocks. He twisted violently, screaming murderous profanity, mouth bruised and muffled against the table, teeth scraping the steel.

I'll kill you.

He meant that. That was the scary part, not the heartless questions, not the impending violation. His own fierce reaction. His own bloodlust. His own utter sincerity.

He kicked hard, felt his heel sink into something soft, heard one of them grunt and wheeze. "Little shithead." A fist struck his back, driving out his breath. The world caught fire.

When his vision cleared he was lying on his side on the table, alone. The cramp low in his stomach told him the rectal exam had been done while he was unconscious. It felt like they'd been trying to find his fucking lungs.

He sat up in gradual, careful increments. The pain knotted, expanded into a bright flare. He bit back a groan, and stood, stiff and slow. He put on his clothes. It was a useless display, an allowance to dignity he was no longer sure he possessed. His fingers were numb, A horrible taste was running into his throat from his sinuses.

He went to the door with one hand pressed to his stomach.

They'd locked him in again.

He picked up his bag, buried his face in it to smell something familiar. His face left a colorless smear on the vinyl. He put his hands to his cheeks, and discovered he was crying.

The door opened again. A policeman he didn't recognize put his head in, noticed Leander was crying and made a fake throat-clearing noise. "You can come and wait out here."

In the hallway, other kids were lined up along the wall. Leander went and stood with them. The kid with bright red hair whispered, "They stun you?"

"Yeah," Leander scrubbed at his face, not looking at the kid. Something slippery and thick and cold was greasing the flesh of his ass, spreading damp in his favorite bluegreen dress-civilian pants. He shifted his weight from one foot to the other. The wetness began to sting, making his eyes water. He folded his arms.

"Me too. This doctor started touching my dick, and I yelled. I've got asthma and I told them that, but they stunned me anyway."

"Bastards," Leander said, quite loudly and clearly. One of the cops looked at him. Leander returned his cold stare, wishing with all his soul that looks could kill. The man abruptly looked away, glancing at his wristunit.

The red-haired kid was eyeing him. "You're too pretty. You'll probably be one of the ones to go."

"Go where?"

The kid gaped as if he'd said something crazy. "You don't know?"

"How in hell would I know? No one will tell me anything."

"Everybody knows about the tithe. We're candidates to be tithed out to Oberon."

The last word was a whisper.

"Oberon?" This earned Leander several terrified glares and some shushing from the other kids.

He'd heard that name before, years ago. A woman who lived across the street, screaming at her daughter, *Stop that crying, or Oberon will come and get you.* Soren made him come inside when the lady started that, and assured him there was no such thing as Oberon, or any other variety of boogeyman or closet monster. He'd attached no more importance to it than any other silly grownup lies. Tricks to scare you into obedience. Another version of Hell, now with spaceships.

Oberon. The Septarch. Emperor of All Things Unseen. What

kind of game was this, feeding them that Halloween tale?

"That's a kid's story," Leander said, dripping scorn he was not sure he felt. "A fairy tale. He'd have to be hundreds of years old."

"He's immortal. He hasn't come out as far as here in sixty years. This year he came in all the way to New Jerusalem. If the city doesn't give him what he wants, he levels it. That's what happened to Mars!"

"That's not what happened to Mars, the *dome* failed—"

"And to the colony on Zion 4."

"That's bullshit too. That was a meteor."

More shushing. Leander was not in the mood to be shushed. He stared straight at the guilty parties, noticing with faint amusement that this made them stop as though he'd switched them off.

The kid shrugged. "Whatever. I'm glad I've got all this hair and these freckles. No way he'll pick me."

Leander put his hands to his face again. *Features more or less attractive, somewhat feminine.*

His stomach still hurt, a dull thick pain like he'd been kicked. He concentrated on trying *not* to look somewhat feminine, and waited. He wasn't scared. Not at all. All that trembling was from the acid. Maybe this whole thing was from the acid. That was it. He was still lying in his room. It was acid. He'd never expected it to be so vivid, so horribly...believable.

One of the cops was talking into a comm. He gestured at another cop, and he turned and yelled to the waiting children, "Everybody move out!"

Leander did. He was used to this. He stumbled along like a zombie, one hand pressed hard against his stomach. The cop led them out a back door, across a courtyard, and into a gymnasium. The grownups were sitting in folding chairs lined up along one wall. Leander saw his parents, and ran, fell to his knees with his arms around his mother, buried his face in her chest.

She clung to him so tightly it hurt, saying *Leander* and *I'm here* over and over. He inhaled her, that soft sweet scent that only she had, face pressed into her collarbone. His father's hand closed on his shoulder, awkward but sincere.

He raised his head to look at Soren. "They hurt me," he managed. It was not at all what he meant.

Her eyes were bright, liquid. She hugged him again, hard and fast, and pressed a secret kiss to his cheek near his ear. "It's almost over. We're going home soon. Here, sit down."

She doesn't believe that.

There were no more chairs. Leander sat cross-legged on the floor at his mother's feet, his bag cradled in his lap. He sniffled, and tried to look okay. Soren handed him a tissue. Other kids his age were crying too, and not just girls. At least he wasn't the only one making a fool of himself.

"Why not now?"

"They'll tell us when we can go," Soren said, not looking at him.

Leander knew, then.

"It is, isn't it? It's Oberon."

Her face twisted. He thought for an instant she might hit him.

"Leander, hush," his father said.

It wasn't the anger in his voice that made Leander hush.

It was the fear.

Oberon.

He lived on a mountain. In the desert. Under the ocean. In a space station built by aliens. He was a cyborg. An alien. A giant. The Devil. That old book, *Dracula*, forbidden for centuries, was about him.

He ate children. He had a horde of demons. He was a sorcerer. He was immortal. He was evil, and he could do anything.

He was a fairy tale.

An invisible signal passed through the room, and there was silence. Leander pressed his back against his mother's knees. Eyes dropped.

Except for his.

Leander raised his head, looking at the door. What he felt was no longer fear, but wonder.

He sniffed at the air, as if he could catch the scent of immortality.

happily ever after

Four guards came in, dressed in violet plate armor, chrome belts crossing their chests from shoulder to waist. They had crossbows. Real ones with actual, physical bolts.

They were flanking the Septarch.

This spider of a man towered over the tallest of his guards. He wore a sleek black floor-length coat Leander thought might be actual leather. The Septarch's hair was black, almost blue, falling like water down his back. He was eerily serpentine, moving like a precise machine, every joint greased and frictionless. His face was long and made of angles, his skin seamless, white as sunbleached bones. He was painted, his lips the color of chocolate, a symbol etched in black on his forehead, a looped cross with an arrow pointing down the bridge of his nose. His eyes were so dark they looked insectile.

He was so...

(familiar)

alien.

He was no fairy tale. He owned the room and everything in it, and he knew it.

He was a blaze in Leander's eyes, a supernova.

New. Knew.

Oberon.

Something bright and fluid and fierce ignited in his stomach, scorched its way up his throat, settled burning under his tongue. His hand wound itself into a cramp, and he could smell ink and paint and pencil shavings. He *needed* to draw this...creature.

The Septarch's eyes glided over the waiting children, missing nothing, stopping nowhere. His face remained expressionless, and he did not seem to breathe. When he spoke his voice was a shock, low and rich, casual.

"No. None of these."

His mother sagged behind him, almost collapsing under the weight of her relief.

Oberon turned to leave.

Leander said one word.

"Wait."

It was deafening in the stillness, echoing in the vast space of the gym.

Wait. Wait.

Soren made a desperate, terrified sound, more breath than voice. She tried to cover Leander's mouth and missed. Her hand spread awkwardly over her son's face, pulling his head backwards into her lap.

Oberon stopped.

Everything stopped.

The Septarch turned on his heel, pushed one of his startled guards out of his way. It didn't look like a hard push, but the man was moved several feet, and nearly went to one knee.

He stopped so close the toe of his boot brushed Leander's knee.

He looked down.

Leander looked up, his lungs locked.

Oberon's eyes were not just dark. They were without whites, without pupils, black as oil. They reflected nothing. They reached down into his brain, into his gut, burned him there with cold that spread tendrils into all his limbs. Leander felt like a bird, nailed moveless and terrified.

The Septarch said two words.

"Take him."

The guards reached for Leander.

He didn't see them. He'd fallen into Oberon's eyes, and he was still there, small and cold, a voodoo cocktail of acid and adrenaline was thundering through his chest.

Soren grabbed Leander out of their hands, tore him away from them so hard that he sprawled at her feet. "Get away from him!"

She struck the Septarch in the chest, with both fists.

It moved him not at all, but he stepped back, cringed as though she had burned him. Something like terror crossed his face for a microsecond, before the careful mask of coldness closed over it.

Paul's hands moved in slow motion, too late to stop her. It was already done.

Soren raised her hands, poised to hit him the Septarch again.

Oberon raised his left hand, a clipped, practiced gesture. Everything was moving frame by frame, like a series of photographs, and Leander didn't understand any of it.

The sound came, not a wail, not a loud report, not even an antimatter hiss.

Three snicks, so close together they were almost in unison.

Soren never saw the guards move. Three bolts appeared, one below her collarbone, two lower in her chest. She was transfixed, nailed to air, her back arched, head crooked, arms bent and out, her hands limp for the space of a heartbeat.

Leander opened his mouth to scream.

Then, the bolts detonated, and the blood came.

She flew back. A sheet of warm fluid slammed into Leander, Everything went red.

The metal chair behind her collapsed under her with a clatter, taking Paul's chair with it. He made a terrible noise, a hoarse ragged howl. He tried to put his hands on his wife. Instead, he put them in her, in the gaping hole that had replaced her chest. Organs pulsed there, charred, still forcing out obscene liquid.

Leander blinked. Blew out a hard breath he didn't remember taking. Tiny fragments of his mother's bone fell from his lips. He inhaled, tasted acid, copper, chemicals, ashes.

He moved his mouth to say, *Mom*. Nothing came out.

I was known to go in the opium dens when I was a little older than you. Who could blame us, the world being what it is?

Leander's not feeling well. I'm going to help him dress.

Get away.

"Mom," he said. Nobody heard him.

Oberon spoke again. "Take him."

The guards pulled him to his feet.

Leander stumbled forward and fell to his knees. His backpack fell over his shoulder, dragged him down on all fours. He looked up through his hair, and the red-haired kid swam before his eyes, clinging close and safe to his red-haired parents.

Leander's hand slipped in blood, and his chin struck the floor. His teeth snapped closed around his tongue. His father was still screaming, somewhere behind him, but there was no sound, only texture, and it was all tangled together with the pain in his tongue, his knees, his stomach.

Green lines. A basketball court.

He spit, and the green lines were gone.

Red. Green. Christmas. His mother hanging strings of popcorn on their tiny illegal Christmas tree. His father, behind her, laughing too, wrapping his arms around her waist to drag her to the floor, tickling her until she shrieked with laughter.

New. Knew.

Hands under his arms, at his elbows, an arm around his waist. The guards were gentle. He looked for the Septarch. Oberon was standing still, hands in the pockets of that long leather coat. Half his face was splattered crimson, covering his black paint.

Leander hid against a violet suit of armor, eyes open wide, eyelashes brushing steel. Gagging. Air. There was no air.

He fell again. This time, he never made it to the floor.

CAP·TIVE

(kàp¹tîv) noun

1. One, such as a prisoner of war, that is forcibly confined, subjugated, or enslaved.
2. One held in the grip of a strong emotion or passion.

adjective
1. Taken and held prisoner, as in war.
2. Held in bondage; enslaved.
3. Kept under restraint or control; confined: captive birds.
4. Restrained by circumstances that prevent free choice: a captive audience; a captive market.
5. Enraptured, as by beauty; captivated.

fairy tales

Oberon watched that slip of a boy carried away, boneless and bloody, head lolling. He made one clipped gesture towards Soren's body, and said five words to the guard at his left, "Tell medical to get that."

He maintained what he devoutly hoped resembled composure all the way out of the school, all the way across the empty parking lot to his transport. The door closed between him and Earth, and it was safe to gasp and shake and shudder.

Cayle looked at him with deep concern. "Is it safe to touch you?"

"No," he said, and covered his face with his hands. Breathing too hard. "Drugs. Now."

"You going to explain it to me, or do I call—"

"Theren," Oberon nearly moaned, and jabbed at a console until it opened the comm channel to his guard. "One of you meat tell Theren to take that boy back to *Goya* immediately and separate him from the others. He is worth more than all of your lives."

He disconnected without adding that their lives were worth extremely little after that clusterfuck.

Cayle was already setting up a small tank.

Oberon held out one hand, gesturing *hurry* with the other, desperate. Cayle gave him the breather mask after about a thousand years. He slammed it over his mouth and nose, hauling in starving breath after breath, mist already clouding it opaque. He indicated *more, more* until the doctor obliged him. Then he waved for Cayle to get back. Cayle moved to the farthest possible seat, both hands visible and relaxed, palms up and empty.

Oberon panted into the mask until the whirring of his heart slowed. He nodded to Cayle, after a long time, meaning that it was safe to move, and the doctor touched the datascreen to his left, pulled up the immediate briefing.

A moment later he looked at Oberon over the top of his glasses and frowned. "All right, I see. Which is posing the problem, here, being attacked, or being spoken to?"

"Both," Oberon said, and raised the mask to his face again. He said into it, muffled, "He's yours as soon as you're both on board. I need to know why that happened. Explain that one to me."

"As you wish, Lord Septarch."

Was he...amused?

Oberon studied the mild, faded-blue eyes behind those ridiculous glasses, and decided that was his own imagination.

"The woman. Pull her neurofile *immediately*. I want Medical *running* with that gurney, do you understand me?"

"Perfectly, Lord."

"And stop with the Lord."

"Oh? Am I talking to Oberon again, and not his Imperial Majesty?"

"You're pushing it."

Cayle thought about this, while rummaging through the bar. He brought a glass for himself and a glass for Oberon, and poured too much Scotch into each. "I am. I could use new hips and a new spine and a new prostate anyway, so go ahead and kill me. But drink with me first."

Oberon sighed. "What just happened?" he said, more to himself than to Cayle. He picked up the drink he did not want and drained it, the mask bleeding lazy tendrils of sedating mist into the air in his hand.

"You got a surprise."

"I don't like surprises."

Cayle tilted his head, weighing this declaration. "No, you don't like to be touched, or disrespected, and that was both, and you don't like things that aren't your idea, but still, somehow, you *do* like surprises."

Oberon was now sure he'd been right the first time. The doctor was amused. "Well, I don't like them often, and I don't want any more of them anytime soon. The boy. I want a report waiting for me when we reach Omega."

Cayle's eyebrows went up. "You want to skip the Pandemonium visit?"

Oberon took Cayle's drink out of his hand and drank that one too. "Yes. Surprise."

Leander was at home in bed. Someone outside was yelling, *Stop that crying. Oberon will get you.*

Something was poking his left knee.

He opened his eyes. They were gummy, and he rubbed at them. Then came the panic.

He was *not* home in bed, and his eyes were sticky because he was covered in blood.

He was sitting up, and he couldn't stand. His hands found the buckles. A harness. Under the straps his favorite suit was stiff with drying gore.

He was in a surface-to-space transport.

He exhaled, aching. His bag was tucked under his feet. He kicked it with his heel, making sure it was really there.

Someone was still crying.

There were faint blue lights overhead running from stem to stern. There were nine other seats, three of them occupied by the dim forms of sleeping children. The poking came again and he looked down. A little girl was sitting in the cramped aisle, tugging at his pants and weeping. "Mister, are you awake?"

He scrubbed at his eyes one more time. "I'm awake."

"Open the door. I wanna go home."

"I can't open the door. The accelerat—um, the transport is going really fast."

"I don't wanna go to jail," she said, smearing snot across her face with the palm of her hand. Leander grimaced, leaned over, the buckles trying to dig holes into his ribs, and dragged her up into his lap. She was wet enough to squish against his thighs.

He got his shirttail out of his pants, found it clean enough to wipe her nose. Dampness began to seep into his pants. "What's your name?" he asked to distract her, groping over his head. There it was. He flicked the switch and a small white light came on.

"Jyana," she said around her fingers, staring at him with frank curiosity. She was adorable, huge blue eyes, hair that was almost white. "Why're you all bloody?"

"I fell down." he said. It wasn't even a lie, he supposed.

She nodded, and her eyes relaxed. She understood that. Then the panic again. "Can't you open the door? I don't wanna go to jail," she begged, the tears starting again.

"We're not going to jail," he said, wishing she would go back to sleep. His head was killing him, and he didn't want to think, at all, about anything.

Jyana chewed her lip. "Where are we going?"

To Hell, in a handbasket, and the most beautiful motherfucker you've ever seen is there waiting for us. He has eyes like ink and he's going to suck out our brains.

Had he really been bored before, really felt trapped? He had the sudden urge to burst out laughing. Or crying.

Or screaming.

"Mister? Where?"

"To Heaven. We're so special that we get to go to Heaven early."

That one was definitely a lie.

"I want Mommy," she said, leaning her head on his chest.

He closed his eyes. "Me too."

"Will she be there in heaven?"

"Yeah. She'll be there," he said, and swallowed hard. Had he ever believed in Heaven?

"You're nice," she mumbled, sleepy.

I'm not that nice.

His hair was drying in spikes. That was where his mother was. In his hair, on his skin, in fragments down in his lungs.

"Knew," he whispered, but Jyana was already asleep.

He listened to her breathing for a long time.

The second time he woke the vibration of the engine had stopped. Jyana's damp warm weight was gone.

He opened his eyes a crack, without moving. The world was busy and jagged, and it noticed his arrival and swarmed in on him.

The transport was empty except for himself and one of the guards. He was still wearing the violet armor, but he'd taken his helmet off. He was a young man, short and slim, with light hair and friendly hazel eyes.

You're one of them. One of the ones who pulled the trigger. And you're also the one who carried me.

He wrapped his arms around his chest. There was a hole there, and he had to keep his insides in and the outside out.

"I know you're awake," the guard said. His voice was not unkind. "I'm not going to hurt you. I've got to take you to Medical."

"I don't want any more doctors."

The guard hesitated. "They won't be from the Republic, but they have to examine you again. I know they hurt you before. It won't be like that this time."

"Yeah, and you know that how?"

Theren sighed again. "I'm your guard." he said, and it sounded as if he were far away, speaking through deep water. "My name is Theren."

"Uh huh. Are you guarding me for, or against?"

"Both. In this case, against the crazed Republic fucks. The film of your, exam, was presented to me as anomalous."

Film. There was film of that being done to him, making the rounds. Leander flushed. He hated them all. There were beasts, then, all around him, in the space between reality and his mind, and he held up his hands, but they couldn't touch him.

He was awake, then.

Leander raised his hand, and pointed at him, or tried to. Either his hand or the guard would not cooperate. "You're a murderer."

Theren had no reply to this.

The doors to the transport hissed, and winged open behind them, letting in a rush of cool, clean, unscented air. Theren moved as though he meant to unfasten Leander's flight harness, and Leander snarled at him so savagely he snatched his hands back as if he feared they might catch fire.

His guard crouched. It looked like an awkward proposition in that armor.

Leander rolled his eyes. "You want to look less threatening, you should keep your fucking crossbow to yourself next time. You touch me and I'll bite whatever I can reach, and I mean I'll bite it *off*. I can unfasten my own seat belt." He was trying to do that already, and was approaching the kind of giggles that were probably a prelude to madness when he found the trick of it and freed himself.

Theren stood again, sighed. "I'm not your enemy, "

Leander only dignified this with the response of a cold green gaze.

Theren led him out of the transport, though an echoing space he realized was a hangar.

Space. I'm in space.

He had ached for this moment since he understood what space was, but now this granted wish moved through him, empty of importance.

A team in medical white was waiting with a half-grav stretcher. Theren hurried towards them. He spoke a few words Leander could not hear to a man who looked more like a fisherman in an old movie than a doctor.

The doctor waved his entourage back, and approached Leander himself, alone. "I'm Cayle. I understand you're not fond of being touched."

"Not by him," Leander agreed. "And probably not by you."

"Well, if you can climb on yourself, we'll keep the touching to a minimum until we've put you under. Deal?"

The stretcher lowered, and Leander shrugged, sat on the edge. He realized he did *not* want to lie back, did not want this sea of faces all around him, over him.

Cayle held up an air injector, and said "It's just a sedative. Here."

To Leander's surprise, the doctor handed it to him.

"Put it against your upper arm, and—"

Leander did it before Cayle could finish explaining it, and the look on the doctor's face when he handed it back made him smirk. "I'm good at drugs. Probably better than you a—"

Then his first real hangar in a real spaceship did a marvelous trick, and folded itself sideways all around him.

He was good at drugs, yes, but no drugs he'd ever had on Earth had been quite this good at *him*. Suddenly lying back was the best idea he'd had in months. The sheets were like snow against his skin, starched and impersonal. He watched the ceiling rushing by.

Then he was in a tunnel.

Then darkness, and the sound of wind running past him, hurrying away to unknown things.

cryptogram

Leander was in a tiny room that spun with fierce, dangerous energy until the centrifugal force threatened to crush his lungs. His mother was there, moving her lips in the shape of his name with the bolts in her chest bobbing up and down. She was as clear and vivid as a holograph. Her lips were white, and she did not blink. He reached his hands out to her, and saw that they had become barbed hooks.

Love is death.

The voice was sourceless, uncanny and familiar, and it spiraled around him like an ion storm.

The bolts detonated. This time there was no blood. Instead Soren exploded in a blizzard of bright confetti shaped like butterflies. Each one was marked with the looped cross Oberon had worn on his forehead. They weren't confetti at all.

They were tabs of acid.

He didn't want to taste them, but thousands of them were flying towards him, and his jaw was locked open.

He woke drenched with sweat, shivering.

For a long time he didn't move. Moving meant thinking, and as long as he stayed still, nothing hurt.

He stretched his arms, opened his eyes. He was in a hospital bed, shockingly white in a gleaming black room.

He was clean, dressed in a pristine white shirt and pants woven of a substance so thin and soft he tugged at it to see if it would tear. It didn't.

His throat tightened.

Even her blood was gone.

Theren was leaning against the wall beside his bed. "It's silk."

"Where's Jyana?"

"Jyana?"

"She had white blonde hair. Little, like four or so. She was crying for her mother. I had her in my lap."

Theren shrugged. "Couldn't say."

He was not, in Leander's opinion, a talented liar.

Theren reached down near his feet, and handed Leander his bag. The weight was different. He opened it and rummaged around inside.

"My journal. It's gone."

"I know. I'm sorry."

Leander shrugged. "Where are we going?"

"To the Sphere."

This meant nothing, and Leander shook his head.

"Past the Reach. It's on a planet called Omega."

Another planet. Past the Reach of the Republic of Earth. Wild space. Real space. *Here there be dragons.*

He felt nothing about it. Nothing at all.

"Does it have moons?"

"One. Moloch."

One. Just the boring same as Earth. Other planets were supposed to have a dozen moons. "Can you breathe the air?"

Theren pulled a face. "Yeah, you can breathe. But I wouldn't. Smells like a match factory. And it's damn cold, all the time."

"Then I can't go. I lost my mask."

Theren shrugged. "You won't be outside much."

Leander's head was heavy, and colors trailed across his vision. He thought, *I understand everything,* and his brain said, "Is it pretty?"

"Pretty?"

"The planet."

"No," Theren said. "It isn't."

Theren led him to a small office that gleamed with black and silver. It looked like it didn't belong to anyone. No personal items, no clutter, just a black desk and an array of chairs. More leather. Leander petted the one he sat in. He had never seen leather up close. It felt unnervingly...alive.

Theren brought him food—chicken soup in a shatterproof bowl, milk, cookies that were made with real sugar. He left Leander alone.

This was a new slow rolling fear to examine. If Theren was willing to do that, the possibility of his escape was zero.

So he might as well eat, he supposed.

Cayle came in after a few minutes, carrying an electric notepad. He gave Leander a crooked smile, and flopped beside him in one of the too-soft chairs, instead of behind the desk.

"Hello again, Leander. Did you get enough to eat?"

Leander shrugged, refusing to be bribed or charmed by fake concern.

"I know you're not in the mood for this, but I have a few questions–"

"I'm fourteen. My State Id is 467-8471Z-12. No, I'm not genetically engineered, and no, I've never had sex, not with girls or boys," he said around a mouthful of cookie. "Anything else?"

Cayle laughed. It wasn't a mean laugh—it was crooked and honest. It was like broken glass hitting Leander. He cringed.

"Not those kinds of questions. You've probably had quite enough of that."

This guy was determined to be friendly. Leander had no intention of returning the favor. "So you're a shrink. I had all *those* questions in recon. Nobody liked my answers. You've probably already got the records."

"I'm not a shrink." Cayle patted the pockets of his white lab coat, and came up with a cigarette case. He glanced up at the enviro sensors, and made a quick trip to the door to deactivate the smoke detectors before he lit up. "And I don't care what the R of E thinks about anything. I'd rather draw my own conclusions."

Leander had never seen an adult smoke without apparent remorse. Maybe he was willing to be a *little* charmed.

"Fine. Ask."

Cayle's notepad had dual screens, and he tilted one of them up so that Leander could see it. An inkblot flickered onto the screen. "All right, Leander. I want you to tell me what each one of these looks like to you. There are no wrong answers. Say whatever pops into your head. Okay?"

Leander did not believe for an instant that the Rorschach was the real test. Cayle's side of the screen was visible, and the doctor made no attempt to shield it. It displayed readings of Leander's heart rate, breaths per minute, and temperature.

Maybe this doctor thought he was too stupid to understand the data, or maybe they wanted to see if he could.

He didn't like this game.

The gears in his head were grinding at overclocked speed. He could lie, but the doctor would know that from some change in his readings. What good would the truth be doing them anyway?

"Okay," Leander said. It sounded more cautious than he'd intended. "Birds."

Cayle nodded, and clicked to the next picture.

"Thunderstorm clouds...a butterfly...one of those gargoyle things they used to have on churches..."

After about a million pictures, Leander decided he'd had enough. "It's an ink blot. Did I pass?"

Cayle folded the screen with the inkblot display down again. "You can't fail, Leander. One more game, and we're done, all right?"

Games. Trying to see how much of that shameful intelligence he had. A word like water filled with sunlight.

He sighed. He wanted to sleep. For days. Years, maybe. Maybe even longer. "Fine."

"I'll say a word, and you say the first word it makes you think of. Okay?"

He nodded, frowning. Something in the back of his mind was droning about *left brain right brain verbal spatial visual unconscious mind*. He was sure it wasn't even speaking English.

"Love."

(bolt butterfly blood bone)

"Danger."

"Danger."

(eyes ink falling falling paint lips eyes)

"New."

"New," Cayle said back to him.

His heart rate went up, and his temperature went up half a degree.

(hands eyes hands fingers falling)

"Wonderful."

When Cayle said this back to him, Leander shifted in his chair. Another half a degree. *Cold blood taste metal falling.* "Fear."

He knew Cayle would repeat it, but it infuriated him anyway. He was tempted to shout a paragraph of nonsense—*Hopscotch! Testicles! Adhesives!*—but he lacked the energy to be a smartass.

(pain guilt despair falling blood butterflies eyes like ink like ink, like)

80

"Love," he mumbled.

"Love," Cayle said.

Leander didn't answer. The readout informed Cayle he'd just had an adrenaline rush.

(pain more and there is no... god torch a dark man in my room in my head eyes eyes)

Then Leander whispered, "Wait."

Cayle didn't understand. He'd read the incident report, but there was no film of Leander's tithe. He didn't know this magick word was Leander's answer.

He waited a long time before he realized Leander had no intention of speaking again.

in loco parentis

Oberon sat at his desk, still exasperatingly on *Goya*. He was tired of travels and tithes and anything else that did not involve being at home in his beloved Sphere where he could

(the boy)

sleep.

He was holding an ivory parchment in his hands.

He'd read it already and was skimming the paper, searching the red ink for traces of erasure, a crooked letter, a space too short or long. On the desk in front of him was a gleaming black enamel box filled with crimson file folders nestling against two smaller boxes: one with an enviro panel that had *better* be a genofile and the memory data for Soren Schaiden.

Behind him, on one of the telescreens, an old film of an evisceration was playing. He'd left it on for the benefit of anyone he dealt with here. General, pervasive fear tended to increase efficiency in most of his extensive staff.

"He was torn. Was he raped?"

The medical tech trapped in front of him swallowed hard. "No, my Lord. It was a minor tear, a scratch, from his...resistance once the exam was already...in progress. It did require closure acceleration. We gave him antibiotics to be safe...but it was a minor injury, no threat to the boy's health. The police found it necessary to restrain him."

People, wretched, wide, stubby human people, slackjawed Republic of Earth people touching the boy he'd taken. Hurting the boy he'd taken. He thought of eyes the color of leaves.

He thought he might ask Victoria to find him something that could still squirm and scream. "He was stunned?"

The words fell into the silence like shrapnel.

The tech coughed, pale. "As I said, my Lord, he resisted...it was necessary..."

It wasn't, and neither was this conversation. Oberon had been enjoying the stammering terror at first, but that was no longer true.

Oh, all right, it was still a little true. He resisted the urge to smirk at himself. Centuries now, and yet he never got tired of it.

"The doctor. Impalement. The policeman, too. The serum, first, to rule out unconsciousness, that last Lot number we used, four-twelve? Make whatever cuts are necessary for successful penetration."

"My Lord?" The tech's voice betrayed him. "My Lord, the doctor has been an examiner for fourteen years—"

Oberon raised his eyebrow. The man fell silent.

"Do you realize that this boy is the first human being to speak to me of his own free will in almost two hundred years?"

This was almost shouting.

Shouting meant blood.

The tech cleared his throat, eyes searching for escape. There was only the wet red image on the telescreen, the Septarch, and the question hanging in the air. "My Lord, I did not realize that, but—"

"Haven't I been clear enough? Do I need to tell Equipment to prepare three stakes, or two?"

The tech closed his eyes.

Equipment didn't prepare the stakes at all.

They prepared oak dowel rods and the proper tools, and the prisoners finished their stakes themselves. Sometimes lovers were forced to shape them for each other. He imagined wood as thick as a man's arm driving into his intestines. What was human decency, against that?

"I'll see to it," he said.

"Do that. Let me know when this is ready. I'll want to see them beforehand. And I want all of this recorded." This last order was unnecessary. Everything was recorded, reviewed, filed, everything that touched his life at all, even in the smallest way. But it was fun, satisfying, to restate his demands at random intervals.

Oberon collected his *Yes, Lord Septarch,* and then waited for a full minute, watching the man suffer before he inclined his head a fraction of an inch towards the door.

The tech fled.

The Septarch returned his attention to the file.

Leander Schaiden.

The Septarch ran one gloved finger over the name. He traced slow, careful circles around it until he could close his eyes and see it etched in neon on his eyelids. He flipped through the rest of the folders. School records. Test results. One that moved as though it were heavier than the others. He fished out a small notebook, with

EXTREMELY SECRET BOOK OF SACRED HOLINESS

written on the front cover.

Something made him hesitate to open it.

He tapped a button on his desk panel. "Have them prepare the Worm Chamber for my arrival."

After a long moment he put the paperwork and the journal back into the black enamel box. He closed it, and stroked the invisible keypad that locked it, tapped in the rhythmic code so that no one but himself would ever be able to unlock it again.

He set it aside on his desk, regarded it, and realized he intended to carry it back onto the Sphere himself. Personally. As in with his actual hands.

He raised one of the hands in question to hide his smile.

sodom

Space.
Transport.
A new planet and no, it isn't pretty.

Three little clicks. Three bolts. one below her collarbone, and two lower in her chest.

Theren drove him across the surface in a hovercar that would have made him crazy with excitement and curiosity a day earlier. Outside there was a lot of...nothing.

Omega was a wasteland.

It looked like rough water they were skimming, but Leander saw that it was gray volcanic rock, sculpted in permanent rifts and cracks. The sky was deep orange, streaked with clouds the color of sewage, and a dim and distant greenish sun was sinking into the horizon.

It definitely wasn't Heaven.

"Is it all like this?"

"All the habitable parts, yes."

Leander kept looking, waiting for grass, ocean, trees, anything but skeletal black stone formations and occasional bubbling pools of molten rock. The entire landscape looked as though it were wounded, rotting.

He sat back, disappointed and vaguely nauseous, clutched his bag close to his chest. "You're right," he said. "It isn't pretty."

Theren reached over and set the controls for window of the cockpit to opaque without a word.

They hummed along in silence for a while.

"You work for Oberon?"

The craft jerked slightly. "You should call him the Septarch. Yes, I work for him. Everyone you see for the rest of your...from now on will, too."

"Will I work for him?"

Theren pressed his lips together. "Sort of."

A million more questions presented themselves. *Why are his eyes so black? Will he eat me? Is he a demon? Why did he fucking make you KILL MY MOTHER?*

Leander drew in a long, shuddering breath. "Is it far?"

Theren toggled the window transparent again in answer.

The Sphere was a shallow black dome so vast it could have been a part of a fallen moon. Four crooked, twisted towers marked the corners of an invisible square around it. The surrounding land was absolutely flat, even more scorched than the rest of the planet. Something at the top of the hemisphere jutted out into the air, spinning like a complex gyroscope. Leander guessed it was a relay system for a satellite.

"It's huge," Leander whispered, his knuckles white on the straps of his backpack.

"Yeah. And that's not even a fifth of it. Most of the Sphere is underground."

Meaning the ground had been a liquid when the Sphere landed and sank. He tried to conceive of a *fire* big enough to do that, and realized they were flying over what it looked like when you burned a *planet* to the ground. A globe of dreamlike terror settled in him somewhere south of his navel.

They drew nearer. Soon the dome was so tall Leander couldn't see the top of it anymore no matter how he craned his neck. "Does it have a shield?"

"Doesn't need one. It would take a supernova to burn through that. You can hit it with a pulse cannon from a foot away, and then put your hand right on it. It won't even be warm."

Weird, for a surface structure. Expensive, too. Useful, though, if you wanted to land in the planet you'd just melted. He wondered what this motherfucker had for *guns*.

Leander studied the satellite relay again, turned his head to look back at the nearest of the four towers jutting up from the ground. It looked, to his Undernet trained eyes, like a nacelle housing for a...

"Mercury gyre drive?"

Theren gave a nervous laugh. "You ask too many questions, kid."

A wedge opened along an invisible seam in the side of the Sphere, wide enough for the craft to slip inside. There was a humming whine of gargantuan mechanics moving the plates of the dome. It closed behind them. The blade of dull light vanished.

It was absolutely dark. The lights of the control panel hovered in space, a tiny navigational screen tracing a line for Theren to follow.

"I'm never going back to Earth again, am I?"

Theren adjusted readings that didn't need adjusting, pretended he hadn't heard the question.

The hovercraft pulled into a docking bay. It jolted as the clamps closed on it. The recharge cycle began. The cockpit dome slid open. Theren climbed out and helped Leander out, ignoring the face he made. "I'm supposed to restrain you. I don't like that, and I won't do it if you give me your solemn promise that you won't do anything stupid."

"Like run?"

"Exactly. It's both our necks if you try that."

Leander paled at that, but he nodded. "I promise. No running."

He meant it. There was no point in running, now, anyway. Where would he run to?

What was he running *from*?

Theren led him into an elevator. It descended with such speed Leander put out his hand to grasp the railing. "Where are we going?"

"For now, the Gallery. It's where kids your age are—where they stay."

Are kept.

Leander ran his hand through his hair, trying not to look somewhat feminine.

From the elevator they went through a dark stone hallway. There were torches—actual torches, with real fire—set at regular intervals. Leander tried to stop to examine one, but Theren's hand on his shoulder pushed him forward.

"Is it all like this?"

"No. Just this section. Most of it is…worse."

"Who designed it?"

"The basic structure is…the Septarch made a lot of changes when he took the title."

Leander heard the dodge, but in his line of work you learned that missing data was, itself, data. "Took the title? Is it like, an office?"

"No. There was only one other before him, and he's dead."

"Did Oberon kill him?"

"Kid, everything is recorded here, all right? And unlike the surplus garbage they use on Earth the shit here actually *works,* all the time. You shouldn't use his name like that. Only his doctor gets to do that."

Everything recorded, all powerful sky deity with weird rules, yeah. Leander was beginning to wonder if he'd left Earth behind after all. At least not everything here would be unfamiliar.

"So they're friends, him and this doctor?"

"Friends? No. The Septarch has no friends."

That made Leander sad, and he wasn't sure why. No wonder he was like that. It would suck to be immortal and not have anyone to talk about it with. "Aren't you his friend?"

"Kid, I've had it with the twenty questions, all right?"

Theren's tone of voice that told Leander the answer was *no.*

They went through three sets of huge steel doors, with keypads to unlock them. Then they turned left, and there was an archway with a final locked door.

The room they went into was long and narrow, and separated into cells by iron bars that ran from the floor to the high vaulted ceiling. There were few torches here. Most of the room was in deep shadow. Leander stopped, backed into Theren.

"This is the Gallery?"

"Yes."

"But it's...like a prison."

"It's not as bad as it looks. It's clean, and there aren't rats or anything. Surprised he hasn't had some installed for atmosphere."

Rats.

Leander hadn't thought of that. Long yellow teeth. Wormy pink tails, and little scrabbling feet. All the claustrophobia of recon was clawing at his throat.

"Are there going to be any other kids?"

"Just you and Camille. She's right down here. She'll be in the cell beside yours." He paused. "Camille is...well, she's—"

He was cut off by a bloodcurdling shriek that nearly made Leander forget his promise not to run. There was a terrible clattering. Someone near the end of the row of cells was rattling the bars.

Theren stepped past Leander. "Camille, knock it off," he

snapped. "I've got a new one, and you're scaring the shit out of him. It's not funny."

Silence, then a girl's voice, bitter and hoarse. "Bring him down here. I want to see my replacement."

Leander looked at Theren and shook his head. His throat hurt, and his eyes were bright with tears. "Do I have to stay here?" he pleaded.

Theren grasped Leander's shoulder and squeezed. "Leander, she's crazy," he whispered. "She's been here since she was eleven. She's seventeen now. She always does this to the new ones, but she's harmless. I promise you."

"Leander?" Camille's voice was calmer now. "Is that your name?"

Leander looked at Theren. The guard nodded. "Yeah," Leander called out. "I guess I'm going to live here with you."

Silence. Then, "I like that name. I won't scream anymore. Are you...are you mean?"

Leander didn't know quite what to say to that. "Not unless someone's mean to me first."

"Okay," she said, after a moment. "That's fair enough."

Theren took a torch from the wall, walked towards her cell, and Leander followed.

Camille was tall, so thin she looked ill, with auburn hair and summer blue eyes. She was dressed in the same white silk as Leander. She smiled. He could tell she was crazy by the wild light in her eyes.

Each cell had a small bed, a chair, and a little table. There was a curtain, in the back corner, the same near-black as the walls, probably for whatever passed as a bathroom. A keypad was set into every door, looking very out of place in this dungeon.

Theren went to the last cell on the right, beside Camille's and opened it, shielding it with his cupped hand so Leander couldn't see. He stepped aside. "This one's yours."

Leander couldn't move his feet at first, but the idea of Theren shoving him made him force himself to step inside. He sat on the edge of his bed, his bag cradled in his lap.

Theren closed the door, and Leander bit his lip when the locks clicked into place.

Theren gestured at the keypad. "Push this red one if you need anything. The kitchen will bring your meals during the day. I come in every couple of hours at night, but if you push that, someone should be here in less than a minute."

He turned to leave. Camille caught at his arm as he walked past. "Tell Oberon I hate him! Tell him I hope a tiger eats him!" she said, fierce and almost gleeful. "And ask him why he doesn't love me anymore!"

He removed her fingers, gently. "I'll tell him, Camille."

"Promise me! Cross your heart, Theren!"

"I promise," he said with practiced patience. "Cross my heart. Hope to die."

Camille laughed like an animal's call. "Stick a switchblade in your eye."

What have I done?

Theren returned the torch to its place. He closed and locked the Gallery's door behind him.

Leander stood stricken and alone. He thought he might throw up.

I'm not going to. I'm not going to. I'm not.

He didn't. Instead, he burst into tears.

He buried his face in his backpack. It smelled of

(home)

his room, and that made it worse, and he cried so hard he was almost sick. He could feel Camille watching him, and he didn't give a damn.

He cried for a long time.

"Hey," she said.

He pushed his face harder against his bag, feeling tape against his face, smooth plastic stickers, sharp stitches of wire, familiar lumps inside.

"Hey, Leander, come here."

He scrubbed his face and looked up.

Camille was sitting on the floor next to the bars between their cells. "It's okay. Come here."

He didn't want to move, didn't want to owe her anything, but he was hungry, in a terrible deep way. Contact was better than none, even with her, this lunatic, this fellow prisoner.

He sat down on the floor, stiff and awkward.

She pulled at him until his back was against the bars, reached through, put her arms around him. "Go ahead and cry. It's better to do it now. You might forget how, later."

He was crying still. "What am I doing here? I want to go home," he choked out, sobbing. Saying it out loud made that violent aching wish so much worse, so much more deafening.

"This is home," she said. "I'll be your mom for a little while."

That made him cry even harder.

She was crazy, and she wasn't his mother, and he could feel the bars digging into his shoulder blades, but she was human, and female, and her voice was gentle. She rubbed his shoulders, singing something tuneless. She let him cry himself out.

Her fingers were soft, the tips of them like flower petals, and for a while he let her touch him. There were many things in him, still sharp enough to sting, that demanded he accept this small comfort.

After a while, her hands on his shoulders made the back of his neck feel funny. He couldn't think of a polite way to ask her to stop.

"I'm tired," he said at last.

She kissed the back of his head, and stood up. "The beds are okay. You should try to sleep." She went to her own bed, drew back the covers. White sheets, white blankets, a thick mattress. "See?"

He stumbled over to his own bed. He climbed in with his bag, pulled the blankets up so she couldn't see him and pulled off the white shirt, and threw it.

The bed smelled unfamiliar, faint and clean and impersonal.

His bag smelled like sweat and marijuana and silent masturbation and his mother's favorite laundry soap. Like home.

It was the most precious thing he owned.

It was the only thing he owned.

He held it close, its jagged decorations digging into his chest.

"It'll be all right, Leander. He's a monster, but at least he's beautiful."

He didn't answer. He had no idea what to say to that, but he agreed with her on both counts.

She sang for awhile. Her voice was pretty, even if the few words he caught were mad.

...there was a man who lived in Leeds...who filled his garden full of seeds...garden began to grow...full of snow...

...began to melt, it was like a ship without a belt...
...a bird...without a tail...
...a penknife...in my back...began to bleed...
He closed his eyes so tight it made his head ache, so he couldn't see the flickering of the torches. He inhaled the perfume of his bag, and thought, *I'll wake up soon.*

Camille's singing trailed off.

Leander couldn't sleep.

He was shivering. He drew the bedclothes up tight around him, wished for more blankets. He felt exposed, as if the entire Sphere was watching him, the stone walls studded with invisible eyes.

He could press the button. So what if he needed a blanket?

He wouldn't let himself do it. It wasn't that cold. If he pushed the button it would be to see Theren, a semi-familiar face, and that was chicken.

And chicken was dangerous.

He would just be cold, then.

Every time he drifted into the warm gray place where thought ended, he would remember where he was. A shock like falling into cold dark water would snatch him back into the world, eyes wide and cringing away from the awful space of the Gallery, punctuated by the rows of iron bars.

Oberon.

He gave up and tried to imagine the Septarch, and there were only those eyes, an impression of long white hands, terrible strength. He couldn't imagine Oberon's mouth. He tried, and his mind produced an image of his mother's unspeakable wound, gaping open in nightmare red.

He tried to hold onto that, to hurt, to grieve.

He couldn't.

It was so far away.

Earth. Death. Cram those words together and you got *dearth*, an emptiness, an absence.

He'd known it was coming all his life, expected it deep in his bones.

What had it been like to die that way? Unzipped, unfolded?

That was a mistake, that thought.

His brain produced a wet screenplay on the backs of his eyelids, one that had nothing to do with crossbow bolts.

Those long white hands.

The image made his skin ache for friction, sent a wrenching pull down his spine that made him slide deeper into the bed.

What would the Septarch *do*?

Leander remembered a man who had been on the telecasts for weeks. Appalled, wide-eyed newscasters gave maddening, vague descriptions of his sins: *abominations against children.*

It was the most anticipated execution in Zone Twelve in years.

People had come from as far away as Bethany to see it. Leander's entire school had gone. Attendance had been mandatory.

The man was just a man, with a face no one would look at twice. His expression had been both frantic and oblivious. Like he had been looking at a different world than the narrow view from the stake he was bound to, the jeering crowds of pious onlookers.

Abominations against children.

He got a shadowy image, more a sensation, of a sticky ritual performed under the cover of darkness. Whispered threats, tears, terror.

That desperate wonderful panic took him again. He dug his heels hard into the mattress, twisted the sheet in his hands.

I don't care how beautiful he is. He's a bastard. He killed my mother.

He gritted his teeth, determined to find the rage that had to be there, somewhere. He found only frustration, and inappropriate and intense anger at Soren.

Not Oberon.

Soren.

Why didn't you just let him take me? Did you think you'd punch him in the mouth like the neighborhood bully and he'd start to cry and go home?

Home.

Earth was a feeble story, now. This was real.

He'd always known there was a place like this, behind the slogans and the crosses, crouching hidden underneath everything. He'd always known the State was like a group of children armed with sticks and stones, playing at cruelty with no idea where to even begin.

Emperor of All Things Unseen.

Here, there would be no amateur cruelty.

There was a strange comfort in that.

Leander closed his eyes.

lux et umbra

The boy.

The boy was crazy and desperate and damned.

The boy smelled of tea leaves, and needed darkness, craved it, because it was inside him already. The boy longed to be devoured. The boy was prey, potential pain waiting for teeth and claws, a death addict with eyes the color of the green sun, hair the color of espresso and skin like warm wet silk.

Warm. Wet. Virgin.

Silk.

Dragon, dragon, burning bright, in this temple of the night.

Eat me alive. Swallow me.

Wasn't that how it had happened?

Oberon loaded a needle and knotted the tourniquet, pulled it tight with his teeth. There was a song that went like that, wasn't there? *Tasting rubber, tasting you, in the dying air...*

The boy, kitten face, curious eyes, frightened and eager.

Curiosity. Cat.

He injected far too much heroin, mechanical heart whining in gear-stripping protest. He ignored it. It wasn't as if it would kill him.

Heroin. Something so deadly from something so innocent. Flowers.

Sylvia Plath had called poppies little bloody skirts. The skirts of women raped. She hadn't said anything about little boys. Perhaps in her reality that sticky possibility had not existed.

Forget about the boy.

"Septarch," he said. The word cut his lips. He swallowed a sharp, purple taste. The Emperor of All Things Unseen. That was so much to be the god of that it frightened him sometimes.

God. Ridiculous. The Devil, maybe, if there was one at all.

"Am I, am I?" he asked no one in particular.

It had to stop. No one could see him like this.

The boy.

The boy was nothing. He would collapse the way they all did, into tears and revulsion, begging for mercy that Oberon had never been able to give.

Forget about the boy.

"What boy?" he mumbled, pressing the heels of his hands into his eyes.

What boy? Which boy?

There had been hundreds of boys.

And only this one had ever looked him in the eye.

He hissed through gritted teeth, struck out at the air.

Something's wrong, something's wrong, something's wrong.

No. There wasn't anything wrong.

He wouldn't *let* there be anything wrong.

He left his room, walking crooked and crazy. The heroin bit him with nuclear teeth, flung him headlong into the wall. He slashed at it, blind and snarling. He was dangerous now, oh yes.

Oberon liked to feel dangerous.

He stood for a minute, filled with soft, lethal amusement, his mind a black and red place that pulsed with hunger.

He was at the entrance to the Gallery, with no idea how he'd gotten there.

The boy's scent was here, faint, dormant, sleeping.

The torches were long since extinguished in a single mechanical blink that signified night in the Sphere. Oberon adjusted his sight, and the room blinked into focus, the colors dim but discernible.

The rubber soles of his boots were silent on the stone floor.

Oberon walked past the cages. He could see the ghosts of children there, cringing away, cradling wounds, mouths silent and gaping. Whores, all of them, whining, pouting, pleading with wet lips and wide eyes. He wished he could give them flesh again, go over it, go over *them*, one more time.

The last two cages on the right were occupied. Camille, smelling of gardenias and madness. And the last cage, rich with the warm, bright new aroma of sleeping boy.

The Septarch stopped in front of Leander's cell, closed his hands around the bars, pressed his forehead against them. He inhaled. It was an orange scent, copper and salt, and there was the sharp tang of sweat and fear underneath.

"Wait," Oberon whispered, trying out the word, trying to make it both order and plea. He couldn't make his voice sound like the boy's. He wanted to break open the doors, take this child in his hands, wake him, terrify him.

Wait for what? Didn't you know what you were asking?

He touched the keypad, and the door slid open.

The boy murmured in his sleep. One hand slid off the edge of the bed, his fingertips resting on the floor. He had torn off his white shirt. It was flung across the back of the single chair. Oberon picked it up, held it to his face for a moment, took a fold of silk between his teeth, chewed it, wet it with his tongue, dropped it.

He leaned over Leander.

His hair swung over his shoulder, brushed the skin of the boy's narrow chest. He went still, not even breathing, but the boy didn't move. He pulled back his hair with one hand, with the delicacy of a jewel thief, snagging it a little with his

(claws)

nails.

He bent closer, until he could feel Leander's breath against his neck.

"Wait," he whispered again, trying to get it right, the sound, the pitch. Still wrong. He brought his face so close his eyelashes grazed the boy's forehead, breathing him in. His hands were coming up, open.

No. He didn't touch them. Not the first night.

Maybe he wouldn't have to.

There was a game he loved, always the same, though with infinite variations.

He thought of it as *torture without touch.*

His hands went to his waist, and he keyed open his belt.

"Wake up."

A whisper, but it sounded like an explosion.

Leander woke with a gasp that wanted to be a shriek, freezing and knotted and terrified. "What—"

"Don't talk. Not a word. Get on the floor. On your back."

He got up, with terrified speed. Now it was cold enough to collapse his lungs, and he sat on the floor and then lay down, the stone like ice under the bare skin of his back.

He's here, in here, with me. He's in here with me.

Leander's teeth chattered. He couldn't see Oberon. He couldn't see *anything*. He heard a faint stirring from Camille's cell. He wanted to call out to her, but didn't dare. He wanted to cry, but he was too scared to cry. He kept thinking *past the Reach of the Republic,* and realized that this creature could do anything to him, anything at all.

"Put your legs up. Hold them together, straight up."

He tried. It made him want to fall over sideways, and he spread his arms out for balance.

"No. Keep your hands down. And move faster than that."

He can see me, he can see in the fucking DARK, what is he?

He was trembling, all over. He could already feel the tension in his stomach muscles, in the small of his back.

"You can do better than that. Straighten your knees. Point your toes."

That was much worse. There was pain in the tendons behind his knees, in his thighs, a dull slow burn, and something even worse underneath. The desire to do it perfectly.

"Now count. Count to two hundred."

Leander didn't understand. "What?"

"Count. It's not difficult. You start with one, remember?" came the voice in the dark, sarcastic, amused.

Couldn't I see you? If I could see you I might understand what it is that you want...

"One," he said. His eyes were stinging. *What do I look like, lying here like this? Do I look scared? Do I look as scared as I am?*

He made it to forty-six before his knees bent by themselves.

Oberon made a noise like a snake. "Hold your hand up."

He did. Something brushed across his fingers. It felt like a long heavy strip of leather.

He pulled his hand away like he'd been burned.

No. He can't. No.

"Get your legs straight again. Count."

"I...what...what number was I on?" His voice shuddered in time with his heartbeat.

Oberon laughed. "One. You're on one. And it's five hundred, now."

He didn't have to start over again.

His spine was a string of pain. The front of his neck was a trembling anguish. He couldn't even think about his stomach anymore. He could hear counting, but he was sure it wasn't him anymore. The numbers were coming from the walls, from the air, and someone said, *five hundred,* and he couldn't remember what number came next, and he wanted to scream.

"Put your legs down."

He collapsed. He couldn't do anything but pant until he became afraid of what might happen if he didn't speak. "Now what?"

"Get back in bed."

He did, half-crawling, half-clawing. He curled up with his hands tight behind his knees. The pain was already fading, and that was unfair. He felt cheated, horrified that anything that hurt so much could end so easily.

There was a scrape, and a deafening metallic slam that stopped his breath. The door to his cell, opening again and slamming harder than any human being could close it.

"Sweet dreams," Oberon told him.

Then silence.

He lay there, one aching skein of attention, waiting for a sound that never came.

Camille's teeth drew blood from the inside of her cheek.

"I hate you," she whispered.

She didn't know if she meant Leander, or Oberon, or herself.

phetısh

Oberon had to make himself walk into the Worm Chamber. He was filled with the urge to run, as if he were being *pursued*. Nothing in the known universe would've dared to chase him, but that knowledge did nothing to silence his desperate need to flee.

He struggled with his clothes, dropped them in a careless pile until he stood naked.

The room was ready, as he had ordered. It was a circular shaft, thirty feet across, with a stark four-foot ledge that ran along the wall. A steel walkway led from the doorway to a rectangular platform in the center of the room. Both of these were lit by tiny running lights. Below that, it was a forty-foot drop to the floor, in total darkness.

There was a sense of motion below, as though the entire floor were undulating, busy.

The platform and the connecting walkway were still charged. The path tingled under his feet.

He reached the platform, sat down and then stretched out on his back.

The domed ceiling was a shadow, far above him.

His left hand found the controls and rested there, trembling.

Leander's fingertips brushing the stone floor of his cell. Leander's hand on the controls, covering his own.

He programmed the sequence. He set the timer for four hours, changed his mind, moved it up to six. He chose the lowest possible speed of descent, and activated it.

For an instant there was nothing, then a faint jolt as the walkway slid out of its housing in the side of the platform, retracted into the wall below the doorway. He turned his head, and he could see his clothes there, a crumpled heap of vinyl and chrome.

No way back, now. Even he couldn't jump fifteen feet across empty space, not with any hope of landing on the ledge.

If I pushed you, in here, little boy. If I pushed you in here, and you didn't break your neck on the way down...would you scream? Would you feel them, and cry out for mercy? Would it echo in this room, your screaming?

...my screaming?

The platform began to descend. Gears whined, muffled by inches of stone. The current was strong enough to sting the softest parts of his skin. He flexed his shoulders, turned over onto his stomach, pressed his face, his tongue against the metal.

Ten feet. Eight feet. Six feet.

The air was colder, so damp he could feel water condensing on his skin.

The descent paused. The controls chimed to let him know he had ten seconds to abort the sequence and send the platform up again. Otherwise, it would sink to the bottom of the shaft—and stay there for the next six hours, leaving him there no matter what he did to the controls.

He waited.

The platform sank. It clicked into place a foot below the layer of wet earth covering the floor. The electricity that persuaded the worms away from the platform shut itself off. Clods of dirt crumbled in, sprinkling his arms, his legs, his back. He curled up on his side, his head pillowed on his arm, dragged his free hand through the soil.

In fifteen minutes, the six cylinders set vertically in the walls would begin to open, one by one. Each was ten feet in diameter, filled with thousands and thousands of worms. When each one had been opened, the room would be three feet deep in them.

There were caterpillars, centipedes, infinite variations on the earthworm—every species from the quadrant that couldn't swallow him. The stings wouldn't harm him, and though there would be pain, agony even, pain wasn't the purpose of this chamber. He had other rooms to suit him when he felt the hooks of that particular appetite.

The few worms that were already there began to investigate him. He left them as a prelude, for psychological reasons, though the only one he ever subjected to this torture was himself.

He wondered if they remembered him, or if he was a new discovery to them every time.

They were nuzzling cold at his toes. One of them wriggled against the back of his neck, under his hair. It was no bigger than his little finger. Some of them still up in the pipes were thicker than his arm.

There was a shudder at that thought, either dread or anticipation.

101

He was never sure which.

He found a tiny earthworm as soft as a newborn's liver and laid it across his lips. Horror. Lust. It wriggled there, wandered cold up along his cheekbone, across the bridge of his nose, leaving a damp sticky trail.

A pneumatic hiss. The sound of grating metal.

The first cylinder was opening.

He was breathing harder, faster.

There was the sudden ticklish scrape of myriad tiny legs across the back of his knee. A millipede. He pressed one muddy hand to his mouth, bit hard at his palm, shuddering. More. He looked up at the faint glow of the doorway, miles above him. He would be buried in them, soon, and there was no way out.

It happened the way it always did. He felt two of them, then four, then hundreds. The second cylinder opened, then the third. The prick of more miniature legs. The rough fur of a caterpillar, low on his stomach, and the bright agonizing flare of the first sting in the delicate skin below his navel.

Panic for an instant, and, then, submission.

He spread out his arms, and they were all over him.

There were no individual sensations. It was a blur, a thousand lips and a thousand fingers everywhere, vivid flashes of pain that wound together into a single merciless burning.

He closed his eyes. One of them oozed along his eyelid, curling icy behind his ear, then a rush of them covering his face. He was nothing to them. Geography. Architecture.

Leander's ghost was in the doorway above him, breaking open the casing for the controls.

Wait, Oberon cried up at him. This time his voice was exactly like the boy's.

It was too late.

The boy pulled out bright loops of wire, and flung them down into the shaft, where they were lost, the worms twining around them.

Now the platform would never rise again.

Mercy. Please.

There was none.

The comfort in that closed over him like a warm cocoon.

Oberon opened his mouth, and ceased to breathe.

He didn't need to, not anymore.

Not here.

Five hours later, the electricity in the platform clicked on. It rose four feet and stopped a foot above the surface of the teeming sea of creatures. The running lights came on, and it chimed to let him know would begin its ascent in fifteen minutes, with or without him.

He struggled up onto his hands and knees, his hair hanging in his face, clotted with dirt. He crawled to it, swept aside most of its occupants with his arm and collapsed there, bit back a cry at the burn of the current on his bitten skin. Fleeing worms oozed away from him. He inhaled, and his lungs ached, fighting to stay closed. Inertia. The tendency of a nonmoving object to stay in that state...was that da Vinci? Einstein? Tesla? Newton? Hawking?

The platform began to rise. His arm hung over the edge, his fingers loose and streaked with dirt. There was earth gritting in his teeth, and he was sticky, filthy. He spit, licking mud from his lips.

The plank extended itself, locked into the side of the platform. For an instant he saw Leander again, standing in the shadows of the archway, He covered his face, shaken. When he looked again it was Cayle, old and bent in his violet armor, the only attendant who ever saw him this way.

Oberon couldn't stand. Neurotoxins made him perilously clumsy. Cayle came to him with his eyes fixed on anywhere but *down*.

When the doctor was close enough to hear, he said, "Bring me the boy."

sciscitor

Leander had given up sleeping and was sitting on the edge of his bed with his arms wrapped around his knees, wishing he could draw. The torches lit themselves, silent and eerie, and the great door into the Gallery opened.

Theren walked with alarming speed towards Leander's cell.

He held a bloodred armload of clothes through the bars. "Put these on. You can go behind the curtain, if you want."

That was as far as he got when Camille shrieked, an implausible banshee noise that emptied both her lungs. Leander put both hands over his ears, instinctively, and Theren's eyes went wide and his face went white. She laughed silently at their reactions before drawing in a swooping great breath. "Favorite red. Oh, Leander. You're going to be here for years. Like me."

"Favorite red?" Leander asked Theren.

"Pretty much what it sounds like. Put it on. I really don't want to have to dress you." Theren said, ignoring Camille as hard as he could.

He stood up to take the clothes, and his knees buckled and dropped him back onto the edge of the bed. Camille laughed again hoarsely, sitting in the floor in the far corner of her cell, rocking. "Poor Leander. Too pretty for your own good. Should've broken your nose a few times and you'd still be a snug Earth bug right now. Does it still hurt? I had to start over three times. I got to seven hundred before he was satisfied."

Theren sighed. Now he understood, better than he wanted to.

Leander dressed himself behind the curtain, trembling. His suit was gleaming vinyl, the reddest thing he had ever seen in his life. He zipped it from waist to neck. Red boots and a red red cloak, and this time if there was blood nobody would be able to see it.

Camille waved bye-bye solemnly with the tips of her fingers. Theren led him out.

They stopped in a loud bright room, where Leander submitted to having his hair brushed and his face painted, also at a frightening speed. He was

(wanted)

expected *now*, he gathered, and this data did nothing to soothe his slamming heart.

Couldn't you tell me it's going to be okay? Couldn't you tell me what this is all about?

He gave Theren a longing stare, but the guard only rushed him down a corridor with the same torches, and unknown sigils painted on the walls. "Why do you do this? Why is this your life?"

Theren snorted at this esoteric nonsense. "You won't last a week."

"That's not what Camille thinks."

"Yeah, well, I've seen burnout AIs that made more sense than what Camille thinks."

They stopped in front of a low, square set of doors.

"Welcome to the throne room. You look at the floor unless somebody tells you otherwise. You don't say anything. If he tells you to do anything, you do it, no matter what it is. You got all that?"

"Who else is here?"

"I hope to fuck no one." Theren pulled Leander's arms behind him, took a set of restraints from his belt and clamped Leander's wrists.

Leander twisted around, teeth bared.

"Don't. I don't like this any more than you do, and I don't want to have to drug you." Theren opened a door and marched Leander into a new room, hard enough to make him stumble. There was a long walk across a wide round chamber with a very low ceiling, littered with narrow concrete columns. Things were painted on the walls that made Leander glad to look at the floor. It felt more like a tomb than a throne room. He watched his feet in the red boots, watched the hem of his cloak, and he let Theren push him forward, stop him, and he stood there.

"Closer," the Septarch said. That voice made him shudder, with a thrill that was either murderous or terrified. That voice belonged in a closet in the dark. It wasn't human. There was something else in it, *under* it, something metallic and ancient that had never known Earth or sun or sky.

Magick words that put his to shame: *take him.*

Magick that ended worlds.

He was stopped by a stone dais in front of his feet. He knew

Oberon was mere feet away from him, and that if he...

"Look at me," Oberon said, reading his mind.

Leander did. Eyes as black as space without stars. He clenched his bound hands under the cloak.

You look like exactly what you are, and I still keep looking. Like I want to figure it out, like one of those paintings of a waterfall flowing uphill where you can't quite put your finger on the trick.

The Septarch was sitting on a low platform in a massive but simple chair, an inverted cone of dull metal with control panels by either of his hands. He was dressed in black velvet robes. A starburst bruise decorated the back of one languid hand. He raised that hand to his jawline, brushed the backs of his fingers there, as though deep in thought. His height was a fresh horror in this crypt of a room.

Oberon studied him for a long time, taking in the vinyl, the paint.

Does he even know my name? What is he thinking?

Leander refused to look away. Something was happening in his chest, deep in under his lungs. It felt like his insides were rearranging themselves to press closer to his skin, closer to those eyes.

"They did exactly as I ordered," Oberon said to Theren, as though Leander wasn't there. "I am...very pleased with this."

"We exist to serve you," Theren murmured, pretending to be pleased, but Oberon was looking at Leander again, his eyes heavy-lidded and venomous.

"Leander Schaiden."

His name, in that voice. It was like a blow. It was sorcery.

"Why did you tell me to wait?"

"Because..." Well, that was a great start, but he had no idea why he'd done it. Panic. "Because...I guess...I wasn't finished looking at you yet."

So much for his marvelous brain. *Great. He'll think you're being a smart-ass, and he'll splatter you all over this room.*

Something changed in the Septarch's eyes. Amusement? He raised his hand, covered his painted mouth for an instant. Then he nodded, as though he had reached some decision. "You have your wish. I will be the last thing you ever see."

He stood. Leander cringed and stepped back, but the Septarch only turned his back on the room, gestured at Theren over his shoulder. "Theren. Twenty-one hundred hours. Leave him like that."

"He won't kill you tonight," Camille said.

Leander was lying on his bed with one arm covering his eyes. He could still feel the restraints around his wrists, though Theren had taken them off almost an hour ago. "What?"

This time she spoke slowly, loudly as if Leander were deaf or profoundly stupid. "He wouldn't have had them put you here, let alone dress you in that. He wants to keep you awhile."

Mister, can you open the door? "And the others?"

"If they're not here, they're probably already dead, or they will be, the first time he sees them. He separates us by quick or slow, but he kills us all eventually. No one ever leaves."

He bit his lip, thinking of Jyana's tiny, warm, wet weight, of her cornsilk hair. "You're still here."

"Not for long. I'm too old for him. For a while, I had them shave me, here," she said, pressing her knuckles against her groin, "And that worked for a while, but...not for long."

Leander shuddered, disturbed.

"When I first came, there were two other kids here. They were brother and sister. The girl, Julia...she must have been eight or nine...he fitted her."

"Fitted her for what?"

"She did something to make him angry. She was in that cell across from you. He fitted her and had them bring her back here like that. It took her a week to die. It sounded like a wolf, that noise she was making. It took them two more days to take the body away. I can still smell her."

He did *not* sniff to see if he could still smell her, too. "You said there were two kids."

Something savage crossed her face. He almost understood her for an instant. Then, the insanity descended across her face, like a veil.

"The other one's name was Lucius. He was sixteen. He almost never picks anybody that old, but Lucius was...beautiful. Almost like you. I don't know what happened to him. One night he just...never came back."

Leander's eyes were wide, but he tried to make his voice scornful. "I don't believe you."

Camille shrugged. "He eats some of them. Or he'll take the ones he wants to keep a while and make us watch him kill the others. We're all dead already."

"So, if he isn't going to kill me tonight, what will he do?"

There was poison in her voice when she answered. "Wait and see."

He turned over, his back to her. He put his hands over his ears, but he still heard when she started to sing again.

unknown appetites

When Theren came to take him he wouldn't speak to Leander at all. This time the guard led him up an endless flight of spiral stairs. He stopped outside the door, keyed it open, and gestured for Leander to go inside.

"Should I kneel, or something?" Leander was half-joking.

Theren was already leaving. "He'll let you know," he said over his shoulder.

Was he supposed to knock? Wasn't a page or something supposed to go in first and announce him? The Sphere really needed a little rule book for new prisoners. Leander needed to know what the rules *were* so he could work out which ones he should follow and which ones he should break. This guessing game was just completely unfair.

No one seemed to be sending some blond kid with a horn to make a lot of noise about his arrival. Leander inhaled, exhaled, and went inside. The door closed behind him.

The room felt as medieval as the tower of stairs, complete with fireplaces and thick tapestries. They were smaller than he'd expected. A sitting area, with thick lush couches in black and redviolet, surrounding a massive fur rug with pillows in night shades scattered across it.

A small cluttered desk terminal sat to the right of the entrance, and in the space between a table with two chairs, with places set for two people, and covered platters of food. The smell set his stomach to growling furiously.

He didn't see the Septarch.

There was an archway to his right; he went towards it, and looked inside. A bedroom, with a massive black iron bed, dripping crimson fabric. Another fireplace, with heavy upholstered chairs. A black wardrobe. Everything else was red, the walls set with etched crimson glass in Byzantine arches. It suggested a church in Hell.

There was a statue on a low platform.

Curiosity drew him closer to it.

It was dark blue metal, and he had never seen anything like it. All Leander could make of it was a man turning into a bird turning into an engine. The firelight made it seem to contort, its mouths gaping. He ran his fingertips along shiny metal teeth, a geometric feather, and a knotted conglomeration that might have been flesh or cable.

"Leander."

He jumped, snatched his hand away from the statue as though it had burned him.

The voice was behind him. He wanted to turn around, but he couldn't.

"Leander was the name of a boy who lived on Earth thousands of years ago. He was in love with a priestess named Hero who lived on the opposite side of a river. Every night she would leave a torch in her window to guide him, and he would swim across the river to be with her."

The voice was closer. "They would make love, every night. It went on for almost a year."

"Until one night, when she didn't leave a torch. He tried to swim across anyway, and he drowned."

Oberon was right behind him. "Don't place faith," he whispered. "It's almost always...fatal."

Leander turned his head with mounting terror and watched the Septarch raise his hand. Oberon only reached over his shoulder, and laid his hand on the statue with loving pride. "Do you like it?"

Leander swallowed hard. "It's...um...it's beautiful. Where did you get it?"

"I made it," Oberon said, tracing the agonized lines. His nails were long, and dark gray. They looked unnervingly...functional. He scratched them against the metal and shuddered, his eyes drifting closed.

Leander forced himself to look away from them. He spoke more to distract himself than anything else. "What does it...does it mean anything?"

Oberon looked at him, then, and he was falling again. "Change is almost never for the better," he whispered. And he inclined his head, towards the table.

Leander supposed that was an order. Fine with him. He was distinctly glad to leave the

(bedroom, this is his bedroom)

statue and move back closer to the
(exit)
dining table.

Oberon pulled out a chair and stood beside it. This confused Leander for an instant before he understood that chair was for *him*. He flushed and sat down, staring at his hands. Oberon didn't speak. He took Leander's plate and filled it with dripping pieces of pink meat and something that looked like tiny black marbles. Leander eyed it. "What is that?"

The Septarch raised his eyebrow, seeming to be amused at that, and set it in front of him. "Taste it, and if you like it, maybe I'll tell you."

Leander tried. Whatever it was rolled off his fork. He picked up his spoon instead, and put a tiny bit of the stuff on his tongue. The taste was dark, salty. He chewed, hesitant, and decided he liked it. "Is it poisonous?"

Oberon smiled at that. Leander watched, fascinated. He had never seen him smile. His lips were painted, like a woman's, full and curved, but hard at the corners. His teeth were flawless, straight and white, much too long. "It's caviar," he explained.

Whatever that was. Some kind of mushroom, maybe.

Leander started to take a bigger bite then set his spoon down. "Camille says you eat little kids," he said, all in a rush, before he could stop himself.

Oberon cut himself a bite of meat, lifted it to his mouth and chewed reflectively. "Does she?"

He cut another bite, stabbed it with his fork and held it out to Leander.

Leander looked at the Septarch, searching for any clues. Oberon's face was blank.

If he tells you to do something, you do it, no matter what it is.

Leander took the meat from the fork with his teeth. He held it in his mouth as though it were a live spider. His stomach knotted, and his throat closed. He gritted his teeth and drew in a hard desperate breath, and forced himself to chew it.

The result was astounding.

It was the softest meat he'd ever had, and the taste made the caviar seem like protein cubes in comparison. He'd never tasted anything like it. Whatever it was, it was his new favorite food.

He swallowed twice, and cut himself another bite from his own plate.

Oberon smiled as though he'd learned a secret.

He lifted a black bottle, poured something green into two crystal glasses. "It's absinthe," he said.

Leander tasted it. It was sweet, but bitter, like licorice, and it did interesting things with the flavor of the meat.

He finished everything Oberon gave him, and the absinthe made him sleepy and dizzy. He drew his knees up to his chest, wrapped his arms around them, his feet in the chair. "What should I call you?"

"Don't you know my name?"

Leander nodded. "Theren said I should call you the Septarch."

Oberon thought about that. "That would be a little like me calling you the Slave."

Leander hugged his knees tighter. "If I'm your slave, what kind of, um, work will I be doing?"

"Say my name," the Septarch ordered him, so sharply that he flinched.

"Oberon," he whispered, and it did something to his insides, that same shifting that had happened in the throne room.

"No. Not like that."

"Oberon," he said again, more clearly, and he licked at his lips, tasting bitter and sweet.

"Come here."

Leander moaned, afraid he couldn't stand, but he managed it, and went to stand in front of the Septarch, his hand on the table to steady him.

The Septarch reached for him. That was the hand he'd used to make that one little gesture, before three clicks and three bolts. Leander cringed, tears scorching his throat.

If he touches me, I'll go crazy.

Oberon put his hand on Leander's cheek. His skin was too smooth, his flesh too hot, too inflexible. It was like being touched by that deranged statue. It did something to Leander, in his head, in his chest, and it felt nothing like he'd imagined it would to go mad.

He had time to think, *he'll bite me.*

Oberon picked him up and set Leander down in his lap.

That improbable warmth closed around him. Leander was rigid, his eyes shut tight. Oberon leaned in and put his teeth against Leander's neck, drew one line with the tip of his tongue. His breath much too hot to be human. "This is the kind of work you'll be doing."

Leander was still expecting to be bitten, and probably would have preferred that to his first kiss.

He had no idea what to do with his lips, his breath. His eyes opened and then closed again by themselves. He was not bitten. This felt more like a, greeting, a question he had no idea how to answer. His head fell back. His hands and his mouth opened, and he tasted caviar and wormwood and smoke. *Fires, there are fires inside him.*

Oberon took this as an invitation, and he licked Leander's teeth, slid his tongue into his mouth, one long languid taste.

Leander was not quite so new as to be unaware of an erection when he inspired one. He imitated that tongue-gesture, and Oberon inhaled against his mouth, giving him chills.

"Say my name." Different this time. *Did I change him too?*

"Oberon." Leander leaned into his hands. Later he would wonder if that was why it ended.

Oberon set him on his feet. He opened his eyes to that liquid black stare. "Go. The door's open, and Theren is waiting for you."

Something broke in his chest. He had done it wrong. Of course. And now he was being sent back to his cell. Other people were fucking complicated.

He trudged towards the door, hoping Oberon would stop him, knowing he wouldn't. The Septarch had turned away from him, and was staring into the fire.

Leander stopped in the doorway.

Say something clever to fix it.

"What does fitted mean?" he blurted out.

That was all kinds of *not* what he'd had in mind.

"Go."

What he heard in Oberon's voice made his hands fumble in panic at the door.

Theren was sitting in the hallway, his back against the wall. He raised his head, and there were tired lines at the corners of his mouth. He tried to smile. It didn't work. "Are you all right?"

"No," said Leander. Then he was crying again.

Oberon stared into the fire until he was sure the boy was back in the Gallery. He picked up Leander's empty plate, turned it in his hands, lowered his head and licked it, with slow concentration. When he could taste nothing but porcelain he pondered throwing it into the fireplace, but instead set it down beside his own. The absinthe was next. He drained the last of it from Leander's glass, ran his tongue around the rim both inside and out.

He could not stay in his rooms.

He could smell the boy here.

Insanity

They could hear Camille before Theren opened the door to the Gallery. She was howling, and banging something into the bars.

Theren sighed. "Sometimes she...throws stuff. I'll go first."

He went inside, and Leander heard him saying something to Camille in an irritated voice. He caught echoes of it: *if you don't want...and you stop...or I'll...he won't...*

She stopped.

Theren gestured Leander forward, let him into his cell. "You remember what I said," he told Camille, before he turned and left, locking them in.

Camille stood in the center of her cell, with the heels of her hands pressed into her temples. She glared at Leander, with so much hatred that he backed away from her.

Her mouth moved around a single word, over and over. He couldn't hear her, couldn't stand the blazing accusation in her eyes.

"Camille, I didn't—"

Camille shrieked and ran at the bars between them as hard as she could. She bounced off, her neck snapping backwards, and crumpled to the floor.

Leander waited for her to get up.

She didn't.

"Camille," he whispered, and he went over and put his foot through the bars to reach her, and poked her with the toe of his boot. She didn't flinch.

He couldn't tell if she was breathing.

He went to his keypad. The red button.

If he didn't push it, she might die.

He hesitated a moment. He could not have said why. There was a tangle in his head, of Oberon's mouth against his own, of Camille holding him through the bars while he wept. He felt as though he were deciding something important and irrevocable.

He pushed it once, the movement feeling like a convulsion in his hand.

He sat on his bed, watching her.

She didn't move.

Theren came in almost at once. He hadn't had time to get far. "What is it?"

"It's Camille."

"Shit," Theren snapped, seeing her on the floor. "What did you say to her?"

"Nothing!" Leander said, feeling both indignant and guilty. He wondered for the first time where the cameras were in the Gallery, wondered if Oberon would see how he'd hesitated. Wondered what the Septarch would make of that.

Theren pulled a comm from his belt. "What set her off, then?"

"How should I know? She's crazy." It felt like a lie as soon as he'd said it. He knew damn well what had set her off, but he wasn't going to try to explain it to Theren, though it would take two little words: *she's jealous.*

Theren rolled his eyes and spoke into the receiver. "Cayle. I need you in the Gallery, right now. It's Camille again," he said, clicked it off and keyed open Camille's cell.

Cayle took longer to arrive than Theren had. He ignored Leander, who was beginning to feel quite invisible. The doctor knelt by Camille before looking up at Theren in disgust. "You could've told me to bring a stretcher. You'll have to help me. I can't carry her."

Theren lifted Camille in his arms. She hung limp, her hair covering her face.

After they were gone the silence was heavy. Leander pulled off the red cloak, crumpled it, thought better of it and folded it at the foot of his bed. He couldn't manage the zipper behind his neck to get the vinyl bodysuit off, though he did manage to open it to somewhere between his shoulderblades. He struggled out of the boots. That was a little better.

He picked up the cloak, raised it to his face. He could smell Oberon there, dark and sweet, like incense and damp earth. He climbed into bed, still holding the cloak, tangling it around his legs.

He fell asleep with his face buried in it, his bag forgotten on the floor.

116

amychophilia

The Septarch
(fled)
relocated to his office and locked the door. The first thing he saw was Leander's journal. He did not sigh, but the long exhale through his nose was perilously close.

He found a pipe, and an etched metal box provided him with an array of things to put in it. He keyed on the flame, and smoked until his eyes felt large and strange in their sockets, his breath and heartbeat distant and meaningless.

He put the pipe down. Beside the journal.

No escape.

EXTREMELY SECRET BOOK OF SACRED HOLINESS.

What did that mean, to a fourteen-year-old boy? A boy who hadn't screamed, who had tried to kiss him back?

He picked it up, put it down again, sifted instead through the rest of the boy's file, now upholstering his desk.

He almost ignored the test results, but the papers slid apart and he saw the edge of Leander's answer to *How do you feel about the church?*

He picked up the papers, holding them as if the drawn fires might burn him, flipped to the mural that answered that single question.

At that moment he had a look on his face he would have committed genocide to conceal—a wide, childlike smile, in some kind of dopey...wonder. The dinosaurs were what broke the spell, or rather the laughter they inspired, bright and genuine, and something his Sphere had little occasion to record. He would have to show the boy the Zoo levels someday.

The journal.

He took it in his hands. He raised it to his face, smelled it, fanned the pages with his thumb, sniffed again. Licked the covers, front and back, where he guessed the boy's thumbs tended to land.

The first page was emblazoned with the words:

IF YOU READ THIS YOU ARE CURSED. IT'S VOODOO.

This was followed by a cartoon man with a look of anguish on his face. Presumably he had been cursed.

Oberon was smiling without knowing it. This was like...looking into the boy's mind.

March 18

Because of all that time I missed in counseling I have to do twice as much work. The teacher called me stupid in front of everybody. She's a fucking bitch. Her cunt is probably sewn together.

Oberon's smile folded into a frown that would have terrified his guards and his court. He'd been told that the boy had been flagged as having dangerous levels of creativity, courage, violence, and independent thought. No mention of counseling. He could imagine what *that* would be like on Christian Earth. The omission did not please him at all.

March 20

Something bad happened. This other kid he

Something was scrawled out hard enough to gouge into the paper. Oberon could make out two words: *said* and *laughed*.

and then I hit him smash bang on the mouth. His lips

squished and there was blood squirting everywhere, and it hurt my hand so bad I thought I broke my fingers, but I didn't care. Everything was flat and nothing was the right color. I was up inside my head and my body was doing stuff all by itself. He was crying and I hit him again just to see if it would work. And I partly hit his hand and partly his nose.

He was bleeding fucking EVERYWHERE. I wonder if maybe I'm possessed.

I used to think they say that to scare you, until this started happening. I keep thinking about it and the only way I would have felt like it was a bad thing is if I'd gotten caught and I didn't.

I don't feel guilty.

March 22

I should tear out that whole thing because if I ever become a serial killer and they find stuff like this I think you get in even more trouble.

Sometimes I get this happy feeling all over me like I know something wonderful is gonna happen. But that has to do with the fury too. It's so bad.

They'll find out what I'm like because they watch you all

the time and I'm sure they can see it in my face.

March 24

I drew a picture about it and then burned it to sort of get it out of my system. That's illegal too because it's practicing witchcraft. Stupid motherfuckers stupid rules about everything. It didn't even fucking work anyway.

I'm always wanting to look in the mirror all the time to see if I look crazy. It has to make me look different somehow.

It does, Oberon thought. *But only other crazy people can see it.*
His face, once again, was doing something without his knowledge, that would've horrified him if he'd been aware of it. Another genuine smile, one that signified something far more dangerous than simple amusement.

March 3Ø

Got another bootleg game for my computer. It's about this French person who wrote all these sicko books about Sodom. The one they threw in prison and he lived there his whole life. the State would have me in prison for MY whole life if they even knew I have this game.

April 2

Made a copy of the de Sade game and traded it to this kid for an illegal audio disk.

It took me twenty minutes to get my computer to play it.

It's ancient. I never heard anything like it.

I love it. It's like they feel like I do. Furious because they could tell the Christians were taking over the place and they were like me and they knew what other people like them would be in for once THAT happened.

But it happened anyway.

I looked it up, the history of that year. The Christians couldn't make any laws and they couldn't force anybody to be Christian. They just used a lot of propaganda to try and make you want to be. I thought it had to be made up that they used to not own the whole system but now I know they never could have made music like that otherwise. So I guess the propaganda works. It must because boy do they ever still do it.

I wish I had lived then instead of now.

April 3

It happened again.

I was in my room this time. Way earlier this morning in school one of my teachers saw me reading this little thing on autopsies. We weren't even doing anything in the damn class and everybody else was pulling up junk too but she reached over me and turned my computer off and gave me one of those long hard mean looks. Like I'm scared of the bitch. That kid I took out was way bigger than her, and he was EXPECTING me to hit him.

I was SO mad. I was curled up on my bed and I dug my fingernails into my thighs and then the weirdest thing happened. I got hard. And I was scratching hard enough that I knew it SHOULD hurt but it didn't It felt like my whole skin was connected to my dick.

I pretended they were holding me down and scratching me hard, all over. I pretended they said they would choke me to death if I screamed.

I never got off like that before. I almost did scream.

What's wrong with me?!

I know this isn't even fucking CLOSE to normal. The only thing worse than doing that at all is I guess doing it while thinking about a guy. TWO guys.

That has to be why I got so mad when that kid called me that. I guess I knew it was true. What if it gets worse and I get so crazy I don't even know I'm crazy anymore?

I scratched myself all over and I had all these marks. I wish my nails were longer. And I had to sneak a towel past my Mom to clean the come off the bed. It still left a mark even though I wet it and I took off the whole sheet and turned it over. I know Mom wouldn't say anything about it but it's gross to know your Mom knows you do that.

I had that disk playing the whole time.

Maybe all of them left fucking Earth in a spaceship. Maybe they started their own colony and their great-great-great-grandkids are still there. I wonder what it would look like. I wish they would come and get me. Or come here and start a big war.

April 12

I'm possessed.

I know I'm going to Hell and I'm not all that upset about it. I think those singers were witches. I think I am one, too.

I cut myself with a piece of glass. On purpose. And I liked it. Sort of even loved it.

Somebody might find this. I should tear it up but I don't want to. It's MINE.

I don't think I'm going to write in this anymore.

Oberon reread *cut myself with a piece of glass* several times. He was making a long, low, desperate moan in his throat. The rest of the pages were blank, except for a two-page spread in the center. This appeared to be an elaborate space battle between ornate starships and giant mutant bees.

How old would he have been? Twelve? Thirteen? Was it last year, or the year before? Not yet fourteen, living in State-controlled Earth, with a desperate crush on two musicians who had died centuries ago.

It was exquisite, the thought of Leander in his room, alone, his hands on himself, guilty and frantic. His fantasy. Caught by phantoms, who threatened to kill him unless he submitted. Helpless in the grip of evil—and not entirely unwilling to be there.

Oberon felt something in his chest unfold, spreading a blaze of wings, glittering, merciless, bright enough to blind him.

Wait.

That single, magickal word.

He knew. He knew what he was asking.

He opened his comm, and configured it for another cross-Reach call to Earth.

This time, to Leander's old school.

erode

Theren was in his office, sitting in front of blank screens with his head in his hands. He was reflecting upon—or perhaps *mourning* would be better—the general state of his existence.

He had grown up in desperate poverty, in a dying colony on the edge of the Reach, ignored by the Republic of Earth. He'd been Leander's age when he'd agreed to be trained for the Septarch's guard, unable to imagine any farther than food, water, air and medical care for himself and a family he could now hardly remember. Gone, too, was whatever he might have imagined this life would be like, but he was certain he had been almost *completely* wrong, whatever he'd expected to find.

Lovely last few weeks he'd been having. The end of the second tithe had left new gaping wounds in his psyche. And Camille lost what little remained of her sanity whenever there was a new slave in the Gallery, and he was sure this most recent, dramatic trip to sickbay wouldn't be her last.

He found himself wishing The Septarch would kill one or the other, and how *easily* this thought came to him made him groan.

He heard Leander's voice. *Why is this your life?*

"I have no fucking idea," he whispered to himself, and hoped no one would notice this on any recordings.

One of his telescreens activated itself.

His worry blossomed into a wide hot sick weight in his stomach. He knew it was the Septarch, and he swallowed and did his best to make his face a polite blank, and accepted the call. "Yes, Lord Septarch?"

Oberon was typing into a handscreen, the red display gleaming in his black eyes. "Bring him to me. One hour."

"As you wish, Lord Septarch."

There was a leisurely pause. Theren told himself he was imagining the sadism in that.

"Does the boy require anything?"

A heresy happened inside Theren then. *He fucking requires that you never happened to him.* He was unsure how perceptive Oberon was, with that much hardware inside him, but even *thoughts* such as that one scared him, for fear Oberon would read it in his face, his eyes.

"I believe he has everything he needs, Lord"

The Septarch was quiet for so long Theren had plenty of time to be terrified he'd *heard* that angry thought.

"I want everything. All of his belongings. All of his records this time, not this minimalist insult they've given me. School, hospital, police, medical, film. Everything."

The razorsharp edge under these words made Theren's tongue knot in his mouth. He'd never received orders like these. "Yes, Septarch," he said, around a dry click in his throat.

When Oberon replied the edge in his voice was gone. Now there was something softer and even more dangerous. "If I feel anything has been omitted this time I will return to Earth to retrieve his records myself."

The Septarch disconnected, leaving Theren looking through a black screen while seeing a blinding, vivid mental image.

Earth, aflame, atmosphere burning off into space.

curiouser and curiouser

Leander was in Oberon's cryptcolored office, painted within an inch of his life, feeling both beautiful and ridiculous in blackred silk.

The Septarch was sitting behind his black marble desk in a dark leather chair, the gleam of the terminal displays flickering in his eyes. His paint was simple, black with touches of ocher. He wore deep scarlet, a leather suit with the looped cross insignia glittering in silver at each shoulder.

He was holding an ornate blackviolet stack of curves. Leander thought this was a sculpture until the Septarch raised it to his painted mouth and exhaled smoke.

Leander's tongue did a jealous thing behind his teeth.

Drugs.

He missed drugs almost as much as he missed his mother.

Oberon either saw his mouth move or read his mind. "Do you want some?"

He was trying and failing to imagine a drug he'd be willing to have scramble him in *this* place. "Maybe...not right now."

The Septarch stood and pulled out his own chair, waited for Leander to take it.

He skirted the desk, finding it difficult to get closer to the Septarch, forcing himself to do so anyway. It was a tidy chaos of console and art, with a glass jar with something in fluid that might have been eyeballs. The chair felt much too large for him.

Oberon stood behind him.

Leander kept his hands in his lap, afraid to touch anything. "Are you angry about before?" His voice was faint, and he was embarrassed the minute he spoke.

"Before what?"

"Something before you threw me out of your room, I guess?"

"Oh, I wasn't angry. I was dangerous," he said, with faint surprise—or was that amusement? "I have something for you. I've been watching this, over and over. I'm happy with the way it worked, and I wanted you to see it."

He reached over from behind Leander to run the film. His hair hung over Leander's shoulder. Leander tried to edge away without being obvious. Oberon either ignored that or didn't notice it.

The screen went black, flashed a series of numbers, then a name. *Dr. Edgar Nolan.* A picture assembled itself from random points of color. The man's face made Leander feel sick and furious. "That's the doctor who—"

"I know," Oberon said. "Watch."

Another name. *Jamison Curn.* A photograph of the policeman who'd stunned him. He'd found a mark later, two small circles on the left side of his chest, where the skin was dry and peeling.

Then a silent video. It was the throne room. Oberon was in his seat on the platform, facing out into the room. He was wearing the formal robes, painted, tapping something on the armrest that looked like a miniature mace. Behind him, Leander saw himself projected onto the wall above the throne. He was sitting naked on an examining table. The doctor and the policeman stepped into view.

"I don't want to see this," Leander muttered, looking at his fingernails.

Oberon's hand closed on the back of Leander's neck, under his hair. His fingers were so warm it made Leander gasp. "This isn't to hurt you," he said, the words textured and intricate. "I did this for you."

It was those last few words and not the talons so near his throat that made Leander look up at the screen again. Oberon's hand stayed on his neck, working at the muscles there. Leander could feel his shoulders relaxing. He was beginning to understand why people wanted to touch each other.

The camera panned past Oberon, to the floor in front of his throne.

Both of them were kneeling, arms restrained, mouths bound.

Dr. Edgar Nolan. Jamison Curn.

The doctor was crying.

The Oberon on the screen stood, and the projection of Leander struggling splattered across him. His lips moved, and he gestured to someone off screen. The camera turned to catch the prisoners being dragged out—they either couldn't or wouldn't walk.

The ornate glass pipe appeared over his shoulder, presented in Oberon's clawed hand. Leander took it this time, worked out how to trigger it, drew in smoke like nothing he'd ever tasted or smelled. The effect was immediate, softer edges, sharper urges. Those claws grazed his hand when he returned the pipe, and he lost one winding tendril through his teeth.

The screen went black, and when the picture returned they were outside under the orange sky. A smooth circle had been cut into the rock. There was a small group of spectators, dressed in black, with masks against the wind and the dust.

They were holding them down, and a separate group of guards in black plate armor brought the stakes, each one carried by two men.

When the cutting began Leander drew his knees up, rested his forehead on them, his eyes closed.

He knew what impalement was. He read every bloodthirsty thing he could get his hands on, and he'd seen the State execute plenty of heretics, but he'd never expected to witness anything like this.

Real. This is real.

He showed the video to explain their crime—hurting me. So what is he trying to explain to me?

Oberon touched the controls in the arm of the chair, and then there was audio, perfect surround sound through speakers mounted in the walls. The hiss of wind from the planet's surface. Screaming, metallic and frightfully close. Something wet and soft, ripping. The pressure inside him was unbearable. He would cry, or laugh, or run. "Turn it off."

Oberon did. "I thought you would like it."

He liked it, all right. He liked it so much it felt like something inside him might burst if he didn't find a way to show it.

Leander's hands came up and closed hard in Oberon's jacket, and he tried to kiss him, passionate but clumsy. The Septarch almost pulled away, his hands clutching at the air. Then he held Leander's jaw and kissed him back, deep and hard.

"Nobody ever tried to get them back for me." Oberon nuzzled in to bite his neck. The dazzling little explosion of sensation did not help Leander's struggle to find words for the suffering inside him.

The teeth withdrew, and Oberon pressed a kiss to the bruise he'd left behind. "You were brought here for me. Everyone you dealt with from Earth until here was under my control, and they knew that you were mine. Nobody hurts you but me. Not ever again."

Leander made a strangled sound, pushing closer. "I don't want you to hurt me."

"No?" This was in an awful tone of voice, sweet enough to be a trap. Oberon's mouth was moving over the flesh he'd bruised. "What do you want?"

"You're always biting me," Leander said.

"Yes." Oberon did something like petting with the edges of his teeth. "Maybe I'll eat you."

His eyes weren't working right. His hands came up, all by themselves, and he did what he'd wanted to do since seeing Oberon on Earth for the first time, and buried his hands in all that luscious long hair.

"Answer me."

"I want to know why I'm here. I want to know what you want."

"I want you here. That's why you're here. That's what I want."

"That's not a very helpful answer." Leander felt like he'd been either drugged, or poisoned. Everything was blurry, and breathing was so much work.

"I think you've forgotten who's asking the questions." Oberon paused and licked from Leander's collarbone up to his cheek.. "Here's a question for you, Leander Schaiden—do you still want to know what fitted means?"

Leander made a frightened pleading cry, deep in his throat, and buried his face in Oberon's shoulder. He was holding Oberon's hair too hard, almost pulling.

"I'm not going to do it to you. I only want to show you."

Leander was still. He was hearing his own heartbeat, like something the size of a planet smashing into his ribcage from the inside.

It took her days to die.

He's testing me.

He nodded.

Oberon kept Leander's hand in his own, and led him to a door that opened into a pitch-black hallway. "I can see in here, but you can't. Stay right behind me. There's light up ahead."

He pulled Leander in, and closed the door.

Leander couldn't move. He couldn't tell if his eyes were closed or open. It was a trap. The Septarch would kill him, here, and he would never see the light again.

"Leander," Oberon said. He drew him close, pressed another kiss to his mouth. "Follow me. It's all right."

Of course it wasn't all right. It was dark, for one thing, and the corridor smelled...odd. The air was damp, and thick, and heavy, and it reminded him of the smell of soured dirt, or an animal struck by an electrocar.

He wanted to say something idiotic. *Carry me* or *let's go back* or *can't you just tell me about it?* "Kiss me again," he said, holding his hands out in the darkness.

"You're stalling," The Septarch lifted him off his feet, kissed him one hard time, and put him down again.

Oberon led him for what felt like miles. It was so wet here that the air was sticky, and the floor sloped downhill. Oberon tugged at his hand. "It's here," he said.

Leander heard the muffled notes of a keypad. Then there was a wedge of red light, spilling out into the hallway, and he followed Oberon inside.

There was something laid out on a table in the center of the small room. Leander thought it was another sculpture.

"It's iron," Oberon said, looking at it with deep affection. "These braces immobilize every joint. The corset and these bands go across the ribs. It's impossible to take any but the shallowest of breaths, and you can tighten it, here, with these screws."

He picked up the headpiece, an adjustable iron band dripping with tiny hooks mounted on springs, and a mouthpiece like a flat bit. He tapped something, and the mouthpiece snapped open. "It holds your mouth open, and the hooks pull back your eyelids. The collar can be tightened until it closes almost completely."

What am I thinking? Why don't I know what I'm thinking?

He dropped the headpiece. It clattered back onto the table, the mouthpiece gaping in a silent cry. He lifted the bottom half, unhooked it from the corset. "This was a chastity belt. Antique, from the Dark Ages, on Earth. I redesigned it."

Two iron phalluses jutted in, thicker than Leander's wrist. They were stained black in the red light. "The anterior one is removable," he said, and unclamped it and held it in his hand. Leander could tell how heavy it was by the tension in Oberon's wrist. "There are other...accessories, but these are the ones I used last time."

He looked at Leander, his eyes reflecting nothing. "Want to ask me again what fitted means?"

Leander was looking at the mouthpiece, still, hypnotized. "What did Julia do that made you do that to her?"

"Didn't Camille tell you? Her brother did it. Lucius. I gave him a choice between himself or his sister. He chose her."

Leander tried to imagine having a sister. He arrived at someone annoying that you loved, but you wouldn't like until you were grown.

"Will it kill you?" he croaked.

"If it's tight enough, kept on long enough. You die of blood poisoning, asphyxiation, or dehydration, depending."

Leander was pale, the bloodcolored light tracing the edges of his bones. He swallowed hard. "Which one did Julia die of?"

Oberon considered. "Debatable. Maybe one day we'll watch the film."

Theren said, "Your lipstick is ruined."

Leander was staring into space, numb. It felt like there was a bird in his chest, furious wings beating against his ribcage. There was an unbearable, excruciating pressure, like he was struggling against something invisible.

"I'll have them fix it when we come for you and Camille," Theren was saying.

Dark, malicious fury made him clench his teeth together. "Camille? He sent for *her?*"

"He sent for you both this morning. He wants you both in the throne room. He's staging an...amusement of some kind."

"Will you be there?"

"I don't know yet," Theren said. His face told a different story.

hymenoptera

Camille was curled up in the exact center of her bed, doing something elaborate with bits of colored string. She ignored both of them until Theren left the Gallery. As soon as the lock engaged behind him she sprang off the bed, grinning at Leander. "Did he tell you what your rules are?"

"Rules?"

"Yeah, like my rule is I can never put the palms of my hands flat against anything," she said, holding her hand a foot from the wall, like a mime. "That's my rule. He wouldn't let Lucius say any words with the letter 'e' in them. After he slipped up twice he quit talking at all."

His brain was trying to calculate how to speak without using an "e" anywhere. No *love*, no *hate*, no *please*....but *wait*. He forced himself to ignore that. "What if you do it in your sleep?" Leander asked.

"I learned not to."

"But how would he know?"

"Oh, he knows," she said, wide-eyed, as though he'd asked her if water might be wet. "He knows everything that happens on the Sphere, and if you say his name or his title, the Sphere tells him right away, wherever he is. The cameras are everywhere, and most of them are invisible."

Leander was pretty sure an invisible camera would be unable to receive any images. "I don't think—"

"And he can record your dreams. He likes nightmares the best." She'd fallen into a whisper, all the better for telling this ghost story. "That's why the wasps happened to me."

Leander was trying to hide his reaction to this jumbled insanity. Part exasperated amusement, part horror that he might be looking at his own future. Maybe *something* in there was true, but could not begin to guess *which* something. To Camille it was all true, and that gave him a shudder he could not repress.

"So what's yours?" Cheerful, as though they were talking about favorite telecasts.

He blinked, thinking she wanted to know his worst fear and wondering if he knew himself, trying not to imagine iron hinges digging into the corners of his mouth. He was grasping at *any* other phobia to relate to her when he realized they were back to rules again. "I don't think I have any."

Her sunny lunatic cheer vanished, baring something envious and murderous, that was gone as soon as he'd seen it. Camille shrugged. "You will. You better hope he tells you what it is before you break it."

"What was Julia's rule?"

She was quiet for a moment. "I don't know. Why?"

"He showed it to me. That thing. The thing to be...fitted."

He stepped closer to their shared bars, but Camille stepped back, and wouldn't meet his eyes. "Oh," she said.

It was foolish to ask her, he knew it, but there was no one else to ask. "What's wrong with him?"

The pain in his voice frightened him, and he knew too late it had been a mistake to let her hear it.

She did look at him then, and he thought she was going to scream.

The wasps. I wonder if that was the truth, maybe the only truth.

"Wrong?" She shook her head, like a pastor's wife on television who would tell dire and ludicrous tales of Satan. "Wrong?"

Then she collapsed to her knees, covering her face, shrieking into her hands. Leander felt a bolt of longing for Theren or Cayle or his mother or any fucking grownup at all, and then he realized she was *laughing*, and there was a strong bluewhite flare of anger in him that made him remember the scent of explosives, the sound of panicked alarms.

"Don't," he said.

It came out too low for Camille to hear.

"There's nothing wrong with him, Leander. He's evil."

He got so cold his fingers locked into claws, and he ran at the bars connecting their cells and grabbed them and shook them hard enough to hurt his wrists. "Don't say that!"

She heard that one just fine. She peered at him through her fingers with a vicious grin. She'd found a button that was easy to push. "Evil. Evil," she taunted.

Is he? Then what am I?

He slammed on the bars between them, hard enough to make them clatter in their moorings.

"What's the matter, Leander?" she said, her voice dripping sweetness. "Did he kiss you? Did he *fuck* you? *Do you fucking think you're in love?*"

She was shouting, her voice harsh and hideous, echoes thrown back at both of them by so much stone. Here was that ruined and envious thing, unmasked again.

If she has a true face at all anymore, I'm probably looking at it now.

The cold crept up into his lungs, closed around his voice.

He took his hands away from the bars and stood still and straight, staring at her. He could see her, now, not a little faceless girl, Camille with her jaw forced open hard, head clamped, lips drawn back with hooks to expose the sleek pink meat of her gums.

"I think he'd fit you if I asked him to."

Oh, that felt *exquisite.* The pressure inside him was gone with those magick words. It was as though his voice fit into his mouth for the very first time.

Her eyes got wide, and the laughter was gone like someone had pulled a trapdoor open and dropped it through the floor.

He was quivering. He kept wanting to grin, and then he did.

It made her cringe.

It made him wonder if he was unmasked, too.

"Leander." She shook her head, too fast, for too long, rustcolored hair a storm around her. "Not you."

"You watch your mouth, Camille. Oberon doesn't like you, and I don't think I do either."

He looked up, so the invisible cameras could see his smile, thinking of satellites circling in a dead sky, thinking, *radio, live transmission.*

small cruelties

The Zoo was quiet at that time of night.

There was the long hallway, with the solid doors along one side. Cayle was dozing in a chair, a forgotten handscreen on his knee, displaying a diagram of the occipital lobe.

"Are any of them ready?"

Cayle sat up, scrubbing at his hair with his hand. "I gave Four a full dose half an hour ago—"

"No. Not Four." Even numbers were boys. "How's Seven?"

Cayle pushed up his glasses. His nearsightedness could have been repaired, or he could have worn implants, but he insisted on wearing glasses. Real ones. With glass in them. "Seven...ah, I thought you wanted her kept for—"

"I'm not going that far."

Oberon's hands were shaking. Cayle had assured him that was psychological, an illusion of an addiction that his body was incapable of forming. He'd offered to install a permanent implant that would release a steady dosage, or could be activated by a tiny keypad. Oberon had refused. Probably his fondness for syringes, and other anachronisms, torches, paper documents, physical books. Cayle supposed it was the same stubborn fondness that made him cling to his own eyeglasses. He considered asking Oberon if he wanted the morphine before his audience, but decided against it. Attempting to anticipate Oberon's needs was as dangerous as attempting to predict his moods, if not more so.

"Should I dose her?"

"How long does it take to work?"

Cayle did calculations in his head. Body mass, blood sugar levels, how much he could use without risking unconsciousness... "About fifteen minutes. Maybe twenty."

Oberon nodded once.

Cayle reached under his chair for his kit. It was a clever little chemical of his own design. It relaxed the muscles without inducing sleep or dizziness, and it had no effect on perception of pain. Oberon knew. He had tried it on himself.

Cayle went into the seventh door down, and closed it behind

him.

Silence.

Then a wail, that rose in pitch until it struck hysteria, and stopped.

Cayle stepped out again, wobbling an empty syringe between his thumb and forefinger. "Do you want this?"

Oberon waved it away. He had syringes. There was nothing special about that one. "Are the cameras on?"

"Aren't they always?" Cayle said, his voice dry and caustic.

After the door closed and locked behind the Septarch, Cayle reached into the front pocket of his shirt. He extracted a small plastic case, snapped it open, and took out two little cylinders of foam rubber.

He rolled them up small, and inserted them in his ears. Silence descended.

He settled into his chair, his fingers performing an intricate ballet across the keys of his notepad. He pulled up an analysis of the psychological effects of the use of biological weapons in the Second American Civil War, and read the same line, over and over again.

After a long while it he loosened the plug in his right ear and listened. There was the dark rumble of Oberon's voice, merciless and vicious. Then a choking, gagging cough.

He replaced the earplug, pushed at it hard with his fingertip.

He returned to his handscreen, pulled up a history feed. *In the second civil war, political tension and differences in religious opinion led to the unleashing of...In the second civil war, political tension...*

There was a loud crash in the room behind him.

He drew in a long, steady breath, and forced himself to read the second line. *...chemical and biological weapons, the impact of which...*

Hear no evil.

He thought of another Cayle, one who had not had a number after his name, who had said something hundreds of years ago.

First, do no harm.

Almost an hour passed before Oberon came out into the hall

again. He was stumbling, his eyes half-closed. There was blood on his chin. He was shirtless, and there was something dark smeared on his black pants. His chest was more scar than skin. The last time Cayle had suggested cosmetic surgery for that he'd been a much younger man, and they'd both been drunk. Oberon had broken his jaw.

He took Cayle's kit from him, rummaged through it until he found what he needed. He struggled with the tourniquet until Cayle pushed his hands away and did it for him. Oberon's eyes rolled back when he pushed the plunger in. He pulled it out, dropped it.

"I need you to go over the implants for me. Full diagnostic. Something is wrong," he told Cayle, rubbing at the puncture mark with his fingertips. "There are…inappropriate chemical reactions to certain…stimuli, related to…the boy."

"Oh," Cayle said, with no idea what Oberon was talking about. "Do you want me to look at you now?"

"No," Oberon mumbled. "Not now. Tell someone to print the stills for me. I'm going downstairs," he said, ricocheting off the wall towards the door.

Cayle watched him leave, sighed, and went in to see to Seven.

Life in the Sphere.

He supposed it was preferable to death in the Sphere.

saturnalia

Leander was fending off a gilded bird of a woman armed with a gold-dipped makeup brush. "You said I could ask for anything within reason. I don't want gold. Black and red."

Theren scrubbed his hand over his face. "Only the Septarch wears—"

"I'll squirm so much she won't be able to do any paint at all. And he'll be furious."

Theren studied Leander, and nodded. Leander watched until he saw the brush dipped into crimson, and leaned his head back, satisfied.

They were holding Leander's head still, and he caught a glimpse of Camille's back. Her skin was pale as milk, etched with a deep pink latticework of thick scars. She saw him looking and turned her face away, her lips a thin, hard line.

"Keep your hands behind you. Remember to look down, and be quiet. He's usually in a rage when he arranges this kind of thing," Theren warned. "Whatever he's been letting you get away with, don't try it tonight."

The corridors were more crowded than Leander had ever seen them. There were guards in black and violet, and other people in clothes that looked like they had been designed for a funeral in space. He tried not to look up, but he could feel the eyes on him, and he would have sworn that there were whispers with his name in them when he passed.

The throne room was blazing with light. So many torches had been fixed to the walls that it dazzled Leander.

They stopped him outside the door, and dragged Camille past him. She wouldn't pick up her feet. *Please let me not behave like that*, he thought.

It was his turn. He walked. He looked up through his hair, keeping his head down. He saw them push Camille down on her knees, in front of the throne, and snap a gold collar around her neck.

The collar can be tightened until it closes almost completely.

Leander stopped, rigid, but they pushed him forward. He couldn't let them put anything around his neck. He'd choke, or

139

scream, or faint. He raised his head, frantic.

The Septarch was on his throne, dressed in the formal black velvet robes, with his looped cross insignia embroidered on the chest in silver. He saw Leander looking and shook his head, frowning. Leander dropped his eyes again, terrified, but he heard Oberon say, "No. Just her. I want the boy up here."

The guards were falling into position on either side of the throne. There was a general commotion of people filing into the room, lining up around the walls.

Theren nudged Leander, hissing. He stumbled, and thought *they'll drag me, drag me like they did her,* and he put one foot in front of the other the same old way, forward, then up the low stairs. Oberon was as tall sitting down as Leander was standing. His paint was coalblack, edges impossibly sharp, monochromatic except for a splash of blinding red on his bottom lip.

Oberon leaned close, whispered so that only Leander could hear him. "You look terrified."

"I am terrified," he said, in more of a whisper than he'd intended. He wondered if it might help him disappear if he threw the cloak over his own head like a little kid hiding in bedclothes. He was staring at that single splash of red on that savage mouth.

"Already?"

It was too much information, he knew that, but Leander's hand went to his throat by itself, and his eyes went to Camille.

The Septarch said, "No, I can't imagine that for you. She brings that on herself." He turned Leander's face by cupping his jaw. "The paint is magnificent. I thought I told them gold."

"I wanted it more li—this way." Leander blushed at how close he'd come to saying *more like yours.* Now the Septarch would gesture for the guards to put a few bolts into him, and he thought it might be a mercy.

"The color of desire, the color of despair?" Oberon sounded amused.

"Les Miserables," Leander said, and watched that painted mouth break into a delighted smile. Maybe he wasn't making quite as much of an idiot of himself as he feared? Had he ever actually known how you were supposed to *talk* to other people?

"Look," Oberon said, gesturing over Leander's shoulder.

It was a woman in an emerald dress. Her lips were painted the same deep green as her gown, and were laced closed with neat even stitches of silver wire. A transparent tube ran up her nose, the other end of it looped artfully around her neck. She saw Oberon's attention on her, and made an eloquent gesture that brought her almost to her knees.

"That's Victoria. She eats through that. She has to put the lipstick on with a tiny brush," Oberon told him.

Leander forgot to be frightened. "Did you ask her to do that?"

"That was her own idea. I did approve, however. We'll watch the film if you wish, when I'm not playing host."

The room was filling quickly, a blur of Red and Violet guard, more people inked with makeup, some gleaming with wounds that did not seem to pain them, some cloaked and hooded in black or gray.

"Are they slaves?" *Like me*, was what he wanted to ask, but didn't dare.

Oberon raised his eyebrow at Leander, grinning at the expression on his face. "My court. Most of them are refugees." He glanced at Camille, who had her hands covering her collar and was giving both of them a vicious, murderous stare. "Excuse me, Leander."

He leaned over and grasped Camille's chin hard in his fingers. "Don't," he warned, looking at her intently until she closed her eyes.

Leander almost expected it when Oberon struck her across the face with the flat of his hand, hard enough to make her stumble, the chain catching. She turned away from him, her mouth bleeding, and the stitches in her forehead livid.

It made Leander feel victorious.

The Septarch spoke to Leander again. "Will you sit up here with me?"

"With you?"

"Like you did in my room."

Leander was blushing again, certain everyone in the room was watching him.

Oberon picked him up, arranged him in his lap, with Leander's back tight against his chest, and wrapped his arms around him. He didn't know where to put his hands. And now he was *certain* of the eyes on him, and it made him feel

(lucky)
unsafe.

"Why me and not Camille?"

"We both know how I feel about Camille," Oberon said, loud enough for her to hear him, his voice made of disdain. "Hush. They're about to start."

Most of the torches went out, leaving an illuminated circle in front of the throne with the rest of the room in darkness. Six guards marched in, double file. They were wearing the standard plate armor, but it wasn't violet. It was executioner black, with the full faceplates like gleaming chitinous hoods.

Two guards were carrying someone tiny, each only using a single hand to lift her. Leander caught a flash of white-blonde hair. He stiffened, knotting his hands closed, and struggled. There was a dim vision in his mind, of tearing himself free, going to her, catching her up in his arms and carrying her away.

Where are we going?

To Hell, in a handbasket, and guess what? The most beautiful motherfucker you've ever seen is there waiting for us. He has eyes like ink and he's going to...

Oberon's arms were pinning his, and he closed his knees around Leander's legs. He twisted, teeth gritted, unaware he was doing so, unable to ignore the compulsion to *do* something, anything. He might as well have been struggling against a statue.

These, here, and the braces completely immobilize every joint, whispered the voice in his head, dark, casual.

I didn't know, I didn't know what I was asking...

"Stop it," Oberon whispered to Leander.

He looked at Camille. She was sitting cross-legged on the floor. The gold chain from her collar was draped over her shoulder. She was staring off into space, a bruise darkening on her colorless cheek. "Let go of me," Leander said, pleading.

"Leander," Oberon warned, his voice silky and dangerous, "I would much rather do this to her than you, dearest."

"You're testing me," Leander said.

"Yes. And you're failing."

His eyes stung. He ached.

Leander went still.

Jyana's guards set her on the floor. She lay bonelessly as she was placed. Her hands and her feet were bound, her face streaked with tears. More guards were bringing something else to the middle of the circle; a large wire cage. It took four of them to carry it, one of them struggling at each corner. Leander could see something moving in it, something dark, and he caught a glimpse of pale fingers with long ragged stained claws, clinging to the wire.

Camille sucked in her breath, standing straight and drawn tight, and screamed.

Oberon shifted his grip on Leander, leaned over and struck her again, this time with his fist. She fell onto her side like a broken doll, and lay there, sobbing and screaming whenever she found the breath. He moved his hands back to Leander again. He cringed, half-expecting to be hit himself, but Oberon stroked his back, his hair, his attention on his amusement again.

The guards swung open the door of the cage. Whatever was inside cringed away from the light. One of the guards banged on the cage with his armored hand. The thing growled and snapped at the guard's hand, and crept forward, sniffed the air from behind a thick mat of dark hair.

"What is it?" Leander breathed, clinging tight to the Septarch's hands.

"It's a geek," Oberon told him, grinning.

"It's *Lucius*," Camille cried, her voice a shred.

Lucius crawled out of the cage, crouched on his hands and knees, sniffing. He was dressed in ragged scraps of pale leather, and an iron collar with a heavy chain was around his neck. He wobbled on all fours, then straightened.

"That's Julia's skin he's wearing," Oberon whispered, as if they were watching a play.

Leander thought of that first bright flare of fire, so few years ago and so far away, a boy that no longer existed on an Earth that no longer mattered. Of how magnificent it had been to destroy.

Lucius stood shakily upright. He was thin as a whip, and the lines of his face under the mess of hair might once have been elegant. He looked up at Oberon, raised one hand and pointed at him with a jagged fingernail. He bared a mouthful of teeth, filed to sharp points and caked with gore, and snarled at the Septarch.

143

Then, he dropped back down onto his hands and knees. He scampered over to Camille, sniffed at her stitches, her bleeding face, and her crotch. He made a terrible keening sound at her, and tried to flee back into his cage. The guards had already closed and latched the door.

Leander pushed himself back, hard against Oberon's chest. He was not struggling to escape. Something in him needed to feel the moveless strength, needed to be reassured that he was caught and could not run. Oberon sighed in his ear.

Camille was screaming at Oberon. She rushed at him, and the collar caught and dragged her back to the floor, coughing and crying.

Oberon laughed. He put his mouth on Leander's neck and bit him hard. It went all through him like electricity, and he thought, *What if he hit me? What would that feel like?*

"She's angry because she thought she was in love with him, didn't you, Camille? She came to me one night, still wet from him."

"Is that why you don't like her?" Leander whispered.

Oberon thought about that, bit him again. "No. I never liked her."

He never liked her. He doesn't like her. You're the one in his lap, Leander. Who's the pet now?

"Show him the girl," the Septarch ordered.

One of them caught the chain at Lucius's neck and dragged him over to Jyana. She still didn't move. Her eyes were glazed. She was either drugged or mad. Or both.

Lucius sniffed at her. He began rocking back and forth, frantic, panting, then he threw back his head and howled.

"She smells like me," Oberon told him, his fingers lingering on Leander's collarbone.

"What did you do to her?"

Oberon only smiled.

The guards stepped back, giving him room. Theren had his faceplate turned to the floor.

Lucius shoved at Jyana with one clawed hand. He hissed at her between clenched teeth, leaning over her. A clear string of drool dripped through his teeth, left a dark wet circle on her blue silk shirt.

Then, he lunged forward like a striking snake.

Oberon pulled Leander tighter against him. "Watch."

Lucius buried his face in the girl's stomach.

Leander's breath was sticking in his throat, heavy and frantic. His mouth was wet. He could not think. Oberon was hard, under him, and that meant something important.

Jyana made a thin, wailing cry. It was drowned out by a louder sound, a thick wet ripping squish.

"I taught him how to do that," Oberon said to Leander. "Once you're hungry enough, you'll eat anything."

The girl jerked, caught in a seizure of pain. Her hands twitched in the air. One of them fell against Lucius, grasped at his hair, then went limp.

Lucius shoved his hands into the hole he'd made, pulled out a thick clot of meat.

...virgin reams of color, hidden by skin from all eyes for a lifetime, suddenly in his sight...

Leander made a low, anguished noise.

He had expected a neat rainbow, like the anatomical diagrams in his schoolbooks.

...some bright fascination...

Human organs weren't like that at all. There was no rainbow. It was a wet confusion, all in shades of red.

His stomach twisted hard. He thought he was going to be sick. He took a deep breath...and discovered that what he was feeling wasn't nausea at all.

It was hunger.

He turned his head into Oberon's hand, and bit the base of his thumb. Oberon made a quick startled sound, then smiled, and bent his wrist so that Leander could bite harder.

Lucius ate until Jyana was a limp package of skin and bone and hair. He stopped, without warning, leaned up, over her, and stared down at what was left as if he had never seen it before in his life. Then, he curled on his side like a fetus, eyes closed, keening, his hands and teeth smeared thick and crimson.

Camille was making a rhythmic groan that might have been of passion or agony.

Oberon watched her, and pressed a kiss to Leander's cheek. "Get up for just a minute, dearest," he murmured.

Leander tried. He sank to his knees, his eyes nailed to what was left of Jyana, and his hand came up and trailed along Oberon's thigh. The Septarch ran his nails through Leander's hair, before he stood. "Bring him up here," he said, speaking to the guards, but looking at Camille.

One of them took the chain, pulled at Lucius. He wouldn't move, and the guard had to reach under his arms and drag him. Lucius lay where he was dropped, his eyes wide open.

Oberon reached for Camille. She screamed, trying to twist away, but he had her hair knotted in his hand, and he grasped both her wrists and twisted her arms behind her back, and dragged her over to Lucius, and shoved her on top of him. "Kiss him," he ordered her, pushing her head down. "Don't you love him?"

Lucius bared his teeth at her, still streaked with blood and clotted with strings of tissue. Camille screamed again, her voice metallic and desperate. Oberon yanked her hands up to the middle of her back. Something snapped in one of her shoulders, and this time her cry was pure pain.

"Kiss him, or I'll break them off."

Sobbing, she leaned down to kiss him.

Lucius bit through her bottom lip.

Oberon looked back, over his shoulder at Leander. "Should I let him fuck her?"

Leander tried to swallow and couldn't. He looked at Jyana's corpse, lying still in a spreading pool of fluid. His mouth shaped the word *yes*, all by itself.

"Leander!" she screamed, hysterical at this betrayal. He thought, *do you fucking think you're in love?* and he made a heartless gesture at her, like a shrug. His mouth was doing a new something, all by itself, and he thought if he touched it he would feel a smile.

The Septarch gave him a slow grin, wicked and triumphant, and it made Leander want to lick that one bright lipstick flare. "Let him have Camille. Don't let him kill her."

He gave her into the guards' waiting hands. He went back to Leander, settled him on his lap, and said, "That was the only right answer."

Leander groped for Oberon's hand again, as though he had a right to it. He put his teeth back in the marks he'd made, and watched, without a sound.

146

He was mesmerized.

Execution telecasts. Virtual games, underground comics, banned books. Leander had devoured it all and shredded the Undernet for more, and nothing had ever told him about that noise, the blinding surreal quality of carnage in front of you, the thick coppery warm smell.

Oberon pushed two fingers into his mouth, gagging him, and he sucked on them, choking, and thought, *Now I really am home.*

They carried Camille out.

Lucius crawled back to his cage, dragging what was left of Jyana with him. He rattled the door and howled until they opened it for him, and scrambled inside, pulling her inside after him. They carried him out, and there was a splattering of applause.

Oberon pushed at Leander until he stood up. "Put your hands back behind you. Don't look up, and don't say a word," he said, his voice like ice, his eyes empty holes.

He was trying to impress me. Prove something to me. He's determined to take me apart and see how I work. That's what he was doing to me. That entire...thing was engineered and scripted and acted out for my benefit. To see how I would react. If I would react.

He said that was the only right answer.

It happened too fast. It was over too soon.

What did he figure out about me?

Leander turned without meaning to and found that Oberon was looking at him already, with something in his eyes that was fierce and hungry and so cruel that Leander looked back at the ground, shaken.

"That's not what I told you to do. Is it?"

No. Not that voice. Not like that.

Leander could feel the blood rushing into his face, and he was so cold, so cold.

"Is it?"

The shove took him by surprise. He almost fell, and his ankle made an awful noise and pain went through it like a burn.

"Answer me."

"No."

Oberon pushed him again, his hand thudding hard between

Leander's shoulder blades. The guards were watching anything but them. "Weren't you finished looking at me, Leander?" he said. The voice was dangerous now. Oberon was in another place, a place like Hell.

If I looked back, he'd be laughing. He would hit me.

Leander's hands almost moved from behind his back. He tried to will the fury to come, but it didn't. He was alone, and terrified, and outnumbered. He remembered the bolts in his mother, detonating.

This isn't a game. It never has been.

He kept his hands behind him. He walked. He didn't think, and he wasn't sure he was breathing. Oberon's hand was on the back of his neck, and there were guards on either side of them. It had nothing to do with him. He just walked.

Oberon kept his face expressionless. The boy was in front of him, still and quiet and closed.

He's falling apart inside. Now he knows what I am.

His appetite was a raw red fury.

What will you be, after tonight? Will there be anything left?

He would hurt him. He would have to. He would unfold this child, and underneath there would be nothing. And he would be able to think again, able to sleep again. He would be himself again, and Leander would be one more in an endless parade of victims.

Oberon keyed open the door to his rooms. "Inside," he said, pushing Leander past him. "Theren. I'll send for you sometime tomorrow to take him away," he said, and he stepped in, and locked the door, and they were alone.

sigillaricia

The sound of the door locking was deafening, immense. Leander stood where he'd been put, feeling Oberon come closer. He could hear himself breathing. He had never been so afraid in his entire life. He could smell the Septarch, dark and sweet like chocolate, tempting and revolting like old books and abandoned houses. *Centuries,* he thought, the word jangling around in his head as if it wanted to escape. *That's what that smell is, it's centuries...*

Oberon walked around him in a slow circle. "You're beautiful."

This was not what Leander expected, that dangerous predator-polished voice carrying a word he longed for. He was trying not to cry, and failing. "Please..."

"Please what?" Oberon put his hand under Leander's jaw, tilted his head back. Leander shut his eyes, too slowly to escape that lipstick flare. "Don't hurt you? Let you go? Or kiss you again?" He bent lower still, folded his impossible long body until his mouth was inches from Leander's.

The tears came, then. He couldn't help it. "Don't," he said, crying, and stood up on his toes to be kissed. He felt Oberon's hand move to the small of his back, closing around both his wrists. Still room to spare. Long teeth nipped at him, hard enough to hurt, mocking Lucius and Camille.

This isn't the same. He didn't kiss me like this before.

It's like he's serious, now.

The kiss became ruthless. The taste of blood, tangled in his head with the scent of abattoir, red everywhere. He opened his mouth, let himself go limp, let the small bright pain roll through him, let Oberon hold him up.

After nowhere near long enough Oberon let him breathe. "Tell me what you thought of what you saw."

Leander opened his eyes to the silver ansate cross embroidered on Oberon's chest. He made himself look higher—ruined lipstick, and a hot fierce flicker of pride at that—higher still, into those spaceblack eyes. "You engineered that. All of it. You knew how each one of us would react." He was straining up on his toes, without meaning to, wanting to be kissed again.

Oberon put his fingertips on Leander's mouth, stopping him. "Except you. I was guessing about you. Now tell me what you thought."

Instead Leander licked at his fingers before Oberon could take them away, dragged his tongue along the gunmetal point of one long nail. It changed those Unseelie eyes in a way he thought he could watch for days. The Septarch made a low wordless noise he felt in his bones.

"Will you kill me like that, when you get tired of me?"

Oberon closed his black eyes. "Not like that. Not someone like you. I would keep your death between us. Make you choose. Torture you for days."

He bit Oberon's fingertip, hard, and pushed forward, leaned his forehead on Oberon's chest. He was devouring the words. "Would you?" he said, his voice muffled.

"Don't tempt me." he warned,

He let go of Leander's wrists, seized a tangle of his hair instead. He was losing control of his voice. *That's me. I'm doing that to him.* It was inconceivable, and it was wonderful.

"Today?"

"No."

"Tomorrow?"

"Stop it," Oberon hissed at him, pushed him out at arm's length by that handful of hair. Leander cringed away from those long teeth, bared in rage. Oberon shook him, once, and then pulled him.

Towards the bedroom.

Leander found his tears again, found his terror right where he'd left it. Oberon snarled, yanked him forward, lifted him off his feet under one arm, as though he was weightless. It was dizzying, unbearable. Oberon was a sketch of bone and wire around him.

"You're hurting me," he said. He meant it to be accusing, but it sounded desperate and small.

Oberon ignored this. They were in the bedroom, the crimson heart of all this promised red. This door, too, closed and locked behind them. He set Leander on his feet again, but kept him wound up tight. His chest was that same solid plane against Leander's back.

That had been so comfortable, in the charnel-house of the throne room. Now in this Hell-colored room it was awful. Panic seized him, emptied his mind, and he struggled as hard as he could, arching, kicking, straining against those immovable arms.

Oberon laughed and let him do it, until enough sanity returned for Leander to realize he was exhausting himself. He gave up, gasping, head rolling back against Oberon's shoulder.

In answer Oberon wrapped one hand around his throat.

Leander sucked in a single horrified breath, certain it would be his last. Thumb and forefinger found the pressure points at the hinge of his jaw, and pressed hard and fast. Leander bit back on the sound in his throat. His spine drew itself concave, tight and sudden against Oberon's chest. He shook, hard, almost a convulsion. The pain was hot and chemical, like an insect sting, spreading down the sides of his neck, making his mouth wet.

He's playing with me.

Anger. The part of him that upended tables and blew up buildings made him grind his teeth together. Oberon pressed in again, a cruel darting stab, and Leander was forced to make a strangled cry. He wrenched himself sideways, as hard as he could. He didn't move. Oberon laughed. "Do you want me to bruise you?"

Leander shook his head, silent, shame and rage making him cry harder, so the room was a scarlet blur.

Oberon shifted his fingers.

Leander did something close to a scream. His fury abandoned him, and he cried in earnest, no more slow leak, no more pretending. He went limp, waited to be strangled, or perhaps to have his neck snapped.

The pain ceased. The Septarch stroked down his neck with his palm, making a soft sound deep in his chest as though he wanted to soothe Leander to sleep. He turned his hand, drew the backs of his nails up from Leander's collarbone up to the tip of his chin, stroked his nose and his cheekbones with the soft pads of his fingertips, smoothed Leander's hair, combed through it with those long nails.

At first it made him wince. He would be hurt again, he knew it, but the Septarch was gentle and persistent. When Leander subsided into sniffling, Oberon let him go, unwinding those arms slowly enough to let Leander find his feet.

He stood, eyes almost closed, balance unsteady. His hand went to his neck, hovered, went back down to his side.

The Septarch was stretched out on the crimson bed. "Come over here."

"I know what you want," Leander told him, trying and failing to meet those inkblack eyes. "I'm not stupid."

"Aren't you? I told you to come over here. Didn't you understand that?"

Leander moved one foot. His chest hitched, and his hands kept wandering back to his throat, astounded that such hurt had left no wound. Oberon looked hard at the floor beside him, then back at Leander.

He walked forward again, stopped where he had been ordered to. He felt synthetic, dehydrated.

Oberon gestured at the red vinyl suit, the cloak. "Take all of that off."

Leander's stomach did a single sudden roll, like a little sad ghost of his rage.

"Now."

Ice in that voice. And nothing at all in the eyes.

The suit zipped in the front, from neck to waist. Leander dragged his numb hands to his collar, fumbled at the zipper. "I wish you wouldn't," he whispered, aching to look behind him, to the door.

Oberon held his eyes. Trapped.

"I don't care what your wishes are."

His voice was devoid of expression. Did his eyes flicker? Mockery? Something else?

Leander pulled the zipper down six inches, stopped just above his sternum. He waited for a reprieve. There was none. He unzipped down to his waist. He glanced at Oberon one more time, struggled until he managed to pull his arms out of the sleeves.

"Stop," Oberon said, his voice a shade less perfect. He sat up, reached out his hand. Leander didn't understand at first, then reached back, tentative. Oberon grasped his fingers, pulled him even closer, their hands still closed together.

Leander tensed, expecting a bite. He could feel Oberon's breath against his shoulder, could feel the Septarch's hair brushing his ribs.

Oberon nuzzled once at the hollow over Leander's sternum,

bent lower still, stopped at Leander's waist. "You're afraid. I can smell it on you. In you." That uncanny voice was fraying at the edges.

"Yes, fine, I'm afraid." In his own ears he sounded strained, jagged. That breath was lapping against his bare skin at his waist, warm and immediate, and now he understood why animals so feared leaving such soft places exposed.

If he bites me there, I'll scream.

Oberon laughed. "I haven't even done anything yet," he said, almost a warning, before he kissed Leander's stomach below his navel.

Heat. Ice. Terror. He knew he was going to be bitten. He could almost feel it, a thick ragged agony. Leander held his breath, afraid to make a sound, shuddering, staring up at the dark vaulted ceiling, but seeing Jyana hollowed out and over.

He waited and waited for teeth. Instead, it was Oberon's tongue, so warm and startling that he made a sound almost like a cry. His mind was struggling to add up the days, to calculate how long he had been here. It felt urgent that he figure out how long ago Earth had ended.

Oberon licked again, a long delicate motion, and tugged at Leander's right foot until he lifted it, wavering, and pulled off his boot. Leander lifted his other foot without being told, his hands coming down to Oberon's shoulders for balance.

"I know what happens now," Leander said, his voice sounding distant and vague in his own ears. Oberon was pulling off the vinyl suit, and he stepped out of it, naked now except for the velvet cloak. He had to say something else, something perfect, but the best he could do was, "Don't you know what you're like to other people?"

Oberon buried his face in Leander's neck and inhaled, hands pressed against the skin of his back. "You don't smell like the others," he said, sounding as though he were analyzing something. "You almost smell like you're sentient."

This was irrational, cryptic, and it made complete sense to Leander. "I want to be sentient," he said, and that was more like begging than all the pleas that had come before it. He ached to wrap his arms around the Septarch, hesitated, and did it anyway. Oberon was kissing his throat, his collarbone, mouth open and wet. Out of a hundred kisses in a dark room he would know Oberon's mouth. His skin had it memorized. He couldn't move correctly. His joints felt unhinged.

Oberon was pulling him onto the bed.

Hadn't he been afraid?

He was on his back, now, the cloak crumpled and uncomfortable under him. He tried to squirm a little, to rearrange it, his eyes closed.

That was a mistake.

Oberon took this for resistance, made a low, furious sound that climbed into a hiss through his teeth. He knelt up and hit him, twice, his hand open, the blows unplanned and awkward. "Don't. Move."

Leander was more startled than hurt. He opened his eyes again, confused, scared, and Oberon caught his wrists, hard, dragged them up over his head. Something grated against something else in his left hand, the pain sickening and stunning, and he didn't have breath to scream. Leander gasped, and managed, "I won't. I'm sorry—"

"What did you expect to find here?"

"I'll be still, I didn't mean to...please..."

Oberon dragged him off the bed and almost threw him onto the floor. Leander twisted away from him, backed away until he was against the wall. He couldn't look up. The room was a heavy scarlet weight around him. He didn't know if he was about to cry again, or lose consciousness. "Stop it," he said, pleading, hating the whine around the edges of the words. He wrapped his arms around his head. He waited to be struck again, really bitten this time, broken in half, waited for Oberon to laugh at him, or call for Theren to take him away and bring him a better slave.

Camille, maybe.

He waited a long time.

When he looked up, Oberon was looking back at him, sitting on the edge of the bed.

"Are you really this frightened?"

The rage flared up like a fire finding air. "I used to fucking blow up buildings on a planet where the penalty for theft is having your hand cut off. I'm used to fear. And I know what you want," he said, accusing. "You want to fuck me."

There. The words were out, alive and unleashed. No swallowing them back again. No painting over the colors they made.

Leander could feel the incandescent blush in his cheeks and his ears, but he made himself hold those inscrutable eyes.

Oberon smiled, and that one looked like a real smile, looked like he was almost, proud.

"Yes. And you want me to fuck you. Come here."

He was beginning to think the Septarch's wildly unhinged moods were contagious. "Don't you understand? I can't do this. I can't...live up to you."

The Septarch slid off the bed, came towards him slowly, sank down to his knees to look into Leander's face.

"No. I don't understand. Explain it to me."

Leander hadn't expected that. It felt like a trap. He swallowed, sent a furtive glance beyond Oberon, seeking an escape that did not exist. Only the red, red room, black steel walls inset with crimson glass, a fireplace with neatly laid wood waiting for flame. He was trying to get his mind around what he was feeling, but it was bigger and stranger than any emotion he knew. He knew all about rage, about frustration, and this was like those, and yet unlike them. "Before this...before here, and you...I was the only person like me. Now—"

He shook his head, losing the sense of it.

Oberon finished for him. "Now, you're no longer the only one like you. That's what frightens you. Alone is all you've ever known, and now that it's gone...you mourn. You miss it, even though you hated it. It had become...familiar. Safe."

Leander's mouth was parchment-dry, his throat clotted. "How? How do you know that?" he demanded, in awe, feeling almost betrayed to hear the secret teased out of his head and laid out in between them like so many bones.

Oberon sighed. He covered his mouth with one hand, drew it away again. "How do you think I know?"

Leander let his arms drop, let his hands come to an uneasy rest in his lap. "What do you want me to say?"

"What do you want? Did anyone ever ask you that?" Oberon whispered to the lipstick ruin in his palm. "People take everything they hate about themselves and make it into a wall they can live inside, and they call it safe," he said. "Aren't you tired of being safe?"

Leander shook his head, speechless, and leaned over until his forehead rested against the cool floor, stretched out his arms like an Egyptian in front of the Pharaoh. "Does it have to be like this? So hateful?"

"How is it hateful?"

"It's like now that you're going to do this you don't li–don't think of me as a person anymore. I guess I thought that you did. Or you were starting to," Leander said, still miserable.

"Don't move." He reached out and touched Leander's face, stroked the hair out of his eyes, smoothed it along the line of his jaw. "I don't know how to think of you. I don't know what I think of you. I've had hundreds of you, and sometimes I don't even remember the names."

"Do you remember my name?"

"Leander Schaiden."

That made Leander's heart do a little unruly bounce.

Oberon was almost smiling. "You seem to think I'm something I'm not. You seem to admire me. I think I hate you."

Leander didn't exactly smile, but the knot in his stomach was beginning to unravel. He sat up, slowly until he was sure Oberon would let him. "I think I hate you too."

Oberon slapped him. Not hard, and not quickly. Leander let it turn his head, let his breath leave him in a long slow rush. "How dare you understand me," he mumbled, through lips that were almost numb.

"I don't think I do. Not yet. But I will."

"Unmake me," Leander said, in a tiny voice. "Take it away. Everything. They've put things in my head that don't belong there."

Oberon stood up so quickly it was almost funny, stared down at him in horror, the expression of a man whose wish had just been granted. "*Unmake* you?"

"Yes." Leander stayed on his knees, staring up along Oberon's impossible height, his eyes frightened and determined. "Yes."

Oberon bent closer, reached down and cupped Leander's face in his hands. "I will give you...this one chance...to take that back."

Silence.

"No," Leander told him. "I won't. I meant it."

"What you are right now, you will never be again," Oberon warned him.

"Good," Leander said. That felt exactly right. That felt fierce and unrepentant. The one chance gone, and now he was beyond it, free of it.

Oberon picked Leander up and carried him back to bed.

Leander put out his hands, trying to catch himself, and clung to Oberon's shoulders. The Septarch found the clasp for the velvet cloak and unfastened it and pulled it away.

He's burning me, Leander thought, and his hands closed in Oberon's hair, pulling his head close. He was lost in texture, velvet robes against his legs, Oberon's hair brushing his ribs.

"You kiss me," the Septarch breathed.

Leander kissed hard, trying to choke him with his tongue. He pulled away so he could speak, and Leander bit at his chin, licking his face, frantic.

"Do you even know what I want to do to you?"

Leander thought, *This is why they always tell you not to get in a transport with a stranger, They're afraid it might be someone like you.*

He did know what Oberon wanted.

Well, he knew in theory.

He was unclear on the details, and completely unsure of what things people really *did.* He'd come to the general conclusion that sex onscreen had as much in common with sex in the real world as old martial-arts movies did with actual fights. The reality was probably far less elaborate, far less photogenic, far less choreographed.

He'd worked out how to masturbate a year or so earlier, but that appetite felt divorced from sex for him, much more tangled with explosions and fires and horror films he had to watch with earphones to avoid parental condemnation. He'd never known anyone he could imagine that kind of interaction with. Only pictures, only the faces of the long-dead and long-forgotten. Though he often summoned those faces, those hands to take the place of his own, he was hazy on what they might do to him, or what he might do in return.

"I think...maybe you want to put your hands on me, and..." his blush was so intense it almost hurt, his heart thudding so hard he was sure Oberon could feel it. "And maybe...put your fingers...in me..."

Oberon laughed. This time there was only delight in it and not malice. "Oh, you're perfect," he said, the words rolling out of him, almost moaning. He pushed Leander onto his back on the bed, studied him intently. "You really don't have any idea, do you?"

Leander shook his head, blushing. "Maybe...kiss me, and lay on top of me?"

Oberon did that, and said against his mouth, "It's not my fingers I want to put inside you."

He took Leander's hand and put it under his robes.

He'd known that. From books and other solitary pleasures. Though that definitely belonged to the mental list of things he'd thought people didn't really do. "Will it hurt?"

"Probably." His voice was rough and heavy. He pushed Leander's hands back over his head.

Leander closed his eyes. Oberon was crushing him. There was a long blissful space of the Septarch's mouth on him, those yards of nightcolored hair surrounding them both like a velvet curtain. That weight on him was luscious and necessary, all that kept him from flying to pieces. Oberon kept biting, sometimes hard enough to make him wail. The pain he'd feared bloomed into intense sweetness that made him desperate for those teeth, wanting them everywhere at once.

The bites grew less intricate and more savage. The world was made of noise and texture. Leander felt his knees pushed up and apart and he wanted to brace himself, but Oberon still had his wrists, and there was nothing to cling to.

Pain ripped up into him, vicious, staggering. Much more than he had feared. He shrieked, pulling, frantic to free his hands, his heels slipping on fur and satin. Oberon pushed into him deeper, harder, and Leander bit his shoulder hard enough to draw blood. It made him dizzy, made the world spin, and he made a noise like an animal that wasn't even words.

Oberon twisted free of Leander's teeth. His hands closed around Leander's neck. "Don't. I'll choke you to death."

Leander gave Oberon a bloody grin in response to this. His body came up off the bed in a liquid arc. "Scratch me."

The same grin given back to him, just as bloody. One luscious squeeze, stopping his breath, stopping his voice, and then Oberon did, gashing the nails of both hands from Leander's neck to his waist.

He was screaming again, sure his throat would burst if he

didn't, less in pain and more in triumph. There was luxury in that, screaming as loud as he wanted, in knowing no one would come to save him.

It has to be this way. He has to destroy me, first, and invent me all over again.

This is the beginning.

obcursus

Oberon drifted back to himself in stages. There was blood in his mouth, both his own and a warmer richer texture, tangled with that snarl of scent that made him think of tea leaves and matches and feline green eyes. The boy. Yes. The boy that gave him troublesome problems like involuntary smiles and a failure to concentrate. The boy that was whimpering underneath him..

Again he felt that human urge to sigh. He knew what came now, yes, he'd done this part hundreds of times, maybe thousands by now. This birdboned creature would crawl away from him if it could, beg him to go away if it could not. Usually he was happy to do just that. Once his appetite for anguish was sated he lost all interest in recriminations, in petitions for death or mercy.

He didn't feel that way this time.

Frowning, Oberon raised his head. His eyes didn't change, couldn't change, but if he'd still been human he'd have been looking into middle distance, listening to an internal space that should've been sleepy, or bored, or silent.

He didn't want the boy to drag himself away. And worse still, he was

(afraid?)

not at all willing to hear this lovely being call him a monster, wail about going home, start that crying business again, dappled with insistence on *mother* or *doctor*.

That was the problem with fucking. It ended, and the space after it was empty at best.

The wriggling underneath him grew more pronounced.

No. No sighing.

He pushed himself up on his elbows, and the miniature struggle subsided. The plaintive little noise did not, and he realized Leander was speaking, muffled into the bedclothes. Oberon had to lean close to hear him.

"Liked what you were doing, but then it hurt so much. Maybe...maybe if next time you wouldn't do it so hard..."

This was so different from what he'd expected to hear that at first he didn't understand it. Oberon assembled *hurt so much* and *wouldn't do it so hard,* and an unfamiliar feeling crept over him.

From the top: this Earth boy, this kitten-creature composed of lines and angles and heat and that addictive scent was showing no sign of loathing. There was no indication that he was about to try to run out of the room in a crazed search for some fatal exit. He was willing for there to be a *next time,* and Oberon had been...

Cruel.

No, not even that.

Careless.

It had been a long time since he'd been with anyone whose pleasure was of any concern to him. He'd forgotten that sex could be a mutual conversation, and not an echo of orders given and undertaken, pain inflicted and endured. He studied Leander, admiring bruises, the imprint of his teeth at chest and hip, the trailing lines he'd left with his beloved claws, some deep enough to bleed bright red into his bloodcolored bed. Too sudden a climb, lost in his own bliss, lost in the habit of viewing this creature as made for his pleasure, and a deeper pleasure cast aside in favor of that single-minded familiar pursuit. Hadn't he often thought sometimes he might as well be alone to play such a game?

Shame had long since been scoured out of him, burned out, bled out, but he was still capable of regret, though unable to predict when it might strike him or why. This time, maybe the *when* of it was *soon enough* and the *why* could wait. It had been a long time since he'd felt apologetic, and it would never be one of his talents, but he could almost remember it if he tried. He thought it had been like this gentle, wistful sadness he was feeling now.

He put his hand on the boy's stomach, made himself move with slow care. No claws now, only soft pressure from his fingers and palm. "Does it still hurt?"

Leander winced, but the flush in his face was more embarrassment than pain. He nodded, and Oberon could see him wondering if that was the correct answer. Soon he would have to explain that not all questions were meant to be a test. Soon, but not now.

"Where?"

"Everywhere."

"Details."

He chewed his lip. "My stomach and my back and my, insides."

"Sharp hurt, or dull ones?"

Leander's brow knitted, and Oberon wanted to put his mouth there, and wondered for the thousandth time since he'd stolen this boy if he was going even more mad.

"Dull, mostly. The sharp ones are—" he trailed into a hiss, because Oberon was stroking a deep scratch, "—yes, like that one, from your nails. You're not poisonous, are you?"

A cold thrill of surprise went through him. This one was even more perceptive than he'd realized, and still so young. "I think you mean venomous, and no, not at the moment." He patted Leander, hoping to convince him this was teasing. "Turn over."

"No...don't...hurts too much to move..."

Oberon ignored this and rolled him over, spread his legs to examine him. A warning stroke with his fingers, another gentle push. "Does that hurt?"

Leander didn't move, didn't seem to breathe. "Yeah. But you could do it again, if you wanted to..."

Oh, he wanted to, but Oberon was working on being the opposite of inconsiderate. He moved his hands until he found muscles knotted tight, rubbed in firm circles. "Relax. Breathe." He kept his voice low, softened the edges of words, made them glide together. He spoke to animals with that voice. Real ones, not the kind you stole from stricken parents. "You're all right. It'll hurt more tomorrow, less tomorrow night. It won't hurt as much next....next time. It's normal."

The boy was unwinding under his hands, little shudders moving through him. Oberon was surprised to find that this pleased him. A softer pleasure than he found in bringing pain, but a deeper one than he expected from such simple contact.

"Your hands are so warm..."

Oberon let himself smile, and made himself warmer still, as easy as shrugging or blinking, a trick he'd never thought to use this way. This won him a long gorgeous moan that took away his smile and stirred his appetite. He ignored it, a decision as simple as it was unthinkable, and kept petting, slow and smooth, finding new knots and coaxing them to untangle.

Pretty sculpture boy, so fragile, so bonelessly relaxed under claws that could shred him with stunning ease. It felt like a gift. That pulling, tender urge came again, and this time he gave in to it, leaned over and shrugged his hair out of the way and pressed his mouth to the little archipelago of Leander's spine.

Now it was Leander who sighed, without showing any worry about what it might reveal. Oberon left kisses until he ran out of vertebrae, and rested his cheek against Leander's ass, nuzzling a little to feel the graze of invisible soft down. His own skin lacked this, had for so long that it was exotic to him on others.

He wanted to give something instead of taking.

Had sex always involved so much negotiation?

Memories of the time when he'd been a creature like the one he held in his hands were made of sun and shadow. Some stood out in his mind, bright and clear as if they'd happened hours ago. Some were so hazed and dim they may as well have been from books, films, hardly his own at all anymore.

Oberon's hands were cupping Leander's ribcage, and he slid them lower to see if he could circle his waist. Yes, with a little room to spare. Tiny, tiny creature. This discovery filled him with an urge towards tenderness.

"I can show you something that won't hurt. If you trust me."

This was followed by the closest thing to shame he yet possessed, an exasperated rage at himself. Trust? The boy was young, made of a lifetime of seconds compared to himself, but he was far from stupid. That word was almost an insult.

Leander shivered a little under his cheek. "Mmm?" Half want, half worry. But the tension did not climb under his hands.

He licked down Leander's spine, to the end of his tailbone, pressed another kiss there. The boy did tense, then, and made a delicate sound that was not quite a word.

Wait. If not for that word the boy wouldn't be here now, and Oberon wondered if he'd really stolen him after all.

He waited.

Leander hesitated, trembling, and raised his hips.

When he felt the kiss in the middle of his back. Leander's eyes opened by themselves. He tried to memorize that single kiss. He didn't know why, but he wanted to keep that sensation.

Another kiss, this one lower. By the time he realized what Oberon intended

(he can't possibly)

his body had rolled by itself, starving, and it was too late for him to do anything but inhale.

The Septarch took one long lick, freezing Leander with delicious shock, and drove his tongue in, almost vicious.

I never even thought of this.

Leander's breath was stuck in his throat, somewhere between inhale and exhale. Then he made a terrible stricken sound. "More..."

He held Leander's hips and pulled him back and pushed his tongue in deeper, and reached under him and slid his hand down his stomach, clawed four bright lines to his erection.

Leander chewed into the pillow, and lost his mind. Nothing left but pieces of thought, *venomous,* and *bite,* but these were like the graze of nails, bright little thrills, more delight than dismay. Oberon had told him there would be no hurt, and there was none, only the ghost complaints of wounds already made. The hands on him were nothing like his own, made of immovable, inhuman strength.

Leander's thoughts fractured into vague impressions of machinery.

Masturbation had been a secret thing, a pleasure that had to be stolen and hidden like all the others, a race against the alarm clock or his mother's knock or the end of the allotted shower-cycle. The orgasm was the purpose and the point, and he'd imagined sex would be much like that. Goal-oriented, a task to be accomplished as quickly as possible.

Oberon would not let him race. He would bring Leander so close the height of it scared him, ease off again, let him breathe and wail in frustration and take hold of him again. At the last he held Leander there

(centuries)

and when Oberon did not stop there was falling, falling.

Oberon slipped out from under Leander's arm.

He couldn't sleep. He wanted something, but was unsure what. He loathed that sensation, and it came more and more often.

He was trying to understand what had just happened to him. He'd have called this sensation excitement, though it carried distressing undertones of worry.

He wanted that. Wanted me. Even when I hurt him.

Oh, he could have any number of sexual partners, here in the Sphere, on any of the other six worlds in his domain, in several little orbital or deep-space cities he'd acquired or constructed. Men, women, children, creatures that were both or neither, creatures that believed themselves far from human until they met the Septarch. He'd indulged at first, still did from time to time, but he'd learned over the centuries in the hardest possible ways that this was an excellent way to acquire the kind of hurt that even he did not find pleasurable.

Consenting adult partners had proven to be dangerous.

And they didn't really want *him*, did they? They wanted the idea of him, they wanted a revenge fantasy, they wanted the Oberon they saw when he decided to telecast something beautiful and depraved.

Now there was an idea.

The terminal woke at his touch. He ignored a ream of communications, sent them into the aether. It was easy enough to find Leander's intake file, and easy enough from there to find what he wanted. He toyed with the comm settings, but he had no desire to wash and dress and paint himself, and it wouldn't do for the humans to have film of him looking almost like anyone did after such a night. Audio only, then.

The console whirred, chirped, considered. Earth was bedecked with security blocks, unsurprising for such a fragile Republic topheavy with wealthy cowards and superstitious fools. It was no match at all for the Sphere, and the terminal soon informed him that it had established a connection.

"Hello?" came a man's voice, rough and hoarse. There was faint static—there always was on an interplanetary line.

"Is this Paul Schaiden?" Oberon asked.

Silence. Static or not, the Septarch knew even his voice did not sound human anymore, though once when they were both stupendously altered on whatever Victoria had brought him to smoke.

He'd asked her if she could find the words to say why. She could not. Maybe a subaudible resonance even he didn't realize he was perceiving. He would mention it to Cayle, next time he was in the mood for a set of new enhancements.

There was a sound that Oberon was pretty sure was a false start at speaking. "Who is this?"

Delightful. Farther away than any Republic ship could reach and he could terrify their little sheep from his own rooms in the middle of the night. "You know who this is," he said, grinning a rictus at the blank screen.

Then tension like a physical presence. Another sound, this one not so much a false start as wordless rage.

"I just fucked your son, Paul. He's as tight as a boy half his age. I have his come in my hair."

More noise, rage sliding headlong into anguish and insanity. Torture without touch was one of the best games. It made him understand why people bothered to write haiku.

"I laid him out on his back and fucked him up the ass. He loved it. You should have heard the noises he made."

A roar of grief and fury. "I swear, I will KILL you."

Oberon's eyes rolled back. He was going to replay this one for weeks, he could already tell. Oh how they all wanted to kill him. Maybe he'd go back to Earth to watch them try. He let Paul go on for a long time. Sometimes he laughed, and that sent the man into absolute incoherency.

When he was sure the man had run empty he said, "Are you jealous, Paul?"

After another twenty seconds or so Oberon muted Paul, found and triggered a black glass pipe whose contents he had forgotten. He sat with smoke drifting out of mouth and nose, wondering what threats or confessions the man was shrieking into empty aether.

"Oberon?" came Leander's voice from the doorway, sleepy and curious. "Who was that?"

His hand moved to disconnect the call—and then he had a better idea, and left it alone. Let Paul listen. Perhaps he would learn something.

He turned in his chair. Leander was naked, yawning, his eyes bright with sleep, his hair mussed. The intimacy of that was made an ache unfold beneath his ribs.

Always this boy, and only this boy.

"Come here," he said. It didn't sound at all the way he'd planned.

Leander did.

Oberon wanted to catch him close, kiss him for hours. Instead he put his hands on the boy's shoulders and pushed him down on his knees. "I want to teach you something," he said, pulling Leander's head into his lap.

desolatus

When Paul Schaiden came back to himself he was curled up on the floor. The comm panel in the wall above him was destroyed, and his hands were bleeding. That was fine. Neither of those things mattered. Why should they? There was no one here to see him, no need for his hands to be well and whole.

Three weeks ago he had gone to work, spent a peaceful eight hours in the calm predictable space of math and physics, designing a causeway for Zone Five.

He had come home, done

(his duty as a loyal citizen of faith and fortitude, was that what the letter had said?)

what They told him, as he always had, and then his life had ended in every sense of the word but one.

He was alive. He breathed. But there was no purpose to either of those things.

The Republic had done what he assumed was standard procedure for people The Monster had destroyed. After the tithe he had been swarmed by police, and a doctor had come at him with an air injector that left a neat blank space in his head. He'd awoken in a hospital, and when he showed no signs of attempting suicide or homicide he'd been driven home.

Well, to this house.

He no longer had a home.

They had explained it to him, Church counselors in expensive suits, that he was now retired, as if he'd been a wounded soldier, his every need and few wants provided for. He was not permitted to speak to any independent media, or discuss what had happened to him on the Overnet, a condition which made him blink. He had no idea why he might care to do either of those things.

They had changed his wristunit. He suspected the new one would alert them if he attempted to break these few incomprehensible rules. When he had noticed the replacement, he took it off, and dropped it in a little bowl on a table in the entryway.

There it sat, though it did not gather dust.

He had always done what They told him.

This was as close to an illegal action as he had ever taken, this tiny crime that he was sure a billion people accidentally committed daily after a shower or a swim.

It was only rebellion when it was deliberate, and it was certainly that.

He did not think about why he'd done it. He only knew he did not want that thing on his body.

Every other day Church staff came to his empty home, colorless women as engineered and placid as his mother had been. They did not trouble him and he did not trouble them. He spoke to them once, the first day, to order them to stay out of the master bedroom and his

(my son my son my son my SON)

son's bedroom and they did so without protest.

He had not entered either room since That Day.

He sat on the couch, where he also slept, staring at the blank telescreen while they did housework around him. They dusted his abandoned wristunit without comment, stocked his fridge unit and his pantry shelves, made meals that he did not eat, offered prayers he did not join.

He waited for them to complain about the wristunit, to order him to attend Church, or see a counselor. He waited to hear the word *funeral*, or asked if he wanted to visit a grave. When none of this was forthcoming he stopped waiting.

At night when they were gone he would turn on the telescreen, find football or soccer or hockey or baseball and turn the volume up as high as it would go. He would drink vodka, because

(Soren will never drink it again)

it was there. The Church neither forbade nor encouraged this, but when his supply ran low his attendants began to replace the bottles for him.

When he drank enough of it, he could cry, if you could call that crying. There were tears, and when he lost the struggle to stay silent he would scream.

He would wake up in his chair, or on the couch, or once in the hallway, miserable with hunger and thirst and nausea. He would shut off the agony of the blaring telescreen, and then lie in the shower, drinking water with his mouth open from time to time, and when the allotted cycle was over he'd press the switch again. It never refused him, and he was never reprimanded for wasting precious water.

Paul's mother had been engineered, his father natural-born to parents too poor to afford better. He had grown up with this stigma, accepted by neither designed children nor the "wild" as they'd called them back then. He'd desperately wanted to be a good Citizen, wanted to be faithful and loyal, productive. He wanted to fit in, to belong. He supposed that had been bred into his mother and passed along to him, though he wasn't inclined to deep analysis (this had almost certainly been bred *out* of his mother) and simply accepted this instinct as a part of himself.

His fixation had led to eventual grudging acceptance, to being chosen for secondary education, and it was there he'd met Soren. She was not a student. She was a groundskeeper, not by choice, but by force. It was that or jail, due to her flat refusal to attend the Church's required training for young women.

Soren was wild, in every sense of that word. He'd known the moment he saw her, grudgingly pretending to sweep, and stopped to ask her for directions he didn't need. He'd looked into those green eyes, lined in defiant black, and he was lost.

That once, just that once, he had not cared what his parents expected, what the Church expected, what the State would think. He only knew for the first time in his life that he was in jail already, and without her he would stay there.

You always did what They told you, except when you married me. And look what it got you, honey. I told you we should run, if you'd listened to me where would we be now?

Soren's voice in his head was the worst in the morning, when he was still drunk enough to listen, but dared not drink more to drown her out. Sometimes he cried then, too, in the shower, though he did not know he was doing it.

Once he could tolerate the thought of food, he would eat, and then just to silence the nausea. Then he would return to the couch, and stare at the telescreen again until nightfall, when he'd start all over again.

Even with one of the couch cushions over his face, even with the sunny voices of sportscasters babbling their maddening inanities, he was sure the neighbors could hear him.

He did not care about that, or about anything else.

At least, he hadn't, until that ominous chime from his comm.

He did not want to think about what The Monster had said to him. He did not want to think about what he'd heard the monster *doing* before that white space in which he supposed he'd destroyed the comm.

He would drink, and never mind the hour, but when he stood up to do so the result sent him running for the kitchen sink, where he was violently ill.

He ran the cold water, groaning, the pain in his hands beginning to register. He closed and opened both—not broken, as far as he could feel—ran them under the stream to clear them of blood. Bruised, cut here and there, but it would heal.

He cupped water onto his face. This was soothing, and he did it over and over, wishing he could do that forever, not thinking, not feeling.

Not seeing Leander in his head, not the sullen and incomprehensible teenager he had become, but the laughing boy made of dimples and those same beloved green eyes, the little miracle his mother had refused to visit that he was sure his long-dead father would have adored.

Leander, six, Paul boosting him to examine the engine of their long-dead first electrocar. Leander drawing on the backs of his drafting sketches, sitting on pillows on a barstool so he could reach Daddy's desk.

Leander, still alive, in a world the sun had never seen, naked and tangled in a bed with The Monster.

His stomach rolled, and he bent over again, There was agonizing heaving, but nothing to bring up. He stood, trembling, scoured out, staring down into the drain, no longer seeing the faucet gushing wasted water for the State to politely ignore.

That night, Paul Schaiden slept on his couch yet again.

This time, he did it sober.

alexithymia

Leander kept his head on Oberon's knee. The boy's mouth was wet, his skin bright with sweat. "I like that. Almost as much as I like kissing," he said.

Like. He kept using that word. Oberon wasn't accustomed to finding this word in association with anything about himself. He supposed he'd have thought it a lie, if he'd been unmodified. It had been impossible for anyone to lie to him for over a hundred years. Even judicious editing was as obvious to him as someone's hair color, a collage of temperature, heart rate, and scent that he no longer had to analyze.

He'd probably have worked out that Leander's willingness was genuine, even without the broad scope of his state-of-the art senses. The boy was quick to learn what Oberon enjoyed, eager to repeat it, all passion and no reticence once he understood what the Septarch wanted. After a moment or two he'd taken his hands away from the boy's head, leaned back and marveled at a sensation he'd forgotten could apply to him. Another person, giving him pleasure and letting him experience it.

He stroked the boy's face with his fingertips, in something like awe. Would that still be true if the boy knew what mischief he'd been enjoying as foreplay?

The boy nuzzled into his hand and grinned those dull white teeth up at him. There was another thing he wasn't used to having directed at himself. "You don't taste like I do." An adorable climb in heat and heart rate, embarrassment at what he'd inadvertently revealed. Leander didn't let it stop him. "Are you sure you're not poisonous?"

Oberon was almost hurt by that until he grasped that he was being teased. "Also not at the moment. Though I could be, if I chose, or if I ate enough poisonous things."

The boy's grin became something Oberon didn't understand. Dismay? "You wouldn't get sick?"

"No. I don't get sick."

He watched the boy think about this. "Are you...were you, a person, like me?"

"Once." That caused a sensation he thought might be his own version of embarrassment. This boy was exhausting, sending all kinds of impressions and impulses hurtling through him from moment to moment.

Exhausting, and exhilarating.

The boy was petting him in return, cautious, but with increasing confidence. At last he reached up, and ran his fingers along the jagged graffiti of scars on Oberon's chest. "What happened?"

"*Don't!*"

He shoved Leander's hand away.

He sounded afraid. He *was* afraid.

He wanted to *run*, as ludicrous as that was, but the boy was between him and escape unless he wanted to tumble over backwards, chair and all. Memory flicker of himself half buried in the Worm Chamber, a ghost Leander conjured above him.

Leander raised his head, and there was that dismay again. "I'm sorry. Does it hurt?"

A cascade of internal errors. Perhaps this was what people meant when they said they were flustered. "No, but I know they're ugly."

Now that was ridiculous, wasn't it? He was quite sure he himself was hideous, grotesquely tall, over seven feet the last time he'd been adjusted, white as paper, thin enough to count his own elongated bones, everything about him sharp and dangerous, and that was even before he spoke and demonstrated what sharp and dangerous really meant. He set his own standards of beauty, and in the centuries since he'd become the Septarch those around him had adapted to him instead of the other way around.

Since when did he care about the opinions of others?

He didn't have to wonder what *that* expression was. Anger. He had an insane urge to say a *sorry* of his own, but before he could Leander reached up and cupped Oberon's face in his hands. "Stop saying that." he ordered. "There's nothing ugly about you."

He was too incredulous to breathe.

This tiny mortal creature just gave me an order.

And then this tiny mortal creature leaned over, and kissed the marred skin of Oberon's chest.

His breath came back in a horrified gasp. There was a

maelstrom in the Septarch's mind.

Kill him. Choke him. Break him. Don't allow this.

He didn't know what to do, and it was this as much as anything else that made him move his hands out of Leander's way.

He's trying to comfort me. No one ever tried to comfort me.

The decision was made, in that moment, but he didn't move. Leander left kisses on several dozen ancient wounds, nuzzling his way along the skin between them before Oberon trusted himself to speak.

"There's a black box, over the fireplace. Bring it to me."

Leander did, leaving one last kiss over Oberon's sternum. He came back with it in one hand. Oberon took it from him and set it on the edge of his desk. The boy tried to sit on the floor again, but Oberon pulled him into his lap instead. "No. Lean your head back. Close your eyes."

The boy tensed when he heard the box open. Oberon took the knife out with slow reverence. It was ancient, an Earth relic from the Third Reich. It had been difficult to acquire, even for him. He had yet to use it. Such monumental evil had to be saved for a worthy purpose.

When cold metal touched his throat the boy's breath left him in a sudden wrench, but he kept his eyes closed, and did not pull away.

"It's all right. Don't you trust me?"

The boy's mouth moved. On his second try he said, "Okay."

Oberon tangled his hand in that fine soft hair, not hard enough to pull, just to steady him. He cut him, with deliberate, measured care. The marks had to be shallow enough to be harmless, but deep enough to scar. He laid three horizontal stripes in a descending row across Leander's throat, each a little shorter than the last, so that the result suggested an inverted triangle. The boy made little worried noises deep in his chest, louder when blood began to trickle down.

He took the knife away, licked both sides, careful of the double-edge, and set it back in its case. "All over," he said.

Leander's eyes opened, and his hand moved to investigate the wounds. Oberon let him discover that his head was still attached and caught his wrist, drew the boy's bloody fingers into his mouth up to Leander's hand, drew them out again and left a kiss in the center of his palm.

"It marks you as my favorite. My only favorite."

MET·A·MOR·PHO·SIS

(mèt´e-môr¹fe-sîs) noun
plural met·a·mor·pho·ses (-sêz´)

1. A transformation, as by magic or sorcery.
2. A marked change in appearance, character, condition, or function.
3. Biology. A change in the form and often habits of an animal during normal development after the embryonic stage.
1. Pathology. A usually degenerative change in the structure of a particular body tissue.

[Latin metamorphosis, from Greek, from metamorphoun, to transform : meta-, meta- + morphê, form.]

Two nights passed, without a word from Oberon, leaving Leander sleepless and inconsolable, sulking in the Gallery until even Camille was cheerful by comparison, until Theren came in carrying, yes, a bright red armload of clothes.

In Oberon's room, the first thing Leander noticed was his sketch. Cybernetic Jesus in all his mild-eyed, rewired glory was over the fireplace in the front room, the drawing flanked by twin torches that did not explain the way it was illuminated. The tear was invisible, and it was matted with black and framed in deep blue metal with etching that suggested more circuitry.

Framed. Like it was actual art.

Somewhere in his head, his mother murmured, *I even drew monsters in the margins.*

"Just for you, and just for Them," he said to himself, his pulse throbbing in the trinity of cuts on his throat.

"I had it restored," said Oberon behind him. He turned to find the Septarch in a black flight suit that made a nightmare of his narrow height. "They cleaned it, and treated it. It's a little yellow, but it—" Oberon stopped.

Leander was making an odd sound that he was hoping Oberon would mistake for laughter.

The Septarch already knew him much better than that.

"Why are you crying?"

There was no answer for that one. Leander kept seeing his teacher's hands grabbing at the drawing, crumpling it, kept standing that image in his mind beside the reality of that ornate frame, the undetectable repairs.

"I really wanted that back, is all." He sniffled, and looked up at Oberon, his cheeks wet. "It looks like your statue."

"Yes. It does." Oberon caught hold of him, scaring him badly, and scooped Leander up to sit in the crook of his arm. "The instant of transformation. Creation and destruction."

Leander clung, mind filled with hazy toddler notions about grownups pretending to drop you, but the Septarch only held him that way, presumably so he could see better.

"My statue was an experiment," he said. Leander had to lean his head close to hear. "This moment of change fascinates me, but my art tends to be more expressive of destruction than creation." There was a dry, wry little twist in those words, though Leander wasn't quick enough to see the facial expression that came with them.

"Event art," Leander said. "That's what I used to call it, when I would, destroy things. Their things."

Speaking of this out loud, even here, far beyond the Reach of the Republic of Earth, felt dangerous. Suicidal, even.

The Septarch traced the bridge of Leander's nose. "The explosions."

Leander blinked, and felt himself go into Authority Figure mode, or try, anyway. It was difficult when you were being held like a little kid at a fairground. "Explosions?"

"You said you used to blow up buildings. Tell me."

"Um..." Why was he blushing? "That's, about all there is to it. The Republic...the Church and the State...um..." Couldn't they just talk about sex again? "I hate them." He'd had no idea his voice could be so tiny.

Oberon bounced his arm under Leander, making him cling and then stare at the Septarch, indignant. "Again," he said.

"I don't..."

"Say that again, if you mean it."

"Of *course* I mean it. I fucking hate them." That was considerably less tiny. "I wanted to be left alone, I wasn't hurting *them* and they *kept* hurting me and I got tired of it, and they deserved it. I mean, *prison* because you don't like my drawing? *Really*?"

He swung a shaking hand in the direction of the cybernetic Jesus. "I don't like your rules, or your idea of fun, or your fucking dress code, or how fucking *nosy* you are about everything."

He paused, because his tone of voice was *not* one he could imagine anyone using in the Septarch's presence, whether or not it was directed at him, but Oberon listened, watching him with those vacuumblack eyes.

"I tried to pick times where nobody was working. They don't let you choose your job and I didn't want to hurt people that were just, trying to be people."

He expected this to have been a dreadful mistake, as that

essentially described Oberon's hobbies, but the Septarch nodded, still listening.

"I could make Their lives more difficult. Good."

He stopped.

Any fragment of that would have meant public execution on Earth.

Here, it apparently meant a kiss.

They shared the same breath, mouth to mouth, until Leander was dizzy. Oberon whispered, "I'm proud of you."

I've always been proud of you.

Damn it. The last thing he wanted to think about was his mother. Guilt folded around him, suffocating, and he buried his face against Oberon's chest, feeling the slick drag of leather against his cheek. Leander listened to his heartbeat, or at least he supposed that was a heartbeat. It sounded like an industrial pump, a precise cadence of thumps, clicks, and hums. *Cyborg,* he thought. It sounded imaginary, unrelated to this warm narrow being who held him with such calm grace.

After too long—had he almost been *dozing?*—Leander raised his head. "This is...a flight suit?" The word *spaceship* was jangling around in his throat.

"It is," Oberon said, as gravely as if he'd been revealing the secret of the universe. "And this is close enough," he said, petting one squeaky fingertip line down the red vinyl arm of Leander's own suit.

Leander understood that, all right, but didn't quite dare to believe it.

Oberon was mercilessly silent, until Leander said, "Can we?"

The Septarch carried him all the way to the hangar bays.

Leander was highly embarrassed by this, until he noticed that anyone they passed was too busy trying to get out of the way to care. Then it was a secret delight, being held so high and so safe, carried along by that long liquid stride.

The torches became less frequent, and then vanished after a complex hatchway, the rough stone replaced by glossy hematite walls, invisibly illuminated in red and amber. Leander found it unsettling, after the determined medieval pageantry of what he supposed must be the residential part of the Sphere. Yes, he was going to *see* spaceships, but he was already IN the biggest one known to humankind.

After a long elevator ascent in which Oberon demanded and received several kisses, Leander was set on his feet before two massive gleaming black doors.

Beyond the doors was a vast, loud Wonderland.

Here was everything Leander had been unable to enjoy on *Goya*.

The ceiling was a rumor too far overhead to see. The floor was scarred concrete, and the ships...oh, the ships, endless identical lines of ships as liquid, as luxurious and heartlessly coalblack as everything of the Septarch's, the scarlet looped cross insignia gleaming at nose and tail. An army of workers in maintenance grays were swarming among these, and the array of languages tangled with the deafening squeal of cutters and other mechanical arias Leander could not identify. It was orderly chaos, punctuated by the orange scent of hot metal and the pale bland undertone of lubricant.

Oberon let him spin in a slow circle, trying and failing not to smile at his neckbreaking awe. After a moment he drew Leander close, led him through this fascinating maelstrom to a smaller, distant door.

Another lift, the trip too short for kisses. This time the doors slid open into silence. A private bay, and a single ship that looked as if it might be descended from the first, with many generations for improvement, a wicked predator shape like a hole cut in spacetime.

"Yours," Leander said.

"Mine," Oberon agreed. He went to the ship, stroked the side, and the cockpit opened like an exotic flower blooming. He pulled himself up and in with practiced ease, and offered Leander his hand.

After too long—fear and delight warring in his throat— Leander took it, and let himself be hoisted up. He discovered, much to his flustered confusion, that the ship was made to hold a single person. Oberon ignored this. Leander wondered if constant blushing could hurt you, and wondered if there was a *protocol* to how you were supposed to sit on a man's lap without—well.

The Septarch made no mention of this little set of internal errors, if he even noticed them. He strapped the harness around both himself and Leander. The cockpit closed again, silent and seamless, and they were sitting in an inkblack reality composed of the sounds of both of them breathing and the crimson gleam of the instrument panel.

Leander watched Oberon's hands eclipse the console, graceful and effortless. There was a faint impact, and then a rising hum. This made Leander nervous, along with his desperate excitement. A flickering blink, and the private hangar reappeared around them, as clear as if they'd been out in the open again. Then a heavier *thump*, from outside the ship, and the first green gleam of sunlight as the dome above them rolled open.

"Ready?" Oberon sounded like he was grinning.

He opened his mouth to say *probably not*, and found he was grinning too. "All my *life*. Go."

Oberon laughed.

And they went.

Leander expected a great roar of engines. Instead, a single profoundly satisfying bass note joined the purring vibration. The volume climbed, and then the *world* snatched itself away from them, as though it were falling, flung down into the void. He was clinging to Oberon's knees, dizzy with the feeling that he might join Omega and the Sphere in falling away into the dark if he lost his hold.

The sky blurred and dimmed above them, a flash of dull orange, a gleaming arc in tones of raspberry and currant, then deepest burgundy.

Then black.

Then he was alone with Oberon in a tight space, in endless black scattered with precious few lights, some near, some unspeakably distant. Omega was a grubby ball sulking far below. He was gasping with joy and panic, shaken, stricken. And then Oberon leaned forward, opened an interface for each hand, and they *really* went.

Leander had only ever felt anything like it on long-lost and deeply mourned drugs. His stomach rolled and fluttered in ways he associated with dangerous vehicular stunts in vacant lots, and it was delicious. He was helpless with delight.

They circled Moloch, stopped with that same, impossible,

simple *cessation* of motion, to the utter terror of a patrol of gunships, executed a set of rotations that made Leander cry out in as much fear as fun, and nosedived back at Omega. Oberon held the dive until Leander was close to hysterical with panicked laughter, and pulled up with a swoop that made him almost bite his tongue in half. "You're, showing off," he said, when they were cruising at a comparatively sane rate, the green sun at their backs.

"I am. Are you impressed?"

"I want to live here."

A soft bump to the back of his head. Was that a kiss? "You do live here."

"I meant on this ship, um...as a way to say, that..."

(you)

"...that it's amazing." Poetry it wasn't, but he was pretty sure he would never breathe correctly again, and he was so happy his face hurt. "I love it."

"Shall we go somewhere you can fly it?"

Leander's eyes went round. Oberon saw this in his pale reflection on the synthsteel dome above him. He drew them up in a lazy, elegant arc on a new course.

Leander watched two more worlds—entire *worlds*—pass them by, Oberon slowing enough to let him take them in. The first one was small and brown and lopsided, one a would-be gas giant swirling deep blue and violet bands from pole to pole.

"I like that one," Leander said, in an attempt to be polite, though honestly he found both planets dull. He was pointing until he realized that was ridiculous and put his hands back in his lap again, where they would remain for perhaps three seconds.

Oberon made a noise Leander was pretty sure was meant to be scornful. "Someday I'll take you to a nebulae field, or a binary system. Omega is a place no tourist would choose to visit."

Their speed increased—at least, the gas giant began to fling itself away from them at an alarming rate.

Leander was working out what he could of the controls, and the long-range was simple enough. "We're leaving the system?"

"Yes. Quite a lot of nothing in interstellar space."

"Yeah, my mom was going to teach me to drive the car in a...a, parking, lot."

Silence.

After eons, Oberon said, "Same principle."

Leander opened his mouth and only found more silence.

The ship did a graceful, musing spiral of a barrel roll.

"I have her genofile. And a neuro that the Republic would consider sorcery. I can give her back to you, if that would please you."

Too much. Leander thought it was bullshit when people kept fainting all over the place on telecasts when they got shocking news, but a gray haze caught him close for a very long moment. "Can you really?"

"I can."

This filled him with dread and dismay.

"I will not, unless that's your wish."

Wish, he thought. Such a tiny bashful word to carry so much meaning.

"She need not remember the tithe. Perhaps, if someone less unnerving than myself were to explain—"

Leander balled his hands into fists. "Why did you?"

Oberon coughed, and there was that soft bump again, but this time it stayed. He sat with his head leaning against Leander's. "It's not permitted."

"It's not like she could have *hurt* you. Can anything hurt you?"

"*Yes*," Oberon said, in a ragged, choking tone that convinced Leander the way only a demonstration could.

He could be hurt. He was hurting right now.

"She could not harm me, Leander, but I do not permit anyone to touch me without my leave, let alone assault me, or attempt to, or plan to. I do not permit anyone to have technology or resources that even *approach* mine, at any time. I could level civilization if I so chose, and build it again in any image I chose, and they know it. Instead I come, and I take what little I wish from them, and I leave them standing, and I do not interfere with their rampant idiocy. I am the Septarch. I am the apex predator, and I intend to stay that way."

That was what did it, at long last, put an end to Leander's time caught between guilt and grief and stranger things he had no business feeling, none of it at home with of the rest.

Apex predator.

He was not to blame, and Oberon was not to blame, and Soren, even, was not to blame. She might as well have tried to fight a whirlwind for possession of Leander. She'd do it again, a thousand times, and die a thousand times, because he was her son.

And because the Septarch was the Septarch.

He sniffled awhile, feeling things rearrange themselves in his mind. Then Leander put his hands over the dark places in the console that were Oberon's hands, and tangled their fingers together.

It took Oberon a moment to understand this meant he was forgiven, but Leander felt it happen, a relieved weight to the head leaning against him, an easing of the unearthly lines of Oberon's spider-limbs under him.

"I don't think I want to bring her...um, to do that, yet." he said, after a moment. "I don't think she's going to like you at all, no matter who explains it to her."

Oberon squeezed both Leander's hands once before disengaging to use the controls. "Most people don't."

They were going so fast now Leander avoided looking at the displays. "Is it safe?"

Oberon chose that moment to slow, and then drift to a stop, much to Leander's relief.

"Hmm?"

"To be this far out here. We don't have real suits."

"The lack of a suit would not kill me, but there's a membrane pack that I should remind them to test for you. Not many things could damage this ship, but as usual—" He touched the console, and indicated the long-range so that Leander didn't miss the flawless V of tiny red gunships that materialized at their immediate six. The Septarch let Leander goggle for a moment, and then signaled his guards to fall away.

He took Leander's hands again. This time he drew them to the console, and left them there.

"Fly," he said.

Leander supposed that was an order.

To call him shaky at first, would have been generous. "I'll break it."

"You can't break it. I doubt I could break it if I tried."

Leander dared the tiniest bit of speed, daunting in this empty place with little to compare his motion to. "I'll hit something."

"That would be a feat, here, one I'd like to see. Do you want to roll, or not?"

"Maybe not this many ways at once."

Oberon reached over his shoulder. "It's here, all three planes at once. Intuitive," he said, and demonstrated, the ship obeying his hand.

The ease of the gesture made Leander shiver with the understanding of how *tiny* he was, how *young*, of how little he knew after fourteen years, when Oberon had *centuries* on him. It was impossible to ignore how trapped he was in such a small space, alone with this

(monster)

man who could do anything to him, everything to him.

(No one could save me) (I'm safe here)

He was drowning in Oberon's scent, mildew and chocolate, myrrh and hot metal. Leander wondered what Oberon might do if he bit him again, took hold of one of those whipcord wrists and drew it to his mouth, sank his teeth hard until he could taste that scent.

Flying was exhausting, at least when you were new and excited and distracted. He was far from hopeless, or so Oberon proclaimed him after twenty minutes or so with no disasters. Leander was sure this was understatement, and also sure he would be about fifty times better at piloting without Oberon over, under, and around him.

The Septarch guided him into turning them back towards

(home)

Omega, then took the controls. Leander settled back into his lap, relieved but a little disappointed. Both sensations vanished, when Oberon lit a new array on the console, and a new set of silent impacts hummed through the ship in reply.

"There."

Leander would have heard the teeth in that word, even if he couldn't see Oberon's reflection in the glass.

"Now we can shoot something."

Leander decided after awhile, with some disappointment, that

Oberon was teasing him about the guns. He was close to dozing, soothed by the warmth of the Septarch, the drifting array of distant starlight, the hypnotic, subaudible purring of flawless machinery around them.

Then they changed course in a motion that was almost a jerk, instead of Oberon's usual smooth, sure patience. Leander opened his eyes to find them hurtling towards what the scanners displayed as a cluster of irregular objects on no particular heading.

"Asteroids?" Leander asked. He was sure he'd chosen the wrong word.

"Rocks. Scientists have about five thousand different names when one would do: rocks."

It was, indeed, a rock that loomed ahead of them, as Oberon had said, lit in spooky high-contrast by the ship's bank of external lights and doing an impressive imitation of Leander's random-axis rolling. There was a sudden change in the ship's background noise, a terrifying sense of power building to a climax. He felt Oberon go still, exhale, saw him move one finger on the controls.

A silent bluegreen pulse left the nose of the ship, billowing outward and forward like a piece of an aurora, like the ghost of silk ribbons scattered on rushing water. No roar, no expected blaze of fire, only an ease in that noise and tension, a sense of softening, subsiding. It reminded Leander of the sound you made when pulling off boots after a rough day: *ahhhh.*

Oberon's rock was large enough to interest mountain climbers planetside, but its billion-year career of being gargantuan and useless ended with neither bang nor whimper.

The bluegreen pulse became invisible, and when Leander was sure Oberon had missed (and terrified of this possibility, somehow) the rock...ceased.

No roar, no fire. Cohesion perfect in one instant and nonexistent the next. A cloud of billowing dust lit in a warm white wedge, like dust in a sunbeam.

Instantaneous and permanent past tense.

Radio. Live transmission.

Oberon did a playful roll through the debris.

"You shoot, and I'll fly."

Leander's succeeded in *not* screeching in ecstasy, but his hands went to the controls so fast he was surprised there wasn't a sonic boom.

He thought, *fire where they're about to be.*

It worked the same as it did with a bow and arrow. He could not contain a crow of triumph when the first one disintegrated.

Or the second. Or the third.

He missed two of twenty-six shots, and one of those he clipped so that part of it vanished and there was a cut as smooth as a razor had left it through one spinning end of the tumbling survivor.

Leander shook his head. "How many like that, before you'd have to...reload, refuel?"

"Thousands."

"Would it...would it do that to a planet?"

Silence.

"Not destroy it, no. A moon, maybe. A city, oh yes. A.....colony."

This was treacherous ground. Leander could feel that same tension in Oberon, those long limbs around him again more cage than cradle. He was beginning to know what that meant. A wound.

And he suspected Oberon had spent centuries, at this point, making damn sure Cayle never saw even half of his wounds.

Oberon's clawed hands left the controls to unfasten the harness that was around them both. He spent a few seconds leaning so far forward so that they were both crowded and thumped and awkward (though only Leander felt the need to giggle about it) to reach a compartment near the floor on the port side. Leander was not at all surprised to see him retrieve a pipe like the one he'd taken for sculpture in Oberon's office.

"Zion 4?"

Does it hurt here? Little bit?

A click, and a new scent in the cockpit, familiar, opium and marijuana and the bright plastic-sweet scent of an indole.

"Zion 4," the Septarch agreed.

Leander took the pipe when it was presented to him, but did not inhale. "Mars?"

Oberon was locked tight under him, motionless. "No." Sharp and narrow, gritted out through his teeth, riding on smoke.

Leander knew he would step on a land mine any minute now,

at which point Oberon would possibly eject him into space. He decided he'd rather die stoned, and hit the pipe twice in rapid succession.

And waited.

Oberon took back his pipe. A moment later, more words in smoke, drifting around Leander's head.

"The Sphere, for the Samar colony, and for Omega. A gunship will put a serious kink in your civilization plans, and enough of them are perfectly adequate for a mass extinction, but they won't destroy the planet itself, or render it unrecoverable."

Click of the pipe.

"You won't find so much as a microbe on Omega, outside my Sphere. Or within fifty kilometers of the Samar Crater."

This would have been seen as threats, as boasting, by any major media outlet in the whole of the Republic *or* the Colonies, but Leander knew it was not.

Because he knew a secret now.

Can anything hurt you?

Yes.

"I could've left nothing but holes in the sky," Oberon said. This, too, should have sounded hostile, arrogant, but it didn't. It sounded tired, exasperated and sad. "I chose to leave the warnings."

Leander came to one of those physical decisions Oberon inspired in him, a reply without analysis and without words. He arched his back, happy to be free of the harness, and reached back behind his own head. He managed to cup Oberon's neck, and arch upward to lean their heads together again, one of the only feasible forms of embrace in a single-seater gunship.

It was completely unsatisfactory, and it was unthinkable to end it. Finally Leander said, "Do you think I could....maybe...um, turn around?"

Oberon laughed, close to his neck, sending a ricochet of shudders through him. "I have no idea. Let's try."

The pipe vanished in the resulting debacle, and the struggle left Leander stricken with helpless giggles. Oberon keyed on an interior light, a pale red blaze after so much darkness. This helped a little. Leander managed to kneel up, and from there it was a controlled fall and an inadvertent wrestling match.

The end result was several new bruises to add to Leander's collection, utterly worthwhile once he was straddling Oberon's lap, and could hug him properly.

He wanted to steal kisses of his own, but Oberon was hesitant. He said, "Lean back a second," and reached up to his right eye with his fingertips. When he took his hand away, Leander nearly screamed in shock.

The ink-black of Oberon's right eye was gone. That eye was now a complicated glittering mesh, silver painted a baleful red in this carmine light.

"What happened?"

"They're UV shields. To protect the implants. Light will damage them eventually." Oberon explained, slipping out the other one, pondering them a moment and then flicking them aside to fall where they might. "They're also quite unpleasant after I wear them for too long."

Later, Leander would notice that Oberon had swerved around that question, but at the moment he had more pressing curiosities. "Are you a robot?"

Oberon laughed at that. "No. Cyborg, though I think that's fallen out of fashion. I was born as human as you were. These, and my lungs, heart, other things are implants, or have been modified, like my bones, my skin. Immortality comes at a price."

"What about...um..."

Leander's eyes were drawn downward to the subject of his question. Oberon laughed. "No. That's flesh. I saw no need for improvements."

Leander leaned forward again, hesitant, his curiosity about the implants too strong to resist. "Can I see?"

"My eyes, maybe. Letting you see the rest would require extensive surgery." Oberon reached past him, made the interior light brighten.

Leander peered closer at these new eyes. What would have been the white of a human eye was like a spherical circuit board, and little flashes of electricity leapt from one node to the other. The iris was miniscule slats of metal, and as he watched it spiraled shut like a valve or a pinwheel. He leaned back, startled. "Did you do that on purpose?"

Oberon did it with both eyes, slower. He wasn't smiling. "Does it disgust you?"

"Of course not!" He was appalled at the idea anyone could react with disgust. He drew in a long, stunned breath, in reverence for the brilliance that had gone into creating these marvelous eyes. The twin intricacies were different from the canopy of stars, different from seeing with your own eyes that other planets were real. They looked both impossibly futuristic and impossibly *old*, a priceless set of alien antiques that belonged in a museum made of marble floors, velvet ropes and low voices.

"They're beautiful. Unbelievable. How do they—" Leander reached up with one curious finger, without thinking. He pulled his hand back, blushing. "Sorry."

Oberon hesitated, and then took Leander's hand and put it on his face. "You can touch if you want to."

"Oh, I want to." Underneath this sense of awe was a warm busy feeling, far less noble, that Leander was beginning to understand was sexual.

He stroked Oberon's eyelid, the faint, flawless eyebrow, before he wet his finger in his mouth and touched the eye itself near the outer corner. There was a soft transparent covering, slick and warm like flesh. He traced around the iris. He could feel energy thrumming under his fingertip, and it seemed the same to him as the eager, kinetic quiver in ship around them, one vibratory field in which almost anything was possible.

Oberon made a low noise, deep in his throat. Leander stopped, about to apologize, and Oberon's hand closed over his, hard, and drew his fingers back to his eye.

"Does it hurt?" Leander breathed, fascinated.

"Yes. It hurts. Don't stop."

He pulled back Oberon's lower eyelid, to see how far in the implant went. He expected an edge, but the sclera persisted and then submerged like sand meeting sea. Under the eyeball there was dark pink flesh like in Leander's own eye. He scratched his fingernail along it, seeking an edge to the illusion.

Oberon groaned, and pulled Leander hard against him, grinding up into him. His head fell back, and Leander pushed back his hair and held his eye wide open with his fingertips. He wanted to—kiss?—but that didn't seem quite right at all.

Instead he decided to touch with the tip of his tongue.

Touch, and then stroke.

He could *taste* this, not quite like tears, an exotic undertaste that made him think of the smell inside the hangar bay, the scent of *mechanical,* and then his brain gave him a flickersense of junkyards, gasoline and rust and mysteries, and Leander knew machines.

Leander was crazy about machines.

His fear dissolved into fascination and appetite. The shuddering wonder under his tongue made him think of

(butterflies)

impossibly intricate gears, engines small enough to swallow whole, of that bluegreen pulse that left nothing but dust in its wake.

Leander's universe collapsed into this wet intersection, mapping the miniature dome of the iris, feeling it wander under his tongue.

It wasn't enough.

He licked Oberon's eyelashes. "I want you to fuck me while I do this."

That was wrong, wasn't it? You weren't supposed to just *say* that, were you?

Apparently wrong was fine, here. Oberon said "Oh, you're *perfect,*" and dug his fingernails into Leander's back.

That was cheating. Leander made a rolling, longing noise that Oberon could *feel* through the tongue in his eye. Oberon's response was a grating hiss that shaped no words.

I'm making him do that.

Leander held Oberon's eye open wider, licking with delicate violent strokes. He drew in a damp lungful of air around his tongue, to sustain that noise that pleased Oberon so utterly. The Septarch shuddered under him, inspiring new games with breath and moisture that made him claw harder. Leander realized he was leaving one eye bereft, and switched sides, leaving a damp finger on the right side still, in place of his tongue, wanting

(all)

to see if he could make Oberon as insane as the Septarch could make him.

More of that insistent grating hiss. Oberon heaved up

underneath him, and Leander understood. He put his hand between them and rubbed hard, clumsy, between lack of space and lack of expertise. Oberon's uncooperative flight suit was no help. He couldn't even find anything *to* unfasten. "Fuck," he said, exasperated, and then laughed because that was exactly what they were failing to do.

Oberon swatted Leander's hands aside to unfasten his own pants. Leander knelt up to let him manage it, unzipped his suit, and said, "Fuck!" again, this time with more vehemence. He would never get this thing off, or even down, not like this. Why couldn't they have put him in that ridiculous tissue-paper silk today?

Now Oberon's cock was between them, silken and bare and frighteningly hard. Before Leander could explain the problem Oberon solved it with violence, seizing the vinyl with both hands, destroying it ripping slashes that left burning lines on the skin beneath.

Silence again, save for unsteady breathing from both of them.

Oberon's hands were on his hips, pushing him down, and Leander had one hand between them, trying and failing to help, mouth open against Oberon's neck.

One shove, and one slide, and Oberon was inside him, excruciating and exquisite.

Leander was pulling his head down, wanting his mouth against those eyes again, wanting that mechanical taste, that inhuman electricity. Oberon stayed in him, merciless and deep, grinding with slow ferocious rolls of his hips. He was holding Leander too hard, hurting him, bruising his flesh against his bones. Leander found that he loved this, that he should be so fragile, and yet so capable of eroding Oberon's frozen surface to find this blazing hunger behind it.

At last this near-motionless friction was not enough, and Oberon leaned his head away from Leander's mouth, lifted him by his hips, slammed him down hard, again and again. Leander's hands found his own cock, too far gone to give a damn if that, too, was wrong.

He came with his teeth failing to hold back a scream, came hard and for too long, came thinking, *fly.*

The gunship drifted.

They were tangled, sticky. Leander was still straddling him, though there was more in it now of koala than harlot.

Oberon shut everything off, even the console lights, leaving them in darkness except for the scattered glory of stars.

Leander held him that way while the galaxies waltzed around them.

An unimaginable distance away, Paul was sitting at the house terminal. He was drinking, yes, but from a glass this time, not the bottle, and when he raised it to his lips the ice cubes in it did not chatter.

He was searching the Undernet, for the first time in all his life, for a way to acquire something Leander had just begun to receive.

Flying lessons.

"He wants me to wear *that*?"

Theren dropped an armload of gray Earth Standard-issue clothes on Leander's bed. Pants and shirt. His school uniform. "Yes. And no paint."

Camille had not spoken to Leander since he'd come in some days earlier, wearing the shredded remains of a favorite-red vinyl suit, an array of favorite-red clawmarks, and the sort of smile he'd have needed drugs to achieve on Earth. Now she was lying on her bed, pretending to stare up at the ceiling, but this exchange made her exhale in one indignant puff and fling herself over onto her side, her back to them, dragging her pillow over her head for good measure. Leander and Theren both ignored her.

After a moment of study, he concluded Theren was serious. Leander shrugged, and carried the armload of clothes behind the curtain. This was a visual lie for the sake of the hypothetical cameras. He took off the boring white silk that he now thought of as pajamas, chewing the inside of his cheek to keep from giggling. A schoolboy fetish? Really? How was he going to manage not to laugh? It was just so...so *Earth*. So constant in the kind of porn that had convinced him he didn't enjoy porn. So unlike anything he'd have guessed Oberon might want.

So, very unlike.

So very unlike that maybe that was not, in fact, what Oberon wanted from him at all.

The urge to giggle vanished.

He lost the ability to operate buttons. His stomach did that slow gliding roll again, and this time it was composed almost entirely of fear.

Almost.

Twenty-three minutes later, Leander was in Oberon's front room, fidgeting in the embarrassing outfit. It felt more like a costume than a uniform, coarse and badly made. Weird how not-so-long ago, he'd felt the other way around, wearing silk and vinyl.

A light clicked on in the bedroom, deep red, just enough light for him to see Oberon's silhouette in the doorway.

Just enough for Leander to see what he was holding.

He turned in one frantic motion and began struggling with the latch in the door behind him.

"It's locked. And if it wasn't, my guards would bring you back before you made it out of the corridor."

Oberon stepped out of the doorway, and the door to the bedroom closed behind him. Utter darkness.

Leander couldn't see him at all, couldn't hear him, had no idea how close he might be. He stood with his back pressed against the door. "Get away."

"It's the same one. I had it shipped from Earth," he said, so close that Leander tried to run. He tripped almost at once, sprawled hard on the stone floor in the dark.

"You don't understand. It's not funny," he cried out at the room.

And Oberon had him, and Leander screamed and kicked, and his arms were pinned at his side, and he could feel the paddle cold against his leg, still in Oberon's hand. Leander kicked harder with no effect at all. "I won't let you!"

"*Let* me?" Bright with humor, as though this were absurd.

He gave up kicking, sagged in Oberon's arms. "You don't *understand*," Leander repeated, breathless and hurting. "I can't."

Oberon kissed him.

Leander kept his mouth closed and tried to turn his face away for an eternity, but he couldn't keep it up.

He gave in, his mouth open.

Oberon said against his lips, "I want to be the most terrible thing that's ever happened to you. Can you understand that? I want to be the only nightmare you ever have."

It left him stricken, breath motionless in his throat.

Oberon set him on his feet, and reached past him and touched the wall control. The bedroom door opened behind them, casting dim scarlet light into the room. "Go in there and wait for me," he said, his voice like Halloween.

"Bastard," Leander mumbled, his lips paralyzed. He covered his face and turned away, stumbled into the bedroom and lay on the bed, numb. He could hear them, in his head, hundreds of children. They were never on your side.

He heard footsteps, felt the mattress sink beside him. He cringed, his arms covering his head.

He felt it on his ankle, cold and wicked, sliding up along his leg, over his ass, up his spine, against the back of his neck. He was crying again, and the paddle was gone, and Oberon drew him up close, and whispered, "How did they do it?"

"Why? Why do you have to do this? Why are you like this?"

"Tell me how."

"Please," he said his chest hitching. "I'll suck you again. You can fuck me as hard as you want. Please not this."

"Leander."

"Damn you anyway!" Leander cried at him, and he struggled again, his foot shoving the paddle across the bed, but Oberon had his wrists, and he reached under the back of Leander's legs and held him cradled that way, rocking him.

Leander gave up. "What does it matter? Go ahead and do it. I can't stop you. Get it over with," he sobbed, in staccato. "And don't fucking hold me like you're being nice to me when you're not!"

Oberon murmured into his hair. All Leander caught was *tears* and *terror*. Then he said, "Tell me how."

"You want to know how?" he snapped, squirming one hand free and scrubbing at his face. "How. Okay, here's how. They sat me in this little room and then this guy comes in with that goddamned paddle you have, and he grabs me by the collar. And I realize, he's going to hit me. This motherfucker twice my size I've never seen before in my life is going to hit me. And just when I think it can't get any worse, he fucking drags me into the auditorium. And there are a million kids there. The principal's telling them all about me, and he's holding my drawing, and he turned and looked at me like he hated me. And I didn't even know why."

Leander drew in a long, unsteady breath. "So then they make me take my pants down, and lean over this chair. That's when I knew it was going to be bad. They always make you grab your ankles, even girls. They use the chair if they think you're going to fall."

He didn't say anything else for a long time. Then, he said, "That's how they did it, all right?"

Oberon had his hand up the back of Leander's shirt, tracing tiny circles on the skin over his spine. "How many?"

"Damn it—"

"How many times?"

"Fifty, all right? You know how I know that? They had every fucking person there counting. Backwards. From fifty."

He was nuzzled in reward for that. "Did you cry out?"

"I hate you."

"Did—"

"No. I didn't. I sort of screamed with just air, but I didn't make a sound they could hear. Because I knew they wanted me to. Because they would *win* if I did."

Oberon kissed him hard, and let him go.

He got up and left the room.

Leander closed his eyes, and he heard a scraping sound, and it *couldn't* be what he thought it was.

He sat up.

Oberon dragged one of the heavy chairs from his small dining table into the bedroom, set it at the foot of the bed. "Stand up," he said, the paddle in his hand.

Leander swallowed, and then he stood up.

He had no choice, he reasoned. At least this was for only Oberon's eyes, though of course there would be cameras. He would not think about those. He would tell himself he had to, and he would not wonder why part of him wanted to see if he *could*. A challenge. A difficult hack, a risky sabotage.

He took two miniscule steps towards the chair. Oberon inclined his head, those onyx eyes expressionless and insectile, patient and infuriating. Leander tried to make a face, but instead his mouth trembled. "Will you promise not to do it like you hate me?"

He regretted it as soon as he said it, expected puzzlement or mockery or perhaps worse, sympathy, but Oberon only tilted that inhuman head another degree and said, "I promise."

That loosened something inside him, enough to move his feet, anyway. He made it all the way to the chair this time before he stopped.

"Look at me." More request than order.

He didn't want to look at Oberon, but he did, for the sake of how gently he'd been asked. He was caught again by that void of a gaze.

Oberon told him, "You can."

Just as softly, and with utter certainty.

Leander found that he could.

This chair was a great deal taller and more solid than the one at school. It was heavier than he was, and it had arms he could hold on to, so he had none of the previous fear of spilling over, chair and all. Once he succeeded in leaning over the back, he was on tiptoe.

He heard Oberon come closer, and closed his eyes. One of those long hands steadied him, and he opened his eyes in time to see the paddle set on the floor beside him. Oberon unfastened his pants and drew them down. He chewed his lip at this—the school had allowed him to leave his underwear on, but this was a perilous time to argue minor points.

"Turn your head so I can see your face."

Hideous. Leander made an anguished, exasperated noise, and turned his head in almost defiance. Oberon combed his hair back with his talons.

"Stay here with me. Not in the past, and not in your head. All right?"

The intense urge to say something flippant rose and fell in him. He couldn't do it, not with those eyes softened like that.

He isn't pretending to be nice to me. Not now, and not before.

He nodded. Swallowed.

"You do know that I don't hate you?"

That sounded almost forlorn. Leander nodded again, and felt a pang of remorse. "You know I don't....hate you..."

It was Oberon's turn to nod. "I know. You're angry and embarrassed and frightened, and that's exactly as it should be." He leaned in and licked Leander's cheek, making him smile a little in spite of himself. "You may change your mind in a minute, though," he added, too close to Leander's ear.

He straightened, and Leander closed his eyes again, waited to be forbidden this, and when he wasn't, just...waited.

Nothing.

"Don't," he said, miserable. "If you're going to do it, do it."

"Perfect boy. I was waiting for that."

Cold, smooth wood against his ass.

A pat, a pause.

The first blow brought his head up, snapped his eyes open in horrified understanding. That was too hard, *much* too hard, much harder than they'd hit him in school and that had been pretty fucking hard to begin with. He drew in a breath and the second blow drove it out of him in a tight, high sound he could not prevent.

He endured the third in silence. The fourth was too much.

He made an ugly angry wail, hid his face in reflex.

"No." Oberon leaned over him, turned his head back with one gentle hand. "And you don't have to fight that, beautiful boy. Cry out all you like. There's no one to hear you but me, and I'll never tell."

"You're not supposed to," he said, his words uneven and his mouth wet. "It means that you're weak."

"No one decides 'supposed to' here but me, and I am well aware that you are far from weak."

There was no arguing with *that* logic. He wanted to ask about *far from weak*, but Oberon swung again, and then again, and thought, along with silence, became impossible.

At first he managed a shout or a shriek, or something deeper and lower. Each stroke was regular, neither quick nor slow. He had time for several breaths between them. Soon enough he lost control, there, too, unable to keep little hitches of misery and pain from escaping out into the world.

He understood now why Oberon had told him to *stay with me.* This was different from what had happened to him at school, and yet familiar enough to rouse dusty nightmares in his head. It helped to keep his eyes on the glow of the fireplace on the rug, the sleeve of Oberon's robe. He *did* succeed in not reaching behind himself, though the instinct to do so was enormous and deafening. His terror of something happening to his

(art)

hands was louder still, and he clung to the arms of the chair like he was trying to keep from getting sucked out of an airlock.

Soon enough he reached another familiar place, that point at which it went from awful to excruciating, because he was fresh out of places that weren't already bruised. One spot in particular—the right side of his ass, where the end of the paddle was catching him—was an utter horror, and he spent the short gasping space between blows praying the next one would not catch him there. Sometimes he was spared, sometimes not.

Three successive blows landed *right* where he wished they wouldn't. A storm rose in his throat that he thought was rage, until he burst into messy tears.

That has to be what he wanted. Now he'll stop.

Oberon made a soft sound at him, a crooning hum low in his throat.

He did not stop.

It was that intolerable spot that made Leander straighten twice. Each time Oberon stopped swinging and looked at him, waiting, not saying a word, and when Leander leaned over the chair again he went on hitting him.

Leander lost count long past fifty.

The third time his hands and knees surrendered in the same instant. He crumpled to the floor like a blanket cast out of bed.

"Leander."

"I can't," he rasped. Now Oberon would insist that he could, and he would be right, and Oberon would go on hitting him and he would lose whatever was left of his mind.

"Try."

He did try, and he made it up onto his hands and knees. His stomach knotted, and he gritted his teeth, but it didn't help. He puked until he was choking up bile. He felt Oberon beside him, those long hands steadying him again, his hair held out of his face. He made one broken piece of humiliated wail at this, a protest Oberon ignored.

He managed to push himself away from his mess before his arms gave out, and lay with his face pressed hard into the cold floor, too empty of everything even for tears.

Oberon knelt beside Leander again, probing at his neck until he found the pulse. A pause, long enough for counting. Steady and strong, and already slowing.

He dragged the rug over from in front of the fireplace, and dropped it over the vomit so that Leander wouldn't have to look at it. He picked him up, with infinite care, and put him on the bed on his stomach, and pulled his pants from around his ankles, and took off the gray shirt, and pitched both into the fireplace.

Leander opened his eyes, and watched him break the paddle over his knee, and toss it in after his clothes. He closed his eyes again then, and smiled.

Oberon was a wreck of his own. Pride and love and lust and worry were a maelstrom in his chest, and the result was this unfamiliar *tenderness* that he could not resist.

He brought a cold wet cloth, and a glass of water from the bathroom. Leander wanted to take the glass from him, but he didn't permit that, holding it for him to take measured sips, and then wiped the boy's face, mouth, neck.

"Was it like that?" he asked, stroking Leander's hair.

A long silence, in which Leander was presumably thinking. "No," he said at last, so low Oberon had to lean even closer. "It was nothing like that."

He reached out with one arm, groped in the air as though his targeting system was shot, until Oberon understood what he wanted and lay beside him, propped on one elbow, careful not to jostle him. He pressed kisses on Leander's spine, the nape of his neck, his hair, rubbed his back and his shoulders, seeking knotted, exhausted places, humming low in his throat because the boy seemed to find that calming. He could sense the chemicals beginning to untangle Leander, could almost feel the aftershocks of fight or flight dissolving under his hands.

"You have no idea how I cherish you. I have never had a slave even remotely like you."

That was true, but but a mere scratch in the surface of what he wanted to say. But Leander wriggled closer until his entire side was pressed against Oberon, and then sighed, the remaining tension melting out of him like snow in a sunbeam.

"I thought you were going to kill me. I thought...you weren't ever going to stop," he said, and began to cry again, ragged, like a small tired child.

Oberon closed his eyes, and found that they were *wet*, which he had most certainly not authorized. Things were happening in his chest that made him wonder if he needed new hardware.

"I'm just beginning to unmake you."

Leander made a strangled sound at that, that wasn't quite a word, and then *"Beginning* to?"

Oberon laughed a little at the outraged disbelief in that. He put his hand at Leander's waist, but no lower. "Does it hurt?"

"Fuck you. How can you even ask me that?"

Oberon felt his smile widen. This boy had *infected* him with happiness, frequent and unreasonable and unstoppable. "The minute I tell you I cherish you, you think you can talk to me all kinds of ways," he said, and moved his fingertips down, past Leander's waist, placing his palm flat on his buttocks.

"What color were your eyes before?"

Oberon's smile disappeared without a trace. "Brown," he whispered, after too long a pause. There was a malfunction in his throat. "They were brown."

He got up, his fingers trailing down the back of Leander's leg, went to an ebony bureau and rummaged through until he found a flat leather case. He opened it. Seated in a red velvet lining were a syringe and several vials.

He chose a vial, filled a syringe, added a dash from a second vial, tapped out the bubble. Leander watched him. "What is it?"

"It's for pain," he said, kneeling by the bed. "And to calm you a little. Give me your arm."

"Why?"

"Because, Leander, I can't give it to you in your ass right now. You're a bruise from your waist to your knees. You're bleeding in places."

"Why not?"

Oberon saw that he was serious. "I could really get to like you."

He drove the needle in hard, wringing a cry out of Leander. He chose the worst place, where the right cheek of the boy's buttocks met with the back of his thigh. The bruises there were already darkening to a furious blackviolet. He pushed the plunger in slow, and pulled it out and rubbed the knot with his fingers, put his mouth over the puncture and sucked once, hard, chemicals numbing his mouth. Leander's back arched, pushing him closer.

Oberon loaded the syringe again for himself. "I want to do it," Leander said, still watching him.

He put the needle in the crook of his arm, since he was several centuries beyond the point where anything but mainlining would do. He leaned over and held it steady, and let Leander push the plunger in. "Really get to like you," he murmured again, his eyes rolling back.

He put the syringe back in its case, shoved it in the drawer and crawled into bed. "Move your legs apart," he whispered to Leander, and he wet two fingers in his mouth and pushed them up inside him, moving close, his face against the boy's ribs. "You're mine now. There's nothing you can do to get away."

Leander whimpered, low in his chest. "Say that again."

"Mine. You'll never get away. Nothing can stop me. No one will save you. I'll do things to you that will make you forget this ever happened."

"I won't forget," the boy whispered, and added with delightful ferocity, "I don't want you to ever send for Camille again. I hate her."

He wants me to do this? Me? And only to him?

Oberon pushed his fingers in deeper, until he found the place inside where Leander was sticky, and hot enough to burn him. "There is no Camille."

The boy made a rolling, rise-and-fall sound in his chest that Oberon knew he would lose sleep replaying in his head. He tried to arch his back, and gave this up as a bad idea at once.

"Shhh, no, precious. Lie still." He kept drawing that same, slow internal circle, petted Leander with his free hand until the boy relaxed again. He arranged himself between Leander's knees, cheek pillowed against warm bruised flesh, until the boy was mewling and clenching around his fingers, doing adorable things with his toes against the bedspread.

"Don't tease," Leander pleaded, drugs and pleasure blurring the words.

"No, not a tease. A reward."

Leander made a muffled sound that was cobbled together from laugh and whine. Oberon coaxed Leander to raise up, enough to make room for his hand around the boy's cock, and he keychanged back into that fluid sinewave moan.

Oberon licked the worst bruise. Set his teeth against it, a wordless threat that made Leander's breath come faster. He was slow, and patient, and merciless. When he felt Leander tighten inside, an instant from orgasm, he finally let himself bite.

Theren waited outside with a stretcher, looking at his feet while Oberon kissed Leander goodbye. "Take him to Cayle," Oberon said, still looking at the boy.

Leander turned and saw the stretcher. He whirled back to Oberon and clung, his eyes were filling with tears. "I don't want to go."

"He has to look at you. I might have—"

"Come with me. Please. I'll go if you come with me."

He wants me there. I did that to him, and he wants me there to...what? Comfort him? Guard him?

"If I go, will you do as Cayle asks?"

"Yes," Leander promised.

Theren was fine until Cayle undressed Leander, and he saw the bruises.

He stood drymouthed and longing to leave, but for whatever reason Oberon had not dismissed him. Oversight, or cruelty, the result was the same. He stood obedient and silent, and watched Cayle. The doctor spoke to Leander at first, his voice low and gentle, and the boy's face went from furious and defensive to a hesitant, reluctant trust.

Theren could hear them, but he didn't understand a word of it. He was blinded by the bruises, bleeding in places—bleeding, for Christ's sake—and the boy's quiet consent to being examined, and the occasional looks of worship and hunger that he gave Oberon.

The way he looks at him. He thinks he's in love. That's the bastard that did this to him, and he thinks he's in love. What kind of a man are you to watch this happen?

He sat there, sick and still. He didn't move.

The answer, of course, was no kind.

ars longa vita brevis

When Leander got back to his cell he stared, stunned.

His little table and chair had been replaced.

Now there was a drawing table with a gooseneck lamp, laden with little cubbyholes filled with pencils, paint, and brushes. A small easel was beside it. There was a tall stack of expensive smooth paper, and an intricate box of deep red polished wood on at the foot of his bed.

Inside the box was his journal.

He seized it, and then he hugged it to chest, aware it was ridiculous and irrational, but so happy to have it back that he didn't care. He flipped it open. All there. But there was elegant, angular handwriting in red ink on the first blank page.

Leander,

There's nothing wrong with you. You're like me. Some of us were born different. Better, maybe, than everyone else.

Yes, I read your journal.

I also changed your security status.

You can access most consoles in the Sphere, now, as well as open your cell and almost every other door in this section.

Come to my room tonight. I'm sure you know the way by now.

There are pictures for you in the envelope to add to your collection. I don't know if you'll like them, but I suspect you will.

Until tonight.

There was no other signature, only the looped cross in ink the color of blood, arrow pointing down, down down.

Leander did not know he was smiling.

In the box was an envelope.

Photographs. Actual paper photographs, thick and glossy and slippery in his hands.

It was Jyana.

And Oberon.

He looked at them for a long time.

There was a battle going on inside him.

The part of him that couldn't answer when Oberon had asked, *Should I let him fuck her?* was screaming.

In the end, the screaming was drowned out.

Leander got up, carrying the photographs. He went to the drawing table and sat in the little chair, and he tilted the table up at a sharp angle, and set the photographs in the little pencil tray.

He picked up a dark red pencil, and began to draw.

"Leander."

He was startled out of it. His hand was one terrible cramp, and his neck and his back and his eyes were aching.

Oberon was standing outside his cell, watching him with his eyes soft and his mouth amused. "It's late. I waited for you."

"Oh, God...I'm sorry, I forgot, and I was..." He was embarrassed, flustered, groping for a blank sheet of paper and putting it in front of his half-finished sketch. He spared a glance for Camille, but she was heavily drugged and had been motionless and silent for hours, for which he was grateful. Peace and quiet. "How long have you been there?"

"A few minutes. You didn't even know I was here. Your face..." Oberon stopped, made a sound as if he was clearing his throat. "You were absolutely absorbed in what you were doing. And you were talking to yourself, but I couldn't understand any of it."

"I never got to draw like this before. Really draw, whatever I want, with supplies like these. The colors are perfect, and they don't skip or gouge..." Leander stopped. He was babbling. He blushed, feeling like an idiot. "I guess...thank you."

Oberon opened the door. Leander was rubbing his cramped hand, closing and opening the fingers, and Oberon's fingers wrapped around his. "Don't thank me. You needed these things."

"How much of it did you see?"

"Don't worry. I was watching you, not what you were doing. I didn't look at it. It's...unfair to do that until it's finished."

"Yes. Exactly," Leander said. "But I want you to see it when it is. Finished, I mean."

Oberon nodded. "I could show you some of my...work. If you want."

Leander tried to stand. His feet were asleep, and he had to clutch at Oberon to keep from sitting down again. "Of course I want to. Is it more sculptures, like the one in your room?"

"Some of it. It's...unpleasant," Oberon warned him.

Leander sighed. "When are you going to figure out that I don't see things the way the rest of them do?"

"I've figured it out," he said, and they were leaving the Gallery. "I don't know if I believe it yet."

He didn't *dare* to believe it yet.

The entrance to the Museum was a pair of vast double doors, like the doors of a cathedral. There was no keypad. Oberon pulled one of them open, and it swung outward without a sound. He let Leander go in first.

A thousand things rushed into his mouth, wanting to be said.

No. I want to see him react, without interference.

They were in the vestibule, and there were twin torches, and a silver bowl on a stand, filled with dark liquid. Leander went to this, dipped his fingers in, sniffed at them. And then he smiled, and touched his forehead, and his throat, and his fingers left crimson smears, and he turned to Oberon, and went up on tiptoe, and marked him the same way, and left a red thumbprint on his mouth. "Leander, don't," he said, breathing hard.

Leander had already turned. On the black wall above there was a skeleton, spread out flat, each bone separated from the other, laid out in careful precise order. "Can I?" he whispered, raising one hand, hesitating.

"Go ahead. It's not just for looking. None of it is."

"How did you do it?"

"I separated each joint from the others. Every one of them. The skull was the hardest part. The joints there are completely fused, and it kept splintering on me. I kept ruining it after I had everything else done, and it took about a week each time, and it's not easy to get them clean. Chemicals will ruin the bone after a year or two. You have to use water, mostly, and sodium bicarbonate, and really scrub. Finally it occurred to me to do the skull first, and—"

He stopped. He couldn't remember the last time he'd spoken that many sentences in a row without most of them being orders. It was alluring, the idea of speaking entire thoughts that did not contain imperatives, knowing someone was listening.

Leander was running his fingers along ribs, the femur, and the tiny mosaic of teeth. "I guess you couldn't use a different skull."

"Mmm. No. That would be—" He searched for the word. "Incoherent. Not expressive at all." *Shaking! I am fucking shaking! Why?*

"What are these?"

"They're the bones from the inside of the ear."

Oberon could not believe how hard this was, how nervous it was making him. He was desperate to have this boy's...what? Approval? It was a new sensation, desiring something he could not take by force, and he was almost positive he didn't like it. Not at all.

Leander nodded, still entranced. "They look like...like pieces of sea shells." He turned, and looked at Oberon then, and said, "You could use ants."

Oberon blinked, not comprehending. "Ants? For what?"

"To clean them. Ants would do it and I don't think it would damage the bone at all. It might take them a couple of months, though."

He's faking that! He has to be! But how would he? Nobody can MAKE their mind work that way...

His heart was slamming into his ribs, and he said, "I never thought of that." It struck him hard, without warning. He was going to fall and he reached out wavering, covered his ears and went down on his knees.

He felt Leander put his arms around him, and the boy whispered, "It happens to you too, doesn't it?"

"What?" he said, his face against the boy's shoulder, and his mouth wasn't working right, and he was afraid he'd said *help*, and he said "What?" again, louder and with great care.

"I used to call it the Fury. It's like the world is too loud and too bright and big, and it's like the whole world is doing it on purpose, and it makes you so mad you can't even see, but it's scary, because it feels like you're—"

"Falling," Oberon finished. "And it hurts." He was breathing like the air was escaping through an open hatch. He felt Leander pulling at him, and he was lying on his back looking up at the dissected skeleton, and his head was resting in the boy's lap. Leander was stroking his hair, rubbing at his temples, tracing around his eye sockets. His fingers were cool and soft and gentle, and it...helped.

Nothing else had ever helped, except the heroin, and even that was never a sure thing.

"It's okay," Leander was saying, the way you would talk to a small child who was afraid...*very afraid*, he thought, and then oh God he thought he would start laughing, his throat was convulsing, and Leander put his hand there, over his throat, and it stopped, and it left him like a demon exorcised, and he was limp and still, eyes drifting closed.

He reached up and closed his hands over the boy's, and pulled them to his mouth and was kissing his fingers.

"...when you do it?"

"What?"

Leander's voice shook, but he was trying to be calm. "I said, how will you kill me when you do it?"

"I'm not," he whispered. "I'm not going to kill you."

He realized he meant it.

"Oh," said Leander, and then he didn't say anything.

"It's just that...if I did kill you..." This was a new concept for him, and he was struggling to find words for it. "If I did...you wouldn't be here anymore, ever again. I wouldn't like that. I wouldn't like it at all."

"Oh," Leander said again. "I wouldn't like it either. Not being here, I mean."

Beyond the vestibule there was a hall with a high vaulted ceiling, housing a dizzying array of illuminated displays.

There were airtight glass cases, with bodies sprawled inside,

211

each in various stages of mutilation and decomposition. "Event art," Oberon told Leander, and the boy laughed at that. "Why aren't you scared?" he asked.

"I don't know. It's like...I always knew there was a place like this. Part of me knows that I should be scared, but I'm not. I guess I should be puking or going crazy but I have no desire to do that." He shrugged. "I guess I'm weird."

"Were you always...like this?" *Like me?*

"I think so," the boy said, after a moment. "I think you're born that way. When I was really, really little, I remember—wow, that's incredible," he said, distracted. It was several skeletons wired together into a spider, each leg made of six femurs, and the body a careful assembly of ribcages, the head a human skull with the mouth redesigned, with the long bones from the palm of the hand sharpened and fitted there as fangs. The entire thing was hanging from the ceiling, swaying in a nonexistent breeze.

The boy made a nervous laugh. "Here I am in your museum, and I'm embarrassed to tell you this? I think we're both crazy." He thought a moment. "I was in my first year in school. I must have been about four. There was this other kid I hated. I still remember exactly how he looked. I don't know why I hated him. Now I think it was probably because I liked him, uh, like boys aren't supposed to like boys."

His voice became slow and careful. "I don't know where I got the idea. I never got to see or read anything like it. I invented this machine. In my head, I mean, not like, in a garage. It was this long factory, all chrome and rust in a big metal building. Gears and things. And what would happen was I would tie the kid down on this conveyor belt, naked, and once you started the machine there was no way to stop it. And it would pull you through and stick you full of needles. Everywhere."

He sounded like his throat was hurting. "And it was...sexual, I guess. The placement of the needles, I mean, yeah, but the effect it had on me...I would think about it, until I got every detail perfect, but sometimes I would have to stop thinking about it because of how weird it made me. I would feel like I itched all over. I wish I'd known how to jerk off. But I don't think that works when you're that little."

Oberon reached up and slipped out one of his UV shields, put it in his mouth to wet it, and slipped it back in. Leander watched this jealously. "Next time I want to do that," he said.

"Was it him you wanted to do that to, that kid...or yourself?"

Leander covered his face. "You know," he said, muffled behind his hands, "I always consciously thought about it being him, but what would make me so...so frantic...was imagining how it would feel if it were me."

He looked up at Oberon through his fingers. "Don't you dare. I'm still not entirely happy with you about the paddle. If you stick me full of needles I won't speak to you for a month."

That made Oberon laugh so hard he had to lean against a glass case of severed hands.

"It's not funny!"

That made it so funny that he was getting a headache, and his eyes were streaming. He reached for Leander, and laid his hand along the boy's face, thinking, *nothing ever makes me laugh.* "Don't ever change."

There were gigantic paintings, some of the canvases thirty feet across, and they were scenes of unimaginable torture. Leander stopped at one, turned his head sideways, leaned his whole body over to try and look at it upside down. "That has to be impossible."

"Not if you dislocate the hips, saw through the pelvic bone."

"What about shock?"

"Cayle is a chemical genius. You can do anything, unless you destroy the heart or the brain, or they bleed to death."

He's so calm about it, Oberon thought. *So matter-of-fact. And he wonders about shock at fourteen. What will he be like at twenty?*

Leander looked at him through his eyelashes, reading his mind. "I like the way you think." He stopped at another one, tongues nailed in a spiral to a piece of white oak. "Do you ever...regret any of it?"

"When I do it wrong. Or I get too...involved, and do it too quickly. Are you asking me about guilt?"

"I think so. I think that's what I mean."

Oberon shrugged. "What's the point? I'd eventually do it anyway. Why be miserable for weeks?"

"It makes you miserable if you don't do it?"

He nodded. "It's an addiction. Once you try it...once someone like us tries it...it's impossible to stop."

Someone like us, Leander thought, and it made him so happy, *us.* "Do you think..." he began, and he didn't know what he was asking.

"Yes. You could. And yes, you would love it." Oberon told him. "And no, you'd never be able to stop."

"What am I to you?" Leander asked, afraid of the answer.

"Lover," Oberon said, pulling him close, pushing his head back, and the boy was looking at the bone spider when he felt Oberon's teeth. "You're my lover. The first one I've had in centuries."

"Centuries," Leander said, suitably awed. "Weren't you lonely?"

Oberon bit harder, rather than answer with *every single second of every single day.* He settled on, "Not anymore."

Leander cupped his head, raised his wounded throat into the Septarch's teeth, and corrected him.

"Not ever again."

Oberon closed his eyes. He thought *this is madness, this will end as it always does,* and decided to ignore it.

They paused in front of a long glass case, with tiny bones strewn over black velvet. Oberon had intended it to be reminiscent of a starfield. Leander cupped his hands on the glass for a closer look, and then attempted to remove the smudges with his sleeve.

"Why is it always children?"

The Septarch opened his mouth, and a slow turning gyre inside him made him close it again. He considered an easy escape, answers that were true but far from whole.

It isn't ALWAYS children. True, but rare and never wise, and it would lead to questions he could not answer.

You're all children to me anyway. True, with Cayle a bit of a gray area, though that was certainly *not* what kept him off the menu.

He suspected Leander would not be content with either reply, would know Oberon was hiding the worst answer under these gentler offerings. He began doing yet another thing because of this boy that he had not done in several lifetimes: trying to come up with a lie.

Oberon did not lie as a general rule. He had done so when he had been human, as any human must, but the Septarch had no need to fear what anyone thought of him now. He'd left them behind long ago.

So he was quite out of practice.

Leander, perhaps pitying his silence, said, "I just wonder because I don't think I could. Not if they were much younger than me, I guess."

Evil was useful for making people lose interest in things. This boy was different from the others, but he couldn't be *that* different. Honesty with a generous dose of wickedness seemed to please this one. He would try that.

"They're so tiny you can hold them down with one hand. They smell wonderful. They get so frightened so easily, and scream so beautifully, and they all get the same look. Like they just learned the universe has never been safe, and never will be. One day I want to try every single thing in the Kama Sutra with a little girl, six or seven. It would probably take a few of them, actually. They tend to be so fragile."

This was supposed to send Leander into a fit of horrified giggles, but the boy ignored this bait. "Why else?"

Damn it.

Dangerous. Yes, this one was dangerous.

The worst and most important answer was both simple and infinitely complex, a single thread that would tug on a thousand others, each one tied to a memory he would rather not examine.

He wanted to rage, but found only a new smile that felt both sad and proud. He licked one finger, traced the boy's nose, each eyelid. Stalling. One sentence, no particularly complex words or challenging pronunciations, how could it still be so difficult to *say*?

"I can't bear to be touched by adults."

Oh, there were stories behind that one not-so-complex sentence. Years of them, a long skein of shame and madness. Now the boy would ask for these stories, and his traitorous mouth would open, and he would tell.

Leander rolled those peridot eyes, conjuring more questions.

Oberon waited, heavy with dread.

"What's a Kama Sutra?"

It changed Oberon's smile, leached the sadness out of it and left only tired, grateful wonder. "An ancient book from Earth with hundreds of sexual variations."

Leander smacked him for that one, and it sent a rippling flare of

(......)

distress through him that he decided to ignore.

"You wouldn't try them with me?"

An exit, and a kindness. Oberon let himself take it. "Now, there's an idea."

He lunged. Leander squealed and tried to escape. Oberon wrestled him to the floor and pinned him, made a mock-ferocious face at him, and said, "Just a few needles?"

Leander was trying desperately not to laugh, squirming, his boots squeaking on the marble as he failed to get away.

"Just one needle, lots of times?" he suggested, near the boy's ear.

And there was an unspeakable massive crashing cacophony and a thunderous vibration that shook the entire Sphere.

Instinct made Oberon cover the boy's body with his own invulnerable one at the instant of impact.

All the lights went out, then began to strobe in a jarring amber. There was a crash of breaking glass close to them and the sudden explosive reek of chemicals and decay. The bone spider chattered and swayed above them, casting a strobelight deadfall of shadows. There was a light pattering of falling bones on Oberon's back, his shoulders, a chorus of clicks on the marble floor.

"What—" Leander began, petrified.

A chaos of alarms went off in discordant pulses.

Oberon spoke with terrible, reasonable calm.

"Someone is shooting at my Sphere."

green eyed monster

Oberon and Theren were moving at military speed down the corridor, trailed by several of the elite guard. "How did they get in?" Oberon demanded.

"Cut engines. Space suits. Drifted in like garbage, right past the sensors. First thing they powered was weapons."

"They would have gotten caught in the gravity and crashed here."

"I think they knew that, Lord Septarch," Theren said.

"You got them yet?"

"Six coming down in transport. Five minutes, maybe ten. Their ship's docked at Moloch."

"Fuckers," Oberon muttered. "Any idea why?"

Because, you're a fucking interstellar child molester, why the hell do you think? "Cult. Survivors of Zion 4."

"More survivors?" Oberon grabbed a torch as they passed, tore it free of the sconce and slammed it several times into the wall in a shower of sparks. Then he flung it behind him without looking to see where it went. "This is the second time this *year. Why* are they still getting through?"

No one had an answer for that. Fortunately, Oberon did not sincerely want one.

He groped in his pocket, pulled out a tube of red lipstick and slashed it onto his mouth, without looking, smacked his lips together, and threw that over his shoulder too. "Somebody pick that up," he said, as an afterthought. Two guards almost collided attempting to do so.

"Are they all alive?" he asked Theren.

"Not even a scratch."

"My Sphere?"

"Not even a scratch."

"I want the receiving area at forty degrees." He dabbed at his lipstick with his fingertip, glanced at the color, reached over and smeared it on Theren's bottom lip and pinched his cheek. "Happy...birthday...to me," he said, half-singing, and grinned like a skull.

My God, Theren thought, aching to scrub at his mouth, *you'd think we were going to a party.*

Leander was kissed hard, ordered to *stay in this room,* and abandoned in Oberon's chambers. And locked in, as he discovered after Oberon's departure.

And he was *furious* about it.

What if it's a war? What if there are hundreds of soldiers out there? What if he gets killed?

He ran his hands through his hair, frantic. How immortal was immortal? Would a detonator kill him? Ordinary metal bullets? Knives?

He sat in Oberon's desk chair, stiff and nervous, helped himself to Oberon's pipe. After several fast, greedy hits he keyed on the console. The terminal flashed through a dazzling array of incomprehensible diagrams and schematics, and then sudden, perfect video.

There were six people standing with their backs against a wall, knees bent to the point where they were off balance. Leander knew all about stress positions, from both school and recon. Five of them were men, in their fifties or sixties, all in flight suits.

The last one was a girl with hair like fire.

Oberon was the tallest and the blackest shape in all that featureless gray room. He was talking to Theren, his head inclined towards his guard...but he was looking at the girl.

And only at the girl.

"This is all of them?"

"Yes, Septarch. Their ship had no escape pods."

They were shivering, and trying not to show it. He could smell the girl's terror.

"May I ask why you were shooting at my Sphere?"

"Because...you're the Devil," a man told him. His teeth were chattering. "You destroyed our homeworld. Millions were slaughtered."

"Oh. That." Oberon nodded. Then he turned to the girl. She

clenched her teeth, avoiding his gaze. "What are you doing with them?"

She cringed, and tried to speak, and couldn't.

"What's your name?"

"Felicity," she said.

That was hysterical. He laughed and laughed. Her eyes were the color of her hair, and this made them shinybright with humiliation and resentment. She was still looking straight into his face. That impressed him.

But not enough.

"Felicity. Happiness. Good fortune. And one of the saints, no less," he told her. She still didn't get it, and he gave up. "How old are you?"

"I don't know. I think...seventeen," she said, her chattering teeth making the words into too many syllables.

So that was all right.

"And you've come to kill me, is that it?"

She nodded.

"You're their champion?"

She nodded again, wary, her jaw set hard. Delightful.

He gestured to the guards, and they backed away, weapons down. This was not at all what she expected.

He came closer to her. Closer still.

Entirely too close.

One of the other prisoners made some sound in protest. There was an immediate insectclick of multiple guns locking onto a target. Oberon's guards, clarifying the rules of this game.

He could feel Felicity's breath on his face, hot in the cold room, quick and sweet.

She shut her eyes, pressing back against the wall.

He whispered, for her ears only, "Try."

"I don't understand."

He backed away from her, one long easy step, and unbuckled the armored overshirt. He pulled it over his head and tossed it to Theren. Then he spread his arms out like Jesus, and said, "Go ahead. Try and kill me. I won't even fight you."

She eyed him, suspicious, hesitant.

Then she came at him so fast he almost didn't see her move.

Her fist caught him straight in the jaw, and she swung twice more, and he felt the bones crunch near his temple, and his jaw was hanging crooked, and she waited, clutching her hand, watching him. He hadn't moved.

Not bad. That would have put him on the floor with no interest in further combat, had he been human. He reached up, examined the damage with his fingertips, and slammed the heel of his hand into his chin, and the hinge clicked back into place. He opened his mouth, closed it. It would heal itself within hours. He looked at her, waiting for it.

Her face crumpled, and she screamed, and dove for the floor, rolling. It fascinated him, and he turned to watch her. She snatched a little hand-held energy gun from one of his guards, and up on one knee she shot him, four times in the chest, from less than ten feet away.

He fell obligingly, and lay without moving or breathing, his eyes wide open. It hurt like absolute hell. Oh, she was glorious. It was a shame she wouldn't be staying. He could smell the scorched vinyl of his shirt, could see tendrils of smoke drifting up from his chest. He watched her stand, holding the gun on him in wavering hands.

He sat up, pushed the hair out of his eyes, smiled for her. "Felicity," he said. He did not mean her name.

She was screaming, "God, *God!*" and she fired again, and this one went wild and burned a black streak in the wall behind him, and then the gun was out of charge, but she kept pulling the trigger, backing away, until he took the gun out of her hands and dropped it on the floor.

"Repair their ship. Disconnect the controls and set a course for Zion 4, terminating orbit. Do I still have those cases of wine, the thirty-eight?"

It took Theren a second to catch up to all of that. "Yes...I think there's six or seven left, Lord Septarch."

"Put those on the ship, too, and let them go. Except for her, of course," he added, looking at Felicity.

"You can't," she whispered, not believing it yet. "Zion is a radioactive wasteland—"

He raised his eyebrow at her, and she understood then, and struck at him, crying out in rage. He grabbed her hands and covered her mouth, screams beating against the palm of his hand. He said to Theren, "Leave their screens on receive-only. Felicity and I might want to say hello."

There was one consistent conclusion supported by all of Leander's psychological data no matter how it was interpreted. The boy was not particularly skilled at impulse control. Oberon had exactly enough time to recall this after he opened the door to his rooms before he was nearly decapitated by whatever it was Leander threw at him.

"First I see you look at her like that, and then I thought you were fucking dead, do you know that? Then I see you look at her like that *again!*" He was in a full red rage, and Oberon found this both upsetting and a tiny bit—amusing? charming?

Leander threw the black absinthe bottle next. Oberon knocked it out of the air, and black ceramic and leaf-green liquor splattered everywhere, and the smell of wormwood hung in the air like smoke. He lunged at Leander before he could reload, picked him up and dragged him kicking into the bedroom, put him on the bed and pinned him. "What is wrong with you?"

Leander burst into tears.

"I have never seen a boy—or a girl, for that matter—who cries as much as you do. I am fine. The Sphere is fine. They're prisoners now."

"I know that. I watched."

"Then what is wrong?"

It took the boy a minute. He was crying too hard to speak. "When are you going to kill me? You keep me here, and you call me dearest, but I've seen what you do to people you get tired of! Fucking kill me, all right? I don't want to have to die knowing I was wrong about being important to you—"

You are important to me, Oberon thought.

He tried to slap the boy, but the message got lost between his brain and his arm. He slammed his hand down on the pillow next to Leander's head. Leander shoved him away, or tried to. He was, as usual, immovable. For some reason this pushed Oberon over his internal line into amusement again. He covered his mouth with his hand until the urge to laugh subsided, grateful for once for this odd reflex.

"Why do you want her?"

At last he understood. "Is that what this is about? You think you're being replaced? Leander, I kept her for *you*."

"For...I don't understand."

"I thought she'd be perfect for your first."

"My first *what*?"

"Kill. Your first kill."

AU·TOPH·A·GY

(ô-tòf¹e-jê) noun

The process of self-digestion by a cell through the action of enzymes originating within the same cell.

parabellum

Theren didn't look at the new prisoner. He'd filled his canteen with alcohol and he sat outside her cell, positioned so that he'd have to get up and walk towards her to see her. He drank, and he was trying not to think.

He took a long pull, and it scorched his throat, burning up into his sinuses. And to think that he couldn't really even drink himself to death. Cayle would just give him a new liver. He could probably look forward to another hundred years of this.

"Guard?"

"Don't talk to me. I have nothing to say to you."

He had thousands of things to say to her. That was why he was drinking.

"I saw your face when he was here. You don't like him."

"Are you crazy? Look, there are fucking cameras and microphones everywhere."

"He'll kill me anyway."

She didn't even sound upset about it. She sounded...serene. He'd seen a few of them pull that beatific peace nonsense near the end. He'd seen none of them hold onto it. Not once the knives came out. "Yeah, but at this point he might kill you quickly."

"Does he ever?"

If he's said two words to you, then no. By that time it won't be quick. Otherwise it seems to depend on his mood.

Against his better judgment he went in to look through the bars. She was sitting in one corner of the bare white cell, arms wrapped around her knees. She looked entirely too young, entirely too *clean* to be here.

"I don't care if he kills you, and I don't care how." He drank. He had the insane urge to pass it through to her, and did not.

"You're not fooling me," she said.

He said lamely, "You better shut up," and turned away from her, raised the canteen to his lips again. It didn't taste like anything this time. He supposed he'd scorched his taste buds into submission.

"He's got a boy," he said to her, over his shoulder. He didn't know why he'd said it. "Fourteen. Just a kid."

He heard the rustle of her suit, the thump of her knee as she crawled closer to the bars. "His son?"

Theren laughed at that. "Jesus, no. His whore, I guess. But this kid..."

"What's your name?" she asked.

"Theren."

"Theren," she said, as if making sure she'd gotten it right. She had a beautiful voice, had he noticed that before? "Tell me about this boy."

He was fast becoming completely drunk, and he didn't give a damn because she would be dead in a day or so anyway. She made soft sounds in all the right places, in that infuriatingly lovely voice, and that was all that mattered. "You know what this place is?" he said, gesturing at the entire cellblock. "This is Hell. They took a serial killer and gave him his own fucking planet. Leander is...one too many. I can't do it anymore."

"So take him, and leave."

Theren sighed, killed the last of the vodka. "He'd kill me. Both of us."

"Didn't you say he would do that anyway?"

"Do you have any idea what I've seen?" he shouted at her. He wanted to snap her in half, for having a life that hadn't crossed Oberon's life until now. "He impales people. Puts them in little glass cubes and starves them to death. He films everything, and once a year he piles us all into his claustrophobic throne room to watch his favorites. Like any of us wanted to see any of it ever again."

"So you're telling me he's a monster," she said, softly.

"Yes."

"And what does that make you?"

The button that electrified the floor she was sitting on was right at the top of the door controls, and for the first time in his career, his hand twitched towards it. She noticed it, and she didn't move, and her expression didn't change. She merely waited.

He opened his mouth to answer her, and his comm beeped at him. He pulled it off his belt, dropped it, picked it up and fumbled it on. "Yes?"

That voice. Like rotting candy. It coiled into the room through the tiny speaker and left coldness and a scent that was as sweet as the smell of gangrene.

"Bring her. Room six. One hour."

He turned it off, looking at the silent gray screen in his hand, looking at his boots, looking at his discarded canteen.

Looking at anything but the girl.

Leander watched Oberon turn off the comm. "I can't do this."

"Why not?" His hair was a tangled wreck, and his shirt was scorched. He pulled it off and threw it into the fireplace, and the entire room began to reek of burning plastic. Oberon rifled through drawers, leaving a disaster in his wake, threw a black shirt and heavy black pants at Leander. "Put these on. They should almost fit you."

He did, still arguing. "I'm too little, and I'll freak."

Oberon replaced his own shirt with a black silk one, passed a mirror and frowned at himself. He picked up a brush and dragged it through his hair. "Come here."

Leander did. Oberon sat at his dressing table and pulled Leander to crouch between his knees. Oberon began to brush his hair with businesslike efficiency. It was hard to remember what he was even arguing against. "She's older than you, as you asked."

"She's a *girl*."

"Would you prefer a boy? I gathered you might, overall, but thought your first might be easier for you if we removed lust from the equation."

Leander made a noncommittal noise. There was an oasis of quiet while Oberon painted his face.

He could kill someone he was angry at, he already knew that, and he could watch Oberon kill someone he wasn't angry at. Again, he reminded himself, thinking of Jyana.

But to do it himself, with his own hands? To a girl?

He thought, *I'll disappoint you*, but could not say it out loud.

Oberon finished him off with a few smudges of his thumb, nuzzled him in approval, started in on his own makeup. "Do you want to?"

A person. A human being. A girl. That girl.

Oberon made a face at his sullen quiet, his lips as black as his eyes. Fingers, then lips, on his neck, where the cuts were still closing.

Breath, on his skin. Leander made one chestnoise of protest and dismay, but it was too late. He could feel his reasons, or perhaps just his reason, eroding.

"Do you want to?" Kisses that tasted of fresh lipstick. "You can do anything you want to. This is your first. We have to do this right." Oberon pulled Leander up to stand in the mirror with him, spread out his arms for approval. Head to toe black.

Killing clothes.

"Do you have to carry me everywhere?"

"I do, if I want to move at a normal speed."

"Your normal speed is crazy because, giraffes."

Leander won a laugh for that one, and a hot darting kiss that was far from lipstick-friendly.

Oberon carried him to a corridor that felt familiar. Leander suspected they were near the room where he'd seen The Device.

They went into a room that burned Leander's existing concept of *toy* to the ground.

The left-hand wall was lined with whips, chains, pulleys, shackles, manacles, paddles, oiled switches of multiple kinds of wood, implements of punishment of every possible description. There were lovingly displayed harnesses, corsets, and straps that defied human anatomy. There was an antique taser. There was a loop of green garden hose, coiled neatly on a hook like a dead snake. There was leather, vinyl, wire, long skeins of rope studded with glass and shrapnel.

Facing them was a wall of phalluses like the one that had been fitted to Julia's device. These were arranged according to material: metal, wood, vinyl, leather, jade, glass, even some that an art dealer would have discreetly called ivory. Within these categories they were arranged according to size, from the thickness of a finger to twice as thick as Leander's arm. Some of them were ridged, carved into cruel spirals, geometric sculptures designed for bruises, blood, tears.

The right-hand wall was lined with every possible tool of physical death. Hanging on steel mounts were swords and knives with myriad edges, some gleaming, some rusted. There were scythes and pliers and claw hammers and crossbows and blowguns and crowbars and saws and clubs. There was a wicked loop of piano wire and there were bottles of chemicals, labeled in angular handwriting with crimson ink. Jars of acid were in neat military rows in spill trays on the floor, next to canisters marked only with a wordless pictogram of a gas mask. There were axes. Ice picks. Needles two feet long. Pincers. Blow torches. Enema tubes with copper nozzles and plastic bags of fluid plastered with skull-and-crossbones stickers. Overgrown corkscrews. Clamps and electrodes and batteries and hooks and weights and hedge clippers and a miniature guillotine.

Oberon set Leander on his feet. His lips were stiff, and he was freezing and soaked with icy sweat under his clothes.

His killing clothes.

The Septarch's eyes were half-closed, moving along the walls of tools, and his voice was silken, adoring, indulgent. "Choose something. Several things. Anything. Everything."

"Ohhh..." Leander said, and then he didn't say anything at all.

Room Six was a claustrophobic booth, painted stark white, freezing cold. It contained two pieces of furniture, both chairs. One was ordinary, padded and upholstered in a dark burgundy velvet.

The second was chrome and black leather, bristling with levers and restraints.

Theren cleared his throat. "Um...you have to..."

Felicity started to sit in the chair that wasn't velvet, and Theren's hand on her arm stopped her. "You have to...I mean, you have to take off your clothes," he said, looking at the floor.

She was still wearing the navy one-piece she'd worn under her space suit. She unzipped it from neck to waist with uncooperative hands. She had to contort to do it without brushing against him. She gave it to him. There was nowhere to look but the chair, or the floor with its downhill slope and indiscreet grating.

She sat down, so he wouldn't have to ask her to, put her arms on the armrests, and settled her feet in the footrests. "Go ahead," she told him.

He started at her ankles, buckling the restraints tight enough to hurt her because he had to. She didn't flinch, and she didn't make a sound.

He hesitated at the straps around her upper thighs.

She waited. He fastened them, blushing, and did the rest of them with a quickness that had nothing to do with efficiency. He stopped at the strap that would hold her head tight and motionless against the headrest. "I could let you out. We could go in the hall, and you could attack me, and I could...I could shoot you."

She looked at him, not understanding.

"It's...electrical. Quick."

She still didn't understand.

"It's painless," he whispered, and he started to unbuckle the strap around her chest.

"No."

"Felicity...he'll be angry, but if you hit me, if I'm bleeding, he'll understand." This was probably untrue.

"No," she said again.

He looked at her, and he saw she was serious.

"You don't know—" he began.

"I do know," she told him.

She'll regret this half an hour from now, he thought. He could tell her so, but it wouldn't change her mind. It would only be cruelty on his part when half-an-hour from now actually happened.

"I'm sorry," he said.

He left before she could say something merciless, like, *I forgive you.*

Felicity waited. The chair was positioned so that she couldn't look at anything but the door.

Leander reached out, and tugged at a glittering steel phallus. It was too high for him, and Oberon took it off the wall and handed it to him. He ran his fingers in a circle around the tip.

"Careful," Oberon warned. He pushed Leander's fingers out of the way and turned a metal band around the base. The tip unfolded with a spring-loaded click, into four blades.

Leander sucked in his breath.

"It gets better." Oberon turned the band again, and it exploded into an octagon, a jagged evil flower of razor-sharp edges, three times the circumference of the shaft.

"This one," Leander said, hoarse and stricken. He ran his finger along the new geography of the tip, and it drew immediate blood.

Oberon turned the band again, and it closed with a snap, like a secret, the seams invisible, the surface polished smooth. "Anything. Anything you want," he said again, and he started to put his hand to his face to hide his smile, and didn't.

There was no one to hide it from, now.

Not anymore.

Not ever again.

terror couple kill colonel

They were walking in a corridor Leander had never seen. There were skeletons nailed to the walls, some dripping shreds of dried skin, their hands wired to hold pairs of torches. One of them had red lipstick smeared across its grinning teeth.

They were passing doors, labeled *one, two, three.*

Oberon had a leather case in one hand.

They stopped outside a doorway marked *six.* Oberon put Leander down, produced a loaded syringe and shot up, and slid to the floor with his back against the wall. He reached up and pulled Leander into his lap. "I didn't use it all. Do you want some?"

"What is it?" Leander wanted some, regardless of the answer, but he was still getting used to the idea of an adult who handed him drugs as nonchalantly as if they'd been sharing a candy bar.

Oberon grinned at him. "Guess."

"Will it damage me?"

A shrug, the gesture so human that it looked wrong on the Septarch. "Cayle can replace anything it breaks."

Leander was already rolling up his sleeve.

His black sleeve. His new shadowsuit, and wasn't that what those had always been, too? His killing clothes.

It was different this time. Intense. Oberon was looking straight into his eyes, and he used his hand instead of a tourniquet, and pushed the needle in too slow and too mean. Leander didn't struggle against the pain. He had learned the trick of suffering was to yield, to stop resisting, and that the sensations that followed were as delicious as they were addictive.

The drug scorched its way up his arm, feeling magnetic, as though he wanted to draw his arm and his hand and his fingers tight together. "Will it always be like this?"

"Like it's the first thing that's ever happened to you. Genesis in a syringe."

He hadn't meant the drug, exactly. His life, his future.

His world.

Leander leaned his head back to look at the door to Room Six. "She's in there."

"Yes."

"I'm scared."

"Yes." Oberon dragged a mouthful of Leander's hair through his teeth. It made a metallic singing sound, like bells, like breaking glass.

"We should have brought some for her."

"No." He stood up, pulled Leander up with him. "It tends to dull pain."

"Did you bring it?" Leander was almost frantic. He was hoping they hadn't, that they'd backtrack, delay, stall, anything but go into Room Six.

Oberon patted the leather case, his eyes gleaming. "Ready?"

Leander wasn't sure he was, and wasn't sure he ever would be, which made delay pointless. Oberon opened the door for him with an over-the-top gesture of his arm, and a mock bow.

They went inside.

The door locked behind them.

Felicity's eyes were closed, and her lips were moving. Some of her red hair was caught under the leather strap across her forehead, and she was naked.

Leander had never seen a naked woman, not in person. Camille, in flashes, obscured by Lucius and what remained of her clothes, and then by blood.

It wasn't what he'd expected.

She was so pale, and her skin looked...fake, like rubber, soft and inefficient. There was hair between her legs, a shade darker than that on her head, and there was a blue vein tracing a crooked line on her left breast. Her nipples were stiff with cold, almost as pale as her skin, he could see her ribs.

It's supposed to turn me on, he thought. It didn't. He kept looking at the vein. Her lips were almost the same translucent blue. He thought of Oberon's skin, ivory traced with snow-white scars like the schematic for a circuit board, lean and tense and perfect.

Different. So different.

Oberon took the seat across from her. He put his arm around Leander's waist and pulled him close. "Are you actually praying?" he asked, pretending amazement.

She opened her eyes and gave him a look of pure hate. They were the same color as her hair, and that was interesting. Leander had never seen that before.

He laughed. "How...Christian of you, Felicity," he observed, and Leander knew he was not referring to the prayer.

"I'm not afraid of you," she said. "God is with me."

She's lying, Leander thought, watching her chest, her frantic breathing. *She's terrified.*

"Leander, you didn't tell me God was here. Now, I've gone and given Felicity the best chair."

Leander had a three-second window to say something clever, which he missed. He was fascinated by her continued glare. He wondered how long she'd be able to keep that up.

"I think I've heard more prayers than all the clergy in all the Reach by now. Mothers and children, men and women, entire worlds. So far it's saved not a single soul, but who knows? Maybe you'll be the first."

"You're confusing the soul with the body," she said, each word sounding daintily selected, somehow steady around her bonedeep trembling.

"Am I? I've often been accused of that. We could listen to some of the tapes, if you like. I have quite a lot of audio from Zion in particular. Oh, the relevant part is only about six seconds for any given location–"

"Stop it––"

"--but I think you'd get the idea. Or we could listen to all of them, though that would take years. Quite a lot of help requests going unanswered."

Felicity's face twisted. She took in a deep breath and said, "The fact that we're even here––"

Oberon laughed at that one for a long time. "The fact that you're here strapped to a chair with less than an hour to live proves that this god of yours exists? All right, Felicity's friend God. Go ahead. Strike me down," he taunted the ceiling. He waited, looking upward. After a moment he looked back at her. "He's certainly taking his time about it," he told her in a confiding whisper. "Don't you hate the sort of people who are always late for everything?"

"It doesn't work that way." Felicity's mouth was quivering.

Leander felt himself smile like a knife. *If you cry, it won't even be close to an hour.* He got a sudden vivid flash of what it felt like when Oberon finally slid inside him, the magnificent ache of it, of being torn inside and bleeding and in exquisite pain. He clutched at the arm of the chair, buried his face in Oberon's shoulder to drown out the moan. Oberon ran his nails through Leander's hair. Exhilaration. Dread. Leander found that he loved this secret, silent conversation. *Just his, and just mine. Just ours.*

"No? Suppose you tell me how it does work."

"His..." She made a sound as if she were choking. "Plan. If he lets you kill me here, that's his plan."

Oberon's eyes narrowed. Leander sucked in his breath. "Felicity, darling, nobody *lets* me do anything." He was furious under his pleasant mask.

The playing was over.

Oberon's voice was heavy, cold, and no longer amused. "Don't you think you're a little old to have an imaginary friend?"

He was speaking in a slow deliberate way, choosing each word. He had been taking tiny bites out of her soul. "That sounds like a coward's way to run a universe. He promises you this, promises you that, but when he betrays you he tells you it's all part of some plan? Actually, come to think of it, does he ever really *tell* you...anything?"

The last word was a sudden deep snap. Leander could feel it when Oberon swallowed what he'd torn away.

She's prey.

"Let's have a game of it, hmm? Prove to me that he exists, and I'll let you go. Maidenly virtue intact, blood still inside your body where you'd probably like to keep it. Wouldn't that be lovely?"

Oh, she wanted that, everything in her lunging towards those words, hook and all, before she could stop herself. Oberon watched her begin to bleed and cut her again, more cruelly this time. "Your friends, too. I'll send a ship to rescue them if you prove God to me."

She screamed at him, twisting and slamming her entire weight into the restraints. Oberon enjoyed this tantrum immensely. "Tell him to unstrap you, Felicity. Tell him to cave the ceiling in on me. Tell him to kill you right now with a heart attack. Believe me, it would be a mercy."

She looked at Leander then. Until that moment he had been feeling quite invisible, and the fact that she could see him was an uncomfortable shock. He pressed against Oberon's shoulder.

"He keeps you here," she said, gasping. "He hurts you. Doesn't he?"

He was waiting for Oberon to answer, and when that didn't happen Leander turned to him, helpless.

"Tell her," Oberon said, his voice gentle again, his fingers coming up to Leander's face.

"Yes." His voice surprised him. He sounded calm in his own ears, perfectly...happy. "He does."

"But you don't have to stay here," she said.

"Of course he doesn't," Oberon told her, his eyes narrowing into obsidian splinters.

"I want to stay here," Leander's mouth said all by itself, and that wasn't quite right, no, he'd gotten it exactly right before. "I want to *live* here."

She made a patronizing, stupid little half-laugh. "You're too young to know that."

His hands sculpted themselves into fists, the fingers closing together like lovers, like pieces of an ancient puzzle.

That, *right fucking there,* that was what he hated about them. All of them. Their arrogance. That fucking self-satisfied superiority. Their smug assumptions that they understood what was best for everybody, that they couldn't possibly be wrong.

For the Bible told them so.

In his head, that gleaming, seamless steel, blooming into a thirsty array of blades.

He hated her. Fucking hated her.

He didn't have any doubts, not anymore.

"You don't know what I want," Leander said, almost shouting, furious. "Don't push me." His voice tore his throat on the way out. "I'm not any safer than he is."

At that, Oberon sighed, long and light and joyful. He leaned in close to Leander, touched his neck, his shoulders, whispered, "Should I start?"

"I think we already have," he whispered back, and the taste of that *we* on his tongue was better than any drug had ever been. A feeling came over him, familiar, a sense of impending wonder that itched and ached and grew.

"I meant, should I, or do you want to?"

He didn't know where to begin. "You," he said, with both gratitude and resentment.

Oberon stood up, pushed Leander into his seat. "Watch."

Leander nodded. His neck and his throat were tight. He closed his hands hard on the armrests. He was afraid they could see whatever was glowing in his head gleaming out like a laser through his eyes.

Born again. He raised his hand and covered his mouth. Now he understood why Oberon used that gesture. It was to hold back some new kind of smile that might leave your lips mangled.

Septarch. What an angry, glorious word. He wanted to pull Oberon close, wrap his hands in that long black hair and kiss him hard, until they were both bleeding.

He didn't. He couldn't.

He didn't want to interrupt.

Oberon raised his hand, fluttered his fingers to lure Felicity's gaze, like a stage magician. He kept his eyes on hers and grasped a long iron lever on the side of her chair, rubbed his hand up and down it—all in the wrist—and licked along his teeth, making the gestures obscene to watch her grimace. He slammed the lever back, and the footrests snapped apart, spreading her legs wide open.

She ground her back against the chair, baring her teeth, and he put his fingers half an inch out of biting distance and said, "You hate me, don't you, Felicity, good fortune, dearest?"

The tendons in her legs were taut cords. She was trying so hard to press her knees together so hard that the flesh around the restraints was pressed white. Her sex was like a wound, little folds of skin wrinkled like scar tissue. She revolted him.

There was a division, a vertigo, and Leander was Oberon, and he felt the lever cold and hard and sexual in his hand, and he was Felicity, and the chair was icy leather and the straps hurt him, terrified him.

Oberon pulled the lever outward, and the chair tilted back, enough to have her looking up at the ceiling. She didn't make a sound, and Leander gasped for her, feeling everything fall, feeling unseen gears under the chair lock into place. Teeth.

"Is he up there?" Oberon asked her. "Tell him you're ready for the white horses whenever he is." He glanced at Leander like a secret code. Leander gave him back the same silent magic word. *We are one being, now, one. Him. Me. One being, with one mind.*

And one purpose.

Oberon went around behind her, moving liquid and uncanny and reptilian. She couldn't bear that, being unable to see him. Her whole body went rigid, a line from her sternum down her stomach to the gash between her thighs.

He's going to hurt her. Leander drew his knees up in the chair with fierce, sharp excitement.

Oberon snapped his hands towards her, spreading his fingers out quick with an almost audible sound, as if he were flicking water onto her. Some sixth sense made her cringe, crying out, even though she couldn't see him. His hands stopped inches from her, under complete control. He moved his mouth like a laugh for Leander. "If he's here, Felicity, sweetheart, apparently he intends to watch."

That drove a horrified keen out of her, and she squirmed as low down in the chair as the restraints would allow. Then he did touch her, just her shoulders. She tried to push herself down in the chair. He ran his fingertips up over her collarbone, up her neck, and he cupped her head

He moved her hair back, slid his hands under her breasts, kissed her shoulder, her neck. "Hmm? Now you don't want God here with you, suddenly?" She made a sound like a faded scream, muscles twisting under her skin in a slow seizure.

"She's not being very brave, is she? I'm not even hurting her," he said, without raising his head. Leander could see Oberon's tongue, tracing hieroglyphs on her skin, his thumbs on her nipples. "I think she's worried about what I might make her do."

That's beyond cruel, Leander thought, electricity tasting his nerves.

Oberon bit a pink crescent into her shoulder. She jerked, but did not scream. He circled her again, stroked Leander in passing, went down on his knees, facing her, and Leander slid forward and buried his face between Oberon's shoulderblades, smelling him, and he rasped his tongue against his shirt in a strange kiss before he leaned back to watch.

Felicity was panting through her teeth. Oberon's hands were on her thighs. "You hate me. Don't you?" he asked her again.

"You'd better answer him," Leander said, and his voice was coming from somewhere outside the room. She didn't react, but he knew she'd heard him.

Oberon bit the soft curve of thigh above her knee, pulled with his teeth. She shrieked, her toes curling hard into the metal footrests, and when she found no escape she spit at Oberon in frustrated rage. It struck in his hair and gleamed there. He found it with his fingers, still biting her, and looked up at her and laughed and spit back, leaving a wet line down her stomach. His hands closed on her thighs harder, moved up to her hips, and she was shuddering away from him, frantic.

He pressed his forehead against the line of spit he'd left on her, below her navel.

He's going to bite her there. I know he will. I don't know how he can stand to do that. I wonder what it tastes like.

Oberon didn't bite, but whatever he did made Felicity scream and scream, glassy and hysterical, thrashing like the chair was electrified.

Leander touched the ridge of Oberon's spine, as though he could learn this by osmosis, and when that didn't explain it he looked at Felicity. "What's he doing?"

She was crying all at once, as though she didn't mean to, tears spilling out of her eyes so fast it didn't look real. "Make him stop," she begged Leander.

He was burning with puzzled curiosity, and then that voice in his head whispered the word *kiss*, and he slammed back into the soft chair like he was the one being tortured.

He was laughing. He thought he was. Someone was. It sounded like his own laughter, but there was a noise like solar wind in his ears and it was so complicated to breathe without choking.

"Is he licking you?" Leander asked her.

The color that flushed into her cheeks was so funny that he made a noise that hurt his chest. The puncture in the crook of his arm throbbed like a burn. He could feel what she felt, scorched and helpless and pinned like a butterfly in a dissecting pan. He slammed his head back into the chair to make it all slow down, but it was too soft to hurt enough, and he was being sucked in.

There was nothing to hold onto.

He kept his fingers in his mouth and struggled to get his other hand down inside his killing clothes.

"Does it hurt?" he asked her, ragged, around his mouthful of fingers.

"Answer him," Oberon said, his mouth against her, his voice clotted and wet. "Answer him, or it will."

"No," she said, sobbing now, her short bitten nails digging into the leather under her hands, leaving gray scratches. "No, it doesn't...hurt..."

Leander had his heels under him in the seat of the chair, pushing his hips up, hand wrapped around his cock. "Do you like it?"

"God help me," she strangled out.

He saw it in her eyes when she broke.

It was the noise of a dog, this time, struck with the tip of a heavy boot, an abrupt harsh predator bird cry, then soft liquid infant sounds in her throat, then sudden silence. Her head was back, crooked, the pulse in her neck visible. Her body was one arc from crown to sole, bent like light in an impossible universe. She made a thin brittle wail, and fell back sobbing.

Leander made all the sounds she didn't.

She started screaming again, panic-stricken.

He's biting her, now.

He felt it close down his spine, into his balls, and he thought, *It's heroin. I'm coming pure heroin.*

Oberon was leaning with his back against Leander's knees. *Like I was sitting with Mom,* he thought, and he took his hand sticky with semen and sweat and spread it over Oberon's mouth, loose and wet now, no longer painted black.

He'd left a black feather kiss on Felicity's thigh, another above that dripping nest of auburn hair. Her sex was gleaming, swollen and violet. She was crying, hopeless. Her nose was running, and her chin was inked with red where she'd bitten her lips.

Oberon's tongue was on his hand, tasting his fingers. The Septarch licked one last circle in his palm, and put something heavy and cold there and wrapped Leander's fingers around it.

It was the phallus.

"No, I can't," he whispered, but he was tilting it to see it in the light.

"She's already wet. Point it towards her heart and push it in."

"No." It was the only shape his mouth would make.

Oberon didn't look concerned, or angry, or disappointed. His eyes were hot and sharp, driving in, and he said, "You don't have to do anything you don't want to. Not ever again."

Leander made a tiny muffled cry at that.

He wasn't sure he didn't want to.

He wasn't sure.

Felicity saw what he was holding. He unfolded it for her to admire. One click, one glittering complication, and it became the whole of her world.

"Don't."

A tiny word, much too small to save her from all the points in the air between them.

There was an animal in his chest with sharp feet and a gaping mouth. It crawled in a frantic spiral, clawed up towards his throat. He could feel it breathing, could feel its reptile jaws, wide and eager and hungry.

He clicked it all the way open, thinking of streetlights bristling with fangs of ice, of bins of scrap metal shredded into snarling maws that wanted only to bite all the soft places.

Felicity tried one last time. "Leander, that voice you hear, saying you don't want to do this, to be this way? That's the voice of God."

One in front of him, and one behind, tearing him between them. He looked at the device in his hand and closed it, the secret extravagance of blades folding back into the stainless steel.

Felicity burst into heaving, ungainly sobs of relief.

It was much too soon for that.

The trembling started in his toes, and thundered up into his spine and his gut and his throat in a sickening deep rush, like nausea.

Here's your proof of God.

He looked at Oberon. Their eyes were fucking, vicious and hard, like a blow, like the business end of a whip. Leander raised his hand and pointed at his lover. "Say my name."

"Leander," Oberon murmured, in pride and something close to awe.

He already knew.

Leander turned to Felicity, still pointing behind him with his empty hand, and he said, "Do you hear that?" His words, tight and and laden with tears for unknown reasons. "Do you?"

She nodded. She knew.

"That's the voice of God."

The animal was free, wearing his teeth, moving his hands. He was on his knees, all one liquid motion.

It was rape even before he slammed it inside her.

Her entire body shook, as though he were beating her with a hammer. There was resistance, and it made him furious, and he leaned against the phallus with his whole weight. She made an elegant parchment noise. It wasn't bone he was pushing against, too much give for that, but flesh or not it still wouldn't go any deeper. He could feel the texture of her through the metal, like rotting meat.

He hauled upward, and she made a chest-deep frayed moan. It was bone this time that stopped him. He fucked her with it hard and deep and fast, like his own first time. He watched her face, and thought about the fact that he could do anything to her, anything he wanted to. It made his hands feel bigger and his teeth feel longer.

Oberon drank them both in with his eyes, though he saved his doting, beaming pride for Leander. He kept touching Felicity, in ways that would have made Leander set the room on fire if he hadn't known this tenderness was the opposite of kindness. Leander found the perfect stabbing, angry motion that hurt his wrist and his shoulder, made his heartbeat rage in his head and his throat. Her texture changed, the pattern of pressure, and her breath was like a barbed wire pulled up through her lungs.

He went at it faster, rougher, making a savage noise he didn't recognize. She changed again, and it was harder to pull it out, easier to push in.

She's close.

He cried out to Oberon, "Help me," and Oberon's hands were there, the commotion of their struggle moving the phallus inside her. It was impossible now to pull it out or push it in, and her cunt closed around it like teeth. She made begging cries of regret and remorse, pleasure and shame. The only words he understood were *God* and *forgive* and *can't help it.*

The handle was slick with fluid from her. He couldn't turn the little band. Oberon's hands closed around his, and pressed Leander's fingers hard enough, and they both turned it. Ninety degrees.

There was a click like a switchblade, mechanical and heartless, and he felt it all the way up his arm, the blades snapping out, the impact of it, tearing.

It sounded like a wolf, that noise she was making, Camille said in his brain, and now he understood what a noise like that meant.

At last her joints locked, her body breaking-point rigid. Wetness drenched his hand. He twisted the band himself this time. One hundred and eighty degrees. The second spring-loaded snick of the complex octagon unfolding inside her made him come again.

There was nothing of human or animal left in the cries she was making. He was raging, screaming *bitch* and *whore* at her, and worse, words he made up for the sake of their music, for their jagged angles.

She stopped moving. He twisted the phallus with both hands, wicked blades tearing her like wet decayed cloth. There was one metallic snap as one of the delicate evil razors broke off. She wasn't fucking moving, the bitch and he struck the base of the phallus with the side of his fist, hard, harder, and as hard as he could. That flesh that had resisted him gave in. It slid inside her so far he almost lost it.

He thought, *who's invisible now?*

The beast in him was glutting itself. He kept pounding it inside her, the lips of her pussy drawn tight and crimson around the silver edges of it and she was lying there fucking limp and she was *ignoring* him.

She was ignoring him, and nobody fucking ignored him, because he was *not* invisible. and nobody was ever going to ignore him. Not anymore.

Not EVER AGAIN.

He pulled at it, and it came out an inch and stuck. He yanked with both hands, and his feet slid out from under him and he braced them against the base of the chair and fucking hauled at it with his entire body, until a nasty dull hot pain wrenched in his shoulder, exploded in the small of his back, and it wouldn't come out, she had closed her pussy teeth around it and there was a ceramic grating sensation up into his aching wrists, and SHE WOULDN'T FUCKING LET IT GO.

He would show her. Bitch. Whore. Christian fucking syphilitic cunt, he would show her.

He'd shove it down her throat.

Oberon was saying his name, over and over, like a prayer.

Leander jerked at her again, violent and furious. "Help me," he said again, pleading, ordering, shrieking. Oberon's helped him turn the metal band again, and the blades snapped closed.

She didn't move. The bitch was still ignoring him, and he pulled hard, and it slid out of her, greased and easy, and dropped him on his tailbone.

Rage.

He got up with the phallus still dripping in his hand.

He shoved it against her mouth and she was STILL ignoring him, and he battered it against her lips, prying at her jaw. Down her throat. She couldn't scream then, it would be a wet broken slippery rattle, and he smashed it into her teeth and

"Leander," someone was saying, and someone grabbed him, holding him, and held him still, and a familiar luscious voice was saying gently, "She's dead, Leander. She's dead. It's over."

He was clawing at the hands on him, snapping. He couldn't reach anything to bite.

It was over.

The phallus was scarlet, and, and it was still in his hand. It hadn't been quite able to close completely, clotted with shreds of tissue, the seams were no longer invisible. His hands, too, were scarlet, and his arms, redblack ground into his fingernails.

He thought, She wasn't coming. She was bleeding. She was, she was coming, but what you felt, blood, that was blood.

He threw back his head and made a predator's noise, a raven at a kill, a lion over a steaming carcass. He raised the phallus to his mouth and pushed it in, throat deep, gagging, and he pulled it out and crowed again, roared again, and he flung it sidearm and it bang smashed into the wall, so loud, impossibly loud, and it left a red smear where it struck. He looked at Oberon, as though he had never seen him before, his eyes wild.

"It's over. Leander. She's dead," the voice said again, and there were arms around him, warm and gentle. He bit at flesh and felt it between his teeth, the crisp snap of breaking skin, and Oberon groaned and flinched, but he still held Leander close, whispering, "It's over."

Leander was himself again, after a long bright time, and he was breathing like a victim, and he whispered, "More."

Oberon looked at him, to make sure he was serious, and then he kissed him, carefully, away from the mindless teeth the boy now wore. "All right. More. I know, I know exactly what you need," he said.

"I bit you," Leander said, voice unsteady, and he was crying, vaguely, and he kept looking at the wall, at the red splatter there. It looked like a butterfly.

"I know," Oberon said.

"She's dead." He could feel her behind him, suddenly monstrous and terrifying, this murdered thing, and he clung close to Oberon, frightened. "She's—"

"Yes. She's dead. You did that. You killed her," Oberon said, a soft litany.

"I didn't mean it," Leander said, his voice going in unexpected directions.

"Yes you did. You don't have to pretend anything here, don't you know that? You did mean it."

"I want...it was...over so fast...I forgot to notice it and I want to...I wish I could do it over because I didn't do it right..."

"Look. Look at her, Leander, what's left of her."

"No," he said, frantic, but he had already turned his head against Oberon's chest to obey.

"You did that." Triumph. Pride. Comfort.

She was so white, small and collapsed, falling inward. She was streaked from thighs to knees with vermilion, and her head was hanging limp, her mouth smashed. The white floor below the chair was a spreading shout of red, tendrils already winding their way into the drain.

There's one less of Them, now.

That was as important as all the worlds, and nowhere near enough.

Reading his mind, Oberon asked, "Do you still want more?"

"Is there more?" he asked, small and uncertain.

Oberon laughed. "This is the Sphere of Light and Shadow. There is always more."

mille mortibus

Theren forced himself to concentrate on his computer screen.

He would not think of what was being done miles below him, in a room that was too small, to a girl that was too small. He could not afford to remember those amber eyes. His task was too important to allow himself to be distracted by

(one more, it's one more, what's one more?)

anything.

He'd spent half a year's pay to acquire the tiny device hidden in the frame of his chair. It promised a natural-sounding microphone failure within a thirty-foot radius.

He'd survived endless, terrifying days of keeping his face expressionless and his hands steady. Days of managing *Lord* and *Septarch*. Days of trying *not* to think about his treachery, certain the Septarch could indeed read his mind, which of course meant he thought of little else when he was in the Imperial presence.

He had broken no less than six of the Septarch's rules and spent most of the few remaining favors anyone owed him to get the communication code that was blinking now.

And after all that, his finger was poised over the key. One tap, that was all.

And he couldn't move.

His hand was paralyzed.

He suppressed an urge to swat it with his other hand, as if it were being obstinate to defy him.

The kid, he told himself. He thought of blackviolet bruises, of Leander looking at Oberon like the bastard was a saint, and he glared at his finger like a man trying to keep an erection by sheer willpower.

It still didn't move.

The fearful, defeated part of him—most of him really—was a constant mutter in the center of his head. *Rack. Rope. Red-hot irons. Strappado. Rape. Worse. There's always worse. Leave it alone. Because there's always worse, and you've seen enough to know how MUCH worse.*

"The kid," he said through gritted teeth, and in one convulsive motion he slammed his finger down, hitting a lot of other keys in the process. The one that counted beeped at him, and the whirring of invisible voodoo let him know that it was dialing.

It was dialing, and it was now too late to change his mind.

He slumped back into his seat, raked his hands through his dustcolored hair, listened to elaborate computerized rituals, and then there was the Earth insignia, the general one with the cross and the planet insistently still blue despite generations of smog and fallout. "Yes," said the voice through the speaker, already defensive, torn and in terrible pain.

"Paul, please don't hang up. You don't know me. My name is Theren. I want to help you get Leander back."

Silence. Sobbing.

"He's still alive, I knew he was, I knew they wouldn't have come and taken his things if he was dead, not his clothes, not his hairbrush, they even took his sheets and I couldn't smell him anymore, it was like he never happened, my boy, my son, my only, my son..."

Theren scrubbed at his face. His throat was injured. "Sir, please, I want to help you. Please."

"*How do I know that?*" Paul roared in rage. "You people took my *son*, and you killed my *wife*, and how do I know this isn't another fucking game?"

Theren considered trying to explain that Leander was the sole person he'd met in a decade who wanted to know his name, who looked him in the eye and talked to him like he was human, and not just one of the interchangeable Violet Guard, not just one more dangerous thing the Septarch could brandish to get what he wanted.

He considered trying to explain that the kid was funny and bright and brave, and even if Leander hadn't been any of those things, maybe it was finally one fucking kid too many.

He considered trying to explain that in his secret heart, alone at night, all he wanted was to die, preferably *not* while screaming and on display.

He considered trying to explain that he was afraid to do that after the way he'd spent his life, for fear there might be a Hell worse than this one waiting for him, and that thought that maybe, if he could do this *one* thing, that fear would ease. At least enough to give him the strength to turn the gun all the way around, to point at himself.

"I give you my word." Theren hid his face in his hands, knowing what fragile proof that really was, and he waited for the click of disconnection, and the hiss of interstellar static.

It didn't come. He thought *thank you, God,* and meant it.

"I want you to have him back," Theren said into the silence, hoarse and unworthy and desperate. "I don't want him here. He can't stay here. Will you help me?" A beat, and then, "Please?"

Silence. Then, "Leander," in a thin and desolate voice that struck Theren in the base of his skull like a bludgeon.

He knew he would go on with this, coward or not.

"Listen," he said. "This is the plan."

They went over it twice before Theren disconnected.

His hands moved by themselves, digging through his desk drawers. Not for the bottle. Not this time.

He found a smooth stack of paper, and a pen, but when he pulled that out and looked at it, it was a crimson, and he cursed and threw it over his shoulder and wiped his fingers on his thigh.

Tainted. Evil. *Approximate time for clinical death to occur: seventy-six hours, forty-three minutes.*

These things, that unholy pen had written.

These things, his polluted hand had written.

He searched again, and found the stub of a plain ordinary graphite pencil, and he pulled that out and swept his desk clear and began to draw, with difficulty. He was no artist.

He made two lines in the shape of a t, a cross, and a circle and stick arms and legs and body, and it wasn't enough, wasn't right, but it would have to be, because it was the best he could do.

He creased the bottom of the drawing to help it stand up, propped it carefully against his screen.

He sat and looked at it. That wasn't right, and he stood up and shoved his chair aside, so hard it fell over.

He knelt on the floor in front of his desk, his elbows on the edge of the table, and folded his hands, looking at his amateur cross.

God, you don't know me, but my name is Theren. I'm not asking anything for me. I need your help, so please be there, and please listen to me.

He waited.

Nothing.

He felt silly, and that was all.

There was noise, in the hallway, voices and laughter, commotion. Theren stood up, his gun in his hand, an unconscious decision which surprised him. He considered holstering it again. Instead, he clicked off the safety, opened his door a crack, and peered out.

It was Oberon, and Leander, a game that involved a lot of running and stopping, with intervals of shoving and laughing and profanity, each trying to get the other to fall.

Like children, or lovers.

Except that they were both covered in gore, lavishly smeared with it from sole to scalp.

As he watched, Leander pulled himself free, laughing, and sat on the floor right in the middle of the corridor, rolled over on his back with his legs straight up. He drew expectant circles in the air with his toes. It made The Septarch lean against the bulkhead, crippled with mirth. This was unnerving. Theren could not recall having ever seen Oberon *laugh*. Not like that.

Not like he meant it.

When Oberon recovered he seized Leander's ankles and pulled him, while Leander spread his arms and giggled incoherently, leaving a long wavering trail of red in his wake.

Then he understood it. Not fall, but slide. They were trying to get one another to slide.

Theren shut the door. Locked it.

He looked at his drawing, and he couldn't even tell what it was meant to be, anymore.

He picked it up, crumpled it.

Spread it out flat again.

Nope. Still ridiculous.

He pushed it off his desk, and closed his eyes.

occulta

Leander drifted awake, still blissfully high on at least three things, heavy with warmth and exhaustion. He opened his eyes to red and black bedding and the curve of the Septarch's ivory shoulder beside him.

Home.

He burrowed into the addictive warmth of Oberon's back, against the ellipsis of spine. He nuzzled, and when this did not work he licked.

Oberon made an irritated noise. "Leander, go back to sleep. It's early."

"How can you even tell? It's always night here."

"If I am still sleepy, it's too early."

"Do you know what megalomania is?"

Oberon kicked at him, muffled and harmless in a tangle of sheets and furs.

Leander nuzzled him again and quieted, until the Septarch's breathing slowed and his limbs went slack.

This is the Sphere of Light and Shadow.

Oh, how there had been so much more.

A pill that dissolved on his tongue and left most of its magick in his mouth, so that he wanted to bite and lick and swallow all the world.

The taste of own his fingers, still bright with Felicity's blood, and a kiss around them.

A boy with dark soft hair under him, and a nail gun kicking in his hand. Oberon on top of him, inside him, saying *his eyes, do it in his eyes.*

A dark, hot room, filled with the reek of iron and death. Wet ripping sounds. Those talons in his mouth, adorned with shreds of meat. Leander's hands guided into a long gaping wound, slick soft things in there that reminded him of the texture of his own tongue.

Then, a wet red blur.

This made him shudder and twitch, the deluge of it.

So many revelations in so few days, so many maddening pleasures, and no end in sight. The luxury of it.

Always more.

He wished he could give Oberon a gift, after the many gifts the Septarch had given him.

And then he decided to do just that.

The Gallery was silent and empty.

Leander let himself into his cell. It didn't feel like *his*, now. It was hard to understand that he'd slept here so few days ago. His things didn't seem to belong here anymore. He put a smaller sketchbook and a few pencils in his bag. He wanted to take his easel and the massive sketchbook and all the rest of his art supplies

(home)

but wasn't sure if he was allowed to summon guards and boss them around, or upend the Imperial chambers. He decided to wait until Oberon was awake and in less of a kicking mood to ask.

He rummaged through his backpack, pulled out his journal, flipped through it.

Maybe I'm evil.

He didn't feel evil. He didn't feel guilty. He ached all over, but that was about it.

He wished he could write a letter and send it back in time to the old Leander, and tell him there wasn't anything wrong with him, he was just living on the wrong damn planet. People were engineers, teachers, artists, transit drivers, doctors, priests. Why couldn't some people be killers? They had torturers. Executioners. Soldiers. Just another art form.

He wanted to do it again, soon, but maybe not too soon. He wanted to wait for that starving rage again. It would be better that way.

That's what the fury is, why it hurts, like that. It's hunger. I just had no fucking idea what to do about it.

Well, he'd had *some* ideas, he thought, grinning at remembered fires.

He had one thing he *could* give Oberon as a gift, assuming the Septarch had no interest in scraps of Earth machinery, now-useless data sticks, broken drug paraphernalia, or the other flotsam that filled his beloved bag.

Leander lifted the cover sheet from the easel, regarded his drawing of Oberon and Jyana. It was a crimson nightmare, one that pleased him more than he'd dared to hope. With little conscious decision to do so he sat down, the red pencil in his hand, a black one between his teeth.

He added the few last details it lacked, a touch more shading, a smoothed edge, strokes blended with a licked fingertip. When it was finished he left his wheel of three sixes in the right corner, rolled the sketch and the cover sheet into a smooth cylinder, and after some one-handed scavenging, tied it with the string that cinched his bag closed.

Perfect.

Almost.

A memory: Soren, her face alight and stunning with appalled happiness, her arms full of long-stemmed roses, saying *Paul, these must have been a fortune, you know better,* nuzzling into the bright flawless blooms.

He left his cell, and then the Gallery, the sketch in his hand, his bag an odd but familiar weight over his shoulder. He found a wall terminal, and when he inquired *flowers,* was given a map with several illuminated options, each labeled GARDEN, and a string of characters that he assumed specified their location.

What was a garden like?

He remembered the park, when he'd been a toddler, but it had been concrete and wood and metal, not a plant to be found. He could imagine his mother's potted violets. He could imagine a farm, from pictures, but that was as close as he could get, except another toddler memory of *Alice Through the Looking-Glass.*

He chose the nearest GARDEN, and a gentle sourceless line of firecolored light ignited where the wall and the floor met, pulsing in the correct direction. He followed.

It was a long walk. Oberon's impossible legs and embarrassing tendency to carry him everywhere would have been welcome. At last he came to a large pair of double doors, armed with a keypad in the center. It recognized him, and the doors slid open.

He walked through, into Eden.

It dazzled him, so much light, so much color, after the Sphere's soothing palette of night and flame. He drew in a deep breath, and the air was sweet and clear, heavy with the scent of thousands of flowers.

It was green, everywhere, and when he knelt and clutched at the ground there was real soil, rich and brown with a warm smell that made his throat ache.

He looked up, and there was a dome, the bright blue of Earth's sky before the wars.

He had never seen a blue sky.

And there were trees.

He had never seen a tree.

He walked up to one, half-afraid.

The trunk was a rough gray-brown, thicker around than he was, throbbing with life. He reached out, laid his hand on it, rested his head against it. He didn't care if he was being watched. It was so tall, and robed in leaves the color of his mother's eyes.

He reached down and picked a piece of grass, real green grass, not the thin yellow pathetic Earth stuff that sometimes still grew between the cracks in the concrete. He put it to his mouth, and tasted it, and it tasted green and pure.

Here, in this wasteland.

Farther in, Leander found what he was looking for. They were bloodred and flawless, each bloom big enough for him to cup in both hands, perfume as strong as a presence. He broke one off, and the thorns bit at his fingers. He rubbed the blood into the dirt at the base of the bush, in gratitude and apology, and then tied this single rose into the cord binding his drawing.

He could not hand this to Oberon himself. It would unquestionably be fatal, even if the Septarch *didn't* laugh.

He stepped out of the Garden, though it hurt him to do it, and after some thought found a console and attempted to call Theren. The guard arrived, after some minutes, looking puzzled at being so summoned, and then alarmed at Leander's bloody hand. "What happened?"

"It's a scratch. Forget it. Could you take this to him? Please?" Leander asked, and held out the package.

Something sad came over Theren's face, but he held out his hand, and said, "Yes."

He took the Septarch's gift, and went away.

Leander went back into the Garden. He settled himself with his back against

(his)
the tree, took out his sketchbook and pencils and began to draw again, and this time it was his mother, in a thick green forest, and she was young, laughing. The wound had never happened.

Oberon woke, sulked because Leander was gone and because there was no one to see him do it, opted for coffee and drugs in lieu of breakfast, and did useless things at his desk. He sent the film of Felicity to the *Promise Keeper*. Now, he was sifting through ancient Japanese pornography.

He wanted Leander back, wanted to ask what that had been like, his first kill. His own first kill had been a disaster. He'd gotten much better with practice.

He was tempted to send for him, but he knew about being in the middle of a painting or a murder or whatever, and there was a coherency, a flow that couldn't be interrupted.

And yes, because it would look as if he *needed* the boy, and that was untenable.

He considered visiting Victoria, something he did a few times a year. She was soothing company, and her decorative speech impediment made her a very good listener. And she had excellent taste in drugs. He knew she had been patiently trying to instigate a friendship with him for a decade now.

It was that very fact that made him decide against this.

He understood what friends were, and that humans were almost as fixated on having them as they were on having mates. He'd made attempts, but when he tried to interact with others as friends were supposed to do, he felt as though he were trying to perform a dance without knowing any of the steps, to music that everyone but himself could hear. Friendship, he suspected, was something that could only exist between equals.

And he had no equals.

He had almost talked himself into visiting the Arcade, climbing into one of the hideous entertainment devices that only he could survive, when his door chimed. He keyed it open, with unseemly haste, and when it was Theren his discontent threatened to ignite into actual anger.

Theren was a great deal of fun to upset. Oberon often

wondered if the man suspected how many of the things he said or did in his presence were solely to produce that reaction. He tapped his fingernail against the screen. A contorted woman in leather and fishnets, with chemically blonde hair. "I want to get a little girl and do her up like this, like a whore, did I ever tell you that?"

Theren glanced at the screen politely, but Oberon could see him trying not to grit his teeth. Success. "The boy asked me to give this to you, Lord Septarch." He saw the look leveled at him. "You said...if he required anything..."

"Why didn't he bring it himself?"

"I think...he's working on another sketch, my Lord."

Oberon looked at it. A sheet of paper, bound with black cord, and tucked into the knot was

(a lie) (a trap) (a miracle)

a single red rose.

His heart hitched, jolted in his chest, stopped, and then began to run harder, with an uneven and unpleasant jitter in its rhythm.

He reached over his desk and snatched the rolled-up sketch out of Theren's hands. "Get out," he ordered.

He held it a moment, silent alarms triggering in his head, one after another, a cascade failure that made his mouth dry and his hands unwieldy.

He didn't want to open it.

He pulled the rose out of the black string, held it to his face. It smelled of redemption, and it was as soft as Leander was inside, wet and innocent. He licked it to make sure. No. It didn't taste the same. His teeth ached to bite it in half. He did no such thing.

He unrolled the sketch. Himself, angular and elongated and Egyptian. The girl, her name had been Jane or Jaina, with her tiny hands convulsing into claws.

Beautiful. He made me beautiful. Is that how he sees me?

He's talented. Much better than he was for Blue Christ, and he was impressive then, Oberon thought, in the last stable place in his mind.

Then that, too, fell to the dissolution, and the drawing began to blur.

He dropped the paper onto his desk, and fled, the rose still in his hand.

He struck the first doorway he came to, hard with his broken hands, battering against it, kicking at it, screaming, "Get up!"

There were people, stumbling frightened out into the hallway. Most of them were still sleepy-eyed and dazed. His guards. Members of his court. Painted, sticky bedwarmers to both.

He hated every one of them, hated them and *envied* them the imagined silence in the space of their skulls.

He would not suffer madness alone.

"Get up. Everybody. Everybody UP. Nobody sleeps."

They only stared.

"Three days. I want all the fucking cameras on, and *nobody sleeps*. Nobody. If you sleep, you're dead. Every living being in the whole of my fucking SPHERE, you GOT THAT?"

They didn't. They kept staring at him, some terrified, some drowsy and angry, some contemptuous and resentful. Victoria, her flawless doll's face worried and sad, her sewn lips glittering. Kaden in his steel prosthesis, expressionless.

"That's your *penance*."

They still didn't understand.

Leander, in his head: *...looked at me like he hated me, and I didn't even know why....*

He was sobbing, and clutching the flower like a talisman. So much space. So many eyes. He held it out at them, turning and turning, as if it might ward them all off.

"FUCK YOU! YOU HEARD ME!"

Someone was trying to hold him. Theren? Cayle? He struck out hard, was rewarded with a cry of pain, and found himself free.

He left them staring after him. No one dared to follow.

He swarmed into the Crypt, veiled in heavy fury.

Here was his most precious and most hated possession: the corpse of Acharis Maer.

"Why aren't you *dead*?"

He intended a whisper, but it climbed by itself into almost a scream. That felt just right, and he decided to continue it awhile.

Acharis was, of course, still quite dead, yet The First Septarch was never silent. He was an endless litany of questions, of dry and amused accusations, of truths Oberon did not want to hear.

And he was never so loud as when Oberon fractured into dangerous pieces.

He grabbed what was left of Acharis, screaming still, struck out, again and again. Things broke in his hands. He forced his hands closed in the corpse, ignoring the blinding, grating pain of it, and dragged it from the wall. This was demanding even for him, and more pain spilled in a warm gush across his lower back.

He slammed it down, onto the floor, and he was on top of Acharis, screaming still. He had vague intentions of rape, and the utter opposite of an erection. He roared in frustration, and smashed at the body until it was a flat, brown smear. Parts of it were still wet enough to squelch in his hands, and that was fine with him.

Covered in rotting blood, and ancient shit, he stood up, his hands crooked and wounded, and he said, one more time, "Why aren't you dead?"

There was no answer, and yet still, no silence.

He stumbled towards the door. There was a rose on the floor, crumpled and bleeding, but still alive, still beautiful.

Little bloody skirt.

He picked it up in his filthy hands. Something was wrong with his eyes. He smeared the blood away from his cheeks, but the fluid on his fingers was clear. It made no sense to him, and inspired a laugh that was distilled insanity.

Rose. Bleeding. Still alive.

He was wounded.

Safe. There had to be somewhere safe.

Somewhere silent.

The Worm Chamber.

Oberon stood at the edge of the shaft, clutching Leander's flower to his chest.

Little bloody skirts.

Something was wrong, here, in his last safe place.

The sound was faint, delicate, but undeniable. He heard it again, high, near the ceiling. A frenetic, battering flutter.

He knew what it was.

He slammed the door behind him, pressing the rose against his failing lungs, but it was too late. The sound was inside him. Still. Merciless. Fluttering, beating, furious, innocent.

Nowhere. Nowhere was safe. Not now.

Not ever again.

He found a terminal, and between his broken fingers and his inability to remember or express

(who)

what he was looking for it was a wonder he didn't smash that, too. In desperation he pulled up the roll for the last tithe, and to his near-hysterical relief, knew the name when he saw it. He had no need of the light guide his selection activated, and he left it gleaming in his wake.

He reached the doors to the Garden, and couldn't remember how to open them. He left smears of blood and filth on the keypad, trying, and gave up and banged on the door with what was left of his hands, screaming that all-important name.

"Leander!"

The door slid open.

Oberon didn't expect it. He fell into the Garden, and Leander half-caught him, but the Septarch was many times too heavy for him. They were tangled on the ground, half in the hallway, half on green grass and soft warm earth.

The boy was frantic, appalled at his hands, cupping his face, trying to cradle him off the ground. Oberon meant to push him off, and then meant to cling, and found he could do neither.

"What's wrong with you? Why did you give me this?"

The Septarch was sobbing like a human child.

He held up the rose like an accusation.

adflictae

"Don't," Leander pleaded, through tears of sympathy and fear. "Don't cry. I thought it would make you happy. Please don't."

Oberon was clutching at him with those gorgeous hands bent into hideous shapes. He pushed his face into Leander's chest, soaking him with tears. His voice was jagged and terrified. "My eyes..."

Leander tugged at the hem of his shirt and wiped at Oberon's eyes for him. "There's nothing wrong with your eyes, but your *fingers*– "

The Septarch ignored this, did not even seem to hear it. "I'm bleeding. They're gone. He took them out. There was a machine, a claw with hinges and he *took them out!*"

This last was a hysterical shriek. This was no longer the Emperor of All Things Unseen. Only a boy, terribly wounded.

"No," Leander said, and he kissed him all over his face, held him hard and tight. He felt too small to embrace pain like that. "Your eyes are fine. You're okay."

"I'm bleeding. I can't see."

"You're crying," Leander told him, still crying himself. "That's all. I thought it would make you happy. I'm so sorry."

Oberon noticed that the boy was weeping, and he raised a clumsy hand to Leander's face. "Did he hurt you? Which group are you in? I don't remember you," he whispered. "You're beautiful. What's your name?"

"Leander," he said. His heart was breaking. He'd always thought that was garbage they used for poetry, until he felt it happen. It broke like glass and the fragments were ripping him to pieces. "I'm Leander. Nobody hurt me."

"But I killed your mother. You gave me a flower, and I killed your mother..."

"It doesn't matter. I forgive you. It doesn't matter." Leander dared a look out into the corridor, the *empty* fucking corridor. What was the use of having a spaceship bursting at the seams with CAMERAS if you weren't going to send medics after noise like this?

"Stay with me," Oberon said, pleading.

"Yes. Always. Shh, you have to..." To what? Snap out of it?

Calm down? *Seriously I'm fucking fourteen and I was probably high out of my mind the day they covered what to do about this one, could I please get an ADULT for once?*

The Septarch looked at the rose again, holding it between them. "Why did you give this to me?"

Why did you ask me to wait?

He was rocking Oberon now, out of instinct, stroking his clotted skein of hair. "I wanted you to know I was thinking about you. That's all."

"Why were you thinking about me?"

"It makes me happy to think about you," Leander whispered.

"Why?" he whispered, wide-eyed.

Insanely innocent. Innocently insane.

Leander could only shake his head.

The answer was right there, in his throat, on his tongue, but this was not the time to say it.

Oberon tried to stand up, and Leander had to steady him to keep him from sprawling in the dirt again. "My eyes. I need a doctor, they're infected, it could spread into my brain," he said, more to himself than to Leander.

He has no idea what he's doing.

And then a thought even more terrifying than that one. There might be people in the Sphere that would see the Septarch's sickness as weakness.

As an opportunity.

Leander drew in a long breath, in through his nose, out through his mouth. He forced both tears and terror aside, found that still and unstoppable place inside him where fires were born.

"All right. Come on, it's okay. We'll go see a doctor," Leander told him, and other nonsense. He coaxed and steered a staggering, rambling Oberon out of the Garden, and was deciding whether left or right would take them to a terminal sooner when Theren and three other guards drew close in a clicking of bootheels.

He was relieved for an instant. *About fucking time. Maybe they know what to do.*

Then Oberon saw them and began to scream again, his cries high and thin with dread and panic. Leander lost his grip on the black robes, and Oberon *crawled* behind him and tried to hide behind

Leander's legs, covering his face with his mangled hands. "Don't let them," was all Leander could make of the muffled lunacy that followed.

He's afraid of them. He doesn't know who they are. He's not even keeping hold of who I am.

What if he stays like this forever?

What have I done?

No. He could indulge in grief and self-loathing later.

For now, he had things to burn.

Leander looked at Theren and pointed at the gun at his belt. "Give me that," he ordered.

Theren considered, and then shook his head once. "Leander, you're still a slave, there is no way I can hand you my gun—"

"Give that to me *right fucking now* or you will be one sorry motherfucker," Leander snapped. He didn't waver, not at all. It was easy. The animal was there, always had been, and he could slip into it any time he wanted to. They knew their place. Prey.

He heard Oberon break into a panic-stricken wail, behind him. He reached behind himself, until he found and caught a handful of dirty velvet. Either this attempt at comfort worked, or Oberon ran out of breath. The wail dwindled into an intermittent moan.

Theren held Leander's gaze for another infuriating set of seconds, and then handed Leander his gun.

It was heavier than he'd expected, but Leander managed not to show it. He clicked off what he hoped was the safety, and pointed it at the guards. "Get back. Drop the guns. Now."

They looked at Theren. He gestured and three guns hit the floor. Bootheels, clicking in retreat.

"You." Leander pointed the gun at one of then, and the man stiffened. "Go get Cayle. Theren, you stay. The rest of you get out of here."

Oberon was still sitting on the floor, wrapped up small. Leander waited until the guards were out of sight, and then showed the Septarch his prize. "Look," he said, keeping his voice low and even. "It's okay. I've got a gun, see, look. They're leaving. They're going to get you a doctor, all right? Nobody's going to hurt you. Anybody tries anything and I shoot them. Okay?"

Oberon nodded, still crying, but visibly less agitated.

"Promise?"

There was a crashing bloodlust then, and Leander wanted more than anything to have whoever had done it, whatever it was, tied down in a very small room.

"Nobody's doing anything to you. I promise."

"He will, when he catches us," Oberon whispered, staring at invisible things.

"Who will?"

"Acharis. When he finds out we tried to escape."

Leander could feel his muscles wanting to shake, and he ground down with all his will and stood there still and tight, like he imagined a soldier would. Acharis. Oberon's most consistent delusion was that he and Leander were both prisoners of the first Septarch.

He mouthed at Theren, *What's wrong with him?*

"The first Septarch did things to him you would not believe, and he gets like this sometimes," he said, so quietly that Leander almost had to read his lips.

"After this *long*?" Leander whispered. His throat hurt.

Theren nodded.

Leander winked at him, deliberately, and said louder, "Get on the floor. Put your arms behind you."

Theren did.

Leander made a big show of keeping the gun trained on Theren. He sat down beside Oberon and shifted the gun to one hand and pulled him close. Oberon buried his face in Leander's lap, sobbing *he'll kill us all.*

Cayle came around the corner at the end of the corridor in a dead run. Leander snapped the gun on him and he skidded to a stop, his hands up. "What the Hell?"

"Theren, get out of here," Leander said.

"Leander, he might hurt himself, or you—"

"No. He won't. I know he won't."

Theren got up, clearly unhappy about this plan, and left, stopping once to look back at them.

Leander had already forgotten him.

"Oberon, this is Cayle. Do you remember him? He's a doctor. Will you let him look at you?"

Oberon looked up, his face streaked with tears, and shook his head with such vehemence that his hair made a storm around his head. "He might—"

"I'll shoot him if he does," Leander said, looking hard at Cayle to make sure he understood this game.

Cayle understood just fine, and was trying not to smile. He was beginning to think this little slave might actually have a brain.

It took both of them to persuade Oberon onto the examining table. Leander finally gave up and pointed the gun at the doctor (with the safety *on*, this time) while Cayle looked at both of his eyes.

"I need to put these drops in for you, all right?" *Saline*, he mouthed at Leander.

Oberon submitted to that, and to the series of injections after that, and soon he was still, his breath deep and even.

Leander exhaled, one shuddering whoop, and found that his arms were rubbery and perilously feeble when he put the gun down at long last.

"You all right, son?"

Leander found he was not, and managed to fall in the direction of a chair. "I was afraid someone would hurt him while he was....was not okay."

The doctor looked at him with an eyebrow raised, almost doubtfully, but whatever he saw made him give one brief nod. "Commendable, but not necessary. The Sphere locks itself down when it detects that his life signs have stopped, and I have, oh, about an hour to find him and get him running again before it triggers the self-destruct. If he can't have it, nobody can. Nice life insurance policy, if you can get it."

This was comforting, and made Leander feel a little silly. "So he didn't really need me to protect him."

"I wouldn't say that." Cayle made a face at the unconscious Septarch, wrinkling his nose at the smell. He rummaged around for rubbing alcohol and a cotton cloth. "What is this delightful substance he's covered with?"

"I don't know. He was like that when he came to me."

Cayle sighed, and started with Oberon's face. "He's a lunatic," he muttered, but his mouth was soft with sorrow.

"What's wrong with him? Is he crazy, or sick, or what?"

"No one knows what sets him off. He's dead set against talking about his internal life."

That one made Leander quiet for a moment, a little overwhelmed at how much trust Oberon had already shown him. He wondered if Oberon, too, had spent much of his life looking at other people and wondering how and why they could possibly have relationships. "Was he always like this, or did whatever happened to him make him this way?"

Cayle didn't answer for a long time, busying himself with cleaning the Septarch in search of further wounds. "When Acharis bought him, he was eighteen, and in prison serving life for murdering a twelve-year-old girl. No, I don't think it made him like this. But it did make it much, much worse."

"You can't fix it," Leander said, in flat despair.

"I could erase the memories, like I could remove all these, and give him normal-looking eyes," he said, gesturing at the scars. "He won't let me, and I don't suggest you mention it to him. It makes him furious. And he wouldn't be himself anymore, not after that."

"Will he be all right?"

"He has to sleep it off. He's usually fine after that. He's broken his hands again, but that looks like the worst of it." Cayle did things that made terrible noises, pushing and twisting bones back into place. "They'll heal by the time he wakes up."

"But there's nothing you could do, so it doesn't...hurt him like this?"

"His hands?" Cayle made a sound that was suspiciously like a snort. "He's used to that. Probably doesn't even feel it. Or enjoys it, maybe."

"That's not what I meant."

"No. I'm not that kind of doctor and if Oberon wasn't so easily distracted by more amusing pastimes he'd kill every psychologist, psychiatrist, and counselor alive." He stood up to Leander's resentful, mournful green gaze for as long as he could, and sighed. "Kid, don't you think I've tried everything? I'd help him if I could. Believe it. That's why I'm still here." Cayle frowned at a long deep cut on Oberon's forearm. "You could help him, maybe, but I doubt it."

"How?"

"Get him to talk about it," said Cayle. He was looking at Oberon again, with something mournful of his own hidden behind his glasses. "It's just that..."

He stopped himself, waved one hand in the air like a man trying to clear away smoke.

Leander was looking at Oberon, too. His hand moved in what was almost a convulsion, and he took Oberon's broken hand in his own. "Just what?"

"That he's nothing like Acharis was," Cayle finished, more to himself than to the boy. "He seems to...do these things to impress himself, in a way. To remind himself that he survived. He's trying to become Acharis, I suppose, but he'll never manage that one. He has too much...potential."

"Is that why? All of this, I mean," Leander said, motioning with his eyes to indicate the entire Sphere.

Cayle shrugged. "He's insane. I give him too much credit, sometimes. That's all."

That wasn't all, but Leander didn't argue. He felt he had all the information he needed in no particular order. He couldn't see the solution, not even with it right in front of him. He stroked Oberon's hand, tracing the long chrome nails with his own.

Cayle left them that way, without speaking again.

ozymandias

When Oberon woke up he wouldn't talk about anything.

An invisible servant had already brought him a clean black set of robes. He dressed as if he were sore. Leander tried to help, and Oberon responded with such a vicious look that started Leander crying again.

"Come with me. I want to go back to my room," he said.

Leander had to help him. He was moving like he was still wounded, and he stopped sometimes, breathing hard, leaning against the wall. "Please talk to me," Leander said.

"I don't have anything to talk about. I'm sorry I scared you," he muttered. "I want you to go away. To the Gallery, or whatever. I want to be alone."

"You *just* told me you wanted me to come with you!"

Oberon was, expressionless, black eyes motionless.

"I'm not going," Leander told him.

Oberon didn't protest that. He nodded, and whispered, "Fine, whatever."

He's like a zombie. Like he's numb, or too fucking hurt to care anymore.

Once they reached his rooms Oberon lay across his bed and didn't move. Leander tried to lie down beside him, and he said one word. "No."

It was too much. For him to have been so different, so affectionate and interested and *human*, and now this.

"Don't you think I have a right to know what happened?" Leander cried at him. "What did I do wrong? Why are you so angry at me?"

"You think I'm angry at you?"

"Yes," Leander told him. Damn it. He was still crying. Maybe Cayle could remove his tear ducts. "You won't talk to me, and you won't look at me, and you started this when I gave you that fucking picture I wish I never drew. What am I supposed to think?"

269

"On my computer. There's a series of files called The Experiment."

"What are they?"

"Just watch them," he said, his voice lifeless. He pulled a pillow towards him, clutched it to his chest. "Keep the volume down. I don't want to hear them."

Leander nodded, and started to leave the bedroom.

"Wait."

That word. Leander stopped.

"In that drawer. Morphine. I don't think I can...would you..."

He did. It was hard to do that right now, to physically hurt Oberon, even if it was only a needle. He hoped he was doing it right. He laid a kiss on the pinprick when he was finished, thinking of Soren and skinned knees. Oberon touched his hair with clumsy fingers. "I'm not angry. I just need to lay here for a while."

"Okay," Leander said, even though it wasn't. He wanted to say *Am I still your favorite?* but he feared the answer.

He went into the front room, pulled the door to the bedroom closed, but not latched. The statue leered at him as he passed.

He went to the computer, and it woke at his touch. The files were easy enough to find, but when he opened them a text window unfolded on the screen.

LEANDER, AFTER YOU WATCH THESE YOU WILL NEVER WANT ME TO TOUCH YOU AGAIN.

Leander bit his lip. He was tempted to go straight into the bedroom and shake Oberon until he confessed what made him think such a crazy thing.

The film began without introduction.

It was Oberon, sitting strapped into a chair. His hair was pulled back, and he was so thin you could see the bones of his face, his bare chest. The scars were still open wounds, here, and the eyes—

Leander gagged, and got up and wandered in a crooked circle, his face covered, but he could still see it.

There weren't any eyes.

Black holes, lined with red, the eyelids hanging in loose folds, the flesh around then stark and bruised.

And what he'd done, in Oberon's gunship, what Oberon had *let* him do. That must have taken so much courage, so much trust.

His throat tightened.

He sat down again, and he thought, *if I puke I've got to make sure not to do it where he can hear.*

Oberon had asked him to do this, and he would do it.

He made himself watch.

A voice, off camera. "What was that like?"

That had to be Acharis. The First Septarch. It was dry as dust, educated, emotionless. Merciless.

Leander understood, for the first time, how someone could want to end an entire *world* with fire.

"I'll kill you." Oberon was looking at nothing, his voice almost too soft to hear. "I'll kill you."

Oh, and he meant it. Leander shivered. He decided he'd rather remove his *own* eyes with a very dull knife than have Oberon ever say anything to him in that tone of voice.

Acharis, still off camera, said "Do I have to remind you of the rules for acceptable responses?"

Oberon shook his head, fast fast fast, and mouthed *no* over and over. Leander made a fist and drove it hard and fast into his own thigh, too many times to count, until the muscle knotted in protest. That was the broken Oberon he'd seen in the Garden, terrified, childlike. He hated it.

"What was it like?"

"My eyes. Where are they? I want them back."

"Oberon." There was a warning in that faceless voice, and thin amusement.

"Horrible." Oberon's bound hands tried to gesture, and couldn't, moving in underwater motions, in tiny abbreviated circles. He sobbed once, and blinked the wounds in his face. Leander gagged again, violently.

"Horrible. How eloquent of you. Suppose you tell me which part of it exactly was the most horrible."

"Not...not seeing, what it would do next..."

Leander covered his mouth hard and wept in agony. He made

271

himself do it without a sound, and he made himself keep watching.

The rest of the films were much worse.

Some unknown control warned him in time, and he made it into the hallway and was sick there, leaning against the wall and holding his hair out of the way. There was a new atrocity on the screen when he came back inside. He didn't sit down again. He stood with arms around his chest, and he watched until the screen went black.

No wonder he wants to keep the scars. No wonder he doesn't want new eyes. He's keeping it like a badge, like when people get hurt in wars.

Get him to talk about it.

Leander appreciated the sentiment, and the love he suspected was behind it, but while that might help a human he didn't think it would help Oberon. The Septarch was made of stronger, stranger stuff, and he understood wounds far better than he understood words. Leander touched the healing marks across his throat.

He closed the bedroom door between himself and Oberon as quietly as he could. He did not want to be overheard messaging the doctor.

Cayle was not at all pleased with the message. He argued, ordered, and objected. Leander let him do this, restated his message, and waited. Cayle agreed to his request, and hung up on Leander, which made him grin.

Oberon was sleeping, expressions flickering across his face that probably indicated dreams. If so, none of them were pleasant. Leander went to the red glass wall opposite the doorway, imitated the motions he'd seen Oberon use, and discovered an endless corridor of the same red glass. Wrong door. He made a note to himself to investigate this later, before he found the panel that slid aside to admit him to the bathroom.

He considered the sunken tub with longing, thinking of the filth still in the Septarch's hair, under his claws. He suspected attempts at negotiating Oberon into the tub would only lead to another argument, or worse, more of that shattered fear.

He supposed now was as good a time as any to see if Oberon was correct about not being able to get sick.

There was a rainbow of bottles behind the sink, none of them labeled. Leander wondered how many of them were poisonous. He opened drawers overflowing with cosmetics and pointy things until he found a clean black towel. He soaked it with warm water, wrung it out. His own face in the mirror above the long sink looked drawn and tired. Older. He bared his teeth at himself and that was a little better, but it didn't change his eyes. Still worried, haunted, and he'd only had to *watch* those films. The thought of it made his stomach knot, and his struggle to shove the memory away

(redblack holes, blinking)

made him hope this worked quickly, so they could go kill things. Preferably a lot of things. A psychologist. All the psychologists. Everyone on Earth that had no "criminal" record would probably do as an appetizer. He had yet to tire of that wonderful bluegreen pulse cannon and he was feeling highly motivated to continue his lessons as soon as

(his)

the Septarch was himself again.

Oberon was still asleep when he returned to the bedroom. He put his wet towel on one of the glossy black nightstands, stood looking at him for a long time. He knew what he intended to do, and meant to take the idea for a mental test-drive, but he found himself just, looking. Admiring. The Septarch looked like a photograph from an ancient black-and-white-film, impossible monochrome lying in all that red, red bed. Even his scars were colorless, his skin so white under the ocher filth that there couldn't be blood behind it.

Well, he would know in a minute, wouldn't he?

The fire was burning low. He had seen Oberon touch the abstract carvings to the right, and when he cautiously did so it blazed brighter, higher. Oberon stirred behind him, but did not wake.

The glossy black box was back on the marble shelf above the fireplace. He had to stand up on his toes to reach it—flicker of the last time he'd done this, naked and aching and with no idea what it contained.

He opened it, the little click making him wince.

The knife inspired a smile, though it was a weak and wobbly affair. He had no doubt it was real, though either perfectly preserved or flawlessly restored. He took it out of its velvet nook. The weight of it, the age and the darkness of it, the jovial skull, the tiny bolts that had once terrified an entire world. There was a tiny flake of blood on the blade—his own—and his smile steadied a little.

Drawing. That was all it was. Noisy, wet drawing.

The knife felt just right in his hand.

Something wet and light woke Oberon, touching his cheek, his chin. He stretched out his arms, expecting the texture of the worms, reached up and found Leander sitting on the edge of the bed, dabbing at his face with a damp towel.

"Now you know," he said. It was over, of course. No one could ever know that and look at him again. The universe didn't work that way.

Leander nodded once.

Then he put the towel aside and showed Oberon what he had behind his back.

It was the knife.

The sight of it was enough.

Oberon tried to move, to roll away, *he's gone crazy*, but he was trapped, wound up between his throat and his eyes, too weak to move.

Leander laid it down, on the black silk sheet, and leaned over and tugged at Oberon's robes.

Oberon sat up and let Leander undress him. He tried to help, but his hands were still awkward and uncooperative. Leander unlaced the throat, slid it down over his shoulders with gentle reverence. The robe was open to his waist, pooled around his hips and his wrists. He shivered and lay back again, wishing for the blankets. This was not enough, no, the boy wanted all of it, and he sighed and lifted his hips so Leander could pull the robes away, leaving him naked.

Leander straddled him, his knees digging into Oberon's ribs, still staring into Oberon's eyes, and the knife was in his hand again.

Oberon wet his lips with his tongue. He meant to say *what do you think you're doing?* This got mangled along the exit route, and came out, "What are you going to do?"

Leander laid the tip of the knife against Oberon's lips. "Shhh," he mouthed, and kissed him around the blade.

Oberon reached up to put his hands on Leander's back, his shoulders, and the knife pressed harder into his bottom lip, until he put his hands down again. He licked, cutting the tip of his tongue deeply enough for generous bleeding.

The taste wound itself through his mouth, liquid electricity, and he could feel it trickling down his chin, along his neck.

Blood. And it was his own.

And someone *else* had drawn it.

He made a thick gritty sound deep in his lungs.

Leander made a tight rough noise in response, kissing harder, until he was bleeding too. And he said, against the knife, "I'm going to unmake you."

He trailed the tip of the knife down the tracks the blood had made, left it for a heartless instant against the hollow of Oberon's throat, moved it down to the first thick slash of scar tissue along the left side of his collarbone. And he took Oberon's hands in his empty one and moved them up to the headboard.

Iron. The world was a labyrinth of conflicting textures, metal, velvet, and the pressure of the boy against his hips.

Oberon closed his hands around the bars. He opened his mouth to speak, to say *Leander* or *wait* or even *please*. He gripped the bars as hard as he could, trying to brace himself. He could not think of a word to express the way this was, the way it felt, this hybrid new emotion. Doomed. Perfect. Inevitable.

The knife was a luminous chill against his chest. He had time to draw in one crooked breath. A deep cold pressure, then pain as bright as broken glass, fiercer and bigger than he remembered.

The first cut opened like a dark orchid.

He let his head fall back, swallowed a mouthful of blood. He had never reacted this way. Not

(Acharis)

before, and not later, when it was a machine or some unfortunate slave hurting him at his command. This was different, and yet it had been lying under his skin all along, waiting to happen.

He was gasping in rhythm with the cutting, moving against the knife, as if his flesh was involved in this atrocity, in some obscene relationship with the blade.

That mark was done, and Leander was moving down to the next one.

Not all of them. He can't do all of them. I could bleed to death.

He knew he wouldn't. Even if he was bled dry, he would survive, still and cold and waiting for Cayle to transfuse him. It had happened before.

It had never like been like this.

The next scar was deeper, thicker, and Leander had to cut over it twice. The knife scraped one of Oberon's ribs, and his back arched by itself, sending chemical shudders up his spine, into his teeth. He took in a lungful of air too rough and huge to keep, and hissed between his teeth, blood scorching his throat. He could hear the cutting, like scissors through thick wet cloth. Luscious. Gorgeous. And it wasn't cloth, it was those scars, those goddamned hated scars that he kept because of the price he had paid to wear them, and

...and Leander was unmaking them. Erasing them.

And the scars that came after wouldn't be the same at all.

He made a liquid choking sound, his mouth still bleeding. The pain came and went with his heartbeat, no longer cold, and so massive it had to be bigger than he was, reaching out into the air, into the invisible mystery of his aura.

And that was two.

He had *hundreds* of scars.

This revelation made him cry out, afraid, beginning the first tense stirrings of struggle.

Leander cut him hard and deep and fast, and looked at him with murder in his eyes, and hissed, "Don't."

There was a shriek in reverse, deep in his lungs, and he couldn't breathe at all for a horrible instant, could only shudder, his throat quaking.

He couldn't argue with those eyes. He didn't want to. *He thought, right now, this minute, I'm not the Emperor of anything.*

It made some drastic weight vanish, and he could breathe again. He didn't speak. He didn't need to.

He had almost learned to take it, when to inhale, when to grit his teeth, when Leander traced the awful scar down his sternum, along the edge of his ribcage, where it curled in an evil comma along his stomach, the tail cupping his navel, where the skin was soft and laden with nerves.

When the world had faded back into focus, he said, "Gag me. Please."

Leander looked at him. his green eyes filled with the same calm relentless concentration Oberon saw there whenever the boy was drawing. "Why?"

"Because...I'll scream....."

"So scream," Leander told him, his fingertip tracing beside that last cut with secret gentleness. "There's no one to hear you but me, and I'll never tell."

"No," he managed, before he ran out of breath, before he could explain that *scream* wasn't what he'd meant at all. What was about to happen would be irrevocable, would break him in ways not even Cayle could fix.

Leander was pushing at him to turn over, and he already knew to shift his hands and keep hold of the bars on the headboard. And the knife was unmaking the hieroglyphs on his back, painting over them with hard, vicious gashes, cutting deeper than the deepest of the original wounds. He was making an unbearable sound into the black silk pillows, a wet tattered cry that was loud and inelegant and could not be his own.

After years, Leander tugged at him to turn over again. The slashes on his back informed him the silk wasn't soft, not at all, not anymore. It was like lying on gravel puddled with blood.

Leander kissed him again, deeper and almost angry, and laid the blade of the knife across Oberon's tongue and cut him there again.

Then, he pushed him back down on the bed, and pried open his left eye.

That was when Oberon lost hold of his first scream. He tried to fight, but found he'd lost enough blood to cripple him. All he managed was to raise his feeble hands. He dissolved into a loose wail of terror.

"Hush." Leander kissed him again, on his cheekbone, on his frightened wide-open eye. "Stay with me."

"I can't," he said, sobbing, bleeding.

This was familiar ground. "Yes," Leander whispered. "You can."

The knife traced around Oberon's eye, cutting around the implant. It snagged the outer corner of his eyelid for an agonizing instant, made a tiny ragged tear before it steadied, leaving a bleeding circle in the dark pink flesh around his eyeball.

The slice was like an acid.

Oberon screamed again, a softer, slower cry that might have been a moan if it was not so weighted with dread.

Leander moved to his other eye,

...blind, I'm blind, and I can't see what it will do next...

made the same cut,

...no, it's not an IT, it's him, it's Leander, and I am not blind, I can see...everything...but everything is red and all I see is Leander...

and pressed a gentle kiss to each shuddering eyelid.

...over, it's over, it's...

Leander's fingertips were under his chin, pushing his head back, and the three horizontal cuts across his throat were a pale thin epilogue, the memory of agony.

Whispering: "My favorite...my only favorite..." but he didn't know which of them was saying it.

The tears came then, more red than clear, streaking his face. Then a long, safe, silent space, the sanctuary he'd longed for, and he was not alone there. Not anymore.

Not ever again.

Oberon said, "Can I move?"

Leander was rubbing his face against Oberon's neck. He nodded, and Oberon wrapped his arms around the boy and crushed him close, the pressure scorching his wounded chest.

"They're from me, now," Leander was saying, muffled. "All of them. He never happened to you. Only me. The worst nightmare you ever had."

"Am I? Your favorite?" The bed was soaked with blood, the room spinning. He held Leander tighter, to make sure he didn't disappear.

"My only favorite. Didn't I mark you?"

"Yes. Yes you did," Oberon said, crying.

"Did you kill him?" Leander asked him. The boy sounded like

he'd been crying for a long time. Oberon touched his face, his hair.

"Yes."

"It didn't help."

"No. No, it didn't."

"Can...can I help?"

This boy. This birdboned boy, this tiny killer boy with his bright eyes, his endless supply of tears and questions.

His boy.

"You already did," Oberon said. "I hurt. Everywhere. And I can't remember any pain before this one. And I don't want you to go back to the Gallery. Not ever again."

"Oh," Leander said, and then in a plastic cheerful tone, "You know, the blood is starting to dry and I can't carry you, but if you come to the tub I'll—"

"Leander."

The boy stopped.

"I want you to stay here, with me. I don't want you to sleep in a different room."

"Why did you leave that message?" Leander asked, staring at the stained cloth in his hands. "Why wouldn't I want you to touch me?"

"How could you? After knowing...those things."

"Those things are part of who you are. I couldn't...knowing why you are this way doesn't change anything. Not the way you think."

"How does it change it?"

Leander looked up, and then to the side, as if answers were hidden in the etched glass walls. "It makes something...in me...bigger. It hurts me. But it makes me proud of you. It makes me understand you better."

Oberon curled on his side with his limbs drawn in. Spider, wounded. He needed a transfusion, or worse. "Do you know how to call Cayle?"

"He's waiting outside. He almost sent your guards to stop me when I told him what I was going to do. He likes you."

I was safe this entire time, Oberon thought.

"Cayle doesn't like anybody."

"He says."

The door played a single unobtrusive note, but when Leander moved to let Cayle in Oberon called out, "Wait."

It stopped the boy as though he'd been told he was standing in a minefield. The magick word. He turned, and Oberon looked away, unable to meet Leander's eyes, for fear of what he might see there after his next words.

The Septarch moved his lips, as if practicing, and then "I want more than for you not to go back to the Gallery. I want you to not be my slave, any more."

Leander shook his head, not understanding. "But—"

"Leander. I'm asking you. Will you stay with me?"

"Stay with you."

"Yes."

"Not as your slave. Just...stay?"

"Yes." Oberon was doing something in his head he thought a human might call praying, though it was addressed to no one.

"Yes," Leander said, without hesitation. "There isn't anywhere else. This is home."

Light years away, on a ship called the Promise Keeper, five men were arguing. They had gone through three cases of wine. There were four left.

On the viewscreen behind them was the video of Felicity, and Leander. It had been playing for several days, and could not be deactivated. None of then noticed it anymore.

For some reason, God had not yet thrown bread to them from heaven. They had spent an hour having a perfectly reasonable, if one-sided, discussion with God, politely explaining the difficulty this lack of manna was causing them. There was no answer. They had spent the next useless two hours having a drunken theological discussion about the implications of that.

Then, the subject had changed, rather abruptly.

Now, they were arguing over which of them would be the one to be killed and eaten.

The final consensus was an improvised method of drawing straws.

The theory was that this would let God decide.

AL·CHE·MY
(àl¹ke-mê) noun

1. A medieval chemical philosophy having as its asserted aims the transmutation of base metals into gold, the discovery of the panacea, and the preparation of the elixir of longevity.

2. A seemingly magical power or process of transmuting: "He wondered by what alchemy it was changed, so that what sickened him one hour, maddened him with hunger the next" (Marjorie K. Rawlings).

synchronicity

Months passed.

Oberon ordered all of Leander's belongings moved into their rooms. His sketch of Jyana's rape hung beside *Blue Christ*, now both over the fireplace, with Felicity's skull and crossed femurs in the middle, painted by both of them with elaborate hieroglyphs.

The rest of her was given to Lucius.

Camille spent her days sedated, and sang into the empty Gallery.

Ninety-six days after Leander's first kill, a ship crept into orbit around Omega. It ghosted the moon, and devices bought with Theren's credits kept it hidden.

This was not the plan.

Oh my God.

Theren read the message on his screen again, and scrubbed at his face with his palm. "I am not believing this," he said to himself, with utter, utter sincerity.

It didn't go away.

He dialed furiously, and when the invisible ship accepted his comm he hissed, "Are you fucking crazy? You were supposed to stay out of the system! What part of that had to do with next to fucking Moloch? If I had gotten him that far out they'd have taken so much longer to find out—"

The alarms went off.

"Shit," said Theren, half a second after Paul Schaiden said the same thing.

Oberon came into his room—their room—in an absolute fury.

Leander was sprawled on the floor pillows with his feet in a chair. He looked up from a handscreen. "What is it?"

"Security just arrested your father."

"What?"

He had to have misheard that.

"On Earth?"

"No, here, in orbit around my planet," Oberon snapped. He collapsed into one of the leather chairs and sat chewing one of his long nails.

Leander felt the blood drain out of his face. It was possibly bad, possibly so bad. "Did you...are you?"

Oberon looked at him, understood what he was failing to ask. "No, Leander, of course not. I already killed half your parents."

This was meant to make Leander smile, he knew. He tried to, for Oberon's sake, and failed.

"Unless that's your wish?"

Leander tried to speak, and made a noise that scared him. He raised his hands, put them down, raised them again and covered his face.

"Come here," Oberon said.

Leander did, freezing cold. *Why would he come here? What is going on? I don't want, I...*

"I don't know what I want." It sounded broken, as if he might cry as fucking usual, but tears wouldn't come, only this dry earthquake inside him, chattering his teeth, jittering his hands.

Oberon drew him close, stroked his hair. "There are a few options. One, I keep him here—"

"No," Leander said immediately.

Oberon quivered like he was holding back a laugh, but he made no comment to this veto. "Two, I give your mother back to him. We could tell him I had the tech to save her. Neither of them would ever know the difference."

Leander went even colder at that idea. "Could...could you still give her back to me, too?"

"I could, though, again, most hum—people, seem to find that upsetting. I could do both. I could give *you* back to him, too. A copy of you," he clarified, when Leander's death-grip intensified in a stricken spasm.

Leander turned that over in his mind and then shook his head, though it was far less certain than his initial *no*. He tried to imagine a copy of himself, tried to imagine what it would feel like to have known Oberon and to live without him, to think himself exiled, and sucked in a breath. "You're right. Creepy. I don't want another me, and..." He was going to say *I don't want another Mom,* but this refused to leave his lips.

Oberon rocked him. This should've felt silly but didn't. He burrowed, and when that wasn't enough he squirmed until he could wrap his legs around the Septarch. This also should've felt silly, and didn't.

"Three, I keep him a week or so, scare the fuck out of him, and give him a ship with a better chance of not blowing up in his face than the piece of shit he had. I'll send him to Trell. No crime rate. no religion shoved down your throat, no poison count. No surface to space ships of any kind."

Leander kept his face buried in Oberon's shoulder.

Oberon stroked his back. "You don't have to decide anything this instant."

"I don't want to see him. I don't want him here."

"All right, dearest. Whatever you wish."

Leander clung to him. Images of a future on Earth were blinding him. To go back to that, after this. He couldn't. He'd kill himself. That was over, all of it. It had never happened. It could *never* happen again.

"You're shaking. Nothing's going to happen. You're mine."

"I want to stay here, and I don't want to see him." This was close to wail. "Send him away. Right now. Make him go away."

"As soon as they have the ship ready. Maybe a week, favorite boy."

Leander hitched in a horrified noise at that. "Can't you send him right now?"

Oberon held him close. "Precious, I'm not giving your father, or anyone else, any of my own technology, or data, or weaponry. Your father is a fool, or he'd never have come here, but there are others not so empty-headed that do *not* need to know my secrets."

Thinking, insanely, of Atarah Kent, Leander nodded. He couldn't get close enough to Oberon. He climbed higher and bury his face in the Septarch's neck.

"He's locked in a cell. He's safe from me, and you're safe from him. All right?"

Leander nodded, but still he clung. Wristunits. Poison count. Masks. School and church and prisons and that required little sermon you had to key in and listen to twice a day. No more museum of blood and pain, no more garden with real trees, no more kissing and scratching and Oberon with long black hair and electric eyes.

Gray. Fences. Rules.

"Not Earth. Not ever again."

Paul was sitting in the same cell Felicity had been in.

Theren studied the prisoner with pity and contempt. He saw nothing that surprised him, a middle-aged man, sporting an alcoholic's rouge that was a charming preview of Theren's own future, glasses too small for his wide face, shoulders too broad for this small cell. He put his back to the camera, and fervently hoped the tiny silver disk he'd retrieved from his office and tucked into his boot was still killing the microphones.

"Magnificent plan. Much better than my plan. Mine skipped the part where you got arrested."

"You must be Theren."

"Yes. And you must be out of your mind."

A shrug, and a glance. Paul's face was carved out of exhaustion and weary resignation. Theren's contempt faded, but his pity did not.

"He's going to send you to Trell."

Paul blinked. People spent all their lives trying to emigrate to Trell. Compared to Earth and most of the colonies it was an absolute paradise. "They don't accept outsiders—"

"He owns it."

Paul was silent, possibly failing to imagine owning an entire planet, possibly too tired to give a damn.

"Even if he didn't I think they'd be happy to have you. They're working on irrigation, and they need an engineer."

"I don't understand. I thought he was this...killer."

"He is. He never does anything unless he gets something back. What he's getting back for this is Leander." Theren constructed a sentence to follow that, looked at Paul's tortured face, and edited it considerably. "His continued compliance."

Paul heard the unspoken atrocities veiled in those three words. He drew in his breath. "There has to be a way."

"There is."

Paul stood as though he were in pain, shuffled closer, closed his hands around the bars. "Tell me."

"It will probably get us all killed."

"Tell me." Paul was desperate and insistent and a vigilante, all in one breath.

None of it suited him well.

Leander was in the Garden, drawing his tree. He'd named it Soren. He talked to it, sometimes, and that was all right because no one ever came into the Garden except him.

"I almost said it again today," he told Soren, sketching lightly with a brown pencil. "I don't know what he'd do. What if he laughed? Or worse, he might freak like he did when I gave him the rose. But...what if he said it back?"

The response was, of course, silence, unless you counted the faint rustle of green leaves in the sweet warm breeze.

"You know what? You don't talk back very much," Leander told it. "Because of that, you are nothing like my mother."

What would she say?

He didn't know, but he knew what he *wanted* her to say.

"Leander," said Theren behind him.

He sucked in a guilty breath, flipped his paper over, turned to face his guard. "Hi."

"Is there someone here? You were talking—"

"I was talking to myself." He blushed. How much had Theren heard? He studied the man, trying to get a clue from his face.

Theren wasn't wearing the violet armor. He was dressed in a gray one-piece thing that looked like a civilian flight suit.

That wasn't right at all.

"What is it?"

"It's Oberon," Theren told him. "I need you to come with me, right now. It's important."

Leander set his sketch aside, stood up, pale and worried. "Where is he?"

"He's in the hangar bay."

"Why didn't he comm me?"

"There isn't time for this, Leander, it's an emergency."

His stomach did that elevator-plummet, and he felt his face and hands grow cold. "Is he sick again?"

"Just come with me." Theren took the boy's arm and rushed him into the corridor.

His sketchbook lay on the grass behind them, branches without leaves etched in lines that looked like skeleton hands.

That was too easy, Theren thought.

"I've never been here before. My clearance doesn't open some of these doors."

Theren ignored that. "Hurry."

They were almost running now, and the immense double doors into one of the private launch bays slid open in front of them.

Leander saw Paul standing beside a squat gray ship twice the size of a transport, and he understood.

He turned on Theren so fast and so savagely that he damn near got away. Theren grabbed him, and Leander kicked him hard, screaming, and hit him twice in the face, and Theren pinned his hands and picked him up, and he heard Leander's teeth snap together twice, and he was squirming like a snake, and growling.

"Let me the fuck *go*, I will kill you both, LET ME GO!" he shouted, and then he screamed, "HELP! GUARD! OBERON I'M IN HERE AND THEY'RE GOING TO—"

That had definitely carried much farther than thirty feet.

Theren let him go, spun him around and hit him in the back of his head with the handle of his gun. Leander made a noise that broke in the middle. He would have fallen, but Theren caught him and shoved him towards Paul, who was gray and stricken at this violence.

Theren snapped, "Every fucking microphone on this planet just heard that, *hurry the fuck up!*"

Paul took his son, without a word, and they were in the ship and the ceiling slid open, and the engines flung them into the orange sky with a sound like a scream.

Paul put Leander in the little living quarters in the rear of the ship on one of the narrow bunks. His son was unconscious, frowning, his mouth moving without sound.

But was alive. Whole, and alive.

And Paul could see his lost beloved in those eyelashes against his pale cheek.

He touched Leander's face, his hair, crushed him close in one silent hug. There would be time for more, later.

He stumbled up into the front and sat next to Theren. "What now?"

"Now we fly as fast as I fucking can and hope to God we get enough time to hide someplace."

"Run?" Paul sounded, incredulous, almost indignant. "That's your plan, to run?"

Despite his chosen line of work, Theren was not a violent person, but at that moment he experienced a pure, clear, pure, perfect urge to punch another man in the face as hard as he could. "No, *my* plan went out the window when you fucking arrived, so now that we *have* no plan, yes, I'm going with run."

Through the window the sky deepened to crimson, then black, and Moloch glittered like a skull before they passed it, and there were stars.

"You should go check on Leander. I hit him pretty hard," Theren said, without taking his eyes from the controls.

Leander was awake. He sat with his back up against the metal wall and he glared at his father with Hell behind his eyes.

Paul tried to speak. It wasn't all that easy, and all he could manage was, "Leander—"

"He'll come for me," Leander said, with absolute certainty. "When he does we'll kill you both."

Paul's throat was burning, and a sound like a plea came out of his mouth, and he dragged in a deep breath that went solid on him and scorched his lungs. "What did he do to you?"

Leander put his hand over the scars on his neck.

My favorite, my only favorite.

"You have no idea. About anything. You're a complete fucking idiot and you will never, NEVER UNDERSTAND WHAT YOU'VE DONE!"

He stopped it as soon as it had begun.

No. Not now. Not here.

Not yet.

"Leander, it's okay." Paul's voice had serious structural flaws, weak in places, near collapse. "Whatever it is, I'll get you the help you need. They can deprogram you, and—"

"Deprogram me? The help I need?" He said these things like the obscenities they were, and then he laughed. It wasn't a boy's laugh. "Fuck you. You think you're helping me?"

"Leander, please. I came here to save you."

"Whatever made you think I *wanted* to be saved?" Leander turned his face away.

"I'm your father." He put his hand on Leander's shoulder. "You belong with me."

"You're my father? Let me tell you a story, *father*, about when you stopped being my father. I came home, one day, and I took my pants off and showed you bruises like no kid should ever have. I was crying. I thought you would...I don't know. Get fucking angry that somebody hurt me, maybe? Maybe fucking hug me?"

Paul could find nothing to say to this.

"And you know what you did? You fucking patted me, patted my shoulder right where you're touching now, and you said I *should have been more careful about what I drew.*"

The last few words were a strangled snarl of surface rage. Underneath them was a bottomless well of betrayed hurt, of broken trust.

Paul took his hand away. "Leander, son—"

"Then, the same motherfuckers who did it came and took me away. For *MONTHS*. And you let them! Mom tried to stop them, and you stopped *her*. You've been on everybody's side but *mine* for my entire fucking life!"

Paul shook his head. "I know I could have...I can make it up to you, all those things—"

"No. You can't. Especially not THIS. I don't even want you to fucking try. I belong with him. I belong *to* him. Take me back now, and I'll make sure he lets you go."

"I can't do that."

Leander studied him with furious contempt, and then shrugged. "It's your funeral."

Paul went back and sat next to Theren. He strapped himself into the chair. The stars were little blurs and streaks, instead of specks, and he had to reach up to his face to figure out why.

The blank, burned-out emptiness on his face did a great deal to dissolve Theren's anger. He cleared his throat, and when Paul still did not speak, said "You okay?"

Paul choked on a badly disguised sob. "He's so...different."

black hole

Oberon woke up, reached out his arms. The bed was cold. And empty.

He stumbled into the front room. His computer was on. The message read: KISS LOTS, LEANDER.

It had been put there fourteen hours earlier.

He shoved the chair out of the way, already typing with one hand.

The camera feed came up.

Paul's cell was empty.

His hands began to shake.

The room was clicking in and out of focus, his eyes adjusting by themselves, running through all possible visual ranges in rapid sequence in response to his internal sense of *find find find*.

He pulled up the departure log.

One ship. Three passengers. Thirteen hours ago.

He left me.
He left me.

Oberon screamed, and he ripped the entire terminal out of the table, and there were sparks, and smoke, and then a red blank before he was running, running, into the lift, down to the control room.

Into the heart of the Sphere.

Earth.

Again.

Leander curled up small and pulled up his shirt. It was one of Oberon's, and he was swimming in it, and he sniffed hard at it, trying to wrap himself up in that mildew-and-myrrh smell.

What if he didn't come?

Earth. Again. Blank fat pale human faces. An endless scavenger hunt for drugs, forbidden books, underground games. He'd

294

been trying to feed the fury with those pathetic substitutes, and now, now that he knew, now that he'd tasted reality, how could he go back to that?

He wished he'd said it. He should have. He might not get to, now. And Oberon would never know.

"What would you do?" he whispered. "What would you do?"

That voice spoke in his head. Familiar. Casual and dark and like velvet clotted with blood.

He listened. After it was finished he got up and took off Oberon's shirt and stretched it between his hands and spun it the way you did a towel, into a rope, and he tied knots in it, until he had a black silk garrote.

He wanted it to be his father, but logic wouldn't let him do it that way. His father had less of a chance against him, and Paul couldn't fly as well as Theren, probably couldn't fly a ship like this one at all.

He took a series of long deep breaths. Calm. Quiet. Frenzy would be fatal, now. He took one step, and the little squeak-pat sound of it made him reach down and take off his boots. He left the rear compartment, walked up the aisle towards the cockpit in sock feet, the shirt already between his hands. Each step rolled soundlessly from heel to toe. They didn't hear him. Neither of them even moved.

He dropped his weapon over Theren's head, and pulled as hard as he could.

Paul was shouting. Leander kicked at him. Paul stumbled and struck the controls, and the ship jerked and jolted, and Leander slipped. No traction, in socks, on a metal floor.

He fell, screaming in rage, and then they had him.

He did as much damage as he could before they pinned him down. It was nowhere near enough.

Oberon dragged his finger along rows of keys, toggling them all on. He threw back the lever, and terrible pressure smashed into him, and there was a ripping sound like the entire planet was being torn in half, as the Sphere mauled its way through rock that had been magma when it had settled there, centuries.

He couldn't hear himself sobbing anymore.

The sky on the monitors went from orange, to crimson, to black.

They'd fucking tied his wrists to the bunk. With his shirt.

Correction, with *Oberon's* shirt.

He wasn't thinking, wasn't moving. His mind was a fierce litany of unimaginable torture, and underneath it all were the words, *he'll come for me.*

"Shit."

Paul had fallen into a light, uneasy doze in his seat, the harness holding him up. "What is it?"

Theren made a series of faces that Leander would've found amusing. "If there's anything you want to say to Leander, you'd better say it now."

Panic. Cold fear closing in a place in him so deep he hadn't known it existed. "Why?"

Theren tapped the monitor for the sensors. "See that thing the size of a goddamn planet? Can't miss it really, because, yeah. Size of a fucking planet. Coming right at our six as fast as bad news?"

Paul looked, squinting. "What is that?"

Theren sighed. He pulled his canteen off his belt, and rejoiced that it did not contain water. "That's the Sphere. He launched the whole fucking Sphere. Congratulations, we are both dead." He took a long pull, and offered the canteen to Paul.

Behind them, Leander gave a terrible crowing shriek of triumph. "I *told* you he would come for me!"

almost always fatal

Leander was escorted to the throne room in silence, still shirtless, still in sock feet. Oberon not on his throne. He stood in the middle of the room, with his back to Leander. "Leave him."

They did.

Leander was waiting to be caught close, kissed, held, everything, anything.

Oberon didn't move.

"Oberon? I knew, I knew you would—"

He went to him, put his hand up on Oberon's back, smelling mildew, myrrh, blood, feeling that hair like silk straight as rain against his fingers. One touch, just one, and then the Septarch turned on him as liquid quick as a snake. His face was a mask of darkness and fury.

Leander had time to take a single breath. There was one word, beating in his throat, but before he could say it Oberon hit him. There was a crack in his face, near his nose, and there was a wet gush of something that tasted like a bad chemistry experiment. He would have fallen, no, would have *flown* across the room, but Oberon kept hold of him, and hit him again. And again.

And again.

Then he dropped Leander and left him bleeding on the floor.

He looked up at his lover, crumpled and broken, and he tried to hold up his hands. He didn't understand what had happened.

Now I know what it feels like for him to really hit me.

He was all tangled inside, grief and terror and hunger and deep hard sexual fury. None of it was pleasure, because under it all was that terrible difference in Oberon's inkblack eyes.

"How could you?" Oberon's voice was the ghost of something old and heartbroken. "Was any of it real, any of it at all?"

Leander opened his mouth to answer.

The room went from orange, to red, to black.

This time there were no stars.

Dizzy. Pain. Spinning.

He was in the Gallery. The smell, the sense of space was familiar. His hands would go up to his face, now, and his eyes were there, but so swollen they made a blurry slit of the world.

The word was still there. He tried to say it and his mouth wouldn't open the way it used to, and when he tried again there was a crunch that went all the way up into his skull.

Leander wanted to get up. He had to. He would key open the door and go to Oberon's rooms, to *their* rooms, he would crawl there if he had to. Someone had hurt him. Oberon had to know, he would want to know about it. He had to get up.

He managed to sit up, on his bed, and he almost fell, but he managed to turn and his back struck the stone wall behind his bed, and it hurt like crazy, but he stayed sitting up.

The door into the Gallery opened.

Leander knew who it was. He could feel him.

Oberon came in, moving with slow, deliberate grace. He stopped almost at Leander's cell and looked at him through the black UV shields, and there was no expression on his face, no angle to those full painted lips, no emotion in those synthetic eyes.

He was dressed in black.

Killing clothes.

Camille was a drugged sprawl on her bed, a sweaty tangle of white silk and red-gold hair.

He gave Leander that cold empty stare through the bars for a long moment, before he keyed open the door to Camille's cell.

No.

He wanted to look away, but his head wouldn't move, and his eyes wouldn't move. Trapped. He was trapped in his body.

Couldn't you have kissed me, just once, before you hit me?

Oberon picked Camille up with one hand. She was still asleep when he began kissing her, arms and legs hanging loose like a doll, like a corpse. She made a muffled noise, and her hand struck out at the air, then reached up and closed over his shoulder, moved clumsily through his hair.

He was kissing her still, his jaw moving like he was biting her, She moaned and it was like electricity moved through her body. Her arms wound around him. Her legs came up and closed around his waist, and when his mouth moved to her neck she whispered, drugged, "I knew, I knew you'd come back. I knew you wanted me. I knew you did."

Leander's teeth were rattling together, or maybe the bed was shaking, the wall, the floor, the entire fucking Sphere.

It's a game. He's furious at me, he's doing that to punish me, he doesn't really want her, this is a GAME fuck it HAS TO BE A GAME...

He could hear them kissing, a sticky wet sound like a wound being pulled open. He'd heard it that first time, that first kiss in Oberon's lap, his erection hard and scary and wonderful.

New. Knew.

Oberon laid Camille on her bed, tore open the shapeless white silk that covered her. She spread her arms out, growling deep in her throat. Her breasts were bigger than Felicity's, their sole decoration a crooked scar trailing down from her collarbone to disappear along her ribcage. Oberon ran his fingers along her nipples, and they folded tight like the lips of a carnivorous plant.

Camille says you eat little kids.

The museum. Oberon pinning him, teasing him, *Just one needle, lots of times?* The hallway, slick blood, shoving and pulling at each other, laughing. The memories were holograms with forgotten faces and stunned eyes, fluttering down in a technicolor blizzard, into a bottomless pit.

He wanted to scream out in agony. Everything precious to him was being torn away, and he didn't even know why.

I should have said it. Even if he'd laughed, at least he would have known.

Oberon pushed Camille's knees up, his hand was working at the waistband of his pants. He freed an erection the color of a bone-deep bruise. He spread her sex open with his fingers, hard enough to make her cry out, and his eyes found Leander's when he slammed it into her.

But she isn't like you. She's nothing like you.

I'm like you.

He was fucking her. *Her.* Camille. Kissing her cheek, her mouth, with lips that had said *there is no Camille.*

Leander could hear that, too, like the sound of kissing, but more slippery, more violent, and the smacking of flesh against flesh, and he made a desperate sound of sorrow that nobody heard. He put his hands against his mouth, to hold it in, and he thought of his first kill, of watching Oberon with Felicity, of how he'd put his hands on himself, happy and fierce and hungry.

All gone, and he didn't even know why.

Both of them. Moving together like animals, like water, an impact repeated over and over again. Camille, making a vicious hungry sound, like sobbing, without tears. Oberon, silent except for his breath, hissing bright and harsh and quick through too tight a space, his eyes driving into Leander's like a dull blade, the antithesis of light. Hopeless. Merciless.

Confetti, in the shape of butterflies, each one etched with a looped cross. He'd looked up the symbol. Ankh. Ancient Egyptian: water, life, mirror. Immortality.

And the arrow, down, he didn't need to look up. He knew.

Always more.

Camille was making a rough angry sound, her mouth opening and closing like a fish, and Oberon was still grinding against her, staring at Leander. Then his breathing stopped, and he drew her close, hard, into an obscene geometric arc.

He's coming. In her, in her, Camille. Her, and not me.

He was numb, but hurting too much to be numb, watching those black eyes narrow into crescents, watching Oberon's lips twist into shapes that should have been passionate but were only ugly.

Camille was silent, his hand over her mouth, her fist striking the bed in pleasure. The arc collapsed, and Oberon pulled away from her and stood up, and dressed himself. She was squirming on the bed, sticky and gasping, and she held her hand up to him, and he drew it to his lips for a medieval kiss, still looking at Leander.

And he smiled.

Oh no, Leander thought. He knew that smile.

He knew that now would be a *very* good time to look away.

He did not.

Oberon grasped her arm, still holding her hand, and he started twisting. She made a little cry, thinking he was playing, and then the first snap, and she screamed.

Leander made a sound that was almost a gag, and fumbled his hand up to his mouth and pressed the base of his thumb against his lips. He couldn't risk drawing attention to himself. Whatever was about to happen, better her than himself.

He broke her wrist. All right. That's all. He just broke her wrist. He'll probably beat the fuck out of her, and WHEN EXACTLY will this start to have something to do with me?

His ribs started aching. Probably broken, too, and that brittle wet noise had reminded them of it. Leander was breathing in boiling water. It was swishing in and out of his lungs, and his brain and his teeth and his stomach were having a terrified conversation, and *Oberon was not stopping with her wrist.*

He twisted her hand all the way around, and the skin of her wrist wrinkled and darkened and split with a liquid grating scrape. And he went to her elbow, and that didn't take quite as long, one quick jerk, and there was bone gleaming white and startled through her skin.

He couldn't hear her. Leander could tell by her face that she was shrieking, could see her feet slamming useless and spastic against the foot of the bed, but he couldn't hear her. He could only hear what Oberon was doing to her.

He broke her shoulder.

If he doesn't stop he's going to tear off her arm.

He didn't.

He just moved to her other arm.

This already has everything to do with you, the voice in his head told him, sounding flat and drugged and defeated.

Oberon's hair swung forward, into his eyes. He reached up and pushed it back, the gesture casual and familiar, and left a red smear on his forehead. Still no expression, except a vague attention, concentration. After each fracture he would look up at Leander, to make sure he was still watching.

Leander was almost positive she was dead by the time Oberon made it to her hip. That was worse than anything he had ever seen. Oberon braced his foot between her legs, the heel of his boot against her pelvic bone, and he had one hand around the back of her knee and one around her ankle, and he threw his entire weight into the pull. It was like a gunshot, that sound, and Leander could see, actually see the bone slip out of the socket under her flesh.

He had to pull twice to dislocate the other one.

He'd forgotten her fingers, and he broke all of those, calmly, methodically, giving Leander a wilted memory of his mother in their kitchen snapping green beans. He dropped each hand when he was finished, and they left red dashes on the white bed, the fingers at crooked, crazed angles.

He pulled her up by her head and broke her neck in one wrenching turn.

He let her fall.

He stepped back, looked at her, pushed his hair back again and drew in a deep breath. Then he picked her up with swift, sudden violence and slammed her spine across his knee. The sound was like a rock against a windowpane. When he threw her down she looked like someone had folded her, and tried to smooth her out again without success. She was completely the wrong shape, *entirely* the wrong shape, *absolutely* the wrong fucking shape.

He gave Leander one more long look, and he turned and left the Gallery without a word.

When he remembered how to breathe, he whispered, "Camille?"

nadir

The corridors were tactfully empty.

Someone standing behind any of the doors would have heard a glassy, scraping sound, like a ragged bell, and a dark drunken voice singing the words to an ancient rock song from a forgotten planet.

"Laughed at his long black hair.....his animal grace..."

Oberon couldn't remember the words. Not all of them. The song had been on one of Leander's discs. Someone with a bright fragile androgynous voice, and he didn't want to go in his room, and he couldn't remember the singer's name, but he wanted to hear the song, so he would just fucking have to sing it.

The scraping was the bottle. It had been half full of absinthe. He'd topped that off with vodka and what was left of Felicity's blood. Shaken, not stirred. And shaken messily, at that.

He was dragging it along the wall to accompany himself.

"Sang his songs...of darkness and disgrace..."

He couldn't remember any more. Someone named Blue Jean. A stage. Stage fright. Fright night. Night owl. Screech owl.

Spaceships and gas masks and bright shiny stun guns.

He kept singing, random snatches of thought, scattered words.

He needed more heroin. His stash was in his room.

He didn't want to go in his room.

He would never go in his room again.

Not with *Blue Christ*, staring down at him, benevolent, electrical. Not with himself staring out of Hell with Jyana under him on her back. Not with that bed, there, still smelling like a boy with green curious eyes.

He looked at his hand, for some reason. Blood. He thought *shit, I'm bleeding*, and he poured some of the bottle's contents on his hand, and that liquid was a nameless color that didn't help any at all.

It didn't matter.

He would set it on fire. Yes. He would set his room on fire. Actually, fuck it, he would set the whole Sphere on fire.

After he was finished, anyway.

He sang and scraped his way to a room with a locked door. There was blood and absinthe on his chin. He'd stopped singing because he'd discovered he couldn't think of anything that rhymed with *decapitate* except *mutilate* and he'd already used that one.

He regarded the keypad and then kicked the door in. It was far easier than he anticipated, and he damn near dropped the bottle in the process. He'd have to thank Cayle for the adjustment to his mechanical knees before he exploded the Sphere.

There was a smear on one of his UV shields.

He took it out, put it in his mouth, put it back in his eye. That was much worse, between the blood all over it and the fucking alcohol burning like crazy. He took it out again, put it in his mouth, remembered that hadn't helped, and spit the damn thing out in frustration.

Crimson light painted him bloody.

He finished off the bottle, threw it sidearm out into the hall. The crash was wonderful.

He couldn't carry it anyway.

For this, he would need both hands.

auto-da-fe

"You know, did I ever tell you, last year in school, I wrote this essay?"

Leander was talking to Camille. She was a poor substitute for his tree, but since her death she had become a lot easier to talk to, and her replies were a lot less schizoid.

He had no idea how long it had been. A day, three days. He had water, from the little bathroom behind the curtain, but getting it into his mouth and then swallowing it was an ordeal. He could talk, though with great effort and little clarity. He thought he was less swollen, but his hands were no better than his face and he was uncertain of his conclusions.

No one had come in.

Camille's skin had started to look funny and sometimes he thought he could smell her, and he would stop in the middle of whatever story it was and sit sniffing, terrified, but he never could be sure if the smell was real, or if he was imagining it.

"So I wrote this essay, on a poem by this guy named Yeats. About the Antichrist. Well, that's what I thought, though of course, it's about Jesus because everything is, just fucking ask Them."

Camille was in silent agreement.

"Anyway, I loved it. My teacher didn't. I got two weeks of detention, and an F on the paper."

"I used to have the whole thing memorized, but...I can't tell it to you, because...I haven't been feeling all that great."

That was the understatement of the year. His whole body was stiff, and ached in ways that made the room go gray every so often. He was hot and cold simultaneously, and sometimes he got this weird feeling, like he was the bed and he wanted to get off of it, because he was crushing himself. His fever was so high he didn't realize he had one.

"It says there's a strange beast, slouching towards Bethlehem to be born. That's the last line, I think, and that's all I remember. This past...day...that keeps rattling around in my head, you know? Slouching. And...it seems to mean something, like, something important, but I can't quite figure out..."

His voice trailed off.

A metallic rattle, a faint scrape. He thought of a ghost in a burial shroud, dragging chains. His voice was too thin to be a whisper. "Camille there is this noise a noise outside outside the Gallery and it is getting *closer.*"

She didn't answer.

Tears stung his eyes. "No more," he whispered, but not to her. To everything. No more of this, no more talking to a corpse, no more broken ribs, no more. This game wasn't a game anymore, and he was pretty sure he wasn't winning, and never had been.

"You already broke most of them, it shouldn't take as long as it did for her," he whispered bitterly, to no one at all.

The noise. It was right outside, now.

He knew it was Oberon before the door even opened.

Then he saw what the noise was, what Oberon was dragging behind him.

Oh, he thought, with no emotion at all, but he pushed with his feet, sliding in the sheets, until he was pressed up against the wall.

Oberon was dragging the device. The device that came with a single past-tense verb: *fitted.*

He stopped in front of the door to Leander's cell, still looking at him with his eyes like ice. One of his black lenses was missing, and his face was streaked with dark fluid. He dropped the device. It clattered on the stone floor. Oberon keyed in the code without looking, and swung open the bars.

I don't care anymore, Leander told himself, and his jaw got tight and hard. He was still in his black pants, the rest of his clothes who knew where, and he struggled with the snap and the zipper and pulled them off, and he didn't take his eyes from Oberon. *So there*, he thought, and there were insects crawling up his throat, and he couldn't choke them back.

Oberon didn't react at all, but Leander thought he saw the iris of his synthetic eye dilate for a microsecond.

He didn't care. There was no point. He could see in the coldness of the Septarch's face that there was no hope of reason, of mercy. If he resisted, there would be more pain.

He looked up at Oberon, praying his eyes could say, anything. Everything.

Oberon picked up the pieces of his device, dropped them on the bed beside Leander. He flinched, and his eyes cringed closed against his will, and he could not look up again.

He felt Oberon take his arms and raise them up, over his head, and he kept them there, and the corset closed around him, from under his arms to below his hips. He tried to brace himself, and Oberon pulled the first of the straps tight and fastened it, moving down and securing each one with mechanical efficiency.

At first, it made his ribs feel better. Then, Leander felt Oberon move to the other side, tightening something there, too, and there were bands of agony across his lungs, and the terror was immediate. He couldn't breathe. He had to force himself to take calm, shallow breaths. He couldn't afford to panic.

Why not? It's not like you have anything to lose, now. Don't you understand this yet? He's going to kill you. It doesn't matter if you can breathe.

Kill him. It didn't seem to apply to him. He was fourteen. You didn't die at fourteen. That wasn't how it worked. Maybe Oberon would just scare him. Put most of it on him, and leave him awhile.

The collar snapped closed around Leander's neck, Leander leaned his head forward to let Oberon turn the thumbscrew in the back. It was just tight enough to constrict his throat, just tight enough to make it one step harder to breathe.

Leander could feel Oberon's eyes, and he looked up, the iron biting into his neck, and just as he did Oberon looked away and picked up the headpiece.

It'll be all right, Leander. He's a monster, but at least he's beautiful.

The panic started then.

He remembered, in a thick vivid flash, his head in Oberon's lap, Oberon's cock in his mouth, deep and luscious. Not the first time —it was later, after Felicity's execution. Oberon had gotten violent on him, had grabbed his head and choked him, semen spilling into his throat, and he had strangled, the stuff scorching his lungs, and he'd been unable to breathe for an agonizing moment. In that instant every thread in Oberon's shirt, every angle of the stones of the floor had become excruciatingly clear, important, bright enough to blind him.

It was like that now.

You can't, he wanted to scream out, and he tried to draw in breath to do it, and the iron across his throat, his ribs stopped him. Oberon's hands were coming at him again. He tried to thrash, fall, anything, and managed only a slight, convulsive jerk.

The band closed around his forehead, the tiny hooks dangling on their springs cold against his cheek like malevolent jewelry. Oberon was drawing it tighter, tighter, and he could feel it bruising, could feel the fusiondeep surreal pain of it pressing against his skull.

Am I just sitting here? Damn it, am I just SITTING HERE LETTING HIM KILL ME?

He was doing just that.

Mom, he thought, suddenly small, suddenly pleading.

He saw Oberon, saying, *I want you to stay here, with me. I don't want you to sleep in a different room ever again.*

He meant that. I know he did. I could see it in his eyes.

The image changed. Oberon, touching his face, his fingers gentle and frightened and compassionate, whispering secrets of pain and pleasure and isolation.

He meant that, Leander told himself, breaking. *He did. I will believe that he did. I WILL believe.*

The rest of the headpiece. The little part that curled along your jawbone, to the horrible piece that...

Oberon was holding it in his hands, and Leander fell, over onto his back, and it strangled him, the impact, the collar, the corset, choking. He fought to find the magic word.

"Wait," he rasped out, desperate, one hand trembling in the air with frightened fingers, begging.

Oberon looked down at him, one eye black, one eye silver...

...and he waited.

Leander's hands stumbled in the air, fingers closing and opening at the wrong moment, like a broken machine, but he managed it, he gritted his teeth and forced his eyes to focus and he managed it, he did, and that was all that mattered.

He took the mouthpiece out of his lover's hands. Tears were searing at his wounded eyes.

And Oberon waited.

"I love you," Leander whispered.

Oberon didn't move, but his mask began to fracture. The

cracks ran in merciless lines from his face down into his shirt, black and bleeding nameless fluid. He pretended he didn't see them, pretended they were a hallucination for the sake of Oberon's dignity.

Leander opened his mouth, and pushed the terrible bit in himself. He reached to the little button with heartbroken fingers and pressed it, and the iron snapped open, springloaded, merciless, forcing his jaw wide open, sending broken-glass pain shattering up into his skull.

For you. I'm doing this for you.

He could only think these words. He couldn't say them.

He was mute, now. He'd already said the only words that mattered. Oberon hadn't moved to stop him.

I will believe. He won't kill me. He loves me.

I won't fight him.

Every tense and torn muscle in him relaxed. He submitted.

His eyes were open, but he couldn't see. He heard Oberon take two short, quick, hard breaths, and he almost had hope. Almost.

There was no answer except the rattle of the belt with its dreaded phallus.

His jaw was aching already, strained to breaking, and the taste of rust was gagging him. He was freezing cold. Leander caught one blurry glimpse of the belt in Oberon's hands, and he closed his eyes and drew up his knees, and let his hands fall, palms up, fingers open.

He felt small, so small. He pushed his hips up, and the belt closed around his corseted waist, closed with a switchblade click.

The phallus was lying on the bed beside his hand. He curled his fingers, to feel it against his knuckles, and then Oberon picked it up.

The tip of it was against him, pushing hard. It was cold, too.

He thought, *it won't hurt, it's not that much bigger than-*

It hurt like nothing had ever hurt, scraping up into him, dry and heartless. Bright ragged ripping agony, deep hard pain that made his legs convulse, drawing up hard, his feet drawing jagged lines in the air. Oberon shoved it deeper, leaning into it, forcing it in, and there was flesh resisting him, and he slammed his hand into it, like Leander had done to Felicity.

Leander couldn't help his shriek. He was trying with every muscle in his body, every inch of his spine to push it out. He couldn't. The bit was forcing his mouth open, stretching his lips wide, making his scream edgeless and hideous.

It was turned wrong, the little metal loop at the end of the phallus and Oberon twisted it in him, and drew the strap through it, and put it through the waistpiece of the belt and buckled it tight. The pain was a spiral with rows and rows of teeth, snarling in him, winding him tight, dragging him down.

He opened his eyes, and Oberon's fingers were on his eyelids, fumbling with the tiny little hooks on the headpiece.

They weren't meant to go under your eyelids.

They were meant to go through them.

It was a crimson blur, and then Leander's eyes were held wide open, and they would try to blink in reflex, tears pouring down his face, and the hooks through his eyelids would tug, tearing, and green blinding flashes would shatter across his vision. He barely felt the final pieces, braces that held his arms at his sides, his legs straight and pressed together.

It's over.

Oberon stood over him, and why hadn't Leander noticed him, really noticed him before? His hair wasn't black. It was black and blue and green and violet and red, the color of the back of your eyelids in a dark room.

He would never see that again, the backs of his eyelids.

His eyes. Eyes like moon and night, that might collapse into an eclipse at any moment.

Oberon was turning away from him. Leaving.

Leander made a desperate frantic awkward motion, lurching forward with all his weight, iron scraping. Oberon turned back to him, whispered, "What? Haven't you finished looking at me yet?"

Leander made a low brittle sound.

"You *left* me," Oberon's words were less than a whisper, more than a scream. "I hope it takes you weeks to die."

He thinks I...that isn't...can't...I have to tell him...

Oberon was gone, out of his line of vision. He heard the door into the Gallery open and close, and he was still struggling.

He managed to roll off the bed. The stone floor struck him without mercy, and he heard a hundred delicate things in his face, his neck, snapping and tearing, and the room went as bright as if it had been electroplated, blurred, then folded into a single, angry white line.

RAP·TURE

(ràp¹cher) noun

1. the State of being transported by a lofty emotion; ecstasy.
2. Often *raptures*. An expression of ecstatic feeling. See synonyms at *ecstasy*.
3. The transporting of a person from one place to another, especially to heaven.

exit

Oberon sat on the platform in his Worm Chamber. He'd programmed a sequence he'd never used in all his centuries in the Sphere. The gears groaned and whined in metallic protest, then finally submitted with a scraping jerk. The platform rose, until it was a hundred feet above the worm-infested floor.

The fall would break most of his bones. He might even die eventually, if no one found him.

The idea of it was...empty.

He lay back, feet hanging over one side, hair hanging over the other. He could hear them, above him, rustling, beating frenzied and desperate at the dome of the ceiling. The air was as black as ink, damp. Now and then there was a delicate, quick flutter against his face. He could smell them, like tea leaves, like dust exposed to sunlight. A warm brown smell, light and sweet and horrible.

After a long time, he made his platform descend again, and took the walkway back into the Sphere.

There was so much to do, and he was beginning to think there might be so little time.

It was an effort to move. There was grit and blood grinding in his joints. His muscles were sprung and weary, and he had to keep blinking to see through them, the ghosts, crowding him with pleading mouths, accusing eyes. He could almost feel them, now, tiny transparent fingers plucking at the ruin of his clothes, the ends of his hair.

Not his hands, of course. Never his hands.

(one boy wasn't afraid of your hands he fell asleep with your fingers in his mouth, he would chew wet circles into your clothes and touch your face and all those scars like you were a mystery)

(used to he used to he)

He bit through his bottom lip, felt his teeth grate together.

(a puzzle box that only he could open)

He would unplug synapses, rebalance delicate systems of neurochemicals, let Cayle cut out the worst of the best memories. If he survived the process, the boy would have never existed.

(an inscription in hieroglyphics that he could interpret if he

repeated it enough times)

That was what he told himself, anyway.

He was walking towards the dungeons. This was work, now, not art, not sex, not self-expression, not anything he could ever enjoy. This was work, and he was being forced to do it, and he hated *everything*, himself most of all.

Oberon watched Theren in the monitor for a long time. He was chained, suspended almost vertical, with his arms up and twisted back like an interrupted swan dive. He was blindfolded, and his face was set in lines of pretended calm, with sudden tension in his mouth, his jaw, betraying his terror.

Even his anger was empty now. It lacked the bright, wonderful taste he loved so dearly. It was like the memory of an emotion. He felt like he was following a script, acting out the life of someone who no longer lived.

(the boy)

(if you go to him now there is still time)

Time to what? The boy, *his* boy, had never really been his at all. Just like the others, just like all the others. They were a blur around him, less people than flickers of memory, found and treasured and then traitors, every one, suddenly adult, suddenly old, suddenly alien, the faces he'd adored lost forever, too many to remember, too many to count. No one real but himself in the center of this maelstrom, alone.

He'd thought he'd modified himself until they could never hurt him this way again, but he'd been wrong. Only one had ever truly loved him, and that one was ashes in the darkness of space.

The rest would do anything, say anything to save themselves.

That was all.

It was not love. It had never been love. Just fear, just lies he'd believed in spite of his experience and his senses, because he'd been weak enough to *want* to believe them.

Love or not, he had killed them all.

He had known better than to play this game again, had known he would never find what he was looking for, not in an eon of tithes. There were no others. Never would be any others. He had known better than to even look, but he'd wanted so *intensely* to be wrong.

Maybe the Makers had been wiser and crueler than he'd known. Maybe this was their punishment, and his prison: he would be a species of one until the stars went out.

Knowing that would save a lot of trouble. He could skip kisses and gifts, forget the point and the purpose of names, could stop trying to understand what they wanted, what they thought. Be the god they'd been craving since they were monkeys in caves in awe of fire. Fuck them, eat them, kill them, forget them.

There were always more of them.

After awhile he wouldn't even be able to tell them apart. He would change himself until he looked nothing like them, have Cayle make him into a creature of sex and appetite, pain and death, loathing and loneliness. Why shouldn't his form suit his function?

The premonition of a headache was buzzing in his ears. He shook his head, tasting his own hair, and what had happened to his lip? He dug his nails into his scalp until he drew long stinging lines. That didn't work and he struck his forehead with the heel of his hand, hard, over and over until vertigo drowned the voice into silence. He was saying a name as he did so, but the sound of his hand striking his skull drowned out the sound, and he didn't know he had spoken.

His mouth kept moving, but the punishment had stunned his vocal cords into submission, and there was no voice behind it, only his bitten lips shaping a word that no longer had any meaning.

Forget the point and the purpose of names.

There were no magic words. *Revenge,* maybe, was the only one left, unless you had a fucking time machine and you could stop...it...from happening at all.

No torture would equal what Theren deserved.

Oh, the boy would've dropped the pretense eventually. Made a mistake, talked in his sleep the way so many of them did. Tomorrow, next week...or next year, or in a dozen years. He might have had a dozen years to believe he was a species of two. They would have been false years, yes, but he wouldn't have known that. He would have known instead what it would feel like to sleep beside someone like himself. For years.

Judas kiss.

The fucking bastard.

Stole my last delusion.

He would never be able to hurt him enough. Ridiculous to try. Even his lethal innovations were no comparison to what Theren had done to him.

He considered shooting him. Get this over and done, get himself to Cayle, order him to cut away whatever it was that made him fool enough to search, to keep searching.

No. Despair was one thing, but his reputation was all he had left. It would not do to set out to become the ultimate beast with a start like that.

He would improvise. He was sure Theren would be impressed, whatever he did. He would make sure it was messy and merciless, with lots of blood and screaming, and when it was over he would go to his...a new room, and he would order his old room sealed forever, and he would drug himself into a stupor so that he would not have to

(*think about the boy*)

dream anything.

He opened the door to Theren's cell, and forced himself to grin, with lots of smeared teeth showing. The mask was still working.

For now.

Theren's entire body changed, the minute Oberon stepped into the cell. There was instant tension, resistance without actual motion, a frantic contraction of his muscles. There was a flood of the blinding magenta scent of fear, almost nauseating in the confines of the tiny room.

Theren's complex arrangement of chains and cuffs that had been designed with aesthetics in mind. Oberon didn't have aesthetics in mind now.

I could eat him. That would serve him right. He tried to devour me. He found the softest part of me and tore it out with those flat small human teeth, when I almost trusted him.

Yes. That would be perfect. It might even make him feel better, the bright dying taste, blood made thin and sharp with adrenaline, skin salted with sweat.

"I know it's you," The strap around Theren's neck was constricting his words. "Please. I know you'll kill me. Please, first I have to..."

Oberon was not interested in Theren's desired progression of events. He moved in, feeling like an animal, feeling his breath draw in the scent like a chemical skein drawing him in to feed. He didn't care what this meat had to say.

The stomach was tempting, yes, the long line from sternum to navel, the agitated muscles winding tight there. No. Too quick.

He pinched the soft exposed flesh at the back of Theren's left arm. He smiled, and said in a slow cold drizzle of a voice, "Do you know how much it hurts to be bitten? Really bitten?"

Theren tried to shake his head.

"You should. After all, you bit me. Didn't you? Bit me. The hand that feeds you..."

"Wait! For God's sake...you know he said that to you...I'm saying that to you for him, please, WAIT..."

"There is no fucking God," Oberon told Theren. Exasperating, how they all kept bleating that word at him, despite centuries of evidence that it was as useless against him as any other weapon.

He buried his teeth in skin, bit hard and deep in that place where there were so many nerves, until his teeth came together He pulled his head back like a scavenger bird, the scream drowning out the wet gristle tearing sound. Then, he waited, not because he was moved, but because he was chewing. He wasn't listening. He didn't care.

"I don't care what you do to me but Leander had nothing to do with this, it wasn't his idea, he screamed for us to take him back. I swear to you, Septarch, he never wanted to leave you...we had to force him, hit him. He tried to kill us to get back to you...please, God, if he isn't dead yet, don't hurt him."

This incoherent, tearful confession was vaguely interesting. Oberon chewed hard. There was a word in that mattered, and he was trying to remember which one it had been. "Leander?" he mumbled around a mouthful of flesh.

"Yes! Yes, Leander. Don't hurt him. He didn't want to go. Do you even fucking hear me?" Theren was screaming, now.

Oberon licked at his mouth, tongue chasing blood. Hysteria was clouding the words, but that one word, still.

"He didn't want to go!" Theren was shrieking, again.

"Didn't. Want to. Leander?"

"NO! HE DIDN'T WANT TO FUCKING GO!"

It was difficult, going from berserk to rational, an uphill climb to a tiresome destination. The smell of blood and fear made him want to eat first and ask questions later.

"We made him! We kidnapped him! Stole him from you! Are you even fucking *listening* to me?"

Oberon leaned closer, opened his mouth again. The smell. Blood. Soft, warm, cringing flesh in reach of his mouth, but some bastard word, a word like a soft kiss, like breath in darkness, was stopping him.

Leander.

He had a thought to express, some remaining fragment of rationality and reason. It took him a long time to crush all that into two words, "Prove it."

Theren hadn't expected that. Oberon watched him, caught in a moment of gasping panic. He'd decided to eat again when Theren shrieked, "The logs! The ship we took was yours, and you have that goddamn surveillance shit on every fucking thing you OWN, and the logs recorded everything, everything Leander said and did...you have to pull the logs! If I've lied you can do anything, I don't care, but you can't kill him for my mistake, you can't..."

This dissolved into sobbing again, but the necessary words were there. Logs. Proof. And a boy, a soft vicious boy...

Oberon reached up, unhooked the supporting chain through the single pulley, dropped Theren onto the floor. "You come with me," he rasped. "If you're lying, you'll wish I would fucking kill you."

Theren nodded.

"I will give you to my *court*, and I will *forbid* them to kill you, do you understand?"

Theren nodded again, on his hands and knees, the blindfold clinging to his eyes in wet black silk circles.

Oberon sat in the control room, with Theren kneeling beside him, listening to the logs, these voices without faces, again and again.

He'll come for me. When he does, we'll kill you both...You have no idea. About anything. You're a complete fucking idiot and you will never, NEVER UNDERSTAND WHAT YOU'VE DONE!...and you said I should have been more careful about what I drew...

Leander, I know I could have...I can make it up to you, all those things—

No. You can't. Especially not THIS. I don't even want you to fucking try. Take me back now, and I'll make sure he lets you go.

I can't do that.

It's your funeral.

He listened to it four times before he understood.

Then, Oberon screamed.

He screamed so hard and long and loud that only his hands pressed hard against his temples kept his skull from breaking into pieces. He screamed in registers no human throat could manage, and sent several consoles into blackscreened shock.

Theren, with no understanding of what was going on, thought the sound heralded his own death, and he tried to scream too, crumpled on his hands and knees beside Oberon's chair. His nose bled. His eyes swelled in their sockets. His own screams came out in short crooked bursts. He could not draw enough breath to cry out as deeply as he wished to.

Oberon screamed his lungs empty again and again, and now there were words embedded in it. *"I killed him. He didn't WANT to leave me and I killed him I killed him..."*

It degenerated into animal noise, and Oberon was kicking out with his feet, trying to push away the control panel, his chair, everything.

Greatly daring, Theren knelt up, pulled Oberon close, forced the Septarch to look into his face. "What did you do? What did you do?" he demanded.

"Killed him...the device...killed him..."

Theren thought about that, for the briefest instant, and pleaded, "What? Which device? What did you do? Was he alive, when you left him?"

"The device...fitted..."

"Was he *alive?*" Theren demanded.

Oberon was sobbing, for a long moment, before he croaked, "I think so."

"Get up. We have to hurry."

He dragged Oberon to his feet.

321

love which alters

Leander had never thought about death.

He would die. He was mortal.

Oberon could never die, had no reason to fear some nameless retribution in an unknown afterlife.

That afterlife was rising dark and menacing before Leander, and he thought, *I'll go to Hell.*

He saw himself, sitting in a mysterious abyss, with his mother. Alone. No kisses. No teeth. No merciless cock, no voice dark and casual and evil, whispering with that careful, silky, insinuating texture. *Don't you want this? Don't you? You do. You know you do, Leander, little killer, mine, mine, you know you want this. You always have.*

An empty eternity of wanting what he would never have. There would be no deadline, there would be no this-many-days-and-he-will-come-back-to-you. Only a void. Oberon was immortal. He would never die to join Leander.

No. He would not accept that. He would not live without Oberon. He would not go back to that. That...isolation. That vacuum without touch, without piercing merciless eyes, without warm vicious kisses.

Fury, and rage, and what his father had called the Devil in him, screamed out in defiance. He pulled himself back from the place that was a single burning line, and he was in his body again, aching, crying, choking on tears, his eyes pried wide open by metal hooks, the floor cold and hard under him, and the phallus still raping him. He clung to consciousness with a grim determination that pinned him into this place of pain, this place of paralysis and agony and humiliation, this place where he lay on the floor, everything hurting, and he thought again, *he'll come for me. I know he will.*

There was a noise. Outside. Or inside, maybe. He couldn't be sure. He made a thin, warped cry for help, hoping against hope. There was a crooked savage flurry he couldn't understand that might have been movement.

Then Oberon was above him, sobbing like a woman with his hands wound in his own hair. Leander's eyes filled with a burning flood of tears. He had never been so happy in all his life. He was seeing Oberon again, they were together again. The world would be made right again.

"Leander? I didn't know...Leander, are you alive?"

Leander tried to nod his head yes. His head wouldn't move, and it was more a gesture of his eyebrows and his jaw, and that did all kinds of terrible things to his lips, his eyelids. His jaw tried to close, and his lungs started the rhythm of an unknown ritual, and everything was pink and orange. He couldn't breathe.

Oberon unfastened the piece in his mouth, and the pressure forcing his jaw open was miraculously taken away. Metal scraped his teeth and made him cry out, and then his mouth was free, pain was spreading back in dark wings to the base of his skull. He was choking, and Oberon turned him over, sobbing, and it tore at his eyelids. He thought, *there's probably not much of them left, now. Just a meat fringe, hanging in my eyes*, and he thought he was puking, but what he coughed up was slippery and stringy and red.

Punctured, he thought, and wondered what that meant.

Lung, he thought, and wondered what that meant, too. The collar around his neck clicked, tightened for an excruciating second, and then was gone. He dragged in an anguished, grateful breath.

Someone was turning him over, again, and he wanted to scream but he couldn't remember how. He looked up, and someone said, "Jesus," in a whisper that was a sculpture of shock and remorse.

It was Theren. He was almost naked, wearing a weird thing that was like strips of leather crisscrossing over his chest, and the funniest part was the scarf around his neck, like pictures of cowboys in ancient history books. Leander imagined himself laughing and saying, *why the fuck are you dressed like that?* He tried to grin and it did things to the flesh around his eyes that made him wish he was unconscious again.

You were right. He came for you. It's all right to lose it, now.

Leander fought to ignore that voice. Maybe it sounded like his mother, but it *felt* like a trap. If he let go now, he knew, he might not ever return.

Theren did something gentle and excruciating to the hooks in his eyelids, tugged them free with merciful speed. A blackred curtain began scraping across Leander's vision, making gritty strobe-light pictures. Oberon, sobbing, kissing at his chin, his face, his wounded mouth, drawing crimson threads of whatever-it-was he had spit up into webs between them. "Don't die," he was saying, muffled and coming in waves, like a pulsar was sending the words to Leander's ears. "I didn't know you had nothing to do with it...don't die. Please. I'll give you all the stars, Leander. Stay with me. Please."

Leander made a single musical note, that was supposed to mean *don't cry* and *I love you* and *I forgive you.*

Then everything collapsed again, into dark confusion. This time he couldn't stop it, no matter how hard he tried.

A metal tray clattered down beside Oberon's elbow, nearly giving him a mechanical heart attack. His left hand convulsed towards his forehead, and his right hand knotted onto the arm of the chair.

"Take it, you idiot." Cayle ordered, his eyes heavy and bruised.

Oberon did not object to this. He was in complete agreement with Cayle's assessment. He eyed the tray. A syringe, already loaded, and a cup of coffee that had sloshed muddy liquid onto the table. "I don't want anything," he mumbled, his head leaning again against his hand.

"Yes, you do. I need to talk to you."

Oberon covered his mouth with both hands, not hard enough, and the sound tore itself out of his voicebox, half-protest, half-sob. He let one arm fall limp, and he felt the prick of the needle. He picked up the cup and swallowed too much too fast, scalding his throat, his tongue.

Cayle took out the needle, and Oberon felt him rubbing at the puncture for about a thousand years. He snapped, "Tell me."

"He's dying."

The word struck him like a dull blade. The cup hit the floor with a crack, and Oberon let his head fall forward, rubbed his forehead against the metal corner of the table.

He was not surprised.

"Tell me," he said again, muffled against his hands, his hair.

Cayle drew in a ragged breath. "I can keep him alive for another day, maybe two, but he's bleeding internally. Punctured lungs, and an intestinal rupture. He's got so many broken bones it would be faster to tell you which ones aren't broken. There's a fracture in his skull."

"When he's gone, I want you to fit me, and I want you to take everyone out of here. It'll take months for me to be dead enough to trigger the self-destruct, but I want to be alone with him."

"Oberon."

Oberon gestured in the air, not raising his head. The corner of the table was bruising his forehead. He rubbed harder, his hair in his mouth. "You heard me."

He stood. His knees threatened to drop him right back in his seat again, but he forced them to obey. Cayle reached for him, and he swung faster than a human eye could've even seen, and only his blurred vision kept Cayle from joining his dying patient. The doctor got out of his way, and did not try to stop him again.

ice is forming

Oberon walked out of the Sickbay wing, moving like a mortal, slow and rusted. Victoria was outside with a small entourage of members of his court. He didn't have the energy to wonder why. They moved aside to let him pass. He ignored them. They didn't exist.

He found a lift, and it took him three tries to tell it where he wanted to go.

The Gallery was dark, and empty. It reeked of blood and pain. It was standard procedure to leave everything alone until he ordered otherwise, and so Camille's body was still there, limp and fading where he had dropped her.

He stopped at Leander's cell, breathing hard, his eyes closed. He gripped the bars, hard, trying to hold it in, and groped for the keypad and opened it by touch. He raised his hands, covered his eyes, fumbled his fingertips over his face, pressed them against his throat.

Three parallel scars. *My only favorite.*

He opened his eyes, and stepped inside. The scent wrapped around him like an attack, terror and sex and the deep ocean-scent that meant a traumatic wound. Under all of that, the soft orange scent of Leander's skin, his breath, his hair. Oberon put his hand over his mouth, made a sound that was almost choking.

The device was scattered on the floor in a dappled field of blood where he and Theren had dropped it. It scared him to look at it. He crouched, took his hand from his mouth, touched it. It was freezing cold, so heavy, and he had wrapped his fragile, innocent Leander in this atrocity, for something he hadn't even intended to do.

He stood up, still choking. He stepped over the device as if he expected it to strike at him like a cobra. He sat on the edge of Leander's bed, gasping, his eyes trapped in the angles of the jawpiece, thinking a thousand things.

I should have hit him, that first night.

That would have been one more thing to remember.

I should have taken him to Freya, to the art museum there.

I should have ASKED him what happened.

Centuries of education, of learning everything he had ever been curious about, from the best minds in the galaxy, human and otherwise, and Cayle was right: he was an idiot.

Soon there would be one less immortal idiot in the universe, for a grand total of zero.

He lay down, on his side, knees drawn up. He reached over, picked up the device, dragged it onto the bed piece by piece. He had to loosen it almost twice over again to get the corset around his chest. He felt his heart bang into his sternum once, metallic and agonized.

The door to the Gallery chimed.

He'd locked it from the inside. He was working at the buckles on the right side. He ignored it.

There was a hiss-snap. An energy gun. The alarm went off. He ignored that too. Cayle forced the door open, shouldered his way inside in a cloud of smoke and the reek of burning metal. When he saw what Oberon was doing, he snapped, "That's ridiculous." ****SELF DESTRUCT EXPLANATION GOES HERE

"You'll have to help me with it," Oberon told him. He didn't even bother to sit up. "I can't do all of it by myself. And then bring him in here. I want him with me. Take everyone out and set it to explode in one week. You can take anything with you that you want. I don't need any of it." He'd managed the right side himself, and was working on the left. His hands were unsteady, but he persisted.

"God, you're so dramatic. Do you have any idea how much bullshit you could avoid if you would *listen* to people when they are talking?"

Oberon said nothing to this. He was busy with buckles.

"I never said Leander was hopeless."

It took a minute for Oberon to register that.

Hardly daring to believe it, he raised his head.

intervallum

Leander could fly.

There was none of the grinding effort required in his dreams, no sense of struggling through thick air. His ribs didn't hurt anymore, and he didn't seem to need to blink any longer. He had to find Oberon, had to tell him right away. He'd been so upset before. He liked weird things. He'd probably want to learn to fly, too. Maybe that would make him happy again.

This new ability worked a lot like the surveillance system. Leander had no sooner thought Oberon's name than the Sphere flashed into dizzying motion around him. He was in a room he had never seen, floating above a group of people in medical gowns and masks huddled around a table. He recognized Cayle's untidy exclamation of white hair. He tried to call out to him, and he heard a sound like static, and none of the people below him responded.

Cayle stepped back then, gesturing with impatient speed. There had to be sound, but Leander couldn't hear it. He was on the other side of an invisible wall.

He drifted closer, trying to tell them to talk louder. He only made that static sound again. The figure on the table moved, as though startled, pushed a surgical drape away from his face.

It was Oberon.

He looked dazed, drugged, and he looked straight into Leander's eyes, before Cayle pushed him down again, adjusted something on a nearby control panel. There was a flash of color, around Oberon's head, and he lay still.

They're hurting him. He's sick again, and they're hurting him. And I'm stuck up here next to the fucking ceiling.

Leander shouted, furious. A monitor shattered below him, sending the people into a frenzy of motion. They were gaping and waving like mimes. Leander couldn't get any closer. A current was pushing him up towards the ceiling, and he would descend a foot or two, and drift back up again.

Fuck!

He was trying to understand it. There was a field of colors surrounding everyone down there, even a thin dull green one around some of the machines. Oberon's was the brightest, but it was darkening, slowly, flaring less, until it was a dull magenta membrane that didn't move at all.

What did it mean? Had they taken drugs he didn't remember?

Cayle was watching a computer display. He nodded, and did something to a long, thick needle.

They were bringing in another stretcher. Leander didn't want to look at it, but he could no longer control his eyes. It was himself, his own body, bruised and waxen. This was more interesting than distressing.

Wow, I guess I am pretty. I had no idea I was that tiny.

One of the men did something to his discarded body, and there was a blinding noise, or light, or impact, and he was falling.

He was in his flesh again, too heavy to move, too hurt to breath.

"Leander, listen to me. I know you can hear me," Cayle was saying, somewhere behind him. "You're going to be perfectly all right, but you might feel...different...for a while."

Oberon woke up with a knife embedded in the nape of his neck and sand in his eyes. He was in a hospital bed, and Cayle was standing over him.

"I want you to get up and come with me. I want you to see him."

See him. Leander. Yes. "I can't."

"Oh yes, you can and you are," Cayle told him, pulling at him.

"The last time he saw me—the last *memory he has* of me before I..."

"Yes, it's epic, and requires a full symphony orchestra, and you can cry all over him about it right now. Walk."

They passed through a room with four beds. Three of them were empty. Theren was in the last one, his face loose with drugs, his arm bandaged.

Oberon glanced at him, pressed closer to Cayle. "No," he said, and it didn't mean anything. He had done what he had to, and all of this was his fault anyway. He couldn't even figure out where he had gone so wrong.

He knew the beds behind him weren't empty at all. Felicity was there. And Camille. Tiel and Elizabeth and Jude and so many others, a horde of them, silent and accusing.

Cayle felt him stiffen, and he pulled harder at the Septarch's arm. "He's in here," he said, and pushed Oberon into Leander's hospital room.

The doctor didn't follow him.

rediuiuus

Leander in a white geometric room with the worst headache of his short strange life. There was scattered pain in his chest, a sense of pressure in new internal places. He closed his eyes, gritted his teeth against vertigo, opened them again.

Oberon was sitting in a chair beside his bed, his head propped on his hand, sleeping. His face was unpainted, his skin pale as polar ice. There were new tense lines at the corners of his mouth, at the edges of his eyes. He was still smeared with blood and dirt, and his hair was filthy. He made a quick frown in his sleep, and a thin frightened sound deep in his chest.

"Hey," Leander said. His voice was a torn croak, and it hurt like Hell to try and talk. "Oberon?"

The Septarch woke up as if an explosion had startled him awake. Confusion made his eyes blank, until he focused and saw Leander looking at him. He looked back without speaking.

Leander found this understandably disconcerting. "Are you still mad at me?"

Oberon stood up, and walked towards the bed with a look on his face that made Leander cringe back into the mattress. "You are, you're still mad..."

"No." He was touching Leander's face with his fingertips, tracing his mouth, his eyebrows, the line of his jaw. "Are you okay?"

"I feel awful. My head is killing me. What happened?"

"They told me you would die. We had to do it. There was no other way to—"

"Do what?" Leander caught his hand. So far he didn't like this conversation, not one bit. "What did you have to do?"

"Change. Change you. Beautiful you," Oberon murmured. "I missed you. So much. I thought you'd never wake up."

"What did you change?" Leander demanded, frantic now, close to tears. He touched his own face, looked at his hands. Nothing, no difference except bruises and the aching itch of an IV taped to his wrist. He touched his chest, and found smooth synthskin bandages with unsettling seams underneath.

"You're...they copied some of, what was done to me. You're

like me, now."

Leander was trembling. "My eyes—"

Oberon was stroking his neck, sitting on the edge of the bed now, and he caught up the boy's hand in his own. "Your eyes are fine. Still green. Still irresistible. There wasn't any reason to replace your eyes," he said.

"I'm...immortal?"

"As immortal as I am, whatever that means."

"I won't age?"

"No. Not ever."

Leander covered his mouth. Oberon pulled his hand away, and saw that the boy was smiling.

"Can you sit up?"

"I think so." Leander did. It hurt, in many places, but none of them sharp enough to stop him. Oberon put his arms around him, pulled him close. And here were the kisses he had wanted so badly, and there was some difference, now, in the flesh of his mouth, electricity, or magnetism.

A creature like myself.

"It's like...I can read your mind...through your tongue," Leander said between kisses, trying to raise his own arms. The IV in his wrist ached, and he pulled it out, irritated, left the needle stripped and leaking clear fluid on the bedcover.

"Can you? What am I thinking?"

Leander closed his eyes, like a medium reaching for unwilling spirits. "You...need...something..." he managed, struggling to find words for something that was wordless. "It isn't sex exactly, and you're afraid to ask for it."

Oberon pulled away from him, startled, almost afraid. Too close. Too much. "Leander."

"Ask me," Leander whispered to him, pleading. "I'll give you anything you want."

I'll give you the stars.

Anything. He tried to remember the last time anyone other than this boy had given him anything he couldn't have simply seized and claimed. All his memories were of things he had taken.

Taken, and broken.

He searched for words, any words. "When you...in the Gallery,

332

you said—"

He was struggling, and Leander took pity. "I know what I said."

Silence between both of them, threatening to close this doorway before either of them stepped through.

"Did you mean it?" Oberon said, and more than anything in his life he wished he had not asked that question. There was too much at stake behind the answer.

"Yes."

Yes. Then. Before you tried to kill him.

"Do you mean it still, after I—"

"Yes," Leander told him.

"Would you...I didn't, before—"

"I love you," Leander said again, quietly.

There was nothing in him, no part of his throat or lips that knew how to answer that. A familiar something was wrong with his eyes.

He leaned over and kissed Leander again. "Read my mind."

cardınal sın

Three weeks later Leander crept out of bed with nerve-scorching care, and stood waiting. Oberon didn't move, and the rhythm of his breathing did not change.

Leander dressed himself in darkness. He looked back towards the bed one more time, and tiptoed to the door.

Oberon kept still until he heard Leander leave, and he laughed to himself, softly, before he got up and went to the computer.

Paul was behind the wheel of his electrocar, and it was going faster and faster, and nothing he did made it stop. Beyond the windows there was only a not-quite solid blackness that moved like thick greasy smoke.

I just fucked your son, Paul, said a rasp of a voice beside him.

The Septarch was sitting in the passenger seat, with a crossbow in his lap. His face was luminous in the darkness, with a thin green glow like the light of putrescence, and his teeth were too long, the color of chrome. Oberon held up his hand, semen dripping from his fingers, and threw it into Paul's face. He screamed, the sound flat and useless, and when he put his hands to his face they came away wet and red.

The sound of the door opening startled him awake.

His heart was drumming hard. He was still rubbing his fingers together to prove to himself that they weren't really wet at all.

What he saw stopped his breath, latched it cold and solid under his ribcage.

It was Leander.

He was moving exactly as Oberon had, walking into the gym a million years ago, his steps seamless, his motions as smooth as if his joints had been oiled. He was wearing one of Oberon's shirts as a dress; black velvet shot through with threads of silver, chrome at shoulders and waist. He had painted his lips and eyes himself, with black kohl, while the Septarch lay sleeping in the sable bed behind him.

Leander stopped, a foot from the bars, stood utterly still,

staring. "You're not wanted here. You have nothing to do with me, any more."

"Son–"

Leander laughed at that word. It was a hard, sharp, cold sound, too old for such a young throat. It made him tilt his head, exposing the cuts. Oberon had opened them again at his request. Three horizontal red slashes. Wounds that meant a wedding. "Still no, *Dad.* Try 'God' again if you want. Maybe it'll work this time, but I doubt it."

Paul gasped, horrified. One blinding truth was crashing through his mind, those same inadequate and devastating words.

He's so different.

"Leander, I know I could have...I can make it up to you, all those things—" he said, frantic, the same faded promises.

"No."

"On Earth...there are people who could help you..."

Leander grasped the bars, making a face that was too heavy and dark to be called a grin. "What makes you think I would let you take me back to that?"

"What do you think you're going to do?" Paul snapped, angry now, and more frightened than he had ever been in his life "Do you think he'll just let you live here? As his...his..."

"Go ahead and say it," Leander told him. "His whore. That's what you're thinking, isn't it?" He shook his head, that cruel smile still haunting his black mouth, as though Paul refused to learn something simple after many repetitions. "You're made of Earth words, and Earth smells, and Earth stupidity. Always have been."

"You're not in your right mind."

"Oh, yes I am. I finally am," Leander said, showing his teeth again.

"What will you do when you're not his new game anymore?" Paul said, afraid it was obvious how desperate he was. "When you're too old for him? What then?"

Leander hissed at him, his mouth hard, his eyes gleaming. "Want another story? He almost killed me because of your little rescue. By the time he found out I never wanted to leave I was almost dead."

Paul closed his eyes, opened his mouth to deny any or all of this.

"One synthetic lung. Most of my ribs have been replaced. And then, implants. They regulate everything. Every hormone, every chemical, metabolism. I'm almost a machine. And anything that breaks gets...replaced."

Leander's hand went to his chest, where the scars were still smoothing over. "I won't ever be too old for him. Not anymore. I'm like him, now. I guess I should thank you, so, thank you."

"It's not you he loves, Leander. It's that body of yours, and what you let him do to you—"

"Even if that were true, neither one of those will ever change."

Leander turned away from Paul, and eyed the control panel for the cell in a way that Paul found distinctly unsettling. "I know you. I know what you're like. I know you'll never understand the life I have now, and you'll never leave me to it. You're a threat to me."

"Leander, what are you thinking about?"

His son did not answer.

"I don't know what he's done to you, I can't imagine what would make you think I'm dangerous to you—"

"I didn't say that," Leander said sharply. "I said you're a threat. You're not dangerous. Not yet. And I don't think I'll give you the chance to change that."

Oberon leaned closer to the screen, breathless.
Would he?

Paul was prattling on beside him, some incoherent patchwork about trauma and stress and Jesus and Leander doing this because Paul hadn't been attentive enough as a father, and he wasn't acting like himself because of Soren's death, and once they were back on Earth this would all fade away, forgotten, and didn't that sound nice?

No, it sounded like noise pollution, and Leander paid it no mind. He studied the controls, feeling the familiar Tri-Six mentality settle over him, the specific mindset that solved technopuzzles, cracked codes, figured passwords out with an ability that was almost psychic. This little panel was child's play for someone who had

336

hacked the Prime Minister's personal computer and gleefully read his mail for two months. Simple.

There was a display, and a button. That was all there was to it. His fingertips tingled. He was humming to himself, an ancient song about a red door painted black.

Paul was crying now. The noise was distant, irrelevant. He was saying, "Leander, what are you thinking?" over and over.

Leander ignored it.

It was easy to ignore.

He set the current at a hundred and fifty milliamps.

He was sure it wouldn't take that much, but you had to be safe. Too much and he'd likely just survive. There was no point in having to do it all over again.

Besides, he was sleepy, and he wanted to be back in Oberon's warm velvet bed, done with this mess of detention blocks and electrified cells.

"If you see Mom," he said to the inconvenience sobbing in the cell behind him, "Tell her I love her and I miss her, and I'm...home. Tell her I'm home."

He pushed the button.

A delicate thrumming traveled from his fingertip up his arm, into his teeth. He thought again of that bluegreen pulse, billowing across the empty black of space, making dust of what had once been a mountain.

Paul made a crazy, metallic screech, like he was screaming through a mouthful of iron filings. Leander turned to watch him, his face empty. It was interesting. He kept convulsing long after his eyeballs had ruptured, and his hair smoldered and burst into flame.

Leander waited a moment or two longer, then reached over and switched the current off.

Paul's skin had cracked in places, and was weeping colorless fluid. Smoke drifted up from his mouth, the empty sockets of his eyes. The smell was terribly strong, sweet and thick. The only thing that ruined it was the odor of charred cloth.

Leander nodded to himself, turned and left the jail.

Oberon ached everywhere, drawn into furious knots by an

appetite he guessed was lust. And triumph. Lots and lots of that.

He had won.

Leander was his.

By the time Leander came back in, reeking of fire and flesh, he was lying in the bed again, the computer off and silent.

He didn't pretend to be sleeping. He sat up to watch Leander undress. "Is everything all right?" he asked, once he trusted himself to speak.

Leander nodded. "Yeah. Everything is perfect." He picked up a cloth from the dressing table, meaning to wipe off the makeup.

"Leave it," Oberon said, and he was smiling in spite of himself. "Favorite boy."

Leander put the cloth down, closed his eyes. "You know."

"I watched."

"Are you mad?"

In answer, he pulled Leander into the bed, smudging the boy's lipstick with his fingertips. He buried his face in Leander's hair, inhaled deeply. "You smell...wonderful."

perdition

The door into the hospital ward opened and closed.

Theren kept his face turned to the wall. "I know it's you. Come to take me to the jail, or directly to the throne room? Or maybe straight down to the torture chambers, if you—"

There was a clatter that he recognized, that stopped his rehearsed last words. His plate armor, hitting the floor.

He turned over, startled.

The Septarch was standing in front of the pile of armor, holding a small silver briefcase.

Theren was so convinced he would be all in black that he actually saw it for an instant. He closed his hands into hard frightened fists, closed his eyes, opened them again.

Oberon was wearing dark brown vinyl, the looped cross on his right shoulder in gold. Not black. Not killing clothes. He looked pointedly at the stack of armor and ordered, "Get dressed."

Stunned, Theren could only shake his head. "You're crazy," he whispered, finally. "You're just...crazy."

Oberon tilted his head, deliberately overdramatic, making a big show of analyzing this remark. "Irrelevant," he decided. "Cayle told me you're fine. One little bite. Synthskin and antibiotics. I'm not poisonous, though I've been thinking about getting that fixed. You're perfectly fit for duty. Now put your uniform on."

Theren laughed, close to hysteria. "Don't you get it? I'd rather die than be your guard."

Oberon nodded, chewing on the inside of his cheek, as though he had expected that exact response. He sat on the edge of the empty bed across from Theren, and began keying a code into a tiny keypad on the little silver case. Theren sat up, watching him, expecting a bomb. Or worse—knives, needles, venomous insects. It could be anything.

It was worse than all those things.

It was worse than anything.

The Septarch opened the case. It clicked, and Theren flinched, gritting his teeth. There was a soft pressurized hiss, and a plume of white smoke. Liquid nitrogen.

God, no. It's a bluff. It has to be.

He can't actually be this evil.

He just can't.

Oberon could, indeed, be exactly that evil.

Theren could hear himself making a high-pitched repetitive sound, deep in his chest.

The Septarch removed a small glass vial from the case. A medical specimen jar, with a neat computer-chip label. He held it up, grinned, and looked over at Theren. "Recognize this?"

Theren could only stare. He wrapped his arms around himself, shuddering. He'd been unconscious for hours, maybe even days. They'd had plenty of time to get all the information they needed.

The room was spinning. He couldn't breathe. He was drowning in terror. His voice was fragile, scorched, inadequate. "No..."

"It's a genofile," Oberon told him, sounding extremely pleased with himself. His mouth twitched, as though he was resisting laughter, or pretending to. "Welcome to life as a regen, Theren One. Death is no longer an option for you."

"No," Theren said again, staring at the vial as though he could see Hell spinning inside it.

"Here are your choices," Oberon said, "Immortality as my guard, or as my guinea pig. Choose."

Theren One.

He'd die and wake up in a regen chamber. Brand new.

Over and over and over...

Theren stood, his eyes still nailed to the silver case, stumbling, groped for his armor with numb fingers, and began to put it on.

Oberon watched until he was satisfied. He picked up the genofile case and stood to leave. "Camille's body is still in the Gallery. Take care of that," he said over his shoulder.

"I killed the men who built this place." Oberon said, standing in front of a round door.

"What's inside?"

"Something you have to see for yourself,"

The door spiraled open like the iris of one of his mechanical eyes. The air that rushed out was cold and damp, laden with a sweet thick smell that Leander thought he recognized. "Is it...a crypt?"

"No. Come inside."

Leander took Oberon's hand, and the door blinked closed behind them. It was darker than midnight in Hell. Leander privately thought Oberon found this amusing, a bit of a tease about Leander's still-human eyes. "Where are you?" Leander said, whispering instinctively, as though he were in a church.

"Hang on...running lights..."

A circle of light blinked on at floor level, defining the walls of the room. Leander took a step towards them, and felt Oberon grab his arm hard. "Don't move. You'll fall."

"Fall?"

"It's a shaft. Here—"

A row of lights in front of him, marking a path forward. A silken rustle, high overhead.

"What is it?"

Oberon keyed in one last code, one he had never used, and took Leander's hand. "Walk forward. Careful. There's a platform at the end."

Leander did so, Oberon behind him with his hand on the boy's shoulder. "Where are we?"

"Watch."

There was a deep mechanical *thunk* somewhere far below, a grating scrape and an electronic whine above.

The dome of the roof was sliced in half by a single crack of light. It began to hinge open, like an observatory. Outside, the orange sky was streaked with vivid green, peacock blue, sulfur yellow.

"It's sunrise," Oberon said, beside him.

They were flying out into the light. Hundreds of them,

thousands, maybe even millions. Some were invisible specks, others bigger than both his hands, a few the size of his outspread arms.

Butterflies.

Oberon and Leander stood on the platform hand in hand like children, watching. It took forever. The swarm of them was almost thick enough to leave the two of them in darkness again, and it thinned as slowly as a fading illusion.

Finally, the last of them were free, down to the final stragglers, and the sky was gaping open above them.

"Look," Oberon said again. "Down. On the floor."

Leander looked. His eyes refused to make sense of it and he went down on his hands and knees, peering over the edge of the platform. He had suspicions of what he might see, and they proved correct.

"I hate you so much," he told Oberon.

The platform jolted under him, and began to descend.

Leander's first reaction was to climb Oberon like a jungle gym and hang on for dear life. "I can't."

Oberon smiled at what had become a traditional exchange between them. "Yes. You can."

"Oberon...they're *worms.*"

"You're immortal. What will they do, kill you?"

Leander clung harder. "Please..."

"Leander, if you want to lie down, you are going to have to touch the floor."

Leander laughed, surprising himself. "I don't want to lie down! And that sounds like a fucked-up version of the kind of thing teachers have on their desks on plaques."

"Put your feet down."

"I'll freak. I mean it."

"Put your feet down," Oberon ordered, trying not to grin, though he was largely aware that giving orders to his favorite was about as useful as writing them on slips of paper and launching them into orbit.

"I'll *step* on them."

Oberon sighed, exasperated, and losing the battle against the grin. "Put your feet on my feet, then."

Leander did, quivering, still clinging hard to Oberon's shoulders, then his hands, then only one hand. He couldn't stand to squish any of them, so he nudged them aside with the toe of his boot, shuddering, until he had cleared two spaces for his feet.

"Will they bite me?"

"Most of the ones that bite are up there," Oberon told him, pointing at the ominous portals set around the walls.

"Fuck. No. Lots of no. You said I didn't have to do anything I didn't want to. This is about ten things I don't want to do."

Oberon held Leander still to look into his eyes.

"This is the last thing."

"This is worse than the paddle."

"The very last thing. And you will be unmade."

"They're *worms*. How is this not registering for you? Don't you understand that worms are gross?"

Oberon kissed Leander's cheek, his chin, his neck. "I love you." He had taken a long time to be able to say that, and was fond of showing it off at the most inopportune times.

"Don't, you're cheating, don't you dare—"

"I love you...love you..."

"You love me when you want ridiculous, fucked-up things."

"Precious boy. Favorite boy. Please?"

He could sometimes resist *I love you* for a minute or ten, but he had yet to come up with an antidote for *please*. "Damn it." He let go of Oberon's hand. He could not contain his shudders or his wrinkled nose. "I suppose you want me to sit down, now."

Oberon sat down himself, looking up.

Leander sighed.

He sat down and lay back, all in one motion, to get it over with. It was cold, and wet, and soft in the most awful way. And *busy*.

He kept his eyes closed.

He felt Oberon lie down beside him, pull him close, turn him over so that he was lying on top. "Leander..."

"You made me lay in worms when you were going to make me lay on you anyway? Fuck off," Leander said, giggling.

"Leander, look at me."

"I can't. I'm laying on you." This was, of course, untrue, but for some reason he was unsettled now, reticent, and it had nothing to do with the worms.

Oberon pushed Leander up until he could look into the boy's eyes. "Kiss me," he said, trying to communicate other words with his eyes.

Leander saw the attempted telepathy, but he was oblivious
(he can't mean)
to its meaning. He put his mouth against Oberon's and felt a worm against his right pinky finger. It felt like the tongue of a corpse, and he knew damn well he could read Oberon's mind, now, but he couldn't
(mean)
possibly be interpreting this correctly. It was too weird.

Oberon didn't kiss him, exactly. He opened his mouth, a soft wistful sound trilling in his throat, and made a welcoming curve of his spine. He drew up those long legs and wrapped them around Leander in a tangled sweep of velvet robes.

Leander couldn't ignore that. He'd intended to tease, with tickling flicker-licks that drove Oberon mad, but that long lean shape snaring him so utterly made him forget all about this worm business. He kissed hard and deep, the way Oberon kissed him, pressing hard against him, chest against chest, cock against cock. Oberon lifted his hips, moaning. and he put his hands on Leander's back in a new way, just touching with his fingertips. There were worms in his hair.

Above them the first cylinder clicked, jolted, and engaged, moving towards vertical.

He expected Oberon to move, to grind against him, to roll with him, but the Septarch did none of those things. He was passive and yielding under Leander's hands, letting himself be kissed and stroked with a hesitant desire that Leander might have called *shy* on anyone else.

Whatever else Cayle had done to him, Leander was still a teenage boy, and if Oberon would not move his hips Leander would cheerfully do it himself. He tried it, and Oberon made a long starving sound that immediately became Leander's new favorite song. He moved his mouth to Leander's neck, biting in frantic wet hunger up to his ear.

Two words.

"Fuck me."

He pulled his mouth away from Oberon's, gasping, grinding, leaned his head back until he was staring straight up into the blinding sky. Soren was there, with hair the color of new leaves and eyes the color of a luna moth

(and the butterflies, there were hundreds of them, and I was)

and cobwebs covered Leander, like rain, except they didn't burn his skin. He was in a cocoon, and his bones were changing.

The Septarch pulled him down again, eager to be kissed. His hands wound hard in Oberon's hair, and he fumbled one of them free to struggle at his clothing, trying to escape Oberon's legs and straddle him. Oberon's hands closed around his, and those impossible legs held him caught. "No, *you* fuck *me*."

Leander went still, and his eyes went round and wide in something close to horror.

"No," he whispered, desperate. "I mean, you're, *you*, and I'm me, and I..."

Can't, discarded as untrue, *couldn't* the same. His traitorous spine was moving again, the sky still crashing in above them. Oberon arched up against him, shy yielding to shameless, finding all the well-loved hollows on Leander's throat that drove him mad. "You have to, because..."

(the light will damage them eventually)

"...no one ever has, not since him, and you have to, you have to unmake me, Leander. It has to be you, because..."

(because I am you)

"...because I'm yours," Oberon finished, his eyes closed.

"God," Leander said, speaking to the sky, but looking down at Oberon. The light was so bright he could see the gleam of it, on the implants under Oberon's eyelids. Their hands were moving, in synch, the perfect machine, alpha and omega.

This is the last thing. The very last thing.

And you will be unmade.

Leander found that he could.

This was the place between them made of the knife and the scars. This was the final wound, his to remake and claim. The worms grew deeper, and the sun climbed in the sky, and the Emperor of All Things Unseen was under him, around him, open for him, naked for him, helpless for him.

Leander was gentle for as long as Oberon would allow. Then those steel talons dragged eight lines from his shoulders to his waist, and what followed was savage and sweet and endless.

The open sky was above them, with the sun blazing green and pure into this nest of gleaming creatures, shining on nothing human.

Not anymore.

Not ever again.

armageddon

"Don't you ever get tired of this?"

The Septarch was in his desk chair, with Leander over his knees. He had covered the boy in packing tape and was ripping off each strip with varying degrees of speed and violence. Leander's eyes were unfocused, part marijuana and part arousal. His skin was striped with strawberry lines from the past hour or so of this treatment.

"We've only done this one other time. And that was a different kind of tape," Oberon told him, plucking at the corner of a piece of the tape that was across Leander's shoulderblade.

"Not this game. I meant...this. Living in the Sphere, and killing slaves, and doing drugs..."

Oberon ripped off the tape. "Why would I get tired of it?"

Leander choked his way through a moan, and said, "Don't you ever want...more?"

He considered again. The question was terribly familiar, but he couldn't place where he'd heard it before, even though he remembered the correct answer. "Is there more?"

Leander covered his mouth with his hand, and smiled.

"There's Earth."

Isaiah Kel Moriann had been Prime Minister of Earth for fourteen years, three months, and twelve days on The Day of the Black Sun.

He was sitting in the environmentally-controlled, completely automated office that had been built for him a year earlier, in a taupe leather chair that was computerized to adjust itself to his posture. He was drinking coffee imported from Zion Prime, and watching a sermon given two days ago in the Region once known as Washington, in the country once known as America. It was about the evils of the underground culture, the complex system of secrets and supplies and drugs and information that persisted no matter what measures the Church took to obliterate it.

Maybe he could arrange a listing of everyone convicted of any psychological aberration. Require them to be observed and tested weekly, implanted with artificial glands to release sedatives and antipsychotics automatically. With an encoded program to release lethal poison if anyone attempted to remove the implant, he thought, and he'd decided to mention it to the Cardinal when a single monitor in the vast array spread out before him abruptly went black.

He tapped a few keys on his armrest. Annoying. It was a minor thing, a system that showed planetary weather systems. He never even really used it. The point was that it wasn't working.

It didn't work, no matter what he typed.

Another monitor over his head went black, too.

Then two of them, the larger ones that displayed the military launch logs, went to black at the same instant.

Three more.

Twelve.

He touched the comm. Fortunately *that* was still functional. "Jared, there's—"

The chaos of noise that exploded out of the speakers on either side of his head made him scramble out of his chair. He stood there, staring at the speakers, vaguely holding his hands over his ears, and all around him the monitors collapsed into darkness like blinded eyes, one by one.

He was paralyzed by what he was hearing.

Apparently, down at the switchboard, there was a riot going on.

People were screaming. There was the crackling hum of an electrical malfunction, and a cacophony of shouting.

"All down! It's all down! All of them! We have no surface to space capability...took out EVERY airport and spaceport...defense grid is out, it's fucking OUT BECAUSE the satellites are fucking space trash, he blew them into shrapnel before he was even in sensor range...the communication satellites are—"

There wasn't even a click. Just silence.

For the first time in his long, luxurious life, no button he pushed did ANYTHING at all.

Including the one that opened his own door.

The Prime Minister stood there, paralyzed. After a long moment he wandered over to the wide window, transparent steel neatly covered with an opaque shield that was, fortunately, completely manual, and easily raised with one hand.

Looming over it all was the sun.

The edge of it was black.

A tiny slice of the sun was *black*.

And it was growing.

He gaped at this nightmare until the sun was blotted out, black as sack cloth, eclipsed by the Sphere of Light and Shadow.

There was a chime behind him, the signal of an incoming transmission. He turned.

A single monitor was blinking a message at him.

"God, no," he whispered.

GOG AND MAGOG

The letters disappeared, and were replaced by a looped cross over four red words:

HERE ARE OUR DEMANDS.